MILLWALL

d bardsley

A CIP catalogue record for this title is available from the British Library.

Copyright © d bardsley 2014

Published in 2014 by FeedARead.com Publishing.

Printed and Bound by Berforts Information Press Ltd

"Live well for less"
Sainsbury 2014

1

St John's Wood, Friday 4th March

In the basement gloom of 43 Sycamore Drive it was minus two. Alex cleared his throat and swallowed. 'Come on, let's go.'

Crouched over, Vince heard nothing but the screech of aluminium oxide on steel, his eyes fixed on the firework of sparks ejecting from the grinder's disc. Above them, in the future kitchen, a gang of electricians excavated wiring channels in the plasterboard, their dust cascading down and over Vince's head and shoulders. Alex moved in and tapped Vince on the back, and as he did so the end of the metal stringer dropped away. Vince switched off the grinder and removed his safety glasses. 'What was that?'

Alex nodded to the floor above. He was never happy when other trades encroached on his space. 'Let's get a coffee.'

Vince stood, slid his glasses into the pocket of his hoodie – a discard he'd found in the street near his home – and followed Alex out to the van. On the way he blew out his nose and slapped the dust from his hat.

The cube-shaped house had been gutted. Alex and Vince were there to install an elliptical stair up to the first floor and then a helical into the roof space. The skeleton of each was steel, but the finish would be in oak and white plaster. For Alex, a multi-tasking craftsman, day-one on site was always the time of maximum stress; he'd spent weeks, sometimes months, measuring and fabricating, double and treble checking his calculations, but only now would he know if his lengths of twisted steel would fit with the walls and floors.

Five minutes later they were parked up in St John's High Street, on double yellows, thirty yards from Starbucks. As

1

their coffees cooled, Alex checked his emails, occasionally glancing in his side-view mirror on the lookout for traffic wardens.

Vince's phone rang. Straightening his body, he squeezed it from his jean pocket: *Withheld number.*

'Hello.'

'Is that Vince Wynter?'

'Yes it is.'

'Good. My name is Ángel Barros. I am an agent for footballers. I was given your name. I was told you are a writer.'

'Yes,' replied Vince, though he no longer thought of himself as such. 'How can I help?'

'You wrote Kicked in the Park?'

'Kick in the Park,' corrected Vince, 'Jamie Carpenter's story. Did you enjoy it?'

'Well...I never read it, but I have a friend. He read it and says it was very good. I would like you to do a book like this for my client, an autobiography. Is that possible?'

The instant offer of work took Vince by surprise. 'Yes, I suppose...for a fee.'

'Of course, we all need a fee.'

'Who is it for?'

'Kevin Furling. He plays for Chelsea. Can we meet next week? Monday...one o'clock at The Berkeley?'

'One moment.' Vince didn't follow football and he'd never heard of Furling. He turned to Alex, clasping a hand over his phone. 'Can I have a couple of hours on Monday?'

Alex nodded.

'Yes, that would be fine Mr Barros. If you don't mind me asking, where did you get my number?'

'Your agent had it – Miss Sheldon.'

Kathy Sheldon was Vince's ex-agent. He'd not seen or spoken to her for over a year. 'Okay, I'll see you on Monday at The Berkeley.'

Writing, principally for newspapers, had been Vince's first and only career. For eighteen years he'd worked as a columnist and reviewer for national titles, moving from broadsheet to tabloid and back again. The ghost-writing had simply been a sideline that paid well. After Carpenter's, the Arsenal and England goalkeeper, came Richard Tunkey's, an Olympic medallist in the single sculls (Sydney 2000) who, stricken with pancreatic cancer, had admitted in his book, *The Longer the Better*, that he'd secretly used extendable oars. Tunkey's crime, a mere ten millimetres long, was cheating nonetheless. He died two months after publication.

Vince's transition from jobbing writer to jobbing labourer came courtesy of a lost libel case brought by the artist David Spinks. After a shambolic and well-publicised court appearance (Vince's self-defence had been crushed by Spinks' legal team), his freelance work dried up, contracts were terminated, and his phone calls went unanswered. In a matter of weeks he'd been excommunicated. But he lost more than his job and reputation, his social life vanished too, the party invites, the free tickets to premiers, and the all-expenses paid trips to Cannes and Raindance. For six months he did nothing. He waited by the phone, did the crossword, watched TV, read a few books, and deferred the interest payments on his mortgage. He figured that when it all died down, Kathy would call. And she did, but only to say he would have to find another agent. 'No one's going to touch you Vince,' she said. 'Honestly, I've tried. Most people will forgive you once, but not twice.'

What Vince had been slow to appreciate was his status as a two-time offender. The unwritten rule was: two strikes and you're out. His first offence came in 2005, when he libelled the American actor, Edward Larner, accusing him of 'buying' his way into the Broadway production of Spamalot. It was sloppy journalism: while Larner admitted in court that he had close connections with the production company, Vince had no evidence to support his allegation. Following on from the debacle with Spinks, one editor told Kathy that he was *'an accident waiting to happen,'* while another said, *'he's a makeweight, not a Bernstein, we don't need him.'*

Like the Larner case, the Spinks libel was a clumsy self-infliction. In the early hours, when too drunk to know better, he'd written on an internet forum about a conversation he'd had with Spinks at Heathrow Airport. Then, two weeks later, a letter arrived at Kathy Sheldon's office from Brewer and Copthorne LLP, Spinks' lawyers. The letter was brief; it demanded a full and unconditional apology and one million pounds for the reputational damage to their client. It also included a hyperlink to the alleged defamation. She called him and read the letter out, word for word.

'Sounds like bullshit,' said Vince.

'What do you mean bullshit?'

'It must be another Vince Wynter,' he said, 'or someone's fucking me about.'

'Listen Vince, the day Brewer and Copthorne said you met Spinks, you were at Heathrow Airport.'

'Says who?'

'Says me. I booked your flight.'

'So what? That proves nothing.'

'Vince, please?' She'd had enough. 'I've just looked at the website site. It's obviously you. You need to contact them and say you're very sorry. I'll scan the letter and email it.' She put the phone down before he could reply.

When the email arrived, Vince clicked on the hyperlink. It took him straight to the webpage and his poorly argued demolition of Spinks' work. That evening, he wrote back to Brewer and Copthorne, apologising fulsomely for his indiscretion and then posting a full retraction underneath his original article. But his grovelling had no effect; days later the story had been picked up by The Guardian.

He called her. 'Have you seen it?'

'Yes, it doesn't look good. I guess it was bound to leak. It's a good story.'

'Any suggestions?' he said.

'You could try another letter...an open letter to the press. You'll have to say you were drunk and that it was the drink that did it.' Her voice was flat. She didn't think it would work.

'Okay, but then what?'

'I don't know Vince. You need to get a lawyer. How much money have you got?'

'I own half a house. I have a mortgage.'

'So you could offer them that. See if they'll take it and call it quits.'

Vince didn't like it. Though prepared to concede that he'd been disrespectful, he hadn't lied. He had simply repeated, as best he could remember, what Spinks had told him face-to-face. 'I could fight it,' he said. 'If I lose, the outcome's the same. I'm still screwed.'

And screwed he was. Two years on, little had changed. Vince worked with Alex, and in between times he functioned in limp-mode, with no urgency or direction. When at home alone, he'd browse the net or watch and despise daytime TV. Most days he walked to Balham Library to read the daily papers with all the others in Balham that were under-employed. And whether he was in bed or reading or walking to Balham, at some point each day he would ask himself, *why pick on me?*

In contrast to Vince's decline, Larner and Spinks had prospered: Spamalot, helped by weeks of free publicity, broke box-office records, while Spinks' appearance at the Royal Courts of Justice reasserted his position as the country's richest and most recognizable artist.

Days after the court case, on Radio 4's Front Row, Spinks talked about his route to the top. He said, 'I was nineteen. I had ideas and I didn't think anyone at Goldsmiths or Chelsea could teach me anything. I know that sounds arrogant, but no one can teach you ideas...and I didn't want to be contaminated by others. I suppose I wanted to succeed, I was in a hurry, and I thought Art College would have been a waste of time.'

Spinks studied history at Cambridge and then, just two years after, his first London exhibition, *Artgasm,* sold out. He made his first million. But alongside the instant acclaim came the condemnation. After Artgasm the tabloids turned, and ever since, after every exhibition and every commercial success, they mocked his work on behalf of the nation. Working class academics piled in too, sneering at his privileged background, the absence of struggle, and what they saw as Spinks' arrogance. They called him a celebrity, a stunt-artist, a manufacturer. But Spinks pushed through it all, developing new themes, always managing to surprise. And as his reputation grew, like diamonds and pork-bellies, his work became internationally tradable.

The *manufacturer's* tag was not entirely undeserved. Spinks admitted that he'd planned his career. He said to do otherwise would have been an act of stupidity. When at Cambridge he'd known that merely being creative would never be enough. So when not in his room sketching out ideas, he was busy building a network of contacts, and eventually he found Christopher Witherspoon, a hedge-fund manager and art investor. Witherspoon took a punt on the unknown Spinks and put up a hundred thousand to finance Artgasm. It was this relationship, said his critics, which had made him. But Spinks simply countered by pointing out that since Roman times, artists and musicians had had their patrons and backers.

– – – – –

Vince's labouring work came about by accident and an act of kindness. He'd stopped for a morning coffee off Clapham High Street, and for no particular reason he sat outside and turned his chair to face the road. Shortly after that, a white van pulled up on the opposite side, two of its wheels on the pavement. Vince watched the driver unload his tools into a scaffold-clad house and then disappear inside. Two minutes later a traffic warden began circling the van. Vince ran across the road and into the house, and for his good deed, Alex offered him some work. To begin with he carried things, held the tape measure, steadied the plumb-line, swept the floor, and made the tea. And now, ever since that chance meeting, every month or two, for three or four days, Vince helped out with the site work, his contribution having grown from carrying and holding, to drilling, sawing, and grinding, and though his body never adjusted to the work's physical demands, he enjoyed it. It was a welcome break from Balham Library.

Still parked on St John's High Street, Alex sipped his coffee. 'So what's happening on Monday?'

Vince picked at a metal splinter in his finger. 'I'm not sure. I used to write. I was a journalist.'

It was news to Alex. 'But you're not writing now?'

'Not anymore. I was taken to court and the work dried up.'

'You did time?'

Vince smiled. 'I wish I could have. I wasn't a criminal. It just cost me my house because I said something I couldn't prove.'

Their conversation was cut short when a police officer rounded the corner from Ordnance Hill. Vince took the coffees off the dashboard and they headed back to site. Inside the electricians had moved on to the basement and the air had cleared.

By three the heavy lifting was over. The four stringers that defined the inner and outer curves of each stair had been bolted in place. Vince made tea, while Alex stood back, imagining the finished stair, wondering if the plasterers would cope with the tight inner curves. As ever, there was always something for Alex to worry about, if not stairs, it was cash-flow, his son's eyesight, or his own wheezing chest. His thoughts on the plasterers' capabilities were interrupted when a tall, straight-haired brunette walked in and across the open-plan hallway, a small girl at her side. They were both dressed for winter in black tights, puffa jackets, and Ugg boots. The woman placed herself in the space between Alex and the metal stair.

'Where is Michael?' she said. It came out like a demand.

Vince looked at Alex and Alex at the woman.

'The foreman?' said Alex, unnecessarily.

'Michael. I want to see Michael.'

'I saw him earlier,' said Alex.

'I want to see him,' she repeated.

Knowing he wasn't on the ground floor, Alex raised his head and shouted. 'Mike, you've got a visitor.'

After a brief pause, an Essex voice shouted back, 'The fucker's gone home.' It was Karl, one of the plasterers, the only other Brit on site.

Alex looked down and smiled at the woman, wondering if she'd understood.

She had, but she wasn't satisfied. 'When will he be back?'

'Have you got his number?' said Alex. He knew she had.

She didn't respond. She snatched her daughter's hand and left through the front door of her future home.

'Is that the client?' said Vince.

'That's the one. She's got Mike's number. She was here last week. She parked her fucking Range Rover out front on the double-yellows and asked me to watch it.'

'Where's she from?'

'Saudi...the Emirates. Not sure.'

'It's like she's not been socialised.'

'What do you mean?'

'She doesn't know how to behave.'

'Maybe,' said Alex. 'She said the house was too small. They had a bigger stair in Dubai.'

'So they're slumming it?'

Alex nodded.

At four-fifty Vince bolted the last steel tread into place and to Alex's relief, everything that was supposed to be level, was level, and all the heights matched up to within a millimetre. They packed and loaded the power tools and Vince changed his toe-capped boots for trainers.

Alex climbed into his van. 'See you on Monday at six.'

Vince threw his boots in the back, shut the sliding door and slapped his goodbye on the side of the van.

2

He arrived home – a rented two bedroom terrace in Tooting – just after six. Ailish, the legal tenant, was on the sofa, on her laptop, surrounded by bags and boxes of women's shoes. They met on the last day of the Spinks trial and he moved in soon after. To Vince, their relationship, their co-habitation, was another reminder of that singular point in time when his career and life hit the buffers. He first saw her in court, in the front row of the public gallery. She waved at him to catch his eye and then held up her hands with her fingers crossed. And afterwards, as he pushed his way through the crowd, most of who were waiting for a statement from Spinks, she was there again, smiling and blocking his path; short and slim, red-haired with a sprinkling of freckles.

'I guess I didn't help?' she said.

At first he didn't recognise her as the woman from the gallery. He looked left and right and then over her head toward Bush House and Covent Garden. *Which way?*

Then she waved her hands with her fingers crossed in front of his face. 'Powerless against the mighty wigged one,' she said.

He looked down at her, shaking his head, wondering what she wanted.

'Come on, let's go,' and grasping his hand, she led him across The Strand and into Daley's Wine Bar. Inside he stood passively, arms hanging, watching as she read the wine list, and not responding when she asked him, 'Red or white?' She ordered a sixteen pound bottle of Merlot and walked him to a candle-lit table at the back of the bar.

As they sat, he said, 'You're a journalist?'

'No, I'm Ailish. I'm an artist actually.'

'So what?'

'So nothing. You asked, I answered. I'm on your side. I'm not the enemy. I think we should celebrate.'

Vince had heard enough. He stood up. 'I have to go.'

'No don't, I'm sorry. What I mean was...we should celebrate your contribution to the debate.'

Vince shook his head. 'What you on about?'

'Please,' and she patted the table. 'Sit down. Have some wine. Drink with me.' Then lifting his glass, she said, 'It's my birthday.' It was a lie with a smile, but it did the trick. Vince sat down.

For the next two hours Vince did most of the drinking while she did most of the talking. He watched her lips, but didn't listen, and as she talked about the case he tried to work out her age. When she laughed, she looked twenty-five, but when she complained about London, the traffic, the Mayor, and the dog-shit, and how difficult it was to break through as an artist, she could have been forty. With the arrival of their second bottle she began telling her story. And as she talked, now and again, she squeezed his hand, trying to keep him in the present. She told him she was from a family of Irish doctors and that she had followed the same path as her siblings until her second year at med school, when she quit, left Dublin, and came to London. Since then art had been her preferred occupation, but it didn't provide for her. For the past three years she had been buying second-hand designer shoes from boot sales, charity shops, and house clearance companies, and selling them on eBay. In a good month she cleared fifteen hundred, enough to pay the rent and bills. She told him that the competition was building, that her margins were shrinking, and about her USP.

Vince frowned.

'My unique selling point...we all have to have one. I photograph the shoes in different settings.' She went on to explain that while the shoes were always centre stage in her eBay photographs, the backdrop was in some way absurd. She photographed Jimmy Choos in the freezer covered in frost, Pradas on toast, Guccis on a chopping board, and Westwoods in the bath surrounded by bubbles; she called it 'lame-surrealism'. It was simply a marketing ploy to catch the customer's eye and spread the word.

10

'It worked and it was fun at first,' she said. 'Sales took off until I was copied.'

With the second bottle empty, they caught the Northern Line south. Vince's house was in Tooting. In part, it was their very proximity, their shared postcode, which brought them together. Ailish had read about the forthcoming trial in her local paper. The front page, under the headline: TOOTING MAN LIBELS ARTIST had side by side photographs of Vince Wynter and David Spinks. The article ignored the issues of libel and defamation; instead it celebrated the fact that a Tooting man was making international news.

3

Merton College Oxford, Saturday 5th March

Sixty-five miles from London, the Assets Committee of the Commissioners of the Church of England gathered at their usual venue, the Breakfast Room at Merton College, Oxford. The Committee had executive powers, acting as the investment arm of the Church of England. Kenneth Ffooks, the newly appointed Director of Investments, had overall responsibility for the Church's multi-billion pound investment fund, the income from which provided pensions for the living, nursing homes for the infirm, and funerals for the dead. The others seated around the walnut table were Ffooks' senior investment team. The only Church outsiders were Tom Cowly and Phylida Cranson, employees of BSM, a strategy consultancy a tier below the likes of McKinsey and Bain.

Visually, Cowly didn't impress: pudgy-faced with a comb-over, his arms too short for his ill-fitting suit, the seat of his trousers edging towards shiny. He looked more eighties than noughties, more typewriter than ipad. But appearances, in this instance, were misleading. He was a business innovator who just happened to have no interest in fashion or self-image. BSM had made him a partner at thirty-four and ever since he'd been delivering double-digit profits.

Cowly had asked Ffooks to arrange the meeting. 'Good morning everyone,' said Cowly. He rubbed his nose with the back of his hand and scanned the faces round the table. 'Thank you for coming along at such short notice, on a Saturday. I think everyone's made it.' He glanced at Ffooks, who confirmed with a nod that all those invited were present. 'As you know we've been looking at some rather unusual investment opportunities this past month and I'm hoping today we can make a final decision on these. Before we do that, Phylida is going to run through the fund's current position.' He nodded towards the projector.

Taking her cue, Phylida Cranson walked to the head of the table, her dark curly hair bouncing on her shoulders. She was thirty-two, an inch taller than Cowly and almost as broad. As a young teenager she'd been a county swimming champion, before horses and boys intervened. After 'A' levels, she read German and Economics at Durham. She'd been with BSM for five years.

'Hello everyone,' she said. 'Nice to see you all again.' She leant forward, picked up the wireless controller and selected her first slide. 'This is where we were.'

In pounds and percentages, the slide showed the fund's investment portfolio by sector and country for the years 2008 to 2013. Throughout the five-year period the fund had been heavily invested in property, banks, telecoms, and oil and gas, spread across twenty countries and four continents. She smiled at the faces around the table, almost apologetic. Nothing more needed to be said, because the numbers on the slide had changed history; it was the first PowerPoint ever to appear on page 3 of The Sun. On the day of publication, the paper's editor had asked his readers for their patience and forgiveness, saying:

> '...in times of national crisis we all have to make sacrifices....but I give you my word, the gazongas will be back as soon as he's packed his bags...'

The target of the editor's displeasure was on the front page of the same edition. Underneath the 'OH MY GOD' headline was a photograph of the Archbishop of Canterbury, Dr Philip Prendergast. The image had been digitally altered giving Prendergast a purple face to match his shirt.

In the bottom right corner of the infamous slide, the Sun had circled *'less than 1%'* in red marker pen. The percentage represented the Church's investments in UK-based enterprises. On the facing page the paper published an

13

article Prendergast had written for The Church Times two weeks earlier. Much of it covered old ground; Prendergast had castigated the misdeeds of the City, its short-termism, and its hunger for profit at any price. He attacked the retailers that traded on their British heritage, while simultaneously scouring the world for $2-a-day economies from which to source their British-designed goods. He named thirty companies in the FTSE 100 that structured their businesses with the sole purpose of avoiding tax.

He raged most fiercely at the scandal at Bircleys Bank Plc, and its inability to do the right thing. Bircleys had paid out £4 billion to its customers for the mis-selling of Payment Protection Insurance (PPI). And while the bank's CEO had apologised and talked about the future, a whistleblower revealed that behind the scenes the bank had other ideas. Under the CEO's instruction, Bircleys had set up a score of PPI claims companies all registered in the Cayman Islands, each of which was tasked with helping the victims of the PPI mis-selling to claim their rightful compensation. They offered this service for a standard thirty-five percent commission. The whistleblower's killer revelation was that all the commission monies raised by these Cayman-based companies was secretly channelled back to the parent company. In effect, Bircleys had recouped a third of the money they had been forced to pay out. Bircleys, said the Archbishop, had legally profited from their own crimes.

To help the Sun's readers understand why Prendergast was such a colossal hypocrite, the paper had circled key phrases where Prendergast had pleaded for investment in the long-term, in local communities, and in people, young and old. Fine words, said the Sun, except that the Church was a major shareholder in Bircleys. The Church Times article was a monumental blunder.

But Prendergast had other problems besides the Sun. YouGov rushed out a poll showing that regular Church attendance had dropped a further three-percent, year-on-year; with male attendances down seven-percent. Even the poll figures that went up were still bad: fifty-six percent thought Prendergast should resign; the average age of worshippers had risen to sixty-four; and thirty-four percent believed Jesus wrote the Bible, up two-percent on the previous year. The Bishop of York commented: *'If the Church was a business it would be ripe for liquidation'*, while a leader in The Daily Telegraph said: *'the Church will soon be operating in the margins of the margin'*.

In response, the Church of England's Communications Office – their quasi marketing department – held an emergency workshop at the Hotel du Vin in Harrogate. Ninety clergy and laity attended and two days later the Deputy Director of Communications summarised their findings in a report to The Archbishops' Council.

On reading the executive summary, Prendergast dropped it in the bin beside his desk. It said nothing that hadn't been said a dozen times before, that the Church needed to find common ground, increase its relevance, and to embrace social networking. To Prendergast it was all generalities and no solutions. He lifted his feet from his desk and swung round to face his wall of books. He scanned the middle shelf of biographies; Keynes, Churchill, Mandela, Gorbachev, Thatcher, Feynman, Bronowski and more. He'd read them all except for the one on the very end – 'My Life by Bill Clinton'. He pulled it back with his index finger and read the back sleeve. He felt the weight of its nine hundred pages and wondered how the Deputy Director of Communications would capture it all in a powerpoint slide.

- *Fornication?*
- *Near impeachment?*
- *The economy, stupid?*

And there, he thought, was his answer – the economy! The next day he met with Ken Ffooks, and the day after that Ffooks met with Tom Cowly. A further two weeks passed before he broke his silence on the YouGov poll and the infamous slide. To a half-empty House of Lords, he cleared his throat and said, 'My Lordships, this won't take long.'

'That's a blessing,' came a voice from behind. It belonged to Donal Casey, the one and only Catholic Bishop in the house.

Prendergast ignored the heckle. 'If you would indulge me for a few moments, I would like you to imagine a powerpoint slide.' Laughter rippled through the chamber. Even Casey smiled. Prendergast raised his hand. 'No, not that one, another one. This one has just four bullet points and no numbers.' He unfolded a piece of paper. 'Bullet point one, the Church is reassessing its investment policy.' A few cheered. 'Bullet point two, the Church will be investing in British people and enterprise.' This time the cheers were more enthusiastic. 'Bullet point three, the Church will be investing in jobs and prosperity and not profits for the few.' The cheers now so loud they woke the sleeping. Prendergast waited for the room to fall quiet. 'And finally, the Church will define a new moral compass for corporate Britain.' As he sat down, the members applauded.

But Prendergast's new investment strategy had alarmed Ffooks. He feared that with the focus on the UK economy, the fund's overall performance would probably plummet. In response to the challenge, he created a separate investment arm – Church of England Enterprises Limited (CEEL) – that wouldn't be constrained by the 2004 Pensions Act. Ffooks then instructed Cowly and his BSM colleagues to look for UK-based acquisition targets where CEEL would become the majority stakeholder.

In the Breakfast Room, Phylida moved on to her second slide. 'Here is where we are now,' she said. 'As you all know we've made some progress. Our investment in British enterprises has risen to just over five-percent. It's progress, but not at the rate we require. When this quarter's deals are finalised the figure will rise to seven.' She looked at Cowly and he nodded back. Her brief and wholly unnecessary presentation was over. Whatever the situation, whoever the client, Cowly always made sure she was involved. At times it was embarrassing, though she knew he was only following BSM guidelines that required senior managers to mentor their juniors.

'Thank you Phylida,' said Cowly.

She returned to her seat, placing the controller by his arm.

'When we last met I mentioned that I was looking at two acquisitions for CEEL.' He picked up the controller and summoned the next slide.

'The first one is the recently mothballed wind-turbine facility in Eastleigh, together with the wind-farm developer, Boreas Plc. The initial investment for these two assets would be £50 million, with a further £400 million for the development and operation of new onshore and offshore wind-farms. In ten years, and assuming all current planning applications are granted, the combined businesses should have manufactured and installed over one gigawatt of generating capacity. The investment will deliver low-risk returns for at least twenty years. A profitable, made-in-Britain business no less.' He looked around the table at the nodding heads.

'Our second investment opportunity concerns the purchase of Millwall Football Club. They currently lie in second place in the Championship. As you know we've been talking to the club through intermediaries since February and those negotiations have gone well. The provisional offer to the current owners is that through a newly created company the Church will purchase the club for a nominal one pound, with the understanding that the debt and borrowings are settled in full within three months.'

Derek Connelly, one of Ffooks' senior analysts, raised his hand. 'Tom, a question. Have we factored in the cost of paying-off the existing management staff, assuming that is we have to bring in new people?'

'At present,' said Cowly, 'we don't envisage replacing the current manager, though he may decide to leave. His contract expires in the summer, so whatever he or we decide to do, there won't be any compensation. The only additional cost will be for new players.'

Connelly nodded and Cowly continued. 'As you know with promotion comes a broadcasting payment from the Sport Channel via the LPFL (League Premiership Football Limited). That will cover our investment in new players.

17

Our current offer to the Millwall board is conditional on promotion. He smiled briefly. 'We all know the football sector is like no other. It has a reputation for poor governance and financial ineptitude, but I'm still of the opinion that where clubs are run sensibly and sustainably, their asset value will grow. At our last meeting some of you requested some evidence to that effect, so I've put together these two slides.' He clicked the controller. 'This one shows the medium and long-term asset value of ten clubs in the top two divisions.' The figures showed that every club had doubled or trebled in value over a ten-year period. 'Of course, I could show a list of twenty clubs where the opposite is true. The point is, clubs can create value.'

He clicked the controller.

Non-monetary reasons for investing in football:

- *To raise the Church's profile*
- *To provide leadership to the national game*
- *To engage with football fans at all levels*
- *To improve the game's reputation*
- *To make the club a role model for all clubs*
- *To provide opportunities for British players*

BSM/CoE Assets Committee

He pointed at the slide and said, 'These are all very commendable aims, but whether or not they are achievable, I don't know.' He paused and looked round the table, inviting comment.

'I think we understand that,' said Ffooks.

Cowly nodded and continued. 'I believe success with Millwall will require hard work and constant attention. We can't just buy it and hope for the best. Because the game at the top level is awash with money, it doesn't mean it's an easy place to make a profit.

'Unless you're a player,' said Connelly.

Cowly smiled.

'I think we all appreciate that Tom,' said Ffooks. 'Personally, I've no parallels; I've nothing to judge this against.'

'My feeling,' said Cowly, 'is it's less predictable...riskier than other sectors.' He raised his eyebrows. 'But maybe the rewards will be that much greater.'

After further discussion the Committee voted unanimously to go ahead with both acquisitions. One issue, however, remained unresolved: who would take responsibility for Millwall? The wind turbine businesses weren't a problem; the existing board at Boreas would be retained. For Millwall, there was no time to recruitment an outsider. Cowly had a solution, but he felt it was only right that someone else should make the suggestion.

Ffooks duly obliged. 'Tom, would you like to take charge at Millwall, assuming you can get BSM to agree? Say for the first six months?'

Cowly said he'd be happy to.

4

St John's Wood, Monday 7th March

In the backyard of 43 Sycamore Drive, Vince washed his head and hands from a bucket of ice-cold water. He dried his face on the sleeves of his hoodie and then carried his bag of clothes into the small windowless box-room that would soon be the laundry. Standing on some plastic sheeting, he removed his work boots and undressed down to his long-johns, t-shirt and socks. A minute later and close to shivering, he was dressed in a blue shirt, v-neck jumper and grey suit. He pulled on his tan slip-ons, and as he left the room, kicked his work clothes into the corner.

Alex was on the first floor, re-checking the treads with a boat-level.

'I'm off now,' said Vince.

'Okay, see you later...and good luck.'

On the tube via Green Park his thoughts turned to his meeting with Barros. *Did Barros know about Spinks? Did it matter? Tell him it's irrelevant...you can trust me...you need a writer, not a journalist.* Then later, in Knightsbridge, he wondered if Barros had other players that might need a ghost-writer. He walked past the hotel and carried on for a hundred yards before he realised his mistake. The Berkley was on a side street facing away from the main road. Its name, carved into a sandy facade, could only be seen up close.

'Not exactly obvious,' said Vince to the crombie-coated doorman. The doorman looked straight ahead, offering no opinion. Vince turned away, flattened his collar, and pulled on his shirt sleeves. Up the steps he pushed at the revolving door and stopped a few yards inside the foyer. He was immediately struck by the contrast. An hour ago he'd been on a dusty building site where the portaloo was caked in shit and flushed with a bucket. He looked down at the shiny floor and at the pressed and polished staff behind the reception desk. He felt conspicuous, like a contaminant. He glanced at his jacket sleeves and trousers, checking for dust marks. Then he strode across the foyer to the men's room. Inside he removed his jacket, dampened a hand towel and wiped his head, ears and face. Then he leaned in close to the mirror. He wondered again how much Kathy had told Barros. Then he whispered some advice to his reflection, 'Just see what happens, that's all you have to do.' He straightened, pulled back his shoulders, and said, 'Pleased to meet you Señor Barros.' He forced a smile and held out his hand. It was a mistake.

Back in the foyer he called Barros.

'Hello Vince. Have you arrived?'

'Yes.'

'We are in the Caramel Room, on the first floor.'

'I'm on my way.'

From the first floor lift the maitre d' led Vince across the brown carpet, passed the brown sofas, to a table in the far corner of the tea-room.

'Mr Barros, your lunch guest,' said the maitre d'.

In an armchair sat a middle-aged man with a full head of hair, his tanned neck flesh overlapping his shirt collar. He had eight gold rings tight around eight stubby fingers. Slouched opposite was Kevin Furling, dressed in jeans and t-shirt, with a structured but dishevelled haircut. Barros gripped the arms of his chair and rose slowly to his feet. They shook hands. Vince noted the Rolex.

'Pleased to meet you Vince.'

Vince smiled. 'You too.'

They glanced down at Furling who pointed at his mobile and resumed his conversation. Barros looked at Vince and shrugged his shoulders as if to say, where did we go wrong?

'Take a seat,' said Barros.

Vince pulled back a chair and sat bolt-upright, his hands clenched to hide his dirty finger nails.

'Thanks for coming today,' said Barros. 'As I said on the phone, Kevin needs a book. He needs a ghost-writer.'

Vince would eventually learn that Furling was a left-winger with a distinctive over-striding gait. Revered for his whipped-in crosses from the by-line, for a few years he had been touted as a left-sided Beckham. He had twenty England caps, but hadn't been picked since the appointment of the current England manager, Henning Wehn.

Barros continued. 'We have a publisher that is interested and we feel now is a good time for Kevin. He has achieved much, but soon his career will be over.'

Vince turned to Furling expecting some sort of response, but he wasn't listening.

'The deadline is the end of April. We want it ready for the next season, so there is not much time. Your fee is ten thousand. I pay two now and the rest when it is finished.'

Vince nodded. Barros had delivered his terms and it was clear that they weren't for negotiation.

'It would be more,' said Barros, 'but the book has been started. You just need you to finish it. I am afraid the first writer we sacked.'

'I see,' said Vince. He didn't like what he was hearing. First a low fee, and now he's hiring and firing writers. 'What went wrong?'

Barros read Vince's thought. 'Don't worry my friend. It was nothing serious. He got behind and we pulled the plug.' Barros waved his hand, indicating that there was nothing more to say on the matter.

'How far did he get?'

Barros leant forward and handed Vince a blue memory stick. 'There are six chapters on that and I have some background information.' He reached under the table for his navy-blue briefcase. He withdrew a lever-arch file and a scrapbook and placed them both on the table in front of Vince.

'And are you happy with these chapters then?' said Vince, holding up the memory stick.

Barros shook his head.

'What I mean is, would you like me to carry on in the same style or re-write them?'

'Yes, we are happy with the six. You just need to continue to the end.'

Vince placed his hand on top of the scrap book and file. 'And can I take these away?'

'Take the file, but not the scrapbook. That is the only copy and it is Kevin's.' They both turned to Furling, but he was still on the phone.

'Okay, I'll look at what's been done, and then perhaps we should meet again?'

'Yes Vince, but give me a call when you have read the first six...tomorrow or Wednesday? If you cannot do it, we will need to find someone who can.'

'I'll call tomorrow,' said Vince.

They stood and shook hands and Vince nodded a goodbye to Furling.

As he left the tea-room he winked at the maitre d' and ran down the stairs. Outside he tipped the doorman's bowler hat from behind, and not stopping or looking back, he raised both arms above his head, with his thumbs pointing skywards.

Between leaving the Berkley and arriving home his mood changed. He dropped the lever-arch file on the Parker-Knoll.

Ailish shouted from the bathroom. 'How did it go?'

'Not good.'

She pushed the door open and a wave of steam swept across the carpet. 'You serious?'

'Furling never said a word. They're only paying ten thousand. I might not bother.' He shrugged his shoulders.

She shook her head and pulled the door shut.

He prised off his shoes and stared down at the file containing the first six chapters. Fearing the worst, he'd not looked at them on the journey home. He wondered what the first word would be. *Was it I or My or When?* Then he tried to guess the first sentence. *When I was two/three/four...my father/mother/brother...gave me a leather football/Nike boots/Adidas shin-pads.*

Vince had only ever read one book about football and that was the one he'd written. When he finished the first draft of 'Kick in the Park', Carpenter's lawyers deleted whole sections, including all the opinion on other players, managers and clubs. The final version bore no resemblance to the original draft. Like a body dipped in acid, all that remained were the bare-bones of Carpenter's life. The flesh, his voice and personality, had been wiped, and when it was published, the book was rightly panned. Vince assumed that Barros and Furling would want a similar story of banality; of dates, goals, and injury scares, because in the summer, at the book launch, only Furling would be there to answer questions from the media. It wouldn't matter that Furling hadn't written a word; all that mattered was that he understood what had been said on his behalf. Vince blew out his cheeks, sat down and opened the file: *Chapter 1: Playing with Dad.*

As he read, Ailish washed and shaved. When she finally emerged in her towelling bathrobe – untied at the front – Vince had just finished chapter 3. Looking up and then down at her open bathrobe, he said, 'How was it down there?'

'I think I'll get a new razor...something a bit sharper.'

'If it's that painful, leave it. I don't mind.'

'I don't do it for you Vince. I do it because I like the smoothness.'

'What about waxing?'

'Why, are you paying?'

'Can't you do it yourself?'

She changed the subject. 'How was it? She nodded at the file on his lap.

'It's okay. Not as bad as I was expecting. I'll call Barros tomorrow and tell him I'll do it.'

'Good. Why don't you come into the bedroom and tell me about him.' She turned and let the bathrobe fall from her shoulders.

After a quick shower, Vince lay on the bed with Kevin's file on his lap. Ailish dried her hair, while combing it with her fingers.

He turned to chapter 2. 'This section is about where his parents have just moved house.'

Soon after Dad finished playing for Kidderminster we moved down to the South West. He'd been a groundsman at Wolverhampton Racecourse and was offered the head job at Wincanton. I know Mum didn't want to go, she was born and bred in Kidderminster and that's where all her friends and family were. I was nine at the time and I didn't want to go because I knew she didn't. One day we were living in a small semi with a paved patio and the next we were in a bungalow with a racecourse and nine-hole golf-course for a garden. We moved in the summer. That gave Dad a few months to settle in before the jump season started.

I spent that first summer at the racecourse pretty much on my own. I'd no one to play with. I used to follow Dad around, watching him cut the grass, building the steeplechase fences, and lots of other stuff. Mum got a job at the local cheese factory. She hated it. I remember her complaining about having to wear a hairnet and white wellies. Fortunately for her she wasn't there long because she was offered a job at the racecourse.

When September came and I started at school, I was playing football again, first for the school, and then for Wincanton. They ran junior teams up to the age of sixteen. I stayed there a couple of years and then Dad took me to see someone at Yeovil and from then on that's where I played. I captained every side I was in. I didn't really want to be captain. It just seemed to happen that way.

I had a great time playing football, scoring lots of goals and doing okay at school. In the summer, I worked on the racecourse and sometimes on the golf course – mowing, weeding bunkers, painting fences. I learnt to drive a tractor. If I wasn't working or playing for Yeovil, I was kicking a football, doing tricks, running around the track to get fitter. I used to play 'keepie-uppie' between the hurdles, trying to get from one to another without letting the ball touch the

25

grass. Then, when I'd done that once, I set myself the target of doing it between three hurdles. That was about three or four hundred yards. But I made it more difficult. I told myself I had to get over the middle hurdle without dropping the ball. So I used to practice kicking it up high, leaping over the hurdle and then bringing the ball down with my left foot. When I could do that I set myself the target of going round the whole course – which was just over a mile – doing keepie-uppie, and getting over all seven hurdles. I had the skill but not the fitness. It took me a year before I finally did it – I was thirteen and nine months.

So for me Wincanton was a good time. But I do remember causing a big bust-up between my Dad and Henry, the golf course greenkeeper. At the time it seemed really serious, I thought Dad might lose his job. It was also the only time that he ever threatened to hit me. He swung his foot at me, but I don't think he was really trying to connect. He was just very annoyed, though I was never really sure if he was just putting it on. The incident happened at one of the bunkers at the top end of the course. I think it was the fifth hole. Henry used give me a fiver to rake all the small bunkers, pull out any weeds, and clean up any dog mess. A couple of the bunkers seemed to attract the local dogs. Anyway, one Sunday, Henry asked me to do the bunkers. I walked round with a rake, a bucket and a trowel. But that day, when I got to the fifth hole – the bunker with the dog mess – I realised I'd left my trowel behind. It was really messy. Some monster of a dog had left a massive heap of runny poo. It was too messy to move with my foot and I couldn't be bothered to go and find the trowel, so I covered in over with sand and then raked the rest of the bunker. That was that, until Monday morning. According to what I overheard Dad say, one of the members came storming off the golf course...'

'Oh no,' said Ailish, turning around to face Vince.

26

...one of the members came storming off the golf course, through the club house, and straight into Henry's office. I think there must have been a lot of swearing with Henry trying to apologise. The furious golfer was splattered head to toe in dog diarrhoea. As soon as the golfer left Henry's office, Henry went to see my Dad. I guess he gave my Dad a mouthful and when I came home from school it was my turn. That was when my Dad swung his boot at me. So from that Monday I never set foot on the golf course again and Henry never said another word to me.'

Vince stopped and looked up at Ailish.

'Nice one,' she said.

'Shall I carry on?'

'That'll do for now.' She switched off the drier, climbed onto the bed and threw the lever-arch file onto the carpet.

They had sex in her favourite position, from behind, and after, as he traced the line of her spine with his finger, joining up the tiny beads of sweat, he wondered if anyone had ever written a definitive account of the female orgasm and all its variations. He tickled her neck and said, 'What about filming that?

'Filming what?'

'You having an orgasm.'

'For what purpose?' She turned over to face him.

'For the purpose of investigation,' he said. 'Because we need to know.' Playfully, he pinched the side of her thigh.

'Know what?'

'I'd like to know about your orgasm, so it would help if we filmed it.'

'You could just ask me.'

'Well I figure it's impossible to describe it as it happens, but if we filmed it, and then played it back, that would help you remember...like an aide-memoire. We could record your thoughts as you watch yourself come.'

She laughed. 'That's the first time I've heard porn described as an aide-memoire.'

'We could use your camera. I'll film while you have the orgasm.'

'Is that fair?'

'It's not exactly work is it? You'll enjoy it.'

Unconvinced, she rolled onto her back. 'I'm not sure I want you to know what I'm thinking. You might not like it.'

'It's not really about your fantasies or thoughts. It's only about the moment of climax.'

'You're not interested in my fantasies?' She faked a look of disappointment.

'I suppose they might be inseparable...the physical and the mental. We could look at the whole thing.'

'Vince, I know what it's like. And anyway, I won't come, not with you filming.'

'Well if you think you won't, you won't. But it might work the other way. It might turn you on.'

'Sure Vince, you know best.' She'd heard enough. She rose from the bed and went into the bathroom. On the way she said, 'And don't you go messing with my camera.'

5

Brighton, Thursday 10th March

While Alex priced up a stair job in Ascot, Vince travelled by train to Brighton for his first meeting with Kevin Furling. Barros called him as the train pulled out of Gatwick. 'I cannot make it today. Something has come up with another player. I have to deal with it.'

'Okay, so what do...'

'We meet later, when you are back in London. I need to know when the other chapters will be done.' Having delivered his message, Barros cut the call.

Vince stared at his phone and said, 'Have a nice day.'

Outside Brighton Station he passed a line of taxis that stretched up and along Terminus Road. He had time on his hands so he set off down Queens Road towards the seafront, his bag over one shoulder, hands in pockets. Brighton had been Vince's home town for four years: three as a student and one as an out of work graduate. He'd stayed on after university because he thought it would be easier getting a break in Brighton; everyone else on his course seemed to be heading for London. But for twelve months it didn't pay off. He litter-picked in the summer and worked in a bar in the winter. His first break came after he sent some unsolicited film reviews to the Brighton Argus. Though they had no vacancies, a couple of weeks later the Features Editor of the Evening Standard called and offered him a six-month trial as their Arts Correspondent. With that he moved to Croydon and later to Tooting.

At the seafront he turned west and walked along the lower promenade between Kings Road and the pebble beach. All the cafes, bars and shops that faced the sea were shut, waiting for the warmer weather and with it the free spending crowds from London. But Vince knew of one cafe that might be open. He knew the owner, a Scotsman called Andy. They first met at a weekly poetry slam when they were both students. On slam nights they teamed up; Andy would read Vince's apocalyptic poems in an extreme version of Glasgow patter. If the audience's reaction was negative, Andy would stop mid-verse, call them fuckin' jakies and walk off, and if they cheered, he assumed it was ironic and he'd give them the finger.

Andy's business, The World Famous Pump Room, was a humble snack-bar shoe-horned into one of the brick-lined arches that cut underneath the Kings Road. Its grandiose name explained by a large blue plaque above its yellow awning:

> 'The Pump Room was established between 1862-64 to provide seawater to the nearby Grand Hotel when Brighton's seawater was considered to be beneficial to health. Every room in the Grand Hotel had three taps; one hot, one cold and a third for seawater from the Pump room. Today the World Famous Pump Room maintains the tradition of providing high quality health enhancing refreshments to Brighton's residents and visitors.'

Vince turned in by the beach volleyball and said, 'Hi Andy.'

From behind the counter Andy looked up and smiled. 'How you doin?'

Though they hadn't seen each other for three years, they didn't shake hands, they never had. If they'd not met for a decade or two it wouldn't have been any different. Neither was one for visiting, but when they did meet, usually in Brighton, usually at the Pump Room, their friendship resumed.

Vince always looked first at Andy's hair, for signs of grey or thinning. He couldn't see any. 'You look well,' he said.

'Aye, not bad. You want a coffee?' Vince nodded and Andy went back inside. 'What you down for?'

'I'm writing a book for a footballer. He lives in Hove.'

There was no follow-up from Andy, no curiosity, and that was normal too. He put two shots of coffee into the group-handle and then stopped. He glanced at Vince. 'Can you finish off? I'm busting.'

Vince checked the time on his phone. He still had an hour and a half before he was due at Furling's. 'Okay.'

Andy came out onto the pavement and put his hand on Vince's shoulder, 'I won't be long.' He unlocked his rusty bike and as he tucked his trouser bottoms into his socks, he said, 'Where's your dog?' It was an afterthought and he didn't wait for an answer. He rode off in the direction of the Palace Pier towards the public conveniences. Vince's dog had been dead five years.

Behind the Pump Room's counter not much had changed. They were the same appliances from years ago, the walls still needed painting, and the fridge compressor still groaned like an angry old man. Vince topped his coffee with cold milk and then sat out front on one of the Pump Room's chairs. An hour and six customers later Andy returned. 'What happened?' said Vince, unable to hide his irritation.

Andy re-locked his bike. 'I had to see someone at the Council.' It wasn't an apology, just a statement of fact.

'I have to go,' said Vince. 'I put the takings in a mug.'

Andy nodded. There was no smile or frown.

'I should be down again in a week or two. It depends how it goes.' Vince grabbed his bag and continued along the esplanade. A quarter of a mile further on, he crossed over Hove Gardens and onto the lawns of Adelaide Crescent. He turned on the spot. Much like the Pump Room not much seemed to have changed. From the beach, the nineteenth-century crescent spoke of authority and money, but up close, the peeling paint and cracked render told a story more ordinary. It surprised Vince. He thought the location a little downmarket for a millionaire footballer.

He picked out Furling's first floor apartment; the tall sash window at the front opened onto a wrought-iron fenced balcony that offered sideways view of the beach. Vince checked the time on his phone and then his inside jacket pocket for a pen. He was dreading the next few hours. At the Berkeley, Furling had barely said a word. If he couldn't speak in sentences it was going to be a nightmare.

He pressed the buzzer and was met on the landing with a genuine smile and a firm handshake. Barefooted and in shorts, Furling said, 'It's Vince isn't it?'

'Yes.'

'Good journey?'

'Fine thanks. I got the train.'

Vince walked in sensing that this wasn't the man he'd met just three days ago. This version was polite and attentive. He took Vince's coat and then stared down at his shoes. 'If you don't mind,' said Kevin, apologetically. 'It scratches the floor.'

'Of course not.' Vince crouched down to untie his laces.

'Would you like a drink?'

'Tea, no sugar.'

Kevin disappeared into the kitchen and shouted, 'What sort?'

'Ordinary is fine.' Pulling off his left shoe Vince noticed the row of footwear stretching along the edge of the hallway, first trainers, then shoes and then boots, all their toe-ends touching the skirting board, all their laces folded inwards. He wondered if Kevin or perhaps his housekeeper was OCD, and whether it would be okay to add his scruffy brogues to the line up. He pulled off his right shoe and said, 'Bollocks.' His big toe was poking through his sock.

'You alright?' said Kevin from the kitchen.

'Yes, fine.' He twisted his sock round. It looked odd but he had no option.

Kevin walked past carrying two mugs of tea and said, 'This way.'

Vince clenched the toes of his right foot, picked up his bag and followed Kevin through to the conservatory at the rear of the apartment. They sat opposite each other in feather-cushioned armchairs.

'Nice place,' said Vince.

'Thanks. I like it here. I like Brighton.'

'Ángel said that you're down here most of the time.'

Kevin nodded. 'We don't get much time off during the season, so I come here. I usually spend the summer here.'

'Not one for flying off?'

'Not really. We travel a lot anyway, so the last thing I want is to spend more time in airports and hotels.'

They talked about Brighton for a while, Vince mentioning the poetry-slam at The Belmont and pubs he used to drink at when a student. They were all places unfamiliar to Kevin. Kevin said he would probably move down permanently when his career was over. He said he had no plans to stay in football or work his way down the lower leagues. Then he apologised.

'Sorry about the other day. Ángel and me, we don't get on. We disagree over the book. He wants to do it and I don't.'

'Why's that?' said Vince.

'It's about money...it's always about money.'

'I spoke to Ángel this morning. He seems keen. I guess that's what his job is...to make you money.'

'Yes, and he never stops reminding me. But the book's not going to sell, not in big numbers. So we'll take the advance and I reckon that'll be it. Ángel thinks it's easy money.'

'Easy for him you mean?' Kevin nodded. 'You could refuse to do it.' Immediately Vince regretted his words. Much as he didn't want to write Kevin's book, he needed the it to happen regardless of sales or what Kevin wanted.

'No, we'll do it,' said Kevin. 'We may not get on, but we *need* to get on, if you know what I mean? He's working for me on my next contract. I'm thirty now, so it'll probably be my last. Once it's signed, we'll probably go our separate ways. He'll be looking for a younger player.'

'And what happened to the first writer? Ángel said he got behind.'

'He left.' Kevin paused and looked out of the window at the gardens below and the houses on Holland Road. 'It's complicated.'

'Okay, never mind. Personally, I like to finish what I've started.'

Kevin sat forward and looked Vince in the eye. 'If I tell you what happened, I have to know I can trust you. I mean *really* trust you.'

'Kevin, I don't need to know. It's not important to me.'

'I think it's more a case of you having to know.'

Vince shook his head in puzzlement then gestured with an open hand. 'Okay, go ahead. I've signed a non-disclosure agreement so if I break it, I won't get paid. I've been a journalist for twenty years...I'm used to keeping secrets.'

Kevin laughed. 'Vince you're forgetting, I'm a footballer. I know all about journalists and what they say and what they do.'

'Fair enough, but where does that leave us?'

Kevin smiled. 'I'm not sure.'

Vince leant forward. 'Well you can trust me, and I'll tell you why. I need your book to go ahead. I need the work and I won't do anything to jeopardise it.'

'Good,' said Kevin, then he reached out and they shook hands. 'What I have to tell you is that I paid off the first writer. I told him to make an excuse to Barros. I paid him his fee in full and that was it. I don't want the book written, so that was my solution until Barros decided to find someone else...until he found you.'

'So what's the problem?'

'Besides being a dull read, it won't be the truth.'

Vince smiled. 'I know that. I know you can't say what you really think...but I can do any job you like.'

Kevin nodded. 'The main reason it can't be the truth is because I'm bi, and that can't go in the book.'

'What do you mean?'

'Bi-sexual,' said Kevin. 'I'm bi-sexual.'

'Ah. I see. I...'

'I didn't want him finding out about me. It was too risky. He might have sold it. It's still a story worth more than any ghost-writer's fee.' The previous season Derek Portland became the first top-flight player to announce his homosexuality, and though Portland's gayness was no longer headline news, his career had suffered. He lost his place in the Everton first team and was then loaned out to Bury.

Vince shook his head. 'So why you telling me?'

'It has to be a secret between you and me. If I pay you off like the last one, Barros will probably find another. He's already taken the advance. He doesn't like giving money back.' Kevin paused and then added, 'I'm trusting you Vince.'

'And Mr Barros doesn't know you're...?'

'No, he doesn't.'

'Okay, I understand. But what about the book? Relationships? A footballer's story and no mention of WAGS? It'll look a bit odd.' Then he quickly added, 'Not that there's anything odd about being...'

'That's one of the reasons I don't want to do it. The absence of women...of girlfriends. It'll look suspicious.'

'So we'll focus on the football,' said Vince. 'I can do that.'

Relieved, Kevin rolled his shoulders and stretched his arms to the ceiling. 'Perhaps I'll do a sequel when I retire, when I officially come out. I could give a free copy to everyone that bought the first one with an apology.'

'I wouldn't worry about that. They'll probably burn it.'

Kevin frowned.

'Sorry. What I mean is, if you write about being a bi-sexual footballer your readers will be different. It won't be a stocking-filler for young boys. You'd probably get hate mail from Chelsea fans and...' Vince stopped, realising he'd said too much.

'Yes, you're probably right,' said Kevin.

'But if you did do another one, it would sell. You definitely have a story.' Vince was warming to the idea of a sequel. 'I'm curious, so I'm sure lots of others would be too.'

'Bi-curious?' said Kevin, straight-faced.

'Err...no, not that. I mean curious about being in football and having to live...'

Kevin smiled at Vince's embarrassment. 'I know what you mean.' Kevin sipped his tea, holding his mug in two hands. 'I'm pretty much celibate now. I had to pay-off one guy to keep him quiet. I don't want to go through that again.'

'And you handled it?'

'It cost me a few thousand.'

'Tens?'

'Six figures,' said Kevin.

'But if you are bi, then you've had girlfriends? We could write about one of them.'

'I have, but nothing long-term. It wouldn't look right. Why would I tell people about a girl that I only knew for a few months?'

'Fair enough, but you could look for a woman now.'

Kevin laughed.

'What is it?'

'It doesn't really work that way, not for me. It's more about who I meet.'

'But if you went to a bar today, this evening, would you be looking for a man or a woman?'

'It depends on the bar.'

'Of course,' said Vince, remembering that Brighton had bars that catered for all persuasions.

'Actually, I don't go out much,' said Kevin.

'But if we did go out?'

'Right now?' Kevin paused and dropped back in his chair. 'I suppose I'd like to meet a man.'

'But if you met the right woman?'

'What does that mean?'

'Someone that you could marry?'

Kevin smiled. 'I suppose that's possible. But what about you Vince, have you met the right woman?'

Vince didn't need to think about his answer. 'No, not even close.'

'Why's that?'

36

'I don't know. I guess I'm not that type, not a homemaker.' He didn't have a better answer.

'So when did you last live with someone?'

'I am now.'

'But she's not for you?'

'I think it's more a case of I'm not for her. Circumstances sort of brought us together.'

Kevin nodded. 'I was a slow starter. I didn't have sex until I was twenty-two. It didn't bother me. Football and school work took all my time, though I knew when I was fourteen that I was bi. I chose football over sex. It was too dangerous to mix them.'

'But you live in Brighton?'

'I've got a wave board,' said Kevin.

Vince shook his head. He'd never heard of a wave board.

'I like being by the sea and on the beach. I like swimming. That's why I'm here. But you're right, I don't talk to others about where I live. I keep a low profile. I drive a Golf.'

They chatted some more about Brighton, and then Vince suggested they get to work. 'I've some ideas for the next few chapters.' He opened his note book. 'Chapter seven could cover your England career, chapter eight your World Cup, chapter nine your time at Reading, and then another on your two seasons with Chelsea.'

'Sounds okay,' said Kevin.

Vince switched on his voice recorder and they started talking football. Four hours later Vince packed his bag. They agreed to meet the following week and go through the drafts and then develop some more ideas for a final chapter or two.

It was dark when Vince stepped out onto Adelaide Crescent. The temperature had dropped to near zero. Walking slowly along the seafront his ears and toes were soon numb, but he barely noticed. His thoughts were on Kevin and their conversation, and how hard it must be to spend one's life hiding the truth. He passed the Pump Room not noticing that the shutters were down. On the train back to London he called Barros and left a message.

6

M4, Monday 14th March

The following Monday, Vince and Alex were moving stop-start along the westbound carriageway of the M4, on their way to Maidenhead to fit a glass balustrade. Vince was there to help Alex carry and hold the panes of toughened glass. Over the weekend he'd worked solidly on Kevin's book while Ailish was staying with her sister in north London.

'How's the writing?' said Alex, easing into second gear.

'Not bad. As footballers go, he's alright. He talks in sentences.'

'He has things to say?'

'Yes, but he's still playing...he can't speak too freely...there are issues.'

'Like what?'

'Like stuff that I can't mention.'

'So why did he mention them?'

'I guess...he just felt he had to. It's a trust thing.'

Alex shook his head.

'Like with a doctor and patient.'

'I see,' said Alex, unconvinced. He moved up into third. 'I don't really see how anyone can write their life story when they're still playing?'

'It's just about his football career. It's just a money thing. His agent wants to do the book and if he doesn't do it now, it'll never happen. Publishers aren't interested in dull stories from retired players. Basically, it's a stocking-filler.'

'I had Gary Lineker's,' said Alex. 'I just looked at the pictures.'

'There you go.'

'So has anyone else been in touch?'

'How do you mean?'

'Perhaps some of Furling's mates will want one?'

'No, it'll be a one-off. I'm not sure he has any mates...he hasn't mentioned any.'

They didn't talk for a few minutes then Alex said, 'Kirsty wanted to know something.' Kirsty was Alex's partner. They had two kids and a semi in Dorking.

'About Furling?'

'No, about how you ended up in court?'

'Are you sure you want to know?'

'Why not, she does.'

'Okay, for Kirsty then.' Vince lowered his feet from the dash and sat up straight. 'Two years ago I was in the departure lounge at Terminal 1, in a bar.'

'Heathrow?'

'Yes, Heathrow, in Wetherspoons. It was crowded. My flight was delayed and I'd had a couple of Magners.'

'Why?'

'I don't know. I think there was some technical problem with the plane.'

'No, I mean the Magners.' Alex hated cider.

Vince blew out his cheeks. 'Maybe there was a promotion on. Look it doesn't matter, forget I mentioned it.'

Alex nodded.

'The thing was, I'd been drinking and then this tall guy comes up to me. He's wearing sunglasses with his hair combed back. He asks if he can share my table. He looked a bit like an ageing rocker. Anyway, he sat down, pushed his glasses up and I could see his eyes were red. I thought he was either ill or on something. When a waiter came over, he ordered a whisky and pointed to my Magners and the waiter left. His story was like mine. A delayed flight, though he was in transit and heading to New York. He said he'd been in Madrid the night before at a party.'

'Is this for real?' said Alex, sensing that Vince was providing more detail than was really necessary.

'I'm giving you the background. Trust me, Kirsty will need to know.'

'Okay, but why didn't he fly direct from Madrid?'

'How the fuck do I know?' said Vince. 'Maybe he was lying. Anyway, when the drinks arrived I thanked him and we shook hands. He tells me he's David Spinks.'

'Who?'

'He's an artist.'

'What, the cock man?'

'Yes, the cock man,' said Vince, weary of the constant interruptions.

Alex got the message and signalled that his mouth was zipped.

'I'd written about Spinks three or four years earlier. He was featured on this arts programme on BBC2. You wouldn't have seen it. I wasn't complimentary. Anyway, he didn't seem to know me. So we talked, and I told him what I did and he told me who he was, and then I said I thought I recognised him. We had a bit of a chat and a moan about something. Whatever it was, we laughed about it and did that knuckle-knock thing.' Vince shook his head, embarrassed at the memory. 'Spinks got more drinks in. I offered to pay, but he said no. He said something about what goes around. Then I told him about what I was working on.'

'Just one question?' said Alex.

Vince nodded.

'How come you remember all this?'

'This is the story I told in court, to the judge...it's engrained.' Vince tapped the side of his head with his index finger. 'I told Spinks about the stuff I'd ghost-written. I mentioned the one I'd done for Richard Tunkey, the rower. I told him how I made most of it up, but for the bit about the oars. I told Spinks it was easier to make stuff up, rather than waiting for Tunkey to say something interesting.'

'Spinks then said we all do it, we all make stuff up. And I said that of course he made stuff up, he was supposed to make stuff up, that's what artists did. But he said it went further than that. He said he made everything up. Then he said he wasn't really an artist. He called himself a con-artist. I thought it was the drink talking. I've heard all that sort of shit before. Every *creative* (Vince fingered some air quotes)

I've ever met does it. All that fucking self-doubt. I've done it. You do it.'

'No I don't,' said Alex, shaking his head. The van slowed and stopped behind a truck. They looked each other in the eye.

'Yes you do,' said Vince. 'You knock your own work, even when everyone else is saying how good it is. You're just the same. It's a fucking disease and what's worse is that all the fuckers that work with creatives think they're creatives too.' Alex was lost, but Vince carried on. 'Sometimes, I think I'm creative because I help you make stairs, but the reality is, I cut things up and drill a few holes. It's like, if you're not a creative, you're a *nobody.'* He repeated his air quotes.

'I suppose I know what you mean. They're in the building trade too.'

But Vince wasn't listening. His thoughts were back in Wetherspoons.

'So, what next?'

Vince turned to face Alex, 'Sorry?'

'Spinks says he's a con-artist and then what?'

'Spinks said he'd cooked the whole fucking market with someone called Witherspoon. He said Witherspoon bought and sold his work, and paid for his exhibitions.'

'Witherspoon in Wetherspoons?' Alex laughed. 'You're kidding?'

'No. We were in Wetherspoons and his collaborator is Witherspoon.'

'Yes, but it's a bit of a coincidence?'

'No it's not.'

Alex raised his hand. 'Okay, forget it. So why did Witherspoon buy Spinks' art?'

'I don't know. I guess to make money. Spinks said some of his ideas were Witherspoon's. Early on they used to meet up once a fortnight for a sort of progress meeting. They would go out to Mayfair or somewhere, go to a few bars. Sometimes they played snooker at Chelsea Arts Club and then got pissed in the garden. Whatever they got up to, they taped everything they said. They threw around ideas. Spinks

41

said, some were good and some were bad, and some of the good ones were Witherspoon's. And then he told me that the two of them had signed a letter which their lawyers would only make public when they were both dead and buried.'

'I don't get it,' said Alex.

'Spinks said the letter, a sort of death-bed letter, states that they had intentionally manipulated the art market, and that that act itself was a work of art.'

'What, ripping people off is art?'

Vince smiled. 'Good isn't it?'

'Not really. What about the people that bought his work?'

'Spinks said most of them would be dead and he reckoned prices would go up. He said scandal had a market value too. And he's right, people love that shit. I thought the death-bed letter kind of made sense. I believed him.'

'So crime is art?'

Vince put his feet back on the dashboard. 'I don't know about that. That's different. He just said his fiddling with the arts market was art. He didn't mention stealing or killing.'

'And then what?'

'That was pretty much it. I told him that I'd always thought his stuff was shit.'

Alex laughed and hit the steering wheel with the heel of his hand. 'He buys you drinks and you tell him he's shit.'

'Yes, but he didn't seem to mind. He said that's what's so great about it all. No one knows what they're doing. He said that most of the people that buy his work were witless. He called them *sheeple.*'

'Sheeple?'

'People who can't think for themselves, who herd together. That was pretty much it. We had a few more drinks and I gave him some ideas for his next exhibition. We shook hands and he got his flight and I got mine.'

'Okay, so why did you get in trouble?'

'Because I repeated what I've just told you on an internet forum. I told everyone what Spinks had said to me. I said something I couldn't prove. The story about the death-bed letter was the killer. And then it got into the press and

42

everyone in the business knew about it. I went to court and lost my house.'

'You'd got no evidence?'

'Yes, no evidence.'

7

The Den, Monday 21th March

A week later – and two weeks after the Assets Committee's meeting at Merton College, Oxford – an afternoon press conference was underway at The Den, Millwall's stadium in east London. It wasn't full; there were less than twenty journalists, mainly from the local press and radio and the Sport Channel.

The day before Millwall had played West Ham at home and won 4-0. Lonny 'hairy' Harris scored a hat-trick, two with his head and a third with his elbow as he tripped and fell backwards into the net. As Harris was substituted ten minutes before the end, thousands in the Dockers Stand chanted, 'Who's a hairy fucker?' To which the West Stand replied, 'Lonny! Lonny!' The 'hairy' tag had nothing to do with his downy legs and neck, and all to do with his bouffant-like coiffure, an unfortunate consequence of his large domed skull – Lonny's barber was entirely innocent.

The thumping score line had ended a perfect day for Lions' fans: Millwall were fifteen points clear of the third-placed team – plus another point if one counted their vastly superior goal difference – while West Ham dropped into the relegation zone. But none of the fans leaving The Den that afternoon had an inkling of what was to come.

Cowly began with a short statement which simply said, a company called Triboarde has taken over the club and that he was the new CEO. He'd persuaded Ffooks to take a gamble and agree the Millwall purchase even though promotion wasn't yet mathematically guaranteed. He told Ffooks, that if they waited any longer another buyer might step in. Cowly had looked at the stats. No Championship side with a fifteen point lead at the end of March had ever failed to gain promotion to the League Premiership.

When Cowly stopped, Ffooks took over. 'Any questions?' Ffooks pointed to a young reporter from the Docklands Advertiser.

'Mr Cowly, I've just googled Triboarde on my phone.' He raised his phone for all to see. 'There's nothing, it's not even a Googlewhackblatt. You don't exist.'

Cowly nodded and smiled. 'There's nothing on Google because Triboarde is a brand new company. It's wholly owned by the Church of England and under my stewardship I will be seeking to establish Millwall as a successful League Premiership side.' Having dropped the bomb, he looked at Ffooks and raised his eyebrows, as if to say, there's no going back now.

But the anticipated explosion didn't come. Stunned by Cowly's statement, for half a minute, no one said a word. The reporter from the Advertiser went back to his phone looking for confirmation. Mark Groenig from the Sport Channel was the first to speak out. 'Are you saying a bunch of vicars own Millwall?'

Cowly nodded. 'I wouldn't put it that way myself, but in short, yes.'

Some journalists stood up and left the room, others began calling in the story. Phylida handed out a press release which explained the relationship between the Church and the club, and the financial terms of the takeover.

Cowly tapped his microphone and said, 'We'll adjourn for twenty minutes.'

Within an hour all the main broadcasters were camped in the Millwall car park; each demanding an interview with Cowly or Ffooks. Away from the ground, journalists from across the UK were blocking the phone lines to the Church of England's Communications Office. Their Comms Director, Mark Collompton, had been forewarned by Ffooks, but foolishly had taken no preparatory action. After two hours of non-stop calls Collompton had had enough. He set all the phones to voice-mail and recorded a new message referring all callers to a statement on the Church's website. An hour after that the website crashed.

But the media scramble for a definitive view spread much wider than the Den and the offices of the Church of England. Theologians of all faiths, managers and ex-managers, pundits and ex-pundits, professors of philosophy, and experts on the British constitution were all sought out and questioned, generating a flood of cliché and opposing opinion. The two Match of the Day Alans summed it up for most, calling it *unbelievable*.

At the stadium, Cowly had anticipated the response and set up a temporary media centre in the boardroom. Office and retail staff, even the head groundsman, had been brought in to attend the phone lines, each one briefed to keep the conversations short and refer everyone to the Millwall website. A meeting of the Church Commissioners had been pre-arranged for Wednesday. Cowly figured that by then, they would have a better understanding of how the news had been received and how they might need to respond. He instructed his colleagues at BSM to monitor all the press coverage. Phylida had the task of bringing it all together for the Wednesday meeting.

The resumed press conference eventually ended at five. Cowly, Phylida and Ffooks retreated to the Chairman's office.

As Cowly shut the door, he clenched his fist, and said, 'That couldn't have gone better.'

'History in the making?' suggested Phylida. 'Or is that a bit over the top?'

'I think it is,' said Cowly. 'We'll find out soon enough.'

A worried looking Ffooks didn't share their enthusiasm. The relentless questioning on football and religion weren't his idea of fund management. He also felt compromised. From the start he'd not been keen on the Millwall purchase, and though he'd raised concerns during Asset Committee meetings, he hadn't voiced strong opposition or chosen to exercise his veto. He'd not taken on the role as the Director of Investments for the money. After thirty years in the investment business, Ffooks was seeking an easy run up to his retirement. On paper, leading the Church's Asset Committee had looked perfect, but when he discovered during his interview that the Church was overhauling its strategy, he nearly pulled out. He'd asked his friends in the city for advice and pretty much they all had the same opinion: *It won't happen...they'll water it down...they'll do a u-turn.* Sufficiently reassured, Ffooks had accepted the job, but after a month in-post it was clear that his city friends had not understood the groundswell for change. His worry now was that as the newly appointed Director of Investments, he'd be seen as the architect of the new strategy, and he'd be blamed if it all went wrong.

Cowly rubbed his hands together. 'Cheer up Ken. The Church wanted to be talked about and now it is. We've got the engagement that you and the Archbishop wanted.' Cowly's enthusiasm had nothing to do with Millwall or football; he'd never supported a team or watched a game from the terraces. His enthusiasm came from making deals and having an impact – business was his game. He glanced at Phylida and put a hand on Ffooks' shoulder. 'It'll die down, don't you worry. Let's just get through these early days unscathed.'

Ffooks nodded and said, 'My worry is that we don't know where this is heading.'

'I know, but we'll deal with it. Just help us this week with some of the interviews. That's all I'm asking.'

'Okay, I'll do what I can,' said Ffooks.

'We're not doing any more today,' said Phylida, 'other than Newsnight. But tomorrow it'll be full on again.'

The producer of Newsnight had called late afternoon and asked Cowly if he would do a one-to-one with Paul Lakin, the show's new anchor. Cowly said yes to the interview, but had declined to take part in the studio discussion.

'Well good luck with Lakin,' said Ffooks, 'I expect he'll do his damnedest.'

'I'm sure he will,' said Cowly. 'We're doing a mock interview in a little while. I could use your help. The trickier the questions the better.'

'I'll be there,' said Ffooks.

8

At nine a BBC limo dropped Cowly and Phylida outside the u-bend shaped building of Broadcasting House. Phoebe Gillard, the programme's assistant producer, met them in reception and immediately offered the use of the Green Room. Cowly refused. He wanted somewhere private where they wouldn't be disturbed by the programme's other guests. She led them to a box-room with a two-seater sofa, a small television and a table of refreshments that didn't include alcohol.

Gillard pushed the door open and said, 'I'll send someone to get you around ten.'

Cowly removed his jacket and shoes, and stretched out on the sofa, his feet resting on the padded armrest. 'Let me know if anything interesting comes through.' He closed his eyes and, in silence, began practicing his answers. Next to the table of juices, Kitkats and crisps, Phylida powered up her laptop and began reading through the stream of emails forwarded by her media colleagues at BSM. Any that she thought might be important she read aloud, and to remember it and understand it, Cowly repeated the information back to her, word-for-word.

Lakin had a reputation for being weak on numbers, so Cowly rehearsed his answers to the moral issues surrounding the dangers of mixing religion and sport, and the conflict between Christian ethics and a national game that only valued money. He expected that at sometime during the interview Lakin would deploy his trademark tactic. Whenever Lakin thought his interviewee was being too clever or evasive, he'd stare, Benaud-like, into the camera, as if to say – 'Can you hear this twerp, this big-head, with his fancy words and his half-truths?' And occasionally, while his guest was still talking, still being evasive, he'd glance to camera and raise an eyebrow, or turn his lower lip inside out, like a chastised child. In his defence, Lakin said he only looked to camera to make his audience feel like they were part of the discussion. He was, he said, simply acknowledging his viewers' frustration as much as his own.

Barry Princeton, Lakin's predecessor, who four months earlier had moved on to a more lucrative role with Top Gear Magazine (he penned a column featuring interviews with distinguished politicians and entrepreneurs, prising out anecdotes of their motoring highs and lows, a sort of petrol-head version of *Desert Island Discs*) had said that with Lakin's appointment the BBC had gone beyond dumbing down and that 'the boy' – Lakin had cut his journalistic teeth on *The One Show* – wasn't even qualified to interview his dog.

Princeton had intended to keep quiet about his forced departure from the programme, knowing that any criticism of Lakin would come across as sour grapes. But he felt compelled to speak out after seeing the programme's latest innovation. Viewers could now vote, via text or twitter, on whether the programme's guests were telling truths or lies. The so-called RTVO (real-time viewers' opinion) was displayed along the bottom of the screen as an ever changing ratio in green (truths) and red (lies). Princeton assumed it was Lakin's idea.

At ten, Cowly was in make-up, and fifteen minutes later he was sat in studio TD7 waiting for the programme to begin. He pressed a finger to his wrist to check his heart rate. It was higher than normal, but not racing. Across from him, on the other side of the set, were the fifteen experts and opinion formers who had been invited to discuss the relationships and boundaries between sport and religion – eleven men, three women and a teenage boy. To Cowly's right, and centre stage, were Lakin's A-listers: The Bishop of York; John Woodendale MP, the leader of the Culture, Media and Sport Select Committee; and Theo Paphitis, Millwall's Chairman from the late 1990s.

At 10.22 Phylida wished Cowly good luck and returned to the box-room to get a viewer's perspective. At 10.25 an assistant producer asked Cowly if she could have his phone.

'I haven't got one,' said Cowly.

'Are you sure?' Cowly nodded and she nodded back in apology. 'Sorry, but we have to be so careful.'

Lakin walked onto the set with seconds to spare. He shook hands with the bishop and raised an open hand towards Paphitis and Woodendale. Then, as the tally light turned red, he dropped into the swivel seat six feet from Cowly. He smiled to camera and began his opening statement. Cowly followed it on the autocue:

> IT'S BEEN SAID TODAY THAT THE BOUNDARIES OF THIS NATION, DEFINED BY STATE, DOCTRINE AND LORE, HAVE BEEN RE-WRITTEN. FOR CENTURIES, THE CHURCH OF ENGLAND, LIKE A WELL-WORN PAIR OF SLIPPERS, HAS BEEN A COMFORTING AND PREDICTABLE PRESENCE, A BASTION AGAINST THE EXCESSES OF CONTEMPORARY SOCIETY. TODAY THOSE SLIPPERS WERE THROWN ASIDE AND THE CHURCH EMERGED WEARING A PAIR OF HIGH-HEELED DOC MARTINS.

Someone in the darkness at the back of the studio laughed. Lakin didn't falter.

> THE CHURCH HAS BEEN RE-CAST AND TAKEN A RADICAL STEP INTO THE MURKY WORLD OF PROFESSIONAL FOOTBALL. ON TONIGHT'S SHOW...

Yes, thought Cowly. It's a show, a current affairs show.

> ...WE WILL DISCUSS THE CHURCH'S ACQUISITION OF MILLWALL FOOTBALL CLUB. WE'LL BE SPEAKING TO TOM COWLY, MILLWALL'S NEWLY APPOINTED CEO, AND TO THE CLUB'S FORMER CHAIRMAN, THEO PAPHITIS.

WE ALSO HAVE A SPECIALLY SELECTED STUDIO AUDIENCE TO HELP US UNDERSTAND THE RAMIFICATIONS OF RELIGIOUS OWNERSHIP IN PROFESSIONAL SPORT.

As Lakin turned to Cowly, the production room cut to a report from Newsnight's home affairs correspondent, which included a vox-pop with Millwall fans outside the stadium. As it finished, Lakin asked his opening question. 'Tom Cowly, what in God's name is the Church of England doing?'

'Good evening Paul,' said Cowly. Then he waited for Lakin to acknowledge his greeting.

Lakin looked to camera, raised an eyebrow and shook his head in puzzlement. Then, turning back to Cowly, he said, 'It wasn't a difficult question.'

'Good evening Paul,' repeated Cowly. Then accepting that Lakin wasn't about to reciprocate, he began his first prepared answer. 'Millwall Football Club is owned by a company called Triboarde, which itself is wholly-owned by Church of England Enterprises. I'll be seeking to run Millwall sensibly and to make a profit for the club and the Church.'

'Yes, we know that. Triboarde aside, basically the Church owns the club.'

'Yes. The Church is the sole shareholder of CEEL, Church of England Enterprises Limited, so indirectly it does. But the football club will be run and managed by me and my board of directors. And before you ask me, I'm an atheist.'

'Well I'm sure Millwall fans will be heartened to hear that. What's probably concerning them more is that you're a management consultant and you know nothing about football. Do you even know the rules?' Lakin smiled.

'Paul, the CEOs of clubs up and down the country are not ex-footballers. The vast majority are from the private sector, from the business world, so in that respect I'm no different. Triboarde is more than capable of creating and running a successful business and keeping Millwall in the League

51

Premiership. Over the coming weeks and months we'll be making some new appointments.' Cowly paused, as if considering his next statement. 'We won't be looking to appoint from within.' It was bait and Lakin grabbed it.

'So no bishops in the boardroom?' Lakin threw back his head in mild self-amusement.

Cowly countered. 'That's right, and no deacons in the dugout.' The line was Phylida's.

Lakin leant forward ignoring Cowly's riposte. 'So God will be on your side, helping Millwall. Is that fair?'

'We expect God to remain neutral in relation to matters on the field,' said Cowly. 'If we are successful, it will be through hard work and the talent of the players and the backroom staff.'

'You do of course realise, you're entering a world of dubious morality, where greed and lies are endemic. What next for the Church, ethical porn?'

Cowly nearly laughed. 'We know the football industry has its problems, but there are clubs throughout the leagues that are well run, that deliver a good investment return. We aim to make sure Millwall is one of them.'

'It's a pretty short list isn't it?' Lakin picked up his briefing notes and read out his killer facts. 'Over the past ten years, two managers jailed, players banned for drugs offences, fifteen clubs in administration, fights, drunken assaults, it goes on and on.'

'Yes, but it is also the case that some clubs, and I grant you they are a minority, are well managed and return a profit.'

'So it is all about money?' said Lakin. 'How very Christian. Saint Francis will be spinning in his grave.'

'No, it's not, but profit is part of it. The Church Commissioners have decided to invest in and support sustainable businesses, British businesses. Millwall is a British business.'

'So it's a buy-British campaign?'

In truth it was, but Cowly wasn't going to admit it. 'The Church is investing in British enterprise and British skills. Not for the short-term, but the long-term, and a small proportion of the profits from Millwall will feed back into the Church. As you probably know the Church has major overseas investments in property, and oil and gas. Why Paul, do you find that acceptable, but investing in British football so abhorrent?'

'I don't,' snapped Lakin. He hated nothing more than guests asking questions. With exaggerated annoyance, he dropped his notes on the glass table and pointed at Cowly. 'Look, the issue is that while your parishioners are scraping pennies together from jumble sales and raffles, you'll be spending their money, tens of millions, on pampered and ungrateful players.' Lakin quickly glanced to camera and tilted his head, as if acknowledging his viewers' appreciation of a point well made.

Cowly wondered whether Lakin's affectations were scripted. He replied, 'It's not that simple. It's not a one or the other situation. The investment in football will deliver returns for the Church Commissioners and we hope there will be wider benefits to the game itself.'

'Let's be honest,' said Lakin. 'This is a publicity stunt and nothing more. The Church has dumbed down. Church attendances are down and at the current rate of decline you'll soon be nothing more than a minor sect. You'll be irrelevant.'

This was an opportunity Cowly hadn't expected. 'First of all, I don't represent the Church. I'm the CEO of Millwall Football Club. For you to say that the Church is dumbing-down is an insult to the Church and to football. We're investing in Millwall and to criticise the Commissioners for trying to bring positive changes to the national game is ridiculous.' Lakin tried to intervene, but Cowly refused to give way. He raised his finger and pointed back at Lakin. 'The acquisition of Millwall is about engagement with the population. Why shouldn't it be? All faiths engage through education, through community work, through charities, so why not through sport?'

'Yes I know,' conceded Lakin, sitting back in his chair, 'but professional football? Why not other sports? Surely there are others that are more deserving?'

'I think you misunderstand. Millwall isn't a charity, and the Church may do other things in the sporting world, I don't know. Millwall just happens to be their first investment in this sector. The feedback we've had so far is that people see it as a positive step.'

'Well that's not what Frank Hobson, the Chief Executive of the League Premiership said.' Lakin shuffled through his notes. 'Mr Hobson said, we have concerns about this initiative.' Then Lakin held up the front page of the next day's Daily Telegraph. The headline read HANDS OFF OUR GAME. 'What have you got to say about that?'

'I agree there are bound to be concerns, but if you'd read out his full response, your viewers would know that the LPFL welcomed the Church of England's investment in the game.'

'I bet they welcomed it,' said Lakin. 'You have lots of money and they have little interest in anything else.'

'I'm afraid I can't speak on behalf of the LPFL,' said Cowly.

Lakin moved on. 'So you think the Glasgow model is a good idea? A sectarian society, segregated schools, hatred on the terraces? You think the levels of violence on match days are sustainable?'

Cowly assumed Lakin was paraphrasing the Superintendent of Strathclyde Police, who, when interviewed soon after the Millwall news went public, had commented on the problems of policing football in Glasgow. He'd said: 'The violence was unsustainable. It's costing too much.' When Cowly heard the interview he laughed at the implication of the Superintendent's words, i.e. if the costs of policing were lower or his department was better funded, then the violence was sustainable.

Cowly began his prepared answer to the Scottish question. 'Of course violence is unacceptable. I want to make it absolutely clear to Millwall fans that under my stewardship the club will not be a Protestant or a Catholic club, or Muslim or Buddhist club. Millwall will recruit the right people regardless of their faith, but we will expect staff to behave according to certain ethical principles.'

'So Christian ethics but dump all the God stuff?' Lakin folded his arms, pleased with his sound-bite.

This time Cowly agreed. 'Christian ethics yes. I don't think most fans would have a problem with that, even non-Christians.' But Cowly wanted to go back to the situation in Glasgow. He had more to say. 'Look, I think the situation in Scotland is regrettable in many ways, and I know there are no easy answers, but things aren't helped by the lack of competition. The sectarian rivalry there has been exacerbated by the presence of two dominant clubs, and when Rangers eventually climb back up, it'll start again. I can't see that situation arising in England. There's much more competition here, and as I've already said, Millwall isn't and won't be a Christian club. Cowly knew that tomorrow some would probably accuse him of sticking his nose in where it wasn't welcome, but that didn't matter – Phylida had persuaded him that a hostile response from the Scottish press might work in their favour.

Lakin received the cue to wind up. 'Tom Cowly, thank you.' He turned to camera. 'Our Home Affairs correspondent, Margaret Tollard, has been looking at the role of faiths in professional sport in the US and here's her report.'

Cowly was unplugged and escorted back to the box room. Phylida beamed when he walked in. She wanted to hug him, but she held back and patted his shoulder. 'Well done Tom. That was good, really good.'

Cowly shrugged. 'I'm not so sure.'

They sat down to watch the rest of the programme. The studio discussion proceeded much as they'd expected. The invited audience and panel offered a range of opposing and extreme positions. A professor of sports sociology said it was a constitutional crisis, though he was unable to say why; an unemployed manager said he wouldn't take the job at any price; and a Catholic fan said it would be good for the game.

Phylida and Cowly left Broadcasting House at half eleven, weary, but both satisfied that their first day in the spotlight had passed without incident.

9

While the Newsnight credits rolled, Robert Caldicott peered disappointedly into an empty fridge. Caldicott worked in the Cabinet Office, in the small team concerned with Economic, Social and Domestic Affairs (ESDA). He'd just flown in from the US where he'd been on a fact-finding mission examining solutions to voter disengagement. His phone rang.

'Did you see it?' The caller was Mathew Groves, a junior colleague at ESDA.

'See what?' said Caldicott.

'Newsnight.'

'I've only been in an hour. I've not unpacked.'

'Have you seen any British news today?'

'No. What's happened?'

'The Church of England bought Millwall.'

'Millwall what?' said Caldicott.

'The football club! I can't believe they let it happen. They'll be...'

Caldicott cut him off. 'Okay, okay. I can't do anything now. I'll have a look. I'll see you in the morning, the usual time.'

Perched on the edge of his sofa he watched the late news on the Sport Channel. His initial thought was that Groves was probably right; it might be disruptive. And while he brushed his teeth, undressed, and lay in bed, he listed the unintended consequences of the Church's acquisition: copy-cat take-overs, protests, and calls for the disestablishment of the Church. Then to empty his head, he turned on the clock-radio and re-tuned to the World Service.

— — — — — —

In the morning, on window stools in Caffè Nero, Caldicott and Groves peered out across Bridge Street at the Palace of Westminster. Above Victoria Tower the union flag reached out to the east against a flat-grey sky. Caldicott sipped his third coffee of the morning and his right eye started to twitch.

'Okay Matt, what shall we do?'

'The priority,' said Groves, 'is to cover the PM's arse. He's a Commissioner along with the Deputy, the Home Secretary, the Lord Chancellor and...'

'Yes, they're all ex-officio Commissioners, I know all that.'

'Yes, ex-officio, but it still looks bad. He'll be implicated.'

'You're assuming it's a bad thing, it may not be.'

Groves smiled, knowing Caldicott was deliberately taking a contrary line. 'I'm not worried about the Church,' said Groves, 'it's the precedent they're setting, that's the problem. If it goes tits-up, the opposition will blame the PM. I reckon it's a small if.'

Caldicott tore off a bite-sized piece of croissant and nodded that Groves should continue.

'No one saw this. While you were in the States, the PM was in the Far East, The Deputy was defending the Pensions Bill, and the Business Secretary spent the week promoting UK technology companies. Yesterday he opened Twitter's new HQ in Slough.'

'Well if it was commercially sensitive,' said Caldicott, 'and I'm assuming it was, then no one would have known, not even the PM.'

'So what shall we do?'

'I'll contact Sara.' Sara was PA to Sir Terrence Brimler, the Cabinet Secretary, and the most senior civil servant in Whitehall. 'If Sir Terrence knew nothing about it, then you're probably right, it's a fuck-up.' Caldicott pushed aside the remains of his croissant and rubbed his flickering eye, annoyed that on his first day back he had a problem on his hands. He wondered whether he'd missed something. There were always signs. Nothing came from nowhere. 'Okay Matt, let's assume the worst.'

Then Groves was off. 'As I see it, we have the issue of what the Church's action means, constitutionally and culturally.'

'Culturally?' said Caldicott.

'Will it be accepted?' Will there be a snowballing of religious involvement in sport? Will there be a backlash? Perhaps nothing will happen.'

Caldicott nodded, grateful that Groves was in his team.

'Then there's the politics. If the PM didn't know about it, the fact that he's an ex-officio Commissioner won't matter. The opposition will shit on him.'

'We may need to speak to the people who are behind this,' suggested Caldicott. 'Who was on Newsnight?'

'Tom Cowly, their CEO. I did some checks on him last night. He was brought in to manage the takeover. He's a consultant, but he has no background in football.'

'Is he an Anglican?'

'He's an atheist. Do you want to meet him?'

'Probably, but not yet.'

'Who else?'

'The Archbishop,' said Caldicott, 'but don't call his office, just check his speeches and look over his website.'

'I've done that,' said Groves. 'He spoke in the Lords soon after The Sun shafted him. He went on about a local approach to investment.'

'Of course,' Caldicott slapped the edge of the table with his fingers. 'That was the sign.'

'What?'

'These things have predecessors. When Prendergast went on about investing in Britain, none of us thought he meant professional football.'

'I guess not,' said Groves.

'We definitely need someone to clarify the legal position. I'm sure the Church won't have broken any rules, but we need to check. If it owns the club outright, does that make Millwall a charity?'

Groves scribbled some notes.

'And if that's the case, are there competition issues? I guess we need people from DoB (Department of Business) on this and someone on the tax side.' Caldicott paused. 'First though, before you do anything, I'll speak to Sir Terrence.' They left their unfinished coffees and headed out onto Bridge Street. In the chilling westerly they buttoned their coats and turned right onto Parliament Square.

– – – – – – – –

Later that afternoon Caldicott and Groves met again, but this time in The Cross; a stone-floored pub/restaurant close to Whitehall. Caldicott chose The Cross sure in the knowledge that he wouldn't be bumping into any of his work colleagues. Others inside and under-occupying the bar staff, were two glass half-empty men; one, overweight and bearded, engrossed in his phone; and the other, a suited thirty-something, fully engaged in chewing his nails to the quick.

Caldicott stared blankly across the room, exhausted. A hurriedly convened afternoon meeting, to discuss the ramifications of the Millwall situation, had been a resounding flop. Only three had attended and none were senior officers with decision making powers. In hindsight, and with the added clarity induced by beer on an empty stomach, he realised he'd been foolish to expect any other outcome, and he blamed his jet-lag for his poor judgement. There had been no reason to be hasty. He could have left it a day or two, or at last until he'd had a chance to speak to Sir Terrence. He turned to Groves. 'Well Mathew, we raised the flag. We couldn't have done much more.'

'We shouldn't have bothered?' said Groves, who felt equally deflated. Groves had started the day full of enthusiasm, thinking he was about to be involved in his first Government crisis.

'You might be right,' said Caldicott, 'but usually nothing happens until the wonks have had their say.' The so-called wonks were a small independent team, mostly Oxbridge graduates, who reported directly to the PM. They worked on 'high-level' strategy, while everyone else in Whitehall worked in the real world. Caldicott emptied his glass. 'We'll just have to wait until they realise there's a problem.' He knew Sir Terrence watched Newsnight, but he suspected that Sir Terrence would have switched off as soon as Lakin mentioned football. Caldicott had heard him describe it as *'a game for the unpunctuated'*.

'I'll put fifty quid on it that they didn't see it coming,' said Groves.

Caldicott nodded. 'And I'll bet my pension that it isn't on the Register.' The Government's Risk-Register, a document controlled by The Cabinet Office, and compiled in consultation with the Ministry of Defence, the Treasury and the Home Office, listed all the major risks to UK national security, economic development and civil society.

Caldicott rose, slapped Groves gently on the back and left. He walked north to Trafalgar Square, then along The Mall and into St James's Park, his swinging briefcase empty but for some Zeiss binoculars and an old leather-bound notebook. Though not a wild space, the park's open water and greenery provided a habitat for birds and insects. Caldicott liked birds and insects. He liked them more than people.

His parents had been twitchers and most of his early childhood memories were associated with twitching activities, whether it was arguments over mislaid binoculars, their car breaking down on the M6 near Carlisle, or their first trip abroad by coach – a twenty-hour marathon. They had travelled to the Camargue in the South of France when Caldicott was nine. And more than thirty years on, whenever he saw an old coach on the road, he was reminded of a toilet-stop they had made outside Le Mans. He'd complained to his father that the travel company's name, *Ornitholidays,* written in large green letters down the sides of the coach, wasn't a proper word and that it shouldn't be allowed. His father had patted him on the head, and said, 'Well spotted Robert.'

The Caldicott family list – the leather-bound notebook – began on the 12th May 1960 (Blackbird on the rear lawn), the day of his father's tenth birthday. And like a family heirloom, it had been passed on to Caldicott when he turned thirty-five.

He paused on the bridge that crossed the lake and scanned the water's edge looking for coots and mallards. He was no longer interested in adding to the family list. He visited the park simply because it helped him imagine an alternative to London, one of open spaces, of hedgerows and meadows. The only recent entries in the notebook he made each spring on the arrival of the first swallow, swift, and chiffchaff.

He scanned the lake again this time looking for flies and midges. He saw nothing. It was still too cold. He left the park after five minutes, crossed Birdcage Walk and followed the high railings that guarded Wellington Barracks. Thoughts of work returned; he imagined a shiny-faced Prime Minister at the despatch box during Prime Minister's Questions (PMQs), and the leader of the opposition demanding to know why, as a Church Commissioner, the Prime Minister hadn't opposed the Millwall acquisition. Caldicott smiled. The mixture of sport and religion was bound to create some divergent opinion. He decided that tomorrow, if nothing else intervened, he would watch the action from the public gallery.

10

Cowly closed his laptop and pushed back in his castor-mounted chair. His windowless office had previously been occupied by Ted Briggs, the club's former Managing Director. Measuring just twelve by twelve, a glass-doored cabinet occupied an entire wall, its shelves now bare but for the dust-free shadows that hinted at Briggs' personal affects, a circle for a tankard, a rectangle where he'd kept a stack of old match-day programmes, and four pencil-thin lines for the framed photographs of his wife and children. Against the opposite wall stood a dented filing cabinet, on top of which were three plastic trays labelled: Pending, In and Out, and in the Out tray was a mahogany nameplate that had once had pride of place on his desk. It bore his name and honour in full: Edward Hutton Briggs MBE.

Phylida kicked back the door carrying two mugs of tea. She and Cowly had just spent two hours updating the SWOT analysis (strengths, weaknesses, opportunities and threats) that she'd prepared prior to the Millwall purchase.

'So what now?' she said.

'Do some more work on it,' said Cowly. 'Concentrate on the threats.'

'Okay, but much of it will be guesswork.'

'Do what you can. Set up some meetings. We need to get a sense of what people are really thinking, whether they're with us or against us.'

'I could write to the FA and the LPFL...invite them to a game.'

'Good idea,' said Cowly.

11

Caldicott's boss, Sir Terrence Brimler, topped the civil service pay scale. He had a connecting corridor to 10 Downing Street and, in theory, he could be at the Prime Minister's side in less than a minute. In practise, however, he chose never to move that quickly as it would have set a bad precedent.

His large office was empty but for an oak-topped desk and a Turkish silk carpet. He'd selected it, not because of its heritage (in the 1950s, when Sir Terrence had been at prep school, the room had been used to entertain banana, tin and rubber-rich trade delegations from Africa and Asia) or location, but because he needed the space to exercise, bad cholesterol being his motivation. During lunchtimes, on Mondays, Wednesdays and Fridays, he locked the door and told Sara, his PA, to hold all his calls, and for thirty minutes, using the carpet as a mat, he followed a regimen of star-jumps, arm-waves and running on the spot.

At all other times, he sat at his desk working with fountain pen and paper or dictating instructions to Sara. She had been his document controller and organiser for twenty years, and he trusted her implicitly. Caldicott saw it differently, he saw it as exploitation. Sara, he thought, bore the burden of Sir Terrence's office, enabling him to appear competent, and all for a fraction of his salary. Sir Terrence had even persuaded her that it was best that they synchronise their holidays. In no position to disagree, she was forced to take a week in August when Sir Terrence went grouse hunting and two weeks at Easter while he visited his son in San Diego. Caldicott was convinced that without Sara, there would have been no knighthood.

Caldicott smiled as he passed Sara's desk. He assumed Sir Terrence's urgent meeting request was in connection with developments at Millwall. He knocked twice on the open door and walked in.

Sir Terrence was at his desk looking out on a walled garden of lawn and apple trees. 'Ah Robert, take a seat.'

Caldicott pulled back the Queen Anne chair and sat opposite, knees together, hands in his lap.

'I've got this meeting,' said Sir Terrence, 'an invite from the Treasury.'

Caldicott knew immediately what was about to happen.

'It's very important,' said Sir Terrence, stressing the very. 'A top level official is over from the US.'

Caldicott knew there was a but coming.

'But I'm a bit busy just now.'

Caldicott glanced at the empty desk.

'Could you go on my behalf?' and before Caldicott could reply, he added, 'Give them my apologies. It's the PM.'

Caldicott nodded. He'd heard it before. It was another pre-meditated PM situation. Sir Terrence had the habit, at least once or twice a week, of saying to Sara or Caldicott or other junior staff that the PM had just been on the phone. 'I'm just off there now,' he'd say, tapping his nose with his finger, suggesting it was all very hush-hush. But there was a pattern. His urgent and unscheduled meetings with the Prime Minister always coincided with some Treasury seminar or Home Office workshop. Sara was the only person who knew where he really went. One day she found a ticket under his desk for the Odeon in Panton Street. The receipt's time and date matched up with one of Sir Terrence's hush-hush appointments with the Prime Minister. What she didn't know was that he went to the cinema not because he was a fan of *X-Men* or *Happy Feet*. He went simply for a nap. In his briefcase he carried a pillow and earplugs.

'Of course,' said Caldicott, 'I've nothing on.' Even if Caldicott's diary had been full, Sir Terrence would have pulled rank and asked him to make alternative arrangements. 'What's it about?' he asked.

'It's on...it's to do with...' Sir Terrence rubbed his chin, and then held up a finger as if he'd just remembered, but he hadn't. 'I'll get Sara to email the details,' he said. 'She'll tell them to expect you.' Caldicott rose and as he turned to leave, Sir Terrence added, 'And Robert, I think it starts at ten, so you'd better get a move on.'

The very important meeting at the Treasury's offices was a lecture by a visiting Harvard professor who'd been flown over to talk about *Ultraism*. Caldicott expected to be bored witless so he made sure he was first into the lecture room to secure a seat on the back row. According to the professor, Ultraism was an emerging branch of economic theory which explained how globalisation had been responsible for the USA's economic decline. Caldicott listened for a few minutes and then gave up, having decided that it had as much relevance to UK policy, as string-theory to the price of milk. So as the professor got stuck into the detail, Caldicott withdrew his kindle and got stuck in *Colonel Chabert*.

An hour passed. The professor, now with his back to his audience, was scrawling differential equations on a flip chart. In front of Caldicott, a man cradled his head in his hands, and across the room other heads were sagging sideways and forwards. Someone, thought Caldicott, deserves a bollocking.

The Q&A session started at 12.05, but no one in the room had the confidence to ask a sensible question. Following a brief shuffling silence, a hand went up on the front row, but the question was simply about the professor's itinerary. After muted applause Caldicott made for the door. He forwent the free lunch and hurried back to his office arriving just in time to catch PMQs on the BBC News Channel.

Politically, it had been a bad and busy week for the coalition. It began with a damning report by the Work and Pensions Select Committee's on the damning state of UK social services. The latest quarterly bulletin from the Organisation for Economic and Co-operation and Development (OECD) was downbeat on the long-term prospects for the UK economy. Inflation was up half of one percent as food prices spiked, and the employment figures were stagnant. These matters occupied the first twenty-five minutes of PMQs. Then the Right Honourable Dennis McIlroy of the Democratic Unionist Party caught the Speaker's eye.

'Mr McIlroy,' said the Speaker.

McIlroy rose to his feet, his pregnant belly pushing aside his pin-striped jacket. He straightened his tie for the cameras. 'May I congratulate the Prime Minister on his support for the Church of England's entry into the world of professional football.'

Predictable football-themed jeers broke out from all sides.

'Order!' said the Speaker. Then as the noise died down, 'Mr McIlroy.'

McIlroy rose once more still optimistic that his question would make the six o'clock news. 'Thank you Mr Speaker. Can the Prime Minster tell us whether the hand of God, or God himself...'

'God himself?' said the member from Bolsover.

McIlroy's smile failed to hide his irritation, but as he tried again, a shrill Scottish voice cut through the chamber.

'If God is a he with a hand, does it mean he's a he with a willy?' The unmistakeable voice belonged to F.J. Fenton, the cross-gender member and all fronts activist from West Kilbride. Though a despised Liberal Democrat, who dressed in a blazer and skirt, the House roared in appreciation.

McIlroy sat down, fuming. Close on a minute passed before the Speaker regained control.

'Mr McIlroy!'

But McIlroy didn't move, his head now bowed in misery.

'Mr McIlroy, your question please.'

McIlroy stood and in a toneless voice he mumbled his question. 'Prime Minister, will God be...'

'Speak up Mr McIlroy. You've been given a chance. Use it or lose it.'

McIlroy cleared his throat and lifted his head. 'Prime Minister, will God be in the dugout or on the pitch, and what number will he be wearing?' Hearing the groans of disappointment, McIlroy didn't wait for an answer. He shuffled along the bench and made for the exit.

At the despatch box, the Prime Minister stepped forward and nodded towards his departing questioner. 'Mr Speaker, I congratulate the Right Honourable member for his interest in the nation's game, but unfortunately I am not party to the team sheet, and so his guess is as good as mine.'

And that was it. The session, for the most part tense and vindictive, had ended on a cheery note.

Caldicott switched off his TV.

A minute later Groves was on the line. 'Did you watch it?'

'Yes, but it didn't tell us much. Though I'm sure I spotted the PM glance at the Home Secretary, like he'd got off lightly.'

'Yes, I saw that. They were probably expecting more. Have you heard from Sir Terrence?'

'Yes and no. I went to see him this morning but he didn't mention Millwall.'

'Okay,' said Groves, 'I'll see you later.'

'Why?'

'Three o'clock at DoB: Britain and the Digital Economy.'

'Fuck,' said Caldicott.

'What's the matter?'

'Nothing. I'll see you there...get me a seat at the back.'

12

Tooting, Thursday morning 31st March

Vince climbed back into bed, the curtains still drawn. The night before, and with some reluctance, Ailish had agreed that he could film her masturbating. They tried once, failed, had a glass of wine and failed again. She blamed the absence of climax on the camera, saying it was too intrusive. He maintained that it was simply about getting used to it and that next time she wouldn't have a problem. She told him there wouldn't be a next time.

She pushed the duvet clear of her face. 'I dreamt about your experiment last night, only we were doing it live on TV.'

'Oh yes.' Vince rolled onto his side to face her.

'I was the half-time entertainment at a football match.'

'Who was playing?' He laughed at his joke, but she didn't. 'What happened?'

She sat up and reached for her mug of tea. 'I couldn't do it and they refused to pay me.'

'Couldn't do what?'

'Couldn't come,' she said. 'You were there too. We were on a rotating stage in the centre of the pitch. You were holding the camera while I was on my back shoving a vibrator up my fanny. There were giant TVs at either end of the stadium. As we went round, I could see this massive picture of me...my knees were enormous. Then over the tannoy, someone said, 'time's up' and then they cut the power to the vibrator and the spotlight went out. The second-half was about to start. Then because I'd failed, you stood up and turned to apologise to the crowd, and while you were talking, some men rushed up and put a big plastic screen around me, hiding me.'

'A screen?'

'Yes, a screen.'

'What, like they do when they shoot a horse?' Vince's cock started to harden.

She shook her head.

'Like at the races when a horse is...'

'I don't want to know.'

'Perhaps you were just too hot? We could change the duvet?' Vince's explanation, which she'd heard many times, was that her bad dreams were a mechanism for waking her up when she was overheating.

'No, I wasn't too hot. It was your fucking experiment.' She put a finger to her mouth to suggest he kept quiet. 'Are you hard?' she asked, even though she could feel it resting on her thigh.

Vince nodded.

She put her mug down, threw back the duvet and turned onto her hands and knees, Vince moved behind her and she guided him in.

'Can you move?' he said.

She knew what he wanted and while still coupled they edged round so he could put his feet on the carpet and knees against the side of mattress. He gripped her hair in one hand and started thrusting.

After a dozen, she said, 'Come on.' It was more an order than an request.

She braced her neck muscles as Vince re-tightened his grip. She liked to fuck in the morning. She'd said it was more refreshing than a shower and cheaper than a skinny latte. As their bodies slapped, she began to think aloud, 'Perhaps they should open fuck-shops...one next to every Starbucks...give them a bit of competition.'

'Starfucks?' said Vince, joining in.

'What?'

'Starfucks...they could call them Starfucks.' He was no longer thinking about her arse. He was thinking how much per fuck, and then about standing naked in a queue while waiting to be served, and how the staff would check for STDs, and how the loyalty-card system would work.

By nine she was asleep again and Vince was out the door and driving down to Brighton in her old Laguna. She let him borrow it but only on the proviso that he paid for the repairs if it broke down. He parked up on the seafront opposite Adelaide Crescent, half an hour early for his midday meeting with Kevin. Briefly, he considered walking down to the Pump Room to see Andy, but calculated there would only be time to say hello before he'd have to come back. So he sat in the passenger seat and flicked through the chapters he'd written in the three weeks since their last meeting. He'd matched the style of the first six and doubted anyone would know there had been two authors. Exactly on twelve he pressed the intercom buzzer for Kevin's apartment.

Ángel Barros answered. 'Vince?'

'Yes.'

The lock clicked and the door released. All three sat in the lounge, Barros at one end of the sofa, Kevin at the other. Vince noticed that once more Kevin had retreated. He was hunkered down and monosyllabic, the large cushion by his side, like a barricade, emphasising his estrangement. Barros seemed oblivious. He played the *bon viveur,* engaged and entertained by his own small talk. He said he'd been home to Andalucía for a few days to visit see his wife and children and, more importantly, for his mother's birthday. He said his life wouldn't be worth living if he ever missed that. And though he included Kevin in his conversation, occasionally asking him a question, he never waited for an answer. Whatever the problem was between them, Vince doubted it was down to the book deal alone.

When Barros finally ran dry, Vince read through chapters seven to nine. Only a couple of points of fact needed correcting; a signing-on fee and the number of first-team appearances at Chelsea. As soon as the read-through was over, Barros excused himself and left for London. Vince used the break to move the Laguna and buy another parking ticket. Then as before, with Barros gone, the other Kevin slowly emerged. His sentences lengthened, he reclaimed his apartment, and playfully lobbed a tennis ball at the wall above the fire place. Vince switched on his tape recorder.

An hour later, as Vince packed away his notes, he said, 'What is it with Ángel? What's the problem?'

'It's nothing. We just don't have much in common.' He shrugged his shoulders as if to say, it's as simple as that.

'Why don't you get a new agent? Sack him, find someone you like.'

'I can't.'

'Why's that?'

'Because he thinks I'm gay.'

'You said he didn't know.'

'Well he does. I didn't tell him. He found out. He happened to be in Brighton on business and he dropped by unannounced. I wasn't home, but he waited for me in his car. I came back with a male friend and we kissed on the doorstep. It was just a peck, but he must have seen it. He didn't mention it straightaway. He waited a week. When he told me he knew I was gay. He said he wanted half my earnings otherwise he'd go to the papers.'

'He's blackmailing you?'

'Weird, isn't it?'

'No, it's fuckin' crazy.' Vince shook his head. 'He takes half your money?'

'Forty-five percent.'

Half seriously and half joking, Vince said, 'You've got to do another book.'

Kevin jumped up and left the room. Vince could hear him fill the kettle in the kitchen. He called out, 'I'm sorry. That was stupid of me.'

Kevin reappeared, not understanding the apology. 'What do you mean?'

'Journalists...we're always looking for the next story.'

'I know that.'

They sat for a few moments, neither speaking. Kevin thinking for the umpteenth time that he should quit the game, while Vince wondered how the blackmail worked. Vince was first to break their silence. 'I still don't believe it.'

'It's true. Ten per cent wasn't enough.'

'Yes, but why does he want the book. That's risky.'

'He said he'd deal with anyone that wanted to make something of it, and he wasn't talking about enforcing the non-disclosure agreement. He's scary when he wants to be.'

'Yes, I can see that. All the friendly chit-chat, it's bullshit.'

'So until I quit, I'm stuck with him.' Kevin went back to the kitchen and Vince followed.

'I've been fucked over too,' said Vince. Then he told the story of how Spinks had destroyed his career.

And when he'd finished, Kevin said, 'So my book's important to you?'

'Kind of, but I'm not really expecting anything to come of it. It'd be nice, but it probably won't.' Then Vince smiled, apologetically. 'No offence, but as it is, it isn't going to make the bestsellers list.'

'Sure, and that's the way it has to stay.'

It was a subtle warning and Vince understood. 'Of course...don't worry.'

Little more was said. They shook hands and agreed that next time they would meet at Kevin's house in Chiswick. It was six o'clock when Vince joined the M23 north and eight when he arrived back in Tooting.

13

Braney, Thursday 31st March

Phylida drove to the family home in Braney, Hertfordshire. Her father, William Cranson, shared it with his second and much younger wife Eve. It was the house where Phylida had been born, where she learnt to walk and ride, where she lost her virginity on her seventeenth birthday, and where her mother, Linda, had died of breast cancer at fifty-three. She had died a week before Christmas after a two-year struggle of treatments, tears and anger. The anger from a botched diagnoses and a life cut short.

When in her teens and twenties her mother had also been her best friend. They confided on matters of love. She told her mother about the boys at school, and Linda told her about the men she dated before she met her father. They joked about Dad, shopped in London, shared clothes, shoes and boots, and argued about who was the better rider. At times William Cranson felt like an outsider, envying their closeness, sensing that their invitations to join them for a walk, or for a drive to London, were made only out of politeness. He would try to make light of it, saying it was like living with twin wives. And often, if he found them busy in the kitchen or out in the garden, he would grandly announce, 'Today the two wives of William Cranson are baking a cake/digging up onions/pruning the fruit trees,' and with each repeated variation they laughed together.

Phylida quit her job and stayed in Braney after her mother's death, believing her father wouldn't cope on his own. That first year became a year of mere functioning, of boredom. Linda's presence – like gravity, powerful but largely unnoticed – had bound them as a family, and memories alone couldn't fill the void. Too often during those early months their conversations would start with: *'Your mother did this...* or *Mum said that...* ' Then later, they never dared speak her name, only talking to each other on matters of fact, of meals and shopping, and of chores around the house. As the year progressed father and daughter were slowly cast apart, uneasy in each other's company, and it became clear to Phylida that her presence was the problem. When cooking or on the phone or just watching television, she would catch her father staring at her, as if she were her mother's ghost. She was, she thought, simply a reminder of his loss, and that by staying in Braney she was continuing his grief.

She left for London after their second Christmas together, found a flat-share and then work at BSM. She was soon immersed in projects, deadlines, and the culture of long hours. If her father came down to London they would meet for lunch and talk about work, and when lunch was over, and before a tearful parting, he'd encourage her to visit. But whenever she went back for the weekend, she spent most of the time on her own. On Saturdays her father played golf and she wouldn't let him cancel. So while he slogged his way from tee to green, she would dust and vacuum, and weed and mow. She'd do anything to keep busy, anything except walk alone through the fields and lanes.

And so the pattern continued for nearly four years, until the day they met for lunch in Covent Garden. He told her he was dating. 'She's a bit younger than me,' he said. It came out like a guilty admission. He was worried that she would disapprove.

Though surprised at his news, she didn't hesitate. She smiled. 'That's great Dad. Where did you meet her?' She was happy for him that at fifty-eight he might have found a new companion.

'I should have told you before, you might not...'

'Dad, it's your life. You can date whoever you like. Marry her, if you...' She hesitated, afraid to mention love, knowing that love wasn't the only reason to marry. 'Yes, marry her, but don't expect me to be a bridesmaid.' It was intended as a joke.

'Of course not,' he said. 'And anyway, we've not discussed it.'

'Okay, but if it feels right, why not?'

'We'll see. Next time you're up, you'll meet her. Her name's Eve.'

He called a month later and talked mostly of Eve and what they had been doing, and how she was helping him decorate the house, and how he hoped they would get on. After each of his subsequent calls, which were all about Eve, the more Phylida dreaded their meeting. She put off going to Braney for six months, and in the end only met her once before the wedding. But from that one meeting she knew they would never be close or even friends. They had no shared interests, no common ground. Eve was a pasta, cheese and chicken vegetarian, diminutive and anxious, and constantly concerned about her health. The liquids that passed her delicate lips did so solely to purge and cool her liver. She permitted herself just one glass of wine a week, and then only because it strengthened her heart. Phylida eventually concluded that her father had married Eve because she was so different from Linda. He would never make the mistake of comparing the two, because they were opposites in every respect.

After the wedding, Phylida's infrequent visits to Braney ceased. She still met up with him in London and he always called on a Monday evening. Then, one Saturday, he broke with routine.

'Hi Dad, what's up?'

'Nothing,' he said. 'No golf today so I thought I'd call. How are you?'

'A bit sweaty. I'm just back from the gym.'

For five minutes they talked the usual talk of her work and his work and Eve's plans for the house. Then, as their conversation neared its conclusion, he said, 'There is one thing. I have some news.' Then he paused.

'What is it? she said.

'I may have done something foolish.'

Her immediate thought was that Eve must be pregnant. 'Like what?'

'I bought a horse.'

'A horse?'

'Yes, a horse...a family horse.'

'What does that mean?'

'It means you can ride it whenever you're here.'

'I don't get it. You can't ride and I'm never there.'

'I can learn. You can teach me.'

She didn't know what to say. Her father had never expressed any interest in learning to ride and she knew that Eve regarded all equestrian sports as a grave violation of animal rights.

'I mean it,' he said.

'No you don't.'

'Maybe I've changed. Anyway, whether I learn to ride or not, the horse is for you too. I'd like you start riding again. I'm sure your mother would have liked that.'

'Dad, don't say that.'

'Okay, but you need some downtime...something away from work. Why not start again?'

'I don't have time.'

'That's my point. You need to make time. I'll email a picture. She's a chestnut, six years old, fifteen hands with a white blaze.'

Thinking it was a ploy to drag her back to Braney, she wondered if things with Eve weren't going so well. 'Is something wrong? Are you and Eve alright?'

'We're fine. Look, why don't you come and have a look at her? If you're not interested, I'll find someone else to help.'

Whether it was a ploy or an act of kindness, it worked. Phylida went home at least once a month and more often in the spring and summer. She would travel up on Saturday mornings and either go straight to the livery or drop her car at the cottage and cycle in. She became friends with the other owners and the livery staff, and when not riding, she helped with the maintenance and mucking out. Then later, her father converted her old bedroom into an office, with a desk, printer and landline. He told her it was for his own use, but that she was welcome to use it too.

Braney, Friday morning 1st April

Form her desk she looked down at a blackbird prowling the rear lawn, its head tilting one way and then the other like an avian automaton. Then her gaze moved beyond the narrowing lawn and over the stream that marked the garden's southern boundary. Further still, she looked over fields of grazing sheep and finally, on the far horizon, at Rindle Woods.

And when she looked back to the garden she could see her mother carrying a basket of washing, smiling as she passed by, and declining the offer of help. Two-stone lighter now, her shoulders curved forward, her hair thinning, and though frail, she was still being strong, still pegging out the sheets as she had done a thousand times before. Watching from the patio, Phylida had whispered, 'I'm going to cry when you are nothing Mum, cry when I do the washing without you.'

She wiped away a tear, switched on her laptop and checked her emails. Cowly had sent through the club's latest press release. She scanned it and couldn't see how it was any different from the last one. Once more he'd repeated the statement that Millwall welcomed players and fans from all religious denominations. He hoped that through repetition, the sceptics would eventually accept that Millwall wasn't a Christian club. Whenever questioned about the religious make-up of the first-team, Cowly would reply: 'I haven't a clue', and to reinforce the point, he'd make reference to the club's Articles of Association and Clause 5a, which stated: 'matters of belief and faith are of no material interest to the Board of Directors'.

Whether or not the press releases were believed, the received opinion within the business community was that the Church had delivered a masterstroke. Confirmation came on The Media Show, when Sir Martyn Clements (Chairman of PPW, the world's second largest advertising agency) said, 'the millions the Church paid for Millwall has already been recouped ten-fold in free publicity.' There were even unconfirmed reports that Church attendances had increased on the Sunday following the Millwall purchase.

Phylida opened an Excel spreadsheet, reset the column width to thirty and typed the main heading: *'Millwall FC Threats Matrix',* Then on row 3, in columns A to E, she typed: *Football Bodies, Other Religions, Press, Government, Religious Fanatics.* Two hours later she had a first draft. Though many of the cells contained only a question mark, it was a document she could work on and populate. She emailed it to Cowly and logged out.

Looking through the window she could see that the sky had cleared. She opened the door to her room and listened – not a sound. 'Dad?' she shouted. With no response she moved down the landing and into her father's bedroom, a room of frills, pot-pourri, and Jack Vettriano paintings. Like the rest of the house, it had been transformed by Eve. It had taken her several years, but now nothing inside or in the garden had ever been touched by her mother. The furniture, cutlery, door-knocker, even the apple trees had gone. She looked down to the driveway for her father's car. It wasn't there. Back in her bedroom/office she quickly undressed down to her underwear, and then pulled on a red top and some beige breeches. She ran downstairs, pushed on her yard boots and slammed the door. Minutes later, with her hair untied, she was pedalling hard down Garston Hill.

14

The Den, Monday 4th April

Ahead of the Tuesday board meeting, over a lunch of pie, chips and beans, Phylida and Cowly leafed through the week's press cuttings. There had been little on Millwall. Most of the back pages were concerned with the run-in for the LPFL title and the quarter final line-up for the European Cup. But on the Friday, when Phylida had been in Braney, another story broke which made the front and back pages of all the tabloids. The story, which seemed more rumour than fact, concerned the Sport Channel, the satellite broadcaster which each year paid the LPFL £2 billion for exclusive broadcasting rights. The tabloids' excitement centred on a possible re-structuring of the contract. The Mirror reported that the Sport Channel had secretly met with several League Premiership clubs, and that was news because each club was also a shareholder of the LPFL, the body that negotiated the broadcasting rights. On the Saturday the broadsheets had picked up the story. The Financial Times reported that:

> *...while it was constitutionally impossible for the Sport Channel to buy the LPFL, a radical broadcasting deal was being discussed that would extend the broadcasting rights from the current four-year period to ten years. The Sport Channel is known to be cash rich and a longer-term contract could have benefits for both parties. A source at one of the major clubs said, 'the proposal on the table was that payments to each club would be heavily weighted in the early years and that they would tail-off to zero towards the end.' Such an arrangement would be particularly*

attractive to those clubs that were struggling with debt.

The paper went on:

'...The only losers in such an arrangement would be the aspiring clubs in the lower leagues...'

And that:

'...so far the Footballing Association has refused to comment.'

'If that happens,' suggested Cowly, 'we could be in for a windfall.' Millwall, as a newly promoted side, was already guaranteed £60 million under the existing arrangements.

'Would the Footballing Association allow it?' said Phylida. 'It seems a little unfair.'

'I guess fairness doesn't come into it.'

Phylida closed the folder of cuttings and then handed him a printout of the Threats Matrix. It was supposed to be an agenda item for the Tuesday board meeting.

He scanned it and said, 'I think we need to keep this to ourselves. Let's just have an open discussion.'

Phylida frowned. 'Why?'

'I wouldn't want it getting out to the press. It probably won't, but I'd rather not risk it. We can still talk about it, but let's not put anything down on paper.'

15

Chiswick, Friday 15th April

Kevin opened the door and Barros pushed past. Without a
word, he dropped his bag in the hallway and continued on
into the kitchen. He'd texted Kevin five minutes earlier
saying he was on his way to Heathrow, but that he would be
stopping by to discuss their future. Barros went straight to
the fridge.

'Hungry?' said Kevin.

'Thirsty.' Barros grabbed a carton of grape juice and
then a tumbler from a cupboard above the sink. He knew his
way around because the layout was the same as Kevin's
apartment in Brighton.

When Kevin bought in Chiswick he had the house gutted
while he spent the off-season coaching in South Africa.
Before flying out, he gave his Adelaide Crescent keys to his
interior designer and told her to do something similar. He
wasn't expecting replication, but that's what he got: he now
owned two properties that had the same coloured walls, the
same furniture, taps, floors, doors, door handles, and
appliances. So while he split his time between Chiswick and
Brighton, it often felt like he had just the one home. And
some mornings, before it was light and before he opened his
eyes, he would listen out for the 'kuwark caaa caaa' of the
gulls of Brighton to work out where he was. There were
downsides though. One evening Barros had called about a
sponsor's contract that needed signing. Kevin told Barros
that he was at home in Chiswick and that he should drop by.
Then later, Barros called Kevin's mobile.

'Are you going to let me in?' said Barros.

'I'm not a mind reader. Ring the bell.'

'I have, many times.' Barros pressed it again. 'Hear that?'

81

Kevin's assumed the door bell was faulty before realising that he was in Brighton and Barros was in Chiswick. When they met up the next day they laughed about it, but then Barros starting using the story as small-talk, re-telling it to others whenever Kevin was present.

As Barros helped himself to juice and biscuits, Kevin's phone rang.

'Are you okay to talk?' said Vince.

'Sure, what is it?'

'I've done a couple more chapters, so I was wondering about the next read through. When shall we do it?'

'Just a minute.' Kevin pushed his phone against his chest and turned to Barros. 'Vince wants to run through the next few chapters.'

Barros shook his head and waved his hand dismissively.

'Vince, we can't make just now. Something's come up. Can you send what you've done and we'll look at it? Post it to Ángel.'

'Anything I should know about?' said Vince.

'No, nothing.'

'Is Barros with you?'

'Yes.'

'Okay, well send me his address.'

'I'll text it.' Kevin cut the call and forwarded Barros' London address. Then he turned to Barros, 'When are you going to tell him?'

'When I know for sure.' Barros wiped his mouth with the back of his hand. 'It can wait.' He was in no mood to talk about books, because on the previous Monday he'd received a text from a contact at Chelsea: *Furling will be off-loaded in the summer.* The information had cost Barros a grand, but he liked to know such things before they became official. It allowed him to plan ahead, to make contingencies. He had an insider at every club where he had a player.

The news on Kevin's contract hadn't been entirely unexpected as Chelsea had been refusing to talk about an extension for over twelve months. On receiving the text, Barros began calling round the League Premiership clubs that were mid-table, and the two clubs at the top of the Championship.

'I've only heard from Millwall and Southampton,' said Barros. They both knew that a move to either club would kill the book deal. 'I'm waiting on Newcastle and Everton.'

'Ángel, I want to stay in London. You know that.'

'Yes Kevin.' He said it like he was talking to a tiresome child. 'I know you want to stay near Brighton, but if we get a good offer from a northern club, it would be stupid not to take it. It could cost you.'

Kevin smiled. 'Cost you, you mean. Why don't you give Millwall a ring?'

16

Central London, Friday 22ⁿᵈ April

A week later Kevin and Barros were in the offices of Patrice Leconte, Chelsea's Finance Director. Leconte had just confirmed that Kevin was on the transfer list.

'A one-year extension and a twenty per cent wage cut.' suggested Barros. He knew that wherever Kevin went next, they wouldn't get anything like Chelsea wages.

'No.'

'Twenty-five percent?'

'Ángel, I'm afraid we have to sell. We have to cut our wage bill. Others are going too.'

'What price?' said Barros.

'Eight million.'

Kevin had cost Chelsea twelve million three years earlier. He still had fifteen months to run on his contract. 'And if he stays?' said Barros.

Leconte faced Kevin and said, 'You wouldn't want that would you?'

Barros held out his arm, his hand on Kevin's chest. 'He would be happy to stay.' Barros turned to Kevin and smiled, 'Whether it is in the first team or the reserves.'

'I understand,' said Leconte, nodding. 'It would be in the reserve team.'

Little more was said and the three shook hands and agreed to stay in touch. Twenty minutes later Barros and Kevin were in a black cab as it snaked along Park Lane, dipping into gaps, swerving round slow buses and cutting up cyclists. Barros had ordered the driver to hurry up. He had things to do before their one o'clock meeting with Kevin's boot sponsor. As he watched the traffic slip by, his phone rang.

'Hello Junko,' said Barros. She was an account manager at Dodsons, Kevin's publisher.

'Hello Ángel. Can you talk?'

'Go ahead.'

'I'm afraid we have some problems with Kevin's book. We understand he's leaving Chelsea.'

'Not as far as I know,' said Barros. 'We've just come from Stamford Bridge.'

'Okay, well I've been told he's leaving. Perhaps you'd better call them.'

'Who said it?'

'That doesn't matter.'

'We have just met with the Chelsea FD. Kevin is not going anywhere. He has fifteen months still on his contract.'

'Whatever you say Ángel, but the book's off and we'll want the advance back. You've got five working days.'

'I will see what I can do.'

'Do that, and if we don't get a cheque by the end of next week, you'll be hearing from our lawyers.' She cut the call.

'It's off,' said Barros.

'So I gather.'

'Someone must have tipped them. Some *Puñeta* at Chelsea.'

Kevin held back a smile. 'I can't see why. Why would anyone do that?' The day before Kevin had left an anonymous message with the receptionist at Dodsons: '*Kevin Furling is leaving Chelsea in the summer. He's on the transfer list.*' It was petty, but worth it because he knew it would annoy Barros.

As their cab moved off Hyde Park Corner, Kevin asked about Vince. 'Are you going to pay him?'

'Why would I do that? He has to pay back his advance.' He turned his palms upwards. 'He will understand that.'

'But he knows about me. He knows I'm gay.'

'How?'

'I told him.'

'Idiota!' said Barros.

'It was too risky not to. He's a journalist. They have a habit of finding stuff out. I thought it was best he knew. He gave me his word.'

Barros laughed. 'So what is your problem? You have his word.'

'My problem? You're the one about to piss him off.'

'If he tries anything,' Barros twisted his fists, while making the noise of snapping bones, 'I will end him.'

'But he's got nothing to lose. He's broke.'

'We all have something, even Vince.' Then Barros poked Kevin in the chest and smiled. 'Don't you worry my little *joto*, I have the perfect solution. You pay him with your money.'

'Okay, maybe I will.' Kevin moved over to the opposite seat. He hated it when Barros got too close and touched him. He looked out as they sped along Grosvenor Place and whispered, 'Fucking book.'

'What is that?' said Barros.

'I said it was a bad idea.'

'Yes Kevin, blame someone else.' Barros leant forward raising his finger in front of Kevin's face. 'I suppose it is my fault you are a gay boy.' Then he sat back and held up an open hand signalling that their conversation was over.

Their cab pulled up outside The Grosvenor Hotel twenty minutes before their meeting with the boot sponsor. Over the coming days, as news leaked out of his imminent transfer, his other sponsors (*Vita-Burn*, a dietary supplement brand, and *Laissez-Faire*, an internet search engine that didn't spy on its users) would also be in touch.

Barros led the way past the doorman and into the lobby. The Grosvenor's decor, with its ornate rendering, fluted columns and scrolls, was like a shrine to Victoriana. It always reminded Kevin of iced wedding cakes. Barros sat where he always sat, to the left of the central staircase, facing the entrance. He opened his briefcase and took out another phone.

Kevin stood to one side stretching his hamstrings. 'You may as well contact the other two.'

Barros didn't answer. He scrolled down his contact list for Vince's number. Kevin crossed the lobby and sat at an empty table in the far corner.

Vince was at home. He walked through to the back bedroom where the signal was stronger. 'Hi Ángel, did you get the new chapters? I posted them last week.'

'Yes, it was good Vince, very good.' Barros hadn't read them. Seeing Vince's name and address on the back of the envelope he'd tossed it aside unopened. 'But there is a problem Vince. Kevin is moving clubs and the publishers are thinking about cancelling the deal. They think it will not be worth going ahead.'

'That's a shame,' said Vince, not realising the full implications of Barros' words. 'As football books go, I think it's pretty good.'

'Yes it is, but the problem is that we will not be paid and I cannot pay you.'

'But I thought you...'

Barros cut in. 'And your contract with me is dependent on publication. It is regrettable, but these things happen. I need you to give back the advance. We have to repay the publishers.'

'That's bullshit,' said Vince

'Yes Vince, I understand that you are upset, but if you read the contract it is quite clear. I also have to repay the advance.' Barros was calm, his delivery slow. He wasn't about to make threats in a public place.

Hearing Vince's name Kevin crossed the lobby and caught the tail-end of the conversation.

'Look Barros...' said Vince,

Barros cut in again and raised his voice. 'Read your contract Vince. I have to go now.' Then he ended the call.

'I said I'd pay him,' said Kevin.

'I changed my mind.' Barros waved his hand and opened his diary. He called his travel agent and asked them to book a flight to Frankfurt, first-class.

'Fucker!' said Vince, throwing his phone at the bed so hard it bounced and hit the wall.

'What is it?' said Ailish. She was working through a pile of paperwork on the sofa. 'What's happened?'

He picked up his phone and checked it worked. In the doorway, he said, 'The book's been cancelled. Kevin's being transferred.'

She stared at him, waiting for more.

'Barros said the contract was based on publication, so if it's not published, no one gets paid. He wants the advance back.'

'That can't be right. What about Kevin?'

'What about him?'

'Speak to Kevin. See what he says. Barros isn't going to sue you for a couple of thousand.'

'I wouldn't bet on it.'

'Well speak to Kevin. See what he thinks.'

Vince went back into their bedroom and came out holding his coat. 'I'm going for a walk.'

'Vince, sit down and call Kevin.' She gathered up her bills and receipts and placed them on the floor, and then patted the sofa. 'Come on, do it.'

'I wanted it published,' said Vince. 'It would have helped to have something in print. You said it. You said it might lead to other stuff.'

'I know.' She patted the cushion again and this time he sat down.

When Kevin saw the call was from Vince, he moved back across to the far corner of the lobby. 'Hi Vince, sorry about the book.'

'Yes, so am I. Is he right?'

'Yes, Chelsea want me out, so I'll be looking for another club this summer.'

Vince didn't reply.

'Vince, are you there?'

'Sorry, I was just thinking about who owns it. Who owns chapters seven to eleven?'

'I guess you do,' said Kevin. 'Look I'll buy them off you. Maybe I can use them another time.'

'You don't have to do that.'

'I know, but I will. Text me your bank details. I'll transfer the money this evening, but don't tell Barros.'

'He wants the advance back.'

'I know. Repay him and I'll pay you in full.'

'Are you sure?'

'Yes, I'm sure. I'll speak to you soon.'

Vince cut the call and smiled.

'Result?' she said.

'Result. He's a good guy.'

'That's great,' she said, relieved that days of misery had been avoided. 'Shall we go out? Shall we celebrate?'

'But the book's dead.'

'Yes, but you're getting paid. Let's go to the Tate.'

'What's wrong with the pub?'

'I want to do something. I'm not going to the pub. There's an exhibition I'd like to see.'

'Art?'

'Yes, art. What else?'

'Who's on?'

'Spinks' new show...and Miró.'

Since they'd been sharing the same roof and bed they rarely talked about Spinks and the trial. They had argued about it just once when she told him that he should have known better, and that if he'd not been drunk it wouldn't have happened. After that, whenever Vince brought the subject up, she would walk away. She thought he was still in denial.

'Spinks?' said Vince.

'Yes, I heard he's upset the Daily Mail.'

'I'm not interested.'

'You can do the Miró.'

They took the tube to Waterloo and arrived at three. Vince bought the tickets, one for Miró and one for Spinks. Standing at the bottom of the escalator on the second floor they arranged to meet at the restaurant at four-thirty to compare notes. He watched her all the way to the top, wondering again why they were together, why she put up with him.

As she stepped off the escalator and disappeared into the crowd he turned and read the poster for the Miró exhibition. He groaned. There were hundred and fifty paintings and drawings on display. Vince thought that forty or fifty would probably be plenty for anyone, even for Miró's most ardent fans. He equated it to stuffing your face with your favourite food – the more you ate the less you liked it. He figured the large number of exhibits was most likely to do with money and health and safety; if the Tate exhibited fewer paintings, they would be in fewer rooms, and then they would have to limit ticket sales to stop the overcrowding. So a hundred of Miró's works were there simply to maximise revenue and disperse the crowd.

He walked through the first two rooms and in the third found a bench seat. He sat for a minute facing one wall trying to make sense of the patterns, and then swung round to face the opposite wall. The room had fifteen paintings of varying dimensions but all of the same style – thick intersecting lines, straight and curved, forming enclosures filled with drab reds and greens. Bored with the images he watched and listened and waited for the inevitable. Five minutes passed, and then from his left, a middle-aged couple walked across the room hand-in-hand. They didn't stop. The man nodded at one of the walls and said, 'I could do that'. It was said with confidence, but not in-confidence, he wanted everyone nearby to know. His partner smiled and hugged his arm. He was showing off to his lady friend and without breaking stride he'd dismissed years of Miro's work in seconds. Vince wondered why they had paid forty pounds to see something they didn't like. *Why weren't they somewhere else?*

Vince looked again at the images, thinking they might be representative of Miró's *primitive period*. Then he wondered if every artist, acclaimed or otherwise, had their 'primitive period', a euphemism, he thought, for work that never sold or where the critics struggled to find merit. *Why not be honest? Cut the bullshit and arrange the paintings on the basis of good, bad, and mediocre. Give the punters something to argue about.* He decided that he'd been in

90

room three, a bad room, long enough and moved on. Room four was busier and Miró seemed to have moved on too. There were more colours and they were brighter, and the shapes more suggestive of creatures with eyes and antennae. Again they left Vince cold. He graded them mediocre bordering on bad, but then conceded that perhaps he wasn't in the right mood for art appreciation, and like the gobshite and his girlfriend, he was also in the wrong place.

He arrived at the seventh floor restaurant early. Ailish was already there, her glass of wine half-empty.

'How was it?' said Vince, pulling back a chair.

'I can see why the old farts are up in arms. Some people were heading back to the ticket office to demand a refund.'

'What's he done?' said Vince.

'It's really a question of what he hasn't done. He's called it *Art-Vision*. It's some form of extreme minimalism. There are no exhibits, no normal exhibits. The rooms are empty. There's nothing to see.'

'Nothing?'

'There's something to read,' she said. 'He's embedded some large postcards in blocks of glass and mounted them on the wall. The writing is done in dot-matrix and at the corner of each block they're signed and dated, but his signature is in three dimensions, like he's drawn it with melted plastic. Then underneath each signature is a barcode. I guess it's to stop people copying them. So each glass block is a *Vision*.' She paused and said, 'How was Miró?'

Vince stared down at the table, his body frozen.

'What's wrong now?' she said.

He didn't respond.

'Did Barros call?'

He looked at her. 'Nothing in the room? Just cards on the wall?'

She nodded.

'He's left it up to the reader to imagine?'

'Pretty much.' She reached into her leather shoulder-bag and withdrew the Art-Vision guide, a double-sided folded card. She read out Spinks' explanation:

'Until now my ideas have been displayed and communicated through the utilisation of natural and man-made materials that obey the laws of physics and chemistry. The shapes and shades of my work came to you via light-waves, from object to eye, and occasionally through olfactory and touch sensors. While much can be achieved through these means, necessarily, the creative process is constrained and corralled, and with it, our ability to create and appreciate art. This latest exhibition is one in words – not poetry or extracts from a book – but words that describe singular visions that would be impossible to reproduce in two or three dimensions. These creative visions will be constructed by each reader, each one uniquely evolving and transforming.'

When she stopped, Vince said, 'I told him to do that.'

'What do you mean?'

'When I met Spinks at Heathrow. It was a joke really. When he said he was a con-artist I gave him a few ideas. I said he should stick some cards on the wall and let the fuckers that pay to see his stuff do the imagining. I suggested a couple of things he could write about.'

'Like what?'

'I don't know, it was two years ago.'

'Try,' she said.

'I think one was about being inside a sort of floating black box.'

She shook her head. 'I didn't see that one, though I didn't read them all.'

'Another was about a scientist, a Nobel prize winner. He was on a stage talking about temperature and sea-level rise. The room was dark and the scientist was lit by a spotlight. It was just after all that climate bollocks in Copenhagen.' Vince paused.

'What else?' she said.

'What else what?'

'What else about the scientist?'

'He was talking about carbon dioxide. When he finished speaking the lights came on and he's looking out from the stage. I told Spinks the scientist sees rows of chairs, only chairs, stretching into the distance. Then Spinks joined in. We worked out the number of rows and how wide they were. I told Spinks we needed to seat the world.'

'I don't get it.'

'The vision was of a hundred thousand rows stretching back beyond the horizon and in each row there were seventy or eighty thousand chairs. It would have taken weeks to walk round the room. Anyway, there were enough seats so everyone, the entire population of the planet could sit down. But the scientist saw only empty seats. Nobody had come to listen. There was only one person looking back at him and he was on the far right in the distance. He was the man that operated the lights. That was pretty much it. It was just bullshit. I'd been drinking. We'd both been drinking.'

'It's there. That's one of his visions.'

He froze again.

'Vince,' she said, shaking his arm.

'What?'

She read his thoughts and said, 'You can do that. You can't protect an idea. He didn't need your permission.'

'If he did,' said Vince, 'he wouldn't have done it.'

'What do you mean?'

'It's the way he is. Nothing's straightforward. It's a game. Just creating stuff, that's not enough for him.'

'You said he was drunk. Perhaps he thinks it was his idea.' But she didn't believe it. You couldn't replicate something in such detail and not remember when and where it came from. 'They're going for fifty thousand each.' She reached over and put her hand to his face and smiled. 'I'll get you a drink...shall we eat?'

'How many are there?'

'Twenty.'

'So he'll make a million.'

93

She waved to a passing waiter and ordered sandwiches and two glasses of wine. Momentarily, she was taken back to the day they had first met – outside the High Court after the trial – when Vince had been too shocked, too distracted to maintain a conversation. 'Look at it this way,' she said, 'there aren't many people that can say they've exhibited at the Tate.'

'Yes, and I'm not one of them,' he said.

'I think we should meet him. I'm going to do it. I'm going to arrange a meeting with Spinks.'

He raised his head. 'How does that help?'

'I don't know, but he's having an impact on your life, so I think he should know that.'

'He knows it. He's fucking with me...and everyone else.'

'Maybe he is. Let's find out.'

On the Tube home she reminded him to send his bank details to Kevin.

17

In the morning she wrote a letter that she hoped would get her an audience with Spinks. Knowing that a simple request for a meeting would be denied, she wrote to Brewer and Copthorne LLB, Spinks' lawyers at the time of the trial.

Saturday 23rd April

Brewer and Copthorne LLB
Bouverie Street
London
EC4Y 8PD

Dear Messrs Brewer and Copthorne

I wish to bring to your attention a matter concerning your client, the artist, David Spinks. I am a buyer of art and some years ago I purchased a piece of work which I believed to be original. Subsequently, the artist responsible has been in contact with me stating that the work has been copied by your client. While I concede that two similar works could be created independently and contemporaneously, in this case the similarity is so close that such an explanation is not credible. Clearly it is important for me to establish whether one artist has copied another. I will be seeking compensation should I find that your client is at fault.

Please let me know how you would like to proceed. I am willing to attend a meeting with Mr Spinks at which I would bring along the work in question.

Yours in confidence

Ailish Brady

cc. Fitzgerald, Carnie and Skinner LLB, Dublin.

She used her parent's home address in Dublin and called her mother to let her know that she was expecting mail. After two weeks she'd heard nothing, so she sent another letter. It was shorter. It threatened legal action and stated that she now had evidence that the artwork in her possession was conceived several years before the piece produced by Spinks. Five days later her mother phoned to say that a letter had arrived.

'Can you send it over?' said Ailish,

'I can read it to you if you want?'

'You haven't opened it?'

'No, but I can.'

'No Mom, best to send it, send it special delivery. Is that okay?'

It arrived in Tooting two days later. Vince answered the door and signed for it. He flipped it over looking for the sender's name and then dropped it on the sofa beside Ailish. 'It's from your Mammy.'

She glanced at the package and then back at her laptop, aware that Vince hadn't moved. Neither received much post and he was curious.

'Aren't you going to open it?'

She looked up. 'Oh, it's just some legal stuff my mother has asked me to sign.' As Vince moved away into the kitchen, she placed her laptop on the coffee table, grabbed the package and disappeared into the bathroom. Cutting open the special delivery bag with nail scissors, she pulled out a brown A5-sized envelope. She immediately noticed the hand-written address. Other than the London postmark, there were no clues as to who might have sent it.

Inside there were more surprises. The letter had been hand-written and signed by Spinks. Just three sentences: the first thanking her for her letters; the second saying they could meet at the offices of Brewer and Copthorne on the 21st June at one o'clock; and the third asking her to call Brewers to confirm her attendance. She turned it over, sniffed it, and then held it up to the window, looking for a watermark. She read it again and then again. She wondered why he'd replied in person, and why his lawyers weren't handling it.

The next day, she made two decisions: she was going to follow through and meet Spinks, but she wouldn't be telling Vince. She figured it was best that he wasn't involved. That way, if nothing came of it, he would have nothing to get angry about.

18

Zurich/Belgravia, Saturday 30th April

A Frenchman and an Italian, Henri Landuzière and Antonio Spilotti, were monitoring the Millwall situation with growing concern. Spilotti had been the first to spot the problem, believing the Church's involvement in professional football had the potential of destroying their business. The two men had both worked at IntraDex SpA., a Milan-based currency and commodities exchange, but it was through a departmental five-a-side team that they first met. During the game Spilotti had heard Landuzière swear in *Hausa* – a language common across West Africa. After the game they found they had other things in common: they both liked money but didn't make enough; they had both been raised in West Africa (Spilotti in Nigeria, where his father had worked for Shell, and Landuzière in Cote d'Ivoire, where his parents had taught at the Ecole Nationale Supérieure de Statistique et d'Economie Appliquée) and they were both fluent in French, English, Italian, and Arabic.

Their illegal business operation had been inspired by a 2004 report published by the *Groupe d'Action Financière* (GAFI – an intergovernmental body that developed policy on global financial systems). The report, titled: *'Risques de blanchiment dans le secteur du football'*, highlighted the vulnerability of the European football sector to money laundering. Spilotti spotted the opportunity, knowing that international regulation to stamp it out would take decades. Landuzière agreed, and in 2006 they launched their own money laundering operation servicing a handful of clients within the Italian Camorra. They acted as intermediaries, specialising in the trade of players from West Africa into Europe, channelling transfer fees from European clubs – the clean money – through shell companies registered in

Caribbean tax havens. It was via these shell companies that the Camorra's dirty money was laundered. The two men paid fees to agents in Europe and Africa, and in turn received much larger fees from the Camorra. Their operation only functioned because the football industry hated financial transparency and resisted it at every move.

Spilotti was worried that the Church of England's involvement might presage a new era of *etica commerciale* – business ethics. While this would be an unwelcome development, he foresaw other threats. If the Millwall/Church venture succeeded, he was sure other religious groups would follow. He believed the mixing of sport and religion would make the game doubly tribal with the rise of extreme factions, and with that, FIFA and UEFA would be forced to act, bringing in new regulations on club ownership and financing. Spilotti concluded that to maintain the status quo and protect his business, Millwall had to fail.

When not in West Africa, Spilotti lived with his wife and children in Zurich, attracted by the low crime rate, low taxes, and proximity to FIFA headquarters. In contrast, Landuzière led a more solitary life. He'd never married. He split his year between London, Paris and Madrid, spending his days arranging money transactions, and his spare time honing his martial arts skills.

That afternoon in his Belgravia flat, Landuzière sniffed the air and frowned. Then he bent forward, his legs straight, and pushed his face deep into the back cushion of his leather sofa. He held the position, breathing through his nose. The sofa was two weeks from new and smelt of nothing. As he straightened up his phone rang.

'Bonjour.'

'I think it's time we did something,' said Spilotti. From his apartment in Zürichberg, Spilotti scanned the back page of *La Gazzetta dello Sport* and the colour photographs of Tom Cowly and the Pope.

'What about?' said Landuzière.

'Millwall. It's too risky to just wait and see. There is speculation in today's paper that the Vatican is looking to buy Inter.'

'So we do as we discussed?'

'Yes, we make it personal.'

Landuzière rang off and made a call on another mobile.

Morne Goosen answered on the first ring.

'Mr Goosen?'

'Yes.'

'We met before about a year ago...Caffè Nero...do you remember?'

Goosen recognised the voice. 'Yes, what can I do for you?'

'Can we meet...now?'

'Give me an hour,' said Goosen. 'The same place?'

'The same,' said Landuzière.

Landuzière spent forty minutes on the net reading about the people behind the Millwall takeover. He printed photographs of Cowly, Ffooks, The Archbishop of Canterbury, and the LPFL's CEO, Frank Hobson. Then he walked down to the Kings Road and flagged a cab. Where possible, he liked to do his business on the move and out of sight of London's vast CCTV network. Fifteen minutes later the driver pulled up outside Caffè Nero on Curzon Street. Goosen was inside at a window seat. Landuzière flung open the cab's door and seconds later Goosen jumped in. There was no handshake.

Landuzière told the cabby to drive. At the first set of lights, he said, 'I have something urgent.' Then seeing the cabby occupied by a giant poster of a semi-naked Mara Rooney, Landuzière handed Goosen a roll of notes. 'Five in twenties.'

Goosen squeezed it, testing its density, and then slipped it into his trouser pocket.

'I want you to look at Millwall, at these people.' He handed Goosen the printed images. 'They are responsible for the Church of England taking over at Millwall. There may be others, but start with these. I want *calomnie*...you understand?'

'You mean smear?' said Goosen. 'You want me to smear them?' It wasn't what Goosen had been expecting. His

100

previous assignment for Landuzière had been a simple observation job.

'Exactement. Their reputations must be attacked.' Landuzière glanced at the bulge in Goosen's pocket. 'Is that enough?'

'Enough to make a start.'

'Any questions?' said Landuzière.

'How soon?'

'As soon as possible. You have my email address from before?'

Goosen nodded.

Landuzière leant forward, tapped the glass partition, and indicated to the driver that he should pull over.

The cab stopped on Old Brompton Road. As Goosen watched it pull away leaving a trail of grey smoke, he wondered if Landuzière was working for the Vatican.

19

The Den, May

With the Championship season over (Millwall came second – nine points clear of third spot) and the euphoria dying down, Tom Cowly pressed on with preparations for the new season. His first task was to oversee the appointment of a new manager. When there were still two matches to play the club had issued a statement saying that the incumbent manager, Harry Caine, would be leaving with immediate effect. His unforeseen departure was precipitated by two minor stories in the tabloids. On the 21st April, the Sun reported that:

> *...sources at Millwall said Caine was looking forward to working with the new owners, but he hoped they would leave the football to him and his players.*

The Mirror had a slightly different take:

> *...friends of Caine say he is worried that money to strengthen the squad won't be made available and that Caine believes the only reason to bring new players to the club had to be because of their skill with the ball – nothing else mattered.*

When Cowly asked Caine about the stories, Caine denied he'd said anything to anyone. But Cowly was unconvinced. He did some checking and through a business contact that spent millions on newspaper advertising, he discovered that Caine had spoken directly to the journalists who had penned the articles. Cowly assumed Caine was simply angling for a move to a bigger club, with a fatter contract, and that his concern about money and players was a side-show. But the fact that Caine had lied meant he had to go. The vacancy was posted on the club's website an hour after he'd cleared his desk.

While Cowly waited for the applications to come in, he began a series of one-to-ones with the first team squad. Every player that entered his office came with his uninvited agent, and every question that Cowly directed at the player, no matter how trivial – Are you enjoying your football? I hear you've had some knee trouble? Are you going away for the summer? – was answered by his agent. 'Yes, he is...his knee's never been better...he's off to Marbella/Malta/The Maldives.' It was ventriloquism of a sort, though the dummy was flesh and blood and its lips never moved.

Cowly asked each player/agent combo about the Church's involvement. Each agent said it was a good thing and then quickly shifted the conversation on to matters of pay and contract extensions, and each time Cowly replied that all contractual matters were on hold until a new manager was in place.

The club received forty-four expressions of interest for the vacancy. Twelve were short emails where the applicant simply stated that they were available for interview. Even though three of these had League Premiership experience, Cowly rejected them all. He felt that if an applicant couldn't be bothered to submit their career history, he wasn't going to bother to find out who they were. The remaining thirty-two sent in copies of their coaching qualifications, school certificates, and DVDs of their playing days. He handed all the documentation to his HR colleagues at BSM, requesting an appraisal of each candidate's disciplinary record, their charitable and community activities, and their press and TV appearances. By the 20th of May he had a shortlist of five, with three in reserve.

When he wasn't meeting players/agents, sponsors and box-holders, Cowly read about football. In his briefcase he carried the Sport Channel Yearbook; a thick tome packed with footballing facts and figures. He memorised score lines, transfer fees, the names of managers past and present, Cup winners and Cup losers, and the rules of the game. He did it so that if pressed in an interview, he could give sensible answers and ask sensible questions. He realised he needed to know at least as much as the average fan. His motivation came in part from the unfortunate experience of Charles Goodfellow, the hapless Sports Minister from the previous Labour Government. Goodfellow had had a momentary lapse of memory while being interviewed on ESPN News. He'd hesitated when trying to recall the name of the current England Manager. Then sensing an opportunity, the journalist moved off script and asked him who played at Old Trafford.

Goodfellow's mouth tightened and sensing danger, his eyes darted from left to right, searching for an exit. 'I really must be going.'

'Just one more question Minster. Who is Harry Redknapp?'

Goodfellow shook his head and forced a guilty smile. 'I'm sorry, I have to go.' He yanked off his lapel mic and walked off camera. Demotion followed at the next Cabinet reshuffle, and he lost his seat the following year. In less than a minute, he had entered the British Hall of Mockery from which there was no escape.

Cowly also read histories of the game, the biographies of players and managers, and books about failed World Cup campaigns, and the more he read about football, the more he was convinced that a good club manager was much like a good CEO. They both needed presence and strength of character, the ability to listen and command, and the skill to spot talent and let it loose.

The interview panel comprised Cowly, Phylida and two ex-Millwall players: Simon Cordale, the youth team's coach, and Graeme Precious who did match-day hospitality and community work. Of the five shortlisted applicants one dropped out – having taken the vacancy at Stoke City. When the final interview was over, Cowly said, 'I want you to rank them...one to four...and no conferring.' It took seconds. All four put Bryan Hardwick first on their list; the only candidate with a beard and the only one from Yorkshire. His current side, Hartlepool, had been in the Championship one season and had only missed the play-offs on goal difference.

Hardwick was asked back the next day. After a discussion over contract conditions, Cowly told him that, if appointed, the club's new owners would expect all his players to behave, both on and off the pitch.'

'Can you be more specific?' said Hardwick.

'Well to start with, we don't want to see Millwall players diving or arguing with the referee.'

'No problem. I don't like that either. They'll all play fair.'

Cowly nodded and looked down at his notes. 'One last question, are you religious?

'No, I'm not. I'm an atheist. Is that a problem?'

'Not at all. It's not a material consideration for us, but whoever we appoint will be asked about their faith.'

Hardwick nodded.

'Being an atheist will probably make it easier for you, you have no affiliations, though having said that, we need the manager to support the club's ethical aims.'

'So will there be some sort of code of conduct?'

'No. We think a code would be more of a hindrance. Whatever we put in it, it won't be right. It'll either be too vague or too prescriptive, and then we'll be asked what the sanctions are. We're not going down that route.'

With Hardwick still in the room, Cowly turned to the rest of the panel. 'Any thoughts...final questions?'

All three shook their heads.

Cowly turned back to Hardwick and smiled. 'Do you want the job?'

Hardwick accepted without hesitation and leant over the table and shook Cowly's hand. When the congratulations were over Hardwick said that with some new players Millwall could finish mid-table. It was a professional lie. He expected relegation. But on the plus side, he would have at least one year in the spotlight playing Man City and Arsenal. He'd get to shake hands with Wenger and Rogers, and most importantly of all, he'd forever be remembered as the first manager whose boss was the Archbishop of Canterbury.

20

Thursday 26th May

The day after Hardwick accepted the Millwall job, the club held a press conference to announce his appointment. Hardwick politely batted away the questions with typical Yorkshire bluntness: 'I wouldn't know. No comment. You will have to ask Tom. I'm not a vicar. I don't think they played football in Judea.' When asked about his own faith he was more effusive: 'Aye, well I've always been an atheist. My dad was and so was his dad. But it doesn't matter, I'm here to steer Millwall to mid-table safety, I don't think we need help from the supernatural.'

Cowly left the press conference reassured that they had got the best man they could afford. He arrived home at seven-thirty, pushed back the front door and listened. As expected there was no one in. Jocelyn and the twins were in France, though he wasn't sure for how long or what they were doing. He communicated with his wife by email and post-it, and on the rare occasions they met face-to-face, they would limit their discussion to matters of house maintenance and, more recently, to exchange and sign the documents that would finalise their divorce. In effect, he'd been living in a house-share for twenty years. They had never been any love or friendship. She got pregnant the first time they had sex, on their third date, and against the advice of their parents, they married. He was thirty and she'd just turned twenty-two.

Two years after the birth of Aimee and Charlotte they decided to stop the pretence of being husband and wife. They agreed to keep the family home for the sake of the girls, but they moved into separate rooms, and then, when the girls went to boarding school, they lived on separate floors: Jocelyn on the first, with the girls, and Cowly on the second. The only space they shared was the kitchen and

Cowly didn't cook. They divided their labours: she did the child-rearing, while he looked after the bills, and throughout it all, he never fed or dressed his daughters, and when they were older, he never picked them up from school or took them to hockey practice. He was a marginal figure in their lives long before they were teenagers.

Shutting the front door he walked through to the kitchen, his footfall loud on the chequerboard tiles. It was as he left it: the stone worktop surfaces were clear but for a veneer of dust, there were no smells of cooking or cooked food, and the recycling boxes were empty. In the centre of the wooden fruit bowl were two mouldy lemons. When Charlotte and Aimee were away at university, Jocelyn moved out. He didn't know where she stayed or if she had a lover. Her last email said she was taking the girls to see her sister and later that she would drive them to Berlin. They were both studying French and German and Cowly had arranged a six-week work placement at BSM's Berlin office. It was likely he'd not see them again until Christmas.

Mirroring his dysfunctional marriage was a meagre social life. Only out of a sense of duty would he attend a colleague's leaving do or a gathering to celebrate the winning of a new BSM contract. And at such events, he would only ever drink one glass of wine. He never loosened his tie or removed his jacket. He would be visible, but on the periphery, and given the opportunity to slip away, perhaps when the party moved from one venue to another, he'd take it without saying goodbye. He feared parties more than anything, because he feared dancing. The prospect alone would bring on a cold sweat. So whenever a celebration started at a night club, he would send in his apologies, saying that he was feeling ill.

He worked at BSM not for the social camaraderie or the salary and the bonuses, but because he enjoyed it, and because he couldn't envisage doing anything else. And over the years, as he distanced himself from Jocelyn and the girls, he transferred his arm's length paternalism to his junior BSM colleagues. Through the company's continued profitability, he imagined himself as a backstage homemaker, a sort of corporate guardian angel, indirectly helping the company's young graduates pay off their loans and mortgages. But it was nothing more than a grand delusion, a self-deception. He was no one's benefactor. Junior staff, though respectful of his business skills, would joke about his ill-fitting suits, his tassel-brogue loafers, and his heavy two-fingered typing.

None of his BSM colleagues, including Phylida, knew he was married with kids, and none of them knew about his heart condition. His GP had warned him to slow down and think about retiring, but Cowly had just smiled, shaken his doctor's hand and said that he would sort something out. He told himself that there were worse ways to go than dropping dead in the office. He even speculated on how the BSM staff would respond to his demise. He assumed Facilities Management would take control with Kieron Betteley, the head of department, directing operations.

He imagined Betteley panicking as he searches his filing cabinet for the appropriate document: *BSM management system A-134-9001_vers9: Emergency Response Procedure.* Unable to find it, Betteley goes online and prints it off. Then he runs from his office passing the lift doors and down the stairwell to the sixth floor. When he arrives beside the motionless body, he looks reassuringly at Bernadette, Cowly's PA, and asks her to stand back. And then, like a vicar delivering a sermon, he starts reading his procedure:

'Action 1. Record the date and time the emergency was reported.'

Bernadette hands Betteley a pen. He looks at his watch, subtracts three minutes and scribbles the time.

'Action 2. Record nature of emergency.' Betteley looks to Bernadette.

She shrugs and says, 'Heart attack?'

Alongside Action 2, Betteley writes, Cause – undetermined, further investigation required.

'Action 3. Notify line manager.'

'I'll do that,' says Bernadette, and she rushes from the room.

Betteley watches her leave and calmly puts a tick against Action 3. By the time he reaches Action 12: Administer CPR to the victim, the blood in Cowly's cooling heart has turned to treacle. And when the ambulance arrives and his body is laid out on the collapsible stretcher, Betteley turns to Bernadette, puts his arm around her shoulder, and says, 'He was a good man. We did everything we could.'

But it wasn't all gloom for Cowly. There was one person in his life that offered an alternative ending. Her name was Imee. She was his secret. He met her in Manila when working on a project for the World Bank advising on the privatisation of the city's waste management services. She and her co-worker, Camille, were waiting for him in the arrivals lounge at Ninoy Aquino Airport. Their duties were to translate for him, to arrange and attend his meetings, and to ferry him back and forth between his hotel and the various ministries. Both in their early thirties, they spoke near perfect English.

The event that changed Cowly's life happened at the end of the third week. He'd taken Camille and Imee to see a show at the National Theatre as a thank you for their hard work. Then later on, when Camille had gone home, Imee accompanied Cowly to the door of his hotel room. It was unnecessary, but he assumed it was part of her duties. She'd done the same thing every evening of his stay. But on this occasion, instead of shaking hands and bidding him good night, she asked to see inside. 'I should have checked before that is it comfortable for you,' she said.

'It's fine, really,' said Cowly, smiling. 'It's perfect.'

'Just the same it would be best that I see it, and then I can go home and sleep soundly.'

Inside he turned the lights on and then she turned them off. She undressed, and in the semi-darkness removed his clothes. He was passive throughout; lying on the bed with his arms by his side. When he tried to sit up and touch her, she gently pushed him back. 'Relax Tom,' she said, placing a finger to his lips. She caressed his head and brushed his arms and chest with her lips. When he was hard, she sat on him, and when he stopped shaking, she lifted off and went to

110

the bathroom. He remained on the bed, motionless, believing that he'd just made a terrible mistake. Then as she came back into the room wrapped in a towel, he said, 'Imee, what about...'

'Don't worry, I'm clean. I have taken a pill,' and then she smiled, 'I don't need another child.'

Her words made no difference. He looked down at his white legs, at his jellied stomach and then at Imee, at her slim waist, her smooth kayumanggi skin, and the fluffy dark triangle between her thighs. She smiled, embarrassed, but also pleased that he was looking at her. She dressed, kissed his forehead, wished him sweet dreams, and left.

Leaning back against the cushioned headboard, Cowly stared at the slit of light from under the door. He stayed stock-still for five minutes, then ten, then twenty, the room silent but for the hum of the air-con. He felt panic and delight. The signs, that he had initially passed off as cultural – the late evening calls to see if all was well, and the air-kiss greeting each morning whenever Camille was absent – had started at the airport when she'd touched his hand as she offered to carry his suitcase.

With each passing day he had remained polite but unresponsive, not wanting to encourage her subtle advances. But after the first week, he would spend his evenings in his room just to make sure he didn't miss her call. He imagined his hand running through her silky hair, but when he allowed his thoughts to go further; if he imagined her lips on his and their naked bodies together, the fantasy imploded.

He wondered whether to email one of his partners at BSM to let them know what had happened. It was the right thing to do because he'd broken BSM's rules. *But what if it leaked out? Everyone would know. Everyone!* He couldn't risk it. He drank two miniature whiskies from the mini-bar and climbed back into bed. He saw her body again, her hips moving up and down, and the smile on her face when he came. He picked up his phone and sent her a text: *Hello Imee. We need to talk about this. Tom.* A few seconds later, she replied: *Hi Tom. I'll come to your room tomorrow, and don't worry, everything will be fine. Imee xx*

In the three weeks that followed, he visited the village where she was born, he met her parents, her sisters, and her ten-year-old son. She had never been married, and her mother looked after her son while she was at work in the city. She presented her life to him, showing him that she was an honest woman and that he could trust her. In the airport departure lounge, before he flew home, she told him that they should marry when he was free from Jocelyn.

That was all two years ago. Imee now lived in London and attended the Metropolitan University, all paid for by Cowly, including her flat near Finsbury Park and her son's school fees in Manila. When she flew home between terms they Skyped. He told her he would marry her when her studies were over. He figured that if that was what she wanted, there was no harm in waiting a few years, and if he didn't last that long, if his heart gave out, at least she'd have her studies to fall back on.

21

The Den, Tuesday 31st May

First thing on Tuesday morning Hardwick, Cowly and Phylida met in the Director's Box to discuss player transfers. Hardwick was nervous. At his previous club, he only targeted loan players and frees. The most expensive player he had ever pursued had been priced at three hundred thousand, and then the board had turned him down.

'Okay Bryan, let's see what you've got.'

Hardwick spun his list and slid it over to Cowly. 'There are five areas on the pitch that I'd like to strengthen. I don't know if they're all available. The names at the bottom are the players I think we should sell.'

Cowly read the names. None were familiar to him. 'Where they are now?'

'Three are at French sides, two at Hartlepool, and the others at Norwich, West Ham and Newcastle.'

'And do you know if they're in or out of contract?' said Cowly.

'I think they're all in. Some I know are looking for a move. I've had their agents on the phone.' Then he quickly added, 'They called me.' He didn't want Cowly to think he was trying to make deals behind his back.

'We had Kevin Furling's agent call a few weeks ago,' said Cowly. 'Just after the takeover. Chelsea want eight million.'

'Yes, I heard that.'

'And how much for the lot?' said Cowly.

'My old players, about half-a-million each. The French ones are young. It really depends on who else is chasing them. We might get them for fifteen, perhaps twenty.'

Cowly looked down at the list. 'And Cole, Dennis and O'Keefe?

'Maybe three or four million each.'

Phylida tallied the numbers and said, 'That's about thirty-five to forty if we add in Furling.'

'And if we shift eight players?' said Cowly.

'Maybe four million for the lot,' said Hardwick.

'Okay,' said Cowly. 'Let's assume net, it'll cost us thirty if it all went through. That leaves us some contingency. Who's your priority?'

Hardwick smiled and shifted in his chair. 'That's difficult. We need them all.'

'I know that. Let's say you've only got twenty to spend. Who do you want now?'

'I'd go for Furling, my two and Legard'. Arno Legard, just twenty-one years of age, was a left-sided midfielder who had eleven caps as a under-21. Hardwick thought Legard and Furling could work well together.

'I'll work on those today,' said Cowly. 'Are you in tomorrow afternoon?'

'I'll be at the training ground in the morning with the youth squad.'

'I'll call you.'

The three shook hands and Hardwick left the room.

'Can you get BSM to check them over?' said Cowly to Phylida. 'The usual things, disciplinary record, affiliations, et cetera.'

'Anything else?' she said.

'No, I don't think so.' He paused and said, 'How have you been getting on?'

'Slowly. I've set up some meetings with the Footballing Association and the LPFL, but nobody else seems that interested in meeting. They're either on holiday or a bit wary, perhaps scared of backing us.' Then she paused and waved Hardwick's list. 'I think we should move more quickly on these. Rather than do the background checks, let's get their agents in now. If they're not suitable, we can always pull out. I don't think we can assume they'll all want to come here, so there's no point in doing the checks...and I think we should ask Bryan for some reserves.'

'Agreed, I'll speak to him.'

22

The Den, Tuesday 14th June

The previous July when Millwall announced its summer signings, Ted Briggs' secretary sent an email to the South London Press, where the story made the inside back page. She also copied in the Millwall Supporters Club and The Lion Roars and left it at that. Twelve months on and pretty much anything that Millwall did made the headlines. All fifty seats in the club's conference room were taken, with a further twenty or so standing at the back. Even though it was uncomfortably hot − the air-conditioning couldn't cope − most of the journalists were smiling, just as everyone who worked at the club had been smiling for weeks, high on the attention and expectation. The club's postbag had increased a hundred-fold. New branches of the Millwall Supporters Club had sprung up in California, Greenland, Fiji, and North Korea, including a new blog-site called the *Lions of Christ*. And that all made the news too. It seemed to be a win-win-win situation.

The positive mood had also infected Cowly. He had lost count of the number of times he'd been embraced by smiling strangers in the car park. Other fans from a distance, would raise their thumbs or wave, and shout their messages of support. For Cowly it was an alien experience. He found it difficult to respond, because he knew all the good wishes and support had no foundation. The club had achieved nothing; no goals, no points, and no significant increase in profits, and he feared that if they lost their first three or four games, all the goodwill would evaporate. So as he leaned back in his chair and looked out at the journalists, he promised not to dream, and to smile less often.

The club's new summer signings, Arno Legard and Kevin Furling, sat either side of Cowly, the three flanked by Phylida and Hardwick. Looking on from the sidelines were the players' agents, the Chairman, and staff from the club's shop and offices. The event was being covered by the Sport Channel, Radio 5 Live, all the national press, and dozens more from the local media.

Below, in the foyer, Vince had just arrived. He looked down at the young woman behind the reception desk and said, 'My name is Vince Wynter. I've come to see Kevin Furling. He's a friend of mine.'

She looked at her list and shook her head. 'You weren't invited.' She wasn't happy because practically everyone else at the club was up in the conference room.

Vince tried again and lied. 'Kevin asked me to come along today.' He jabbed his chest with his index finger, and said, 'I wrote his autobiography.'

'So what?'

Realising she wouldn't be persuaded, he called Kevin.

'Hi Vince.'

'I'm downstairs in reception. I thought I'd drop by and say hello.'

'Okay, but I'm in a press conference. It's about to start. Can you wait till after?'

'Can you have a word with the receptionist? I'm not on the list.' Vince passed her his phone.

She listened and smiled. 'Sandra...Sandra Davies. I normally work in accounts.' She began filling out a visitor's pass. 'That'd be really nice...tomorrow lunchtime would be good...bye.' Her smile dropped the instant she handed Vince his phone and pass. 'Up the stairs, second on the left.'

'Thank you,' said Vince, as if talking to a small child. He ran up the stairs two steps at a time. Outside the conference room he straightened his collar, took a deep breath, and then knocked on the door. With no response he eased it open. The head of a grey-haired security guard appeared in the gap. 'Have you got a pass?' he whispered. Vince held it up and the guard nodded.

116

As he edged his way to the back of the room, Phylida stood up. 'Ladies and gentlemen.' She waited for the chatter to die away. 'Thank you for coming along today. First of all, Tom Cowly, Millwall's CEO, is going to make a statement. That will be followed by another statement from our new manager, Bryan Hardwick, and then we'll be open to questions. Over to you Tom.' She sat down and someone towards the rear of the room clapped slowly four times.

Cowly leaned in towards the microphone. 'Phy, it seems you have an admirer.' A few in the audience laughed. 'Perhaps I should say before we start, that Phylida Cranson is an invaluable member at the Millwall management team. She'll be assisting me and the rest of the board and I'm very glad she's here.' Phylida smiled, slightly embarrassed by his declaration of support.

Cowly then read out a statement of the club's aims and objectives, once more stressing that Millwall was not, and never would be, a Christian club. When finished he nodded to Hardwick.

'Thank you Tom.' Hardwick held a sheet of paper in both hands. 'First, I'd like to thank everyone at Millwall for making me their new manager and for making me so welcome. Both me and the club are in new territory. My main aim is to make Millwall an established League Premiership side.' He paused and glanced at the front row of journalists. A couple were looking at their phones. No one was making notes.

'It will be difficult for us, we all know that, but I'm confident that with the right players and the right attitude we can stay up.' He paused again. 'Kevin Furling and Arno Legard will be joining the club this summer. They are players with great skill and a desire to win and work hard. I hope to be making some further announcements about other players in the next few weeks.' He looked over to his left at Cowly and nodded.

Phylida stood again, but before she'd uttered a word, several applauded with genuine enthusiasm. As a female with an executive role at a club, she knew she stood out, and

117

that to some she couldn't possibly be there on merit. She smiled and said, 'After questions, we'll be serving refreshments next door and for those that want photos, we'll be doing them down on the pitch.' She had already picked out a local journalist to ask the first question. 'James Rearden from The Messenger.' She pointed to the centre of the second row.

Vince fixed his eyes on Barros who was standing at the front of the room with his back against the left wall. After twenty minutes, during which Furling and Legard had done most of the talking, Phylida said, 'Any more questions?'

Vince shouted, 'You'll never get away with it!' His intervention was unplanned, involuntary, as if someone had briefly taken over his body. As heads turned in puzzlement, Vince looked down at the floor, hoping the moment would pass.

Ignoring the heckle, Phylida said, 'Okay, well if that's all, we'll bring things to a close. The refreshments are next door and in about thirty minutes we'll be down on the pitch.'

While most stood chatting, gathering their belongings and making ready to leave, Vince made for the door. He was second out after the security guard. He stood tight against the corridor wall as everyone moved passed in single file. He selected the camera function on his phone. A few minutes later Cowly and Phylida appeared, closely followed by Hardwick and Legard. On seeing Kevin and Barros, he stepped into the centre of the corridor.

Kevin smiled at Vince, and said, 'I'll see you later.'

Vince nodded. He took a half-step back to let Kevin pass, and then a half-step forward. He put his hand on Barros' chest and straightened his right arm. 'Just a moment Ángel.'

'What?' said Barros. He looked down at Vince's hand, his face contorted, as if sensing some awful stench.

'I want your photograph for my new book.' Vince glanced over his shoulder to check that Kevin was still walking away. Then turning back, he said, 'I didn't get a chance to tell you. I'm writing a new book, it's a sequel and you're in it. It's called 'Cunts in Football'. That's the working title. It may change.'

Barros faked a laugh. 'Yes Vince, very good, now move.' Then, as he raised his left hand to remove Vince's arm, Vince took a step forward and shoved hard. Barros' legs back-pedalled as they tried to catch up with his over-balancing body. He bumped onto the floor, dropping his briefcase, and sending his phone sliding. It was comical, it was Harold Lloyd, but Barros wasn't smiling. He sat motionless, his legs splayed, disbelief on his face. When he looked up, Vince took a photograph.

'Coño,' said Barros.

Vince smiled and took another.

Barros rolled onto his hands and knees, his face flushed. As he stood and bent down to pick up his phone, Kevin was beside them. 'What happened?'

Vince said, 'He tripped, but he's okay. You're okay, aren't you Ángel?' Vince picked up Barros' briefcase and held it out.

Barros rolled his shoulders to straighten his jacket, and then pulling on each sleeve he checked for scuffs and tears. He snatched the briefcase from Vince's hand, and shouted, 'Don't fuck with me.'

Vince looked at Kevin with an expression of innocence and bafflement.

Barros raised his hand, his finger an inch from Vince's face. 'You do or say anything Wynter, you're finished. You hear me?' and he moved his finger across his throat. Then he pushed them both aside and headed off.

Hearing the raised voices, Phylida came out into the corridor. She saw Barros push Kevin and Vince aside, then she stepped back as he bustled past swinging his briefcase. She walked up to Kevin, 'What's going on?'

'Nothing,' said Kevin. 'Mr Barros tripped.'

'Really?' She knew it was lie. She turned to Vince, 'Who are you?'

Kevin said, 'This is Vince Wynter. He's a friend, he's been writing my book.'

Phylida nodded. 'And what happened again?'

119

'I'm sorry,' said Vince. 'Mr Barros and I had a disagreement. It was nothing. He tripped, but he's okay...no lasting damage.'

Unconvinced, she said, 'Kevin, let's get this photo-shoot over.' She turned back to Vince, realising that he'd been the heckler at the back of the room. 'You know the way out?'

Vince nodded and walked away.

She said to Kevin, 'Can we talk about this afterwards, just you and me, without Señor Barros?'

'Yes, of course.'

'I'll be up in the Director's Box after we've finished on the pitch.'

Vince ran down the stairwell and through reception, hoping to catch up with Barros. But just as he reached the front car park, Barros' cab pulled away. Disappointed, he set off along the south side of Brocklehurst Street, towards the tube station. While walking he looked at the photographs on his phone and noticed that his hands were trembling. He stopped and flexed his fingers; forming a fist and then a flat hand and then a fist again. He did it ten times but it made no difference. Annoyed that it wouldn't go away, he walked on with his hands thrust deep into his pockets.

He was soon passing stationary vehicles held up by road works in the north-bound lane; a water main had burst. Then up ahead, he spotted a cab. He quickened his pace and then jogged up to the rear of the vehicle. From ten yards back he could see the passenger's thick dark hair and a light coloured jacket covering broad shoulders – it was Barros. Vince smiled, realising he had another chance to call him a cunt. But then another thought, a completely contrary thought jumped into his head – *I need to apologise*. Then Barros' cab moved forward as the flow-control light turned from red to green.

'Fuck,' said Vince, thinking that again his opportunity had gone. He started running behind the cab, and when it was only four vehicle lengths short of the traffic light, the light changed to red. Three cars carried on disobediently, but the cab stopped. Vince reckoned he had forty seconds to turn things round. He stepped into the road and knocked on the passenger window. Barros turned, and then turned away.

'Ángel, I'm sorry for what happened.' Vince held his hands up, as if to say, I'm harmless. Barros fixed his eyes on the red light. 'Ángel, I have a business proposition. Two minutes, that's all I need.'

Barros wound the window down an inch. 'What is it?'

'We can self-publish Furling's book. It's easy. We can still sell it. You'll make more money by cutting out the publisher. It works. I know lots of writers that have done it. They've made a fortune.'

But Barros was only half-listening. He was still furious, his wrist still sore from when he'd crashed to the floor. 'Be careful Wynter,' he warned.

Vince glanced at the traffic light and tried again. 'You could double your money. All I want is the book published. I'll help you do it.'

When the light turned green, the cabbie knocked on the glass partition. 'We have to go,' he said. 'I can stop on the other side if you want?'

'Okay, do that,' said Barros, and he gestured to Vince that he would see him up ahead beyond the road works.

When Vince caught up with the cab, the near-side door was open. It was an invitation to get in and Vince didn't hesitate. He pulled down a seat and sat opposite, slightly breathless. 'Thanks.' He started to apologise again, but Barros waved his hand.

'Hurry Wynter, I have a plane to catch.'

'The book's ready to publish. I can do that for you. Start with an ebook. It costs nothing. The royalties can go straight into your bank account,' then adding, 'any bank account...offshore, anywhere you like. But we can also self-publish it as a real book.'

'What do you mean an ebook...real book?'

'The ebook is an electronic version. You can read it on your laptop or phone. The market's huge. It's bigger than real books, but we can do a paperback. We can get them printed and posted on demand. You don't have to do anything.'

Barros nodded. 'You send me an email about it and we see.'

'Okay. What about meeting again?'

'I am in Frankfurt for a few days.'

'Seeing a player?' suggested Vince.

'Yes, Malisse, he is about to move like Kevin.'

Vince was tempted to ask who Malisse played for, but it wasn't necessary, the name was enough. He opened the cab door and from the pavement, said, 'I'm sorry about the...' and he pointed back towards the stadium. Barros nodded once and pulled the door shut.

'Wanker,' said Vince, as the cab moved off.

– – – – – –

Back at the Den, Phylida and Kevin were seated in the Director's Box, looking down at the pitch. Most of the journalists and photographers had gone. Hardwick was talking to Legard, his exaggerated hand movements suggestive of a conversation about tactics.

'Kevin, I don't want to pry into your private life, but Tom and I need to know if you have any issues which might reflect badly on the club.'

He frowned.

She tried again. 'All I'm saying is that we're under the spotlight, and if you've got a problem and it's nothing to do with Millwall, then we'd rather you didn't bring it here.'

'I understand. I didn't know Vince was coming here today. It won't happen again. We had a problem over the book. Vince wrote it and then the publishers pulled out because of my transfer here. And because the terms of the contract had been broken, Ángel refused to pay Vince. Business is business to Ángel. He's an agent.'

'So Wynter thinks he's been swindled?'

'He's been paid now. I paid him. He wrote a good book so I thought he deserved something.'

'So why's he still angry?'

'I'm not sure,' said Kevin.

'And what did he mean by, 'you'll never get away with it'.' It was him, wasn't it?'

'I don't know.'

'Is he a Millwall fan?'

'Actually, I don't think he likes football.'

'Religious?'

'I've no idea. We've only met a few times. My guess is no.'

'And where's Mr Barros now?'

'He left after the press conference.'

'Have you got Wynter's number? I'd like to give him a call.'

'I'll send it.' Kevin pulled out his phone and keyed in her mobile number as she called it out.

Then she said, 'I'd better get going.'

He smiled and she smiled back.

'I guess you'll be heading off somewhere now?'

'I'll say goodbye to the new boss.' Kevin nodded toward the pitch and Hardwick, 'and then I'll head home.'

'No, I mean for the summer.'

'Sorry,' said Kevin. 'No, I'm not going away. I'll spend a few weeks in Brighton, and then I'll be back here in July for pre-season training.'

'Brighton's nice,' she said, 'though I've only been there once.'

Do I ask her? Do I want to ask her? 'Well if you're ever down, drop by. I can show you around.'

'Okay, perhaps I will.'

'Do that. Call me.'

23

Central London, Tuesday 14th June

In long shorts, baseball cap, and sunglasses Henri Landuzière entered *Net House*, on Marylebone Road. He'd just left *EnCrypt* on Tottenham Court Road, and before that *Inter-Byte* and *Cafe-Neto*. He kept his cap and glasses on and joined three others sitting round an island of internet terminals. Landuzière brought up YouTube and typed in British Defence League (BDL) in the search box. He clicked on the first video and set the volume to mute. Ignoring the video he scrolled down to the comments box and typed his message:

> *You fucking idiots. It's under your nose. Gülen is buying Chelsea. The ragheads are taking over.*

He copied it and pasted the same message under another 30 BDL videos. Then he searched for videos featuring Izir Manas. He posted a pro-Gülen/pro-Manas message under all the videos connected to Manas and his telecoms business:

> *God is great and God bless Fethullah Gülen and Izir Manas and God bless Chelsea*

The day before, but then dressed in a black suit, shirt, and tie, he'd posted an anti-Gülen message below all the Manas videos:

> *Fuck off back to Turkey. Keep your filthy Gülen hands off our club. Chelsea forever British and Christian*

The campaign of disinformation had been Spilotti's idea. For a week Landuzière had been visiting London's internet cafes posting contradictory messages of lies and hatred about the sale of Chelsea to Izir Manas. He'd started with the Chelsea fanzines, warning that the club was in peril from a Gülen-inspired takeover, putting the blame on the Church of England. Then he'd moved on to the pro and anti-Islamic blog sites. Though tedious, it seemed to be paying off. A Google web search of 'Manas Gülen Chelsea' brought up pages of comments and articles linking the three.

Before leaving, he checked his emails. Amongst the junk was one from *bobby_9753@hotmail.com*. There was no message, just three photographs. Landuzière forwarded the email and then deleted the original. Outside, he flagged a taxi and called Goosen. 'I got the photographs. Who's the woman?'

'That's Cowly with his girlfriend.'

'So what?'

'He's married. He has kids. She's a Filipino.'

'Okay, but I need more.'

'More photographs?' said Goosen.

'Yes, maybe other stuff. Use your imagination.'

'I'll need another five.'

'Thirty minutes.'

As before they met in a cab. Landuzière handed Goosen his second payment, a hundred new fifties.

'I should have something in a week or two,' said Goosen. It was a lie. In his jacket pocket, on a flash drive, he already had photographs of Ken Ffooks and the LPFL boss, Frank Hobson. Goosen liked to drip feed his clients to keep them keen.

'Can you do graffiti?' said Landuzière.

Though Goosen never had, he didn't hesitate. 'Sure, what do you have in mind?'

'Have you heard of Gülen?'

Goosen shook his head.

'Izmir Manas?' said Landuzière.

'Should I?'

125

'Gülen and Manas are Islamists...extremists. Manas is secretly trying to buy Chelsea. I have a client who doesn't want that to happen.'

'I see.'

'He wants the Chelsea fans to know this. We would like to do some graffiti to spread the word.'

'Use the internet,' said Goosen.

'Yes, he is doing that already. So can you do it?'

'I can arrange it.'

Landuzière nodded.

'There's CCTV all along the Fulham Road,' said Goosen. 'It'll need some planning. How many locations? What's the message?'

'Say six or seven locations, large lettering.' Landuzière spread his arms. 'I will email you the message.'

'Nothing too long.'

'D'accord.'

24

Whitehall, Tuesday 14th June.

'Come in Robert,' said Sir Terrence, not looking up. 'Take a seat.' Caldicott sat down. Sir Terrence was catching up with his paperwork, signing his name in blue ink, while Sara dutifully dabbed each document with blotting paper.

Watching their synchronous performance, Caldicott exhaled slowly. Then he eased his legs apart, straightened his back, and then gently lowered the back of each hand onto each knee. Finally, he brought the tips of his index fingers and thumbs together. He was trying out a variation of the *Gyan Mudra*, a yoga hand position that balanced energy levels. YWYW (Yoga While You Work) was the latest initiative from the Civil Service Behaviours Team, a cross-departmental group with a remit to improve productivity and inspire a 'can do' attitude. Their programme was communicated via email and posters; so across Whitehall, in kitchens, on corridor notice boards, near printers and water coolers, posters had appeared depicting adapted yoga positions for those that worked in a 'desk-based' environment. Their rationale was that yoga led to calmness, and calmness was linked to well-being, and well-being led to increased productivity.

Sara gathered the last document and slipped away without a word.

'Sorry Robert.'

Caldicott's eyes were drawn to the beads of sweat on Sir Terrence's top lip. He assumed that either Sir Terrence was cooling down from an unscheduled workout or he was feverish.

Sir Terrence's eyes were drawn to Caldicott's hands. 'Robert...is everything alright?'

'Fine,' said Caldicott, inhaling slowly.

'Are you sure?'

'Absolutely.'

'Good. We'd better crack on then. It's about Millwall. As you've probably gathered the PM's office has been playing down the situation...keeping everyone calm. Soft hands, as it were.' Sir Terrence, a thirty-year member of the MCC, overused and sometimes abused the cricketer's lexicon: if a policy needed ditching, it was time to declare, urgent action required a run-chase, while a blunder was a dropped catch. He despised the current political vernacular (he blamed Blair), unaware that he himself was trapped in an earlier version; the one that had favoured the terminology of warfare and sports to describe the business of the day. He was also an avid finger pointer.

'We are concerned about Millwall,' he continued, 'but right now we're not making that concern public. We're monitoring. Do you understand?'

Caldicott nodded, inhaling through his nose and then out through his mouth.

'The problem Robert is that the Church's intervention is just the sort of engagement that ministers want to see.' He paused and looked out of the window. 'Let me clarify that. The Prime Minister wants to see religions engaging with businesses and the community, but not Millwall. Millwall isn't the right model. It's not what the PM envisaged.'

'Is he an Arsenal fan?' teased Caldicott.

Sir Terrence frowned. 'No, you misunderstand me Robert.'

'Is it the wrong sport?'

'I don't follow you.'

'If it were rugger or cricket?' Caldicott bit into his bottom lip, trying to maintain his Mudra.

Like a Nike swoosh, Sir Terrence swept his hand from right to left, consigning Caldicott's comment to another place. Then the finger came out. 'Robert, I want you to arrange some meetings. I want you to meet the Footballing Association and the LPFL, and then with Millwall, but I don't want you to do anything. Have the meetings and then report back to me. I just want to know who you met, where and when, nothing more.' Then jabbing his finger, he added, 'Is that clear Robert?'

'Yes, that's fine.' Caldicott didn't require further instruction. He recognised it for what it was – a pure and simple arse-covering exercise. Someone close to the PM, possibly Sir Terrence, would have suggested they needed something on record. Then if the Millwall situation blew up badly or was a resounding success, the Government would be able to state that meetings had taken place and that ministers had been working behind the scenes. Then he added, 'And would that be just me or do you want someone else along?'

'On your own would be best.'

'Any particular level?'

'Not that important,' said Sir Terrence. 'Meet anyone that's available....as soon as possible.'

'Fine, I'll get back to you next week.

'Excellent.' Sir Terrence picked up the handset of his phone.

'There is one thing,' said Caldicott.

Sir Terrence looked up, his dial finger poised over the keypad.

'Would you like me to look at the Gülen situation?' Caldicott suspected it was the rumours about Gülen that were making the PM twitchy.

'Gülen? No, you don't need to look at that. That's not a concern.'

25

Outside Colliers Wood tube station Vince turned away from the A24 into Cavendish Road. When clear of the traffic noise he called Kevin.

'Hi Vince.'

'Can you talk?'

'Sure.'

'I want to apologise about earlier on. I lost it.'

'Okay, but try not to do it again.'

'I spoke to Barros outside the ground. I apologised and we had a chat about the book.'

'What about it?'

'I told him we could still publish it. We could do it ourselves as an ebook and cut out the publishers. He said he'd think about it.'

'Thanks,' said Kevin, wearily.

'I was just thinking it was a shame to waste all that effort. It's not a bad book.'

'It doesn't matter Vince. It's not going to sell, not now I've moved.'

'I'm supposed to be meeting him when he gets back from Frankfurt. He was off to see Matisse or someone?'

'Patrick Malisse,' corrected Kevin.

'Yes, that was it. Who does he play for?'

'Eintracht. I think they've been relegated.'

'Doesn't he have any other English players?'

'I don't know,' said Kevin. 'He never talks about them. I think de la Rosa was one of his. He was at Everton for a year then went back to Spain.'

With two names to work with Vince decided not to press any further. 'Okay, well on the ebook, I'll tell him you're not keen...or do you want to speak to him?'

'I'll speak to him.'

'Cheers Kevin, and thanks.'

Vince jogged the rest of the way home, eager to implement the next stage of his plan. Ailish's car was parked out front. He ran up the stairs and pushed back the front door. 'Can I use your laptop?' There was no answer. He had no idea where she might be, the terms of their never discussed relationship didn't involve the exchange of whereabouts. She was out but her laptop was in. Normally the two were inseparable. He hurriedly booked a one-way flight to Frankfurt, and then searched for information on de la Rosa and Malisse. He found that de la Rosa played for Valencia, and according to his wiki-profile, he lived in Puigcerdá (*push-air-the)* in the Pyrenees-Orientales. Malisse came from Marciac, a small town in the foothills of the French Pyrenees. An hour and a beer later, he realised he had just wasted ninety-five pounds. Flying to Frankfurt and hoping for the best had the hallmarks of a plan destined to fail. He couldn't approach Malisse if Barros was around.

Ailish came home just after eight-thirty and without a word or hello she emptied a holdall of shoes onto the sofa. She was tired and annoyed. Her supplier had been two hours late and he only had half the stock he'd promised.

Vince was in the kitchen studying a road map of France. He called out, 'Ail, do you speak German?'

'Don't call me that,' she snapped.

'Yes, okay, but do you speak German?'

'Nein...ich liebe dich.'

'I thought that was Welsh?'

She walked into the kitchen and filled the kettle. 'It means, I love you.'

Surprised, he looked over his shoulder. She'd never said it before. 'That's nice,' he said. It was the best he could do. He couldn't bring himself to return the sentiment.

She laughed. 'No, that's what it means.'

Then he realised, *ich liebe dich* was the only German she knew. Feeling stupid, he folded his map and went into the lounge. Then without thinking why, he said, 'If you want, I'll move out.' He'd never offered before. But they were

131

only together because he'd been homeless, and because she had a sofa bed. It was supposed to have been a temporary arrangement, but on his second night they had sex. And though they had fucked a hundred times since, it was rarely anything more than perfunctory. They rarely kissed mouth to mouth.

Hearing his offer, she was tempted to say, yes, find your own place. She didn't want to let things slip by for another year. She'd had her fill of Tooting and London, but her problem was where to go. Ireland wasn't a consideration, the North and Scotland were too cold, and the Southwest too expensive. South Wales, she thought, was her best option, rental prices were lower and the M4 would make it an easy drive into London to pick up stock. In Wales, she would be able to afford somewhere with space to paint, perhaps with a shed and a garden. But wherever she ended up, she knew it wouldn't be with Vince.

Whilst searching the fridge in search of a treat, she said, 'So what's with the German?'

'I was thinking of going to Frankfurt. It's just an idea.'

She peeled open a pot of yoghurt.

He came back into the kitchen. 'I might have a story on Barros.'

'Like what?'

'I'm not sure. He's just flown to Frankfurt to see one of his players. I want to meet him his player. His name's Malisse. He's French.'

'So you need French and German. That is a problem.'

'I might not go to Germany. I need to see Malisse when Barros isn't there. He's also got another player, Adriano de la Rosa. He's Spanish.'

She licked her spoon clean and placed the half-empty pot back in the fridge. Then she said, 'Como es su español Vince?'

He didn't reply. He knew she was mocking him.

'So what's Barros done?' she said.

'I don't know for sure.'

'Is he gay?'

'What?' She'd surprised him.

132

'Barros...Malisse...are they gay?'

'No...no, of course they're not.' Thinking his denial lacked conviction, he changed the subject. 'Do you want to come along?'

'I'll think about it,' she said, but meaning no. 'Perhaps you should call them first. It might save you some time.'

'They won't talk over the phone. They don't know me.'

'Okay, well have a good trip.' She had her own problems to work out. She was due to meet Spinks in a week and she'd done no prep.

‒ ‒ ‒ ‒ ‒ ‒ ‒ ‒

During the night Vince had a rethink. He decided to call the clubs first and push that route. He rose before eight, made coffee, logged on and found the number for Eintracht Frankfurt FC. At eight-thirty he made the call.

'Guten tag. Do you speak English?'

'Yes I do,' said a female voice.

He presumed he was through to their switchboard. 'Thank you. My name is Mark Groenig. I'm calling from the Sport Channel in England. We'd like to do an interview with Patrick Malisse.' Vince remembered Groenig's name from the press conference at the Den. Groenig had asked Hardwick why he'd been sent to a Catholic school given that his parents were both atheists.

'One moment please,' said the woman.

The phone rang once and then a man answered. 'Klauser.'

'Hello, do you speak English?'

'Yes, I do.'

'That's good. My name is Mark Groenig. I work for the Sport Channel. We'd like to get a statement from Patrick Malisse. We've heard he may be on the move to an English club.'

'You'll have to call his agent. I have his number.'

'Okay, that would help. Do you know where they are? We're after a telephone interview.'

'None of the players are here,' said Klauser. 'They have been away for several weeks.'

133

'I see, I was told his agent, Herr Barros, would be at the club today.'

'That may be true.'

'So you think Malisse will be back home?'

'I do not know.' Klauser read out Barros' number.

'Thanks. Do you know which club he is joining?'

'No, I do not.'

Vince rang off. He decided it wasn't worth calling Valencia. Most likely it would be the same outcome. Then he had another idea. A much better idea. But the downside was he couldn't do it on his own. He'd need Ailish's help.

He googled 'French Footballers League Premiership', and then realised he already knew of one. Arno Legard had just signed for Millwall along with Kevin. Wikipedia stated that Legard and Malisse had played together for the French under-21s.

By nine Ailish was in the kitchen, in her dressing down, gathering her breakfast. They were yet to speak.

'Would you do me a favour?' said Vince.

She turned and raised her eyebrows, and then continued slicing an over-ripe banana onto a bowl of muesli.

He tried again. 'If you wouldn't mind, would you call Ángel Barros? I'd like you to ask his permission to speak to Patrick Malisse.'

At the fridge she said, 'And why would he do that?'

'He probably won't. We need to tell him a lie.'

'You mean I need to lie to him?'

'Yes, a small one. I can't see any other way of doing it. Remember the Sport Channel? The one you dreamt about. They were at a press conference yesterday, at Millwall. I went along to say hello to Kevin. What it is, I'd like you to pose as someone from the Sport Channel who wants to do a profile on Arno Legard. Legard's just signed for Millwall.' Vince waited for a response and then said, 'Are you with me?'

'Go on.'

'So the idea is, you contact Barros and say you'd like to speak to Patrick Malisse about Arno Legard. That's pretty much it.'

'And who am I supposed to be?' she said.

'An assistant producer,' he suggested. 'You're after a filmed interview sometime over the summer. You're doing it for Mark Groenig. Barros was at the press conference. He'll recognise Groenig's name. Hopefully he won't call him.'

'And why?'

He shook his head.

'Why am I telling lies?'

'I'm not sure. I just want to meet up with Malisse. It was something Kevin said that doesn't add up.'

'Doesn't add up?' she said, frowning. 'You want me to tell a pack of lies 'cos something doesn't add up?'

'I know that's not much to go on, but you'll be the first to know.'

She returned the milk to the fridge and said, 'Okay, but you need to write this down, the names and who they are, and my name.' She didn't want to do it, but she didn't want to discourage him.' Then she added, 'I'll need another phone.'

He nodded, recognising the problem. 'I've got an old Nokia,' he said. 'You could use that.'

He retrieved the phone from the kitchen drawer, put it on charge and checked it for credit. On her laptop he sent her an email detailing the subterfuge, including Barros' phone number, and a suggested name: Bríd Collins, her sister. Then he googled de la Rosa. He found a short clip on YouTube titled: 'Puigcerdá honours Adriano'. The twenty-second video showed de la Rosa on a small stage shaking hands with the mayor, surrounded by a crowd waving pennants. Below the video clip, he typed a comment:

'I like your video. Does Adriano still live in Puigcerdá?'

Knowing Ailish would soon want to be online and listing her stock, he logged off.

'I'm going down the library,' he said. 'I've just emailed you the stuff about Barros.'

She didn't reply.

At Balham library, Vince logged back onto YouTube and posted comments below a dozen other videos featuring de la Rosa and Malisse, each time asking where the player lived.

Back at the flat, Ailish had just finished her call to Barros. He had been more than happy to help arrange the Groenig/Vince interview. Barros gave her Malisse's phone number, and said Malisse should be in Marciac until mid-July. Apparently he left before it got busy, before the Jazz Festival kicked off. Barros also said that Malisse had signed for Marseille. And just before their conversation ended, he said, 'Why don't I give you a call when I am back in London. We could have dinner at The Berkeley?'

'Err...maybe, but I have to go now.' She cut the call and staring at the phone said, 'No fuckin' way.'

26

The Gherkin, Thursday 16th June

The LPFL, the company owned by the eighteen clubs in the League Premiership, occupied floors fifteen and sixteen of 30 St Mary Axe, the building more commonly known as The Gherkin. Phylida was there to meet Frank Hobson, their Chief Executive. She had an eleven o'clock appointment and arrived right on the hour.

Hobson's PA, Jeannie, met her from the lift and immediately apologised. 'He's in a taxi now,' she said, 'He shouldn't be more than five minutes.' She led Phylida into Hobson's office and gestured to a leather sofa that faced south to the river. 'Take a seat.'

Ten minutes later and Phylida was still on her own. But it didn't matter. Her next appointment, with the Chairman of the Footballing Association, wasn't until mid-afternoon. She sipped a glass of iced water and let her eyes roam over the Deco furniture and the concertina-like fenestration. Bored, she stood and paced the room's outer curve, from wall to wall. She counted 29 steps, approximately 25 metres. Hobson's radii she estimated at 30 metres. In her head, she did the rough maths. $2\pi r$ was 190ish. 190 divided by 25 was 8ish. 360 degrees divided by 8 gave 45. Hobson, she estimated, had 45° of arc in one of London's most expensive buildings. If it was rented, she reckoned his office alone would be costing a hundred thousand a year. And why, she wondered, was he paid a banker's salary? He was, she thought, nothing more than an administrator. That's all he could be, because all the decision-making authority resided with the shareholders, the eighteen League Premiership clubs.

Hobson finally walked in forty minutes late. She'd seen him interviewed on television a couple of times, but just head shots; she'd imagined him to be taller, fatter and younger. His pinstripe jacket seemed to hang from his shoulders, his thin legs lost in his trousers. He was full of apologies and scathing of the train service from Birmingham to London. He had been to see Aston Villa and Manchester City. He said he travelled a lot and that he was often in Europe.

'Doing what?' she asked.

'Oh, meetings, meetings with FIFA and UEFA and some of our partner organisations.'

'Sounds interesting,' she said, but not really meaning it. She called it business tourism: first class all the way with others picking up the bill.

Jeannie came in with coffee and a plate of digestives.

'You must pass on my apologies to Tom,' said Hobson. 'I normally make a point of visiting each promoted club right after the play-offs, but this year we're a bit behind.'

She knew that Cowly had spoken to one of Hobson's assistants and that Cowly had received, signed, and returned the legal documents that formalised Millwall's shareholding.

Hobson continued. 'As far as I know all the paperwork is in order. You should receive your first broadcasting payment in a few weeks.'

'Yes,' she said, 'I spoke to Tom yesterday. He said everything was fine.'

'Good, so how can I help?'

'Well there are a couple of issues I'd like to cover. The first concerns the talk about the renegotiation of the Sport Channel's broadcasting rights. If they're true, we'd like to know something of the process.'

Hobson nodded and scribbled a couple of words on a notepad.

'For example, is Millwall going to be consulted? Is there any documentation I can take away with me?'

'Documentation?'

'Yes, on what's been proposed or being discussed.'

Hobson nodded again and said, 'Well the story in the FT is partly right. Preliminary discussions on restructuring the payments are underway, but so far we've just been looking at how future payments might be weighted. But I must emphasise that these talks may go nowhere. The current deal has another eighteen months to run, so nothing really needs to be decided just now.'

She started taking notes, but not because she needed to. Note taking, she believed, sent a message to the interviewee. It said, 'I really value your opinion'. Over the years, she'd found that men in particular were inclined to say more than perhaps they should, if she noted their words.

'Like always within the LPFL,' continued Hobson, 'some clubs are in favour while others are not so keen. As far as the process, well I'm involved, together with the nominated representatives from six clubs. That's the negotiating team if you like, though nothing is official until everyone votes. And I can assure you that while Millwall may be new to the League, your opinion and interests have as much weight as any other shareholder. It would be wrong to think that the richer clubs get their way.'

She didn't believe him. She assumed, like any business sector where a handful dominated the market, secret and temporary alliances would be formed driven by shifting self-interests. Millwall, in financial terms, were minnows compared to the likes of Chelsea and Arsenal. She thought it absurd to suggest that the eighteen clubs were equal partners. She nodded, indicating that she was happy with his answer. 'The second matter I'd like to cover is specific to Millwall. We'd like to know if you, as the head of the LPFL, support the Church's acquisition. As you know there's been much talk in the press, but not much from the game's governing bodies.'

He paused briefly and said, 'I don't quite understand what you mean. It's not our role to comment on the ownership structure of clubs. As a new member, the LPFL is really only concerned with your interests. In essence, we are here to serve you and your board. We're never going to tell you whether we think it's a good or bad idea that the Church is involved at Millwall.'

'So you have no opinion? Other shareholders haven't expressed a view?'

'That's right, they haven't.'

'So you wouldn't be concerned if Scientologists or the Moonies took over at Man United?'

'I don't think we would be. We might be concerned about how it was financed. For example, if the club's debt burden had increased, but even then, there is little we could do to prevent it.'

'What if something happened that might be to the detriment of shareholders, something that threatened the well-being of the game?' It was a leading question. She wanted him to open up.

'I don't really know what you mean. The constraints on each shareholder are set out in the Articles of Association. There are procedures for shareholders to make proposals and to vote on those proposals. Members aren't allowed to knowingly damage the League.'

Phylida nodded. She'd read the LPFL's Articles of Association. They focused exclusively on the financial arrangements from broadcasting. The shareholders did have powers to change the rules, so in principle, if there were agreement, they could exclude Millwall. She pressed him again. 'Have the rules ever been changed? Have the Articles ever been rewritten?'

'Not while I've been in-post.' Hobson had been in charge for ten years and during that period turnover had trebled. 'The interests of the shareholders are mainly limited to matters of revenue. I suppose if a club did something which threatened the League's income, then the other clubs could take action, but only if they could agree. I really can't foresee such a circumstance.'

She decided to try one more time. She leant forward and smiled. 'I suppose what it is, is insecurity. At Millwall we don't want any nasty surprises. We would just like to know what you feel about what's happened...off the record.'

He nodded, but offered no opinion.

'So as far you're concerned, the involvement of faiths in football isn't a problem?'

'Not for the LPFL, but if you want my personal view, off the record, I think there should be restrictions. I'm worried, not about Millwall and the Church, but about other groups.'

'Other groups?' she said. 'You mean like Muslim-backed groups?'

He frowned, but kept quiet, not wanting to go further.

'Or the Gülen Movement?' she added.

'The Gülen? No.'

'But you've read the reports about Manas?'

He nodded, rolled his biro between finger and thumb, and then moved his empty coffee cup three inches to the left. 'I know about the web chatter, but I've not read anything substantive. That aside, I think that if there was a trend towards faith ownership in football, whether it's Muslims, Hindus or Catholics, I think it would become an issue for the Government and FIFA.'

'Why not you?'

'Because there could be repercussions for society, civil unrest, who knows. I think there's already a sense that the UK is up for sale and that nothing's sacred. If foreign religious groups acquired our clubs, it might be a step too far.'

She thought it a bit rich. Under Hobson's stewardship, two-thirds of League Premiership clubs were now owned by overseas business interests. Seventy-six percent of LPFL players were born outside the UK. She couldn't help herself. 'So ordinary foreigners are okay, but foreign religions aren't?'

'Let's call them interest groups, extreme interest groups. I don't regard the Church as extreme and most Millwall fans seem to have welcomed the Church's involvement. It's familiar.'

'I know this is a hypothetical, but if Manas tried to buy Chelsea, a man who is a known Gülen Movement supporter, could you and the LPFL stop it?'

He refused to answer and took the conversation back a step. 'Look, if you're worried about your fellow shareholders not welcoming Millwall, don't. Nobody I've spoken to has said a word against you.'

'But if there was a trend involving foreign religions, what then?'

'I suppose, if that were the case, the members could take action.'

'Even though it might be lucrative. There are millions of believers out there, all of them potential kit-buying customers.'

'Yes, but there are risks too. For most of the clubs their core revenue is still here in the UK. They wouldn't want to put that at risk.'

She looked at her notes. 'You said earlier it was a matter for FIFA, why's that?'

'Look, it's a matter for everyone, but perhaps it would be best if there were common rules throughout the game, and that's FIFA's role. We're a company, not a regulator. It's a regulatory issue. Our shareholders wouldn't be comfortable with that type of role. That's my view, off the record.'

Phylida nodded, hoping Hobson would continue, but he didn't. He refilled his coffee. Their meeting was over.

– – – – – – – –

As Phylida headed to Soho Square for her appointment with the Footballing Association, it was Robert Caldicott's turn to meet Frank Hobson. He had emailed Hobson after his meeting with Sir Terrence, stating that the Government wanted to establish closer links with the country's key sporting bodies. And when they spoke on the phone later that day, Caldicott had lied. He said he was also planning to meet with the RFU, UK Athletics and the LTA.

'Fantastic office,' said Caldicott. Then he turned to admire the view.

Hobson stepped forward. 'Yes it is. Sometimes, when the clouds move quickly, you can get that sense of falling backwards.'

'Yes I can imagine. Have you seen any peregrines?' Caldicott pointed to the crescent-shaped tower block opposite the Gherkin. 'Must be just about perfect.'

'Sorry?'

'Peregrine falcons...birds of prey. They like to attack from a height. Stooping on pigeons.'

'No, I've not seen any.'

They turned and sat either side of Hobson's desk.

'What can I do for you Robert?'

As the outcome of Caldicott's meeting was of no consequence, he decided to have some fun and play *Bull*. In essence, *Bull* was a more structured version of Bullshit Bingo. A player's aim was to maximise and tally up all the different clichés uttered during a meeting. A decade old, its origins, rules and how to register were on Wikipedia, together with the current list of approved clichés and their shorthand nomenclature (aligned vision (av), unpack (up), stakeholder engagement (se), real people (rp), strategic strategy (ss), composite programming (cp), and so on). Caldicott, a registered *Shitter* for four years, played under the username: *Sterna dougallii* (the Roseate Tern), the name a reminder of a glorious day spent off the Northumberland coast. Unlike most competitive games, in Bull, there were no prizes, no awards ceremonies, no monthly get together, just a no-frills website with the rules and league tables. Caldicott was currently lying 384th out of 902 in League 1.

The nine rules of Bull were:-

1. You must never reveal your true identity to others
2. You must not conspire with other Shitters
3. You must play fair at all times
4. You must not play to the detriment of your work
5. A declared Bull meeting must be 5 minutes or longer
6. A declared Bull meeting must be scored
7. A scoring meeting must involve two or more people
8. A scoring meeting must be declared before it starts
9. A declared meeting cannot be aborted

A player's score – their conversation score or ConScore – was the total number of approved clichés (TAC) uttered during the meeting divided by the duration of the meeting in minutes. The player then entered their ConScore via the Bull website. Each player's Cumulative Score – their so-called CumScore, the average of their ConScores – determined their relative league position. Caldicott's CumScore stood at 0.384, his highest yet. All new Shitters were classified as novices and automatically placed in League 2, where they remained until they had submitted at least twenty ConScores.

Senior Whitehall civil servants knew about Bull, but they powerless to act because the online league tables and website were managed by an ex-employee. He couldn't be touched. The hierarchy were also worried that any attempt to stamp it out might have the opposite effect, so they simply ignored it in the hope that over time it would go away.

Caldicott usually played it safe; declaring only in small meetings or one-on-ones, where there were usually more opportunities to intervene and score heavily. On one occasion, he had sat in on a seminar at DoB and immediately self-declared. With nearly twenty in the room he thought it might deliver a decent score, largely on account of the department's unrivalled reputation for cliché. But it soon became clear that the meeting would be dominated by their guest speaker, an engineer from Rolls Royce, who proceeded to deliver a long technical presentation on 'The Future of Aviation'. Caldicott feared there would be few opportunities to score. Then, as the man from Rolls began explaining the company's latest developments in aero-engine efficiency, he was interrupted by a blonde to Caldicott's left.

Dressed in a navy trouser suit and white blouse, a typical DoB outfit, she said, 'Is that ballpark?'

The engineer frowned, puzzled by the question. 'It's what it is, seven-percent.'

She hit back immediately. 'Sure ballpark, seven-percent, but going forward, is that the sort of efficiency that real people want?'

When she ticked the notepad resting on her crossed legs, Caldicott knew he had company. At the end of the seminar he scored it a respectable 0.293, thanks largely to the woman from DoB. Later that evening, when scanning through the day's declared scores, he notice a player called *MissSirrius* had also lodged a 0.293. He sent her a message via the Bull

Forum congratulating her on a great performance in difficult circumstances.

Caldicott opened his diary and smiled at Hobson, 'As I said on the phone, it's really just to touch-base.' *Tick*

Hobson frowned. 'In what sense?'

Caldicott added three more ticks and said, 'Going forward, the Government wants to partner with key stakeholders.'

'I see,' replied Hobson, 'Could you be more specific?'

'Well in the case of football, the Government would like to know if there are any opportunities to engage with the grass-roots.' *Tick*

Hobson nodded. 'Perhaps it's best if I give you an overview of what we do here. Would that help?'

'Yes, that would be excellent.'

Twenty-three minutes later Caldicott thanked him for his time and left. Hobson had done most of the talking and unknowingly had come back strongly with a barrage of scoring clichés and won the head-to-head, 12-7, giving a very respectable ConScore of 0.826. Hobson had only mentioned Millwall once, calling it an interesting development. Caldicott didn't bother to ask why.

27

Twenty-eight hours after Ailish (aka Bríd Collins) made the call to Barros, she called Patrick Malisse. Vince had suggested that they left it a day to give Barros a chance to speak to his player.

'Bonjour. Est cela Patrick?'

'Oui,'

'Mon nom est Bríd Collins. Je suis de le Sport Channel. Vous parlez anglais?'

'Oui, un petit. Yes.'

'I spoke to Señor Barros yesterday. We are doing a profile on Arno Legard and we would like to interview you. Did Señor Barros call you?'

'Yes he did. It is okay.'

'When are you available?'

'La semaine prochaine. Next Tuesday.'

'In Marciac?'

'Yes, in Marciac.'

'At your home?'

'Can we do it outside?'

'Just a moment.' Holding her hand over the phone she turned to Vince. 'He wants to do it outside.' Vince nodded. 'Yes that would be fine. Any suggestions where?'

'There is a lake here, Lake Marciac,' said Malisse. 'We could do it there, by the swimming pool. It will be quieter than in the town and the weather is good.'

'Quelle heure?'

'Midi, err...une heure?'

'Okay. Une heure, Mardi?'

'Bien.'

'Au revoir,' and she cut the call. 'Did you get that?'

'Tuesday, one o'clock,' said Vince.

'Near Lake Marciac. He didn't say why, other than the weather should be fine.' Slapping the phone into his open hand, she said, 'No more.'

Vince decided to make himself scarce. He walked to the travel agents in Colliers Wood and booked a flight to Toulouse.

– – – – – – –

Toulouse, Sunday 19th June

He touched down early Sunday evening and with hand luggage only he went straight through to the arrivals lounge. The Sunday bus service to Toulouse was no service, so he joined a queue at the taxi rank, near exit D. In front of him, a young American couple were discussing whether to go for a cheap hotel or an even cheaper hostel. Vince was thinking much the same. 'Excuse me?'

The woman turned, flicking her hair back.

'I was just wondering if you would like to share a taxi...split the fare?'

She shrugged and looked at her boyfriend. 'Jimmy?'

'No problem,' said Jimmy. 'Where you staying?'

'I don't know. I don't have one of those.' Vince nodded at the *Rough Guide to France* in Jimmy's hand. 'The information desk was shut.'

Vince sat in the passenger seat, while in the back the couple continued their discussion over where to stay. When the taxi met the main ring-road, she leant forward and said, 'La Petite Auberge de Compostelle.'

'L'adresse?' said the driver, glancing at Vince.

'Dix-sept, rue d'Embarthe,' she said with more confidence.

'Ah, oui bien,' said the driver.

At the hostel, the young Americans were offered a four bedroom dormitory to themselves, while Vince had to share with three lycra-clad cyclists on their way to the Pyrenees, Berend, Andreas and Sergei. All three were from Duisburg, and through hand signals and a map, they explained how

147

they were going to ride two stages of this year's Tour de France: Cugnaux to Luz-Ardiden, and the day after, Saint Gaudens to Plateau de Beille; both routes included a category 1 climb, though Vince had no idea what that meant.

All four were in their bunks before ten-thirty, but Vince couldn't sleep on account of the short mattress, the heat, and Berend's snoring – Berend had the bunk above. Sometime after midnight Andreas touched Vince on the shoulder and whispered an apology in German. In the half-darkness, he gestured that Vince should push his finger into the mattress above to make Berend change position. He said, *'Er wird nicht vergessen'* – he won't remember. But Vince didn't poke Berend, instead he plugged his ears with tissue paper, jammed his head between two pillows and fell asleep sometime after a church bell chimed one.

Shortly after seven the room shuddered as Berend jumped down from his bunk. Vince bolted upright. Seeing Berend leave the dorm in his underpants, he dropped back onto his pillow, turned on his side and watched the three Germans wash and pack. Their sandals, sleeping sacks and towels went to the bottom of each pannier, followed by clothes and waterproofs, the side pockets were for their smaller items: wallets, passports and sawn-off toothbrushes. Andreas had responsibility for the the shared toothpaste, phone and Swiss Army knife, while Berend had all the maps, and Sergei the first-aid kit. Though all three seemed to be in good spirits, and looking forward to their cycling challenge, Vince wondered if their trip was really just an anti-boredom exercise, undertaken to enliven their otherwise dull lives. It probably didn't matter where they cycled or how high the mountains; the Pyrenees were just a wrapping for their mini adventure. And though he hadn't ridden a bike for twenty years, when they walked away, with their cleats clacking on the wooden floor, he half-wished he could join them.

After an unhurried breakfast of croissant and coffee, followed by a stroll to the Place du Capitole, he caught the 12.23 train to Auch. He waited forty-two minutes for a connecting bus which took him via Laas and Tillac before it picked up the arrow like D3 all the way into Marciac. It was

148

past four when he finally arrived at the town square. His phone rang as he stepped down from the bus.

'Hi. Everything alright?'

'Yes,' said Ailish, 'I'm fine, but I had a call.'

'What do you mean?

'Your old phone rang. The one I used to call Barros. I didn't answer it.'

'Was it his number?'

'It was Malisse's. I thought you should know.'

'If it rings again, don't answer it...switch it off.'

'I already have.'

'Everything else alright?'

'Yes, I guess. Got plenty to do as usual.'

'I might be back tomorrow...depends if I head to Spain or not.'

'Okay, see you when I see you.'

Over the weekend, Ailish had prepared for her Tuesday meeting with Spinks by reading through transcripts of interviews and the articles he'd written. For all his wealth, she thought he came across as perfectly rational, and someone that harboured the usual doubts and insecurities. She read nothing that suggested arrogance or connivance. Only his open acknowledgement to succeed artistically and financially set him apart from his peers. Having done her research and rehearsed her story, she had only one concern; that Spinks' lawyers might sue her for attempted extortion.

– – – – – – –

Back in Marciac, Vince was puzzling over the information he'd just received. *Why would Malisse call? Had Barros spoken to Groenig?* Unsettled by the uncertainty, he crossed the square to a small tabac, bought a fifty-unit telecarte and walked over to one of the phone booths at the square's north corner.

'Bonjour Patrick,' said Vince. 'Je m'appelle Mark Groenig from the Sport Channel.'

'Ah yes.'

'Is tomorrow still okay with you? No problems?'

'No, one o'clock is good. I called just to confirm.'

149

'Yes, sorry about not getting back to you. We were travelling. I'll see you tomorrow.' Vince cut the call not wanting to prolong their conversation.

With his bag over one shoulder he followed rue Joseph Abeilhe north from the town's square and ten minutes later he was standing beside an open-air pool next to Lake Marciac. Out on the far side of the lake, where its shoreline hugged the main road, he could see a father and son in a blue pedalo heading back towards the pedalo marina. Vince nodded. It was a good location for a meeting; open, no hiding places, but with room to run.

– – – – – – – – –

Vince booked in at the campsite near the lake. His chalet had a single bed, fridge, cooker and shower-room. More importantly, it was well away from snorers, church bells, and traffic. He went to bed before nightfall and lay awake speculating. *Was impersonating a reporter a criminal offence? Malisse won't say anything, why would he? Did Barros have a contract that legitimised the blackmail?* Then he imagined Barros in court, fighting his case, getting angry, shouting at his accusers, and justifying his extraordinary fees on account of the extra work he did to keep his client's sexuality a secret.

He woke at eight and breakfasted at Zik's, the cafe by the swimming pool. To kill time he hired a bike from the campsite office and cycled to Marciac. With no map, he picked up the chemin du ronde and after one circuit turned onto the D934, the road to Maubourguet. Flat and straight, he cycled non-stop for twenty minutes, trying to pay attention to the scenery. Then he looked down at his spinning feet and wondered if he was cycling as fast as the Germans from Duisburg. At a crossroads, he turned left onto an ash track that divided fields of maize and sunflowers. He assumed that further along there would be another left turn that would lead him back towards Marciac. He changed gear and slowed his legs to avoid a sweat. Moments later a jet of water from an unseen irrigation sprinkler hit him on the back of the head. He rolled forward and stopped where the road

150

was dry, cursing at the muddy splash marks on his shirt and trousers. He swung the bike around and pedalled at speed back to the campsite.

28

Bouverie Street London, Tuesday 21st June

Outside Fuzzy's Grub, on Bouverie Street, two hours before Vince's meeting with Malisse, Ailish took a deep breath and smiled at her reflection in the window. She had gone for the classy-slut look: a short black skirt, steep Jimmy Choo sandals, a cream blouse open at the neck, and a D&G clutch bag. New, it would have cost her two grand. The ensemble was in part inspired by the Slut's March in Hyde Park the previous weekend. According to the Evening Standard, the march was a carry-over from a sluts demo in New York in April. The paper claimed:

> *'the movement was already having an impact on some city firms which had recently introduced 'dress-like-a-slut Fridays'. One of the organisers, Donna Paignton, said, 'to be honest, I dress like this all the time, but it's great to know we now have the City right behind us.'*

She turned to check her rear view. She nodded, thinking the combination worked well. Then she noticed that the customers and staff in Fuzzy's were nodding too. She reddened and moved on.

Brewer and Copthorne were two doors down. She checked her phone to make sure she was ten minutes late and then pushed at the door. Stopping a few yards inside, she glanced at the lifts, the CCTV camera, the security desk. She whispered, 'Fuck this,' and turned for the door.

'Can I help?' The accent was unmistakably eastern European.

Glancing back she saw a pair of spectacled eyes peering over the top of the security desk. 'Err...it's okay,' she said, 'I can come back another time.' Her hand was flat against the glass door, just inches away from the safety of Bouverie Street.

'Brewer and Copthorne?' guessed the security guard. Though there were five companies sharing the building, in the three years he had been at his desk, he found that most of the middle-aged women that came through the front door were in the midst of a marital dispute. Divorce settlements were one of Brewer's specialisations, while he specialised in bedding their female clients. And for that reason alone he loved his job.

He stood, smiled and beckoned her over. As she closed in on his desk, his eyes were drawn down to her legs and shoes. Then he winked at her, and said, 'They are on the fourth floor. They will sign you in there.' He walked her over to the lifts and pressed the call button, and when the lift doors opened and she stepped inside, he smiled again and said, 'Good luck. I hope everything works out...I'll see you later.'

Other than 'fourth floor' she heard nothing. Left from the lift she faced two sliding glass doors that guarded the entrance to Brewer and Copthorne. On the other side she saw carpet. It was a danger to anyone in stilettos, even the experienced wearer. She paused, and like a diver composing themselves on a high-board, she raised her head, pushed her shoulders back, and placed her feet together. On a silent count of three, she passed through the doors and began a slow-motion catwalk into the reception area, twelve steps of exaggerated lifting and placement.

'Can I help?' said a woman standing to one side of her lectern.

'Yes, I'm here to see David Spinks.'

'Of course.' The woman glanced down at her visitors list. 'Ailish Brady?' Ailish nodded. 'This way please.' She was shown into a side-room with a tinted glass-topped table and seating for six. At its centre were six tumblers and two water jugs, each topped with lemon and ice. She wondered if it would be five against one.

'Someone will be in to see you in a moment,' said the woman.

'How many will there be?'

'As far as I know it's just Mr Spinks and Mr Sommerby.'

When the door closed, she circled the room practicing her carpet walk. She stopped by the window and peered down at a concrete yard where half-a-dozen gulls were fighting over a squashed bag of chips. A minute later the door opened. Spinks, in creased linen, moved round the table to greet her. Like the security guard, his eyes flicked down to her legs a split-second before their hands were joined.

'Hello Ailish, pleased to meet you.'

'And you,' she said.

Following behind and clutching a folder to his chest came an older and greyer man in a blue blazer, his shirt collar biting into his neck.

'This is my agent, Grant Sommerby,' said Spinks.

Spinks knew the basic law on intellectual property and had decided that at least for this first meeting he would get by without a legal adviser. His experience was that a lawyer in the room was usually an impediment to progress, and Brewer and Copthorne were no different, they had no incentive to expedite solutions.

'Pleased to meet you...Ms Brady,' said Sommerby, his hesitation deliberate, aimed at seeking clarification of her marital status. She let the uncertainty ride and sat down crossed-legged, while Spinks poured iced water into three glasses.

Prior to the meeting Sommerby had phoned his many contacts in the art world. None had heard of Ailish Brady, and on the net there was nothing, not even a photograph. For Sommerby, such anonymity wasn't unexpected, he knew many collectors/investors who worked hard to keep a low profile, but his gut feeling was that Brady was a fraud.

Still standing, Sommerby said, 'I have your letter here somewhere, it states that...' Then the letter slipped from his fingers and on a thin layer of air, it skimmed across the table. He reached out, his arm at full-stretch, but too slow to prevent it slipping into Ailish's lap. She didn't move. She looked down at the letter on her stockinged thigh and then up at Sommerby, almost inviting him to come and get it. He stared down through the table, transfixed.

She handed him the letter with a smile. 'There you go Mr Sommerby. I know what it says.'

'Err...thank you.' He sat down and ran two fingers along the inside of his collar.

Spinks looked on, amused at the interplay and the evident agitation in his agent's underpants.

Sommerby straightened his papers and continued. 'Your letter states that you have clear evidence that David has copied another artist's work.'

'Yes I have,' she said.

'Which work are we talking about?'

'His latest exhibition at Tate Modern.'

'I see,' said Sommerby, genuinely surprised. 'But your letter said the work was from a couple of years ago.'

'Yes, that's right. It was from a couple of years ago and now another version, Mr Spinks' version, is in Tate Modern.'

'And which piece in particular?'

'Well, I would say it was the whole show, definitely the whole show.'

Sommerby looked to Spinks, expecting an immediate rebuttal, but Spinks just nodded.

Sommerby turned back. 'Where did this artist exhibit her work?'

'His work,' she corrected. 'I bought it for my house in Dublin.' As the words came out, she started to feel a sense of detachment. She was splitting in two. Her clenched hands, her crossed legs, and her voice, all belonged to someone else.

'And who else saw it?' said Sommerby.

She didn't hear his question.

Sommerby leant forward and raised his voice. 'Ms Brady, who else saw this artwork?'

'Sorry. Err...just some friends of mine, but you're welcome to visit and see for yourself.' She glanced at Spinks and wondered what he was waiting for.

155

'Are you serious?' said Sommerby.

'Serious enough to fly over here from Dublin.'

'You're saying the Art-Vision exhibition was first shown at your house?'

'I'm saying something very similar is in my house. So similar, it can't possibly be a coincidence. I can only presume that someone came to my house, then mentioned it to Mr Spinks. In my opinion, Art-Vision as you call it, is a copy.'

Sommerby forced Spinks to respond, 'David?'

'Grant, we need to talk.' Spinks nodded to the door and then he turned to Ailish. 'Will you excuse us for a moment? We won't be long.'

Out in the corridor they passed through the sliding doors and stopped by the elevator.

Spinks said, 'I don't think she's telling the truth.'

Sommerby frowned. 'What does that mean?' He had been Spinks' agent for fifteen years, he'd dealt with all the tricksters – two or three of them a year – who wrote to Spinks threatening legal action. Sommerby was proud of his record. No one had ever followed through and taken them to court and Spinks had never paid out a penny.

'It means, I think she's lying,' said Spinks, but this time with more conviction. 'We'll ask for her evidence. If she's nothing, she can clear off.'

Sommerby nodded and said, 'She's a bit different than the others. I can't make her out.'

The two men smiled as they re-entered the room. Sommerby sat, while Spinks circled the table and then stopped by the window.

Sommerby said, 'Miss Brady, before we bring in our legal team, we'd like to see some evidence that this private exhibition took place.'

'Of course,' she said, with confidence. 'You'll want affidavits and photographs?' She wanted them to believe that she was perfectly happy to take the next step.

'Well that would be a start,' said Sommerby. 'Someone from Brewer and Copthorne will be in touch, but they will want more, details of the artist, et cetera.'

'Fine, I'll get my legal people to send them through.' She was tempted to leave it there, shake hands and escape. Instead she played her final card. 'I presume you'll be wanting to keep this quiet until a settlement is agreed? Hopefully, we can avoid the courts.' She said it, because she remembered Vince telling her how, after he'd apologised for his libel, the story had been all over the papers in a matter of days. Vince reckoned Spinks had deliberately gone public because it had served his purpose. She thought Art-Vision might be different. It had been Spinks' biggest hit in years, reigniting the old debate about boundaries between the visual and the literary. She calculated that he wouldn't want any publicity, good or bad, and certainly nothing which hinted at plagiarism. 'It's so easy for these things to leak out,' she added.

'Yes,' said Sommerby, recognising her veiled threat. 'I see no reason to go public just yet.'

'Do we have your phone number?' said Spinks.

'No, but I'm happy to exchange.'

Spinks withdrew his mobile from his inside pocket. She called out her number and seconds later her clutch bag chimed.

'Okay,' said Sommerby. 'We'll be in touch.'

When she'd gone, Spinks said, 'I'll give her a call.'

'Don't you think we should wait and see what her lawyers...' he paused and picked up her letter, 'Fitzgerald and Carnie come up with?'

'I'm not sure. She might decide to go straight to the press. She could do anything.'

'If she goes public, we sue her.'

'I know, but I'd rather not. I'll meet her...see if she'll do dinner...try and tease out the full story.'

'Okay, if that's what you want.'

'It is,' said Spinks.

They were both quiet for a moment; Sommerby thinking through their options, whilst Spinks added Ailish Brady to his list of phone contacts.

Then Spinks said, 'I suppose as art goes virtual, it's bound to be harder to control. There's always a downside.'

Sommerby didn't understand what Spinks meant but he nodded anyway.

29

Marciac, Tuesday 21ˢᵗ June

After his soaking from the sprinkler, Vince showered and redressed in yesterday's clothes. He walked over to the lake and hid his bike at the rear of Zik's. On the terrace he ordered a beer. By the pool, there were two women in red bikinis flat-out on sun-loungers, and two men in the pool testing their endurance, alternating between lengths of front crawl and lengths underwater. On the terrace, to Vince's left, an elderly German couple studied a road map.

At 12.55 a black Porsche Cayenne turned off the D3 and into the car park, stopping fifty yards from Zik's. Vince's heart rate jumped. He gulped his beer and stared at the vehicle. With its tinted windows it was impossible to see who or how many were inside. A minute passed before the passenger door opened and Patrick Malisse got out. He was dressed smart-casual, a claret jacket over an open-necked shirt and jeans, and closely shaved. The cornrows that Vince had seen on the internet had gone. When Malisse reached the far side of the pool, Vince stood up and waved. 'Bonjour Patrick.'

Malisse lazily raised a hand and then turned round and raised it again in the direction of the Porsche.

Vince walked the long way round, approaching from the left, away from the car park. He passed the two swimmers who were resting, breathing heavily, their arms spread-eagled over the edge of the pool. They nodded to each other, pleased with their workout, unaware that an international footballer was nearby.

As Vince closed in on Malisse, he forced a smile. 'Hi Patrick. Pleased to meet you.'

They shook hands, but there was no smile or greeting from Malisse. Then over Malisse's shoulder, Vince saw two men climb out of the Porsche, both in dark suits and sunglasses.

'I'm sorry,' said Vince, 'but the TV crew are running late.' He knew immediately that Malisse didn't believe him, but he pressed on. 'They'll be here soon. We can have a drink while we wait,' and he pointed across the pool toward Zik's.

Malisse said nothing, his face blank.

'But...we don't have to. We can just sit and talk. Yes, let's just sit for a while. As I said they won't be long. They...' Then he gestured to the sun-loungers. 'Sit anywhere you like. It's up to you. I don't mind.'

'Who are you?' said Malisse.

Vince smiled guiltily. He needed a reason to stop Malisse from walking away, so he started with the truth. 'I'm writing a book about football. I'm a writer.'

'What?' said Malisse. Then there was a beep.

Vince glanced down and noticed the phone in Malisse's hand. 'It's okay, answer it,' said Vince.

'What do you want?'

'Your agent is Ángel Barros.' Vince's eyes flicked back to the Porsche. One of Malisse's minders was taking photographs, while the other started towards the pool. Vince then realised that the two men had been listening in via Malisse's phone and one of them was about to terminate the meeting. Vince stepped back, and while still facing Malisse, he did a shaka-like hand signal to the side of his head. 'I'll call you,' he said. 'We need to talk.'

Vince turned and ran towards Zik's, skidding on the wet slabs at the head of the pool. He grabbed his bike and ran with it until he reached the tarmaced track that circled the southern edge of the lake. Out of the saddle, he pushed hard for twenty seconds and then stopped. One of Malisse's minders was at the rear of Zik's, while the Porsche was already on the D3 and heading along the north side of the lake. Then the man by Zik's started jogging towards Vince.

Being chased hadn't been wholly unexpected. Vince's escape plan, such as it was, involved jumping on his bike and heading for the woods. He'd considered an alternative;

160

a getaway taxi parked up behind Zik's, but had decided that a taxi was probably easier to follow.

He cycled on a few hundred yards, jumped off the bike and threw it over the trackside fence. He glanced back. Malisse's minder was now sprinting. Vince placed his left hand on a fence post, pivoted over, and cried out as the barbed wire ripped into his calf. Not stopping to check the damage, he ran uphill between lines of conifer with one hand on the saddle and the other on the bucking handlebars. He ran for thirty seconds until he reached a ditch. Gasping, he crouched and looked down through the trees. After a few seconds his chaser appeared at the spot where Vince had jumped the fence. Still bent over, Vince edged backwards into the ditch, sinking to his knees in mud. He dragged the bike with him and scrambled up the far bank onto a cinder track.

Only when clear of the ditch, did he realise he'd lost a shoe. He looked down into the ditch, down at his shoeless foot, and then down into the wood. He turned, mounted the bike and began pedalling asymmetrically, pushing hard on the left and gently on the right. He followed the track until it met the main road, where he turned right, and away from Marciac. With the lopsided motion his shoed left leg started to cramp. He turned into the next farmyard and swung in behind an iron-roofed barn. He listened. No voices, no animal noises, just the reflected heat off the concrete and in the background the ensemble hum of insects.

He dropped the bike. He'd not been chased for thirty years, not since he'd run from Woolworths on Stourbridge High Street clutching a handful of pick 'n' mix. Back then, he ran for half a mile, not daring to stop or look back, all the time thinking the man from Woolies was right behind, with his arm outstretched, reaching for Vince's collar, reaching for the sweets.

He undressed down to his underpants and shirt, and laid his shoe, socks and trousers out to dry. Bloody mud coated his right calf, obscuring the wound. He rocked his jaw from side-to-side and then pinched his cheek. He wondered what the symptoms were for tetanus, and whether there was a hospital in Marciac. Then he sat down with his back against the barn, listening for cars, watching the mud dry on his legs, hoping that perhaps the sun's rays would sterilise the wound. He dozed, dreaming briefly of burning skin.

A few minutes later he scurried across the farmyard to the main road, all the time listening for vehicles. At the yard entrance he spotted a faded sign: *Le Petit Juillac*. He read it out loud and then ran back to the rear of the barn, carefully avoiding the cracks in the concrete.

He made a call and a woman answered. 'Zombie Taxi.'

'Bonjour. Je veux un taxi. Do you speak English?' Zombie Taxis was the company he would have used if he gone with his alternative escape plan.

'Ah non monsieur,' said the woman. 'Quand?'

'Now...maintenant.'

'Et où sont vous?'

Vince assumed she wanted his address. 'Le Petit Juillac,' he said, while trying to remember the word for farm.

'Pardon?'

'A farm...ferme,' he guessed. 'Ferme Le Petit Juillac. Je aller Auch.'

'Ah oui. Votre nom?'

'Monsieur Vince.' He wanted a taxi large enough to carry his bike, but he didn't think it was worth pursuing with his schoolboy French.

'D'accord. Dix minutes monsieur.'

He pulled on his damp socks and trousers. Then he picked up his shoe and flipped it like a jugglers club, trying to decide whether one was better than none at all. As he flipped it again and again, he realised he shouldn't have run. Malisse and his minders wouldn't have done anything violent with witnesses present. At most they would have threatened him, told him to back-off. So his tetanus, his ripped trousers, and his lost shoe were all the result of an unnecessary panic. Annoyed, he circled his arm and flung the shoe over his head. It crashed onto the barn's roof and then tumbled down landing on the bike. 'Fucker,' he said. He bent down, snatched the shoe and slung it underarm into a patch of willow herb.

162

Then kneeling beside the bike, he pulled back the quick release lever on the front wheel and tugged, fully expecting it to come away from the frame – he'd seen Andreas do it at the hostel in Toulouse. Though loose it wouldn't budge. He stood, grabbed the tyre and rim in both hands, raised his arms and shook the whole bike. Still the wheel wouldn't come away. Frustrated, he threw the bike against the barn wall. 'Fucking Germans!'

When the taxi pulled into the yard he swore again. There had been no need to de-wheel the bike. The Zombie taxi was a minibus with room enough for two or three. Back at the campsite he asked the driver to wait while he returned the bike and showered. In the site's shop, he bought sandals and studied a road map pinned to the notice board. It was then that he changed his mind. Back in the taxi, he said, 'We go to Tarbes, not Auch.' Tarbes was 30km south of Marciac. It was on the way to Spain.

'Auch?' said the driver, turning his head.

'Non, nous aller Tarbes.'

'Ça va monsieur. Si vous dites.'

'Yes, that's right,' said Vince, 'Je dis.'

163

30

Braney, Wednesday 22nd June

In the back garden and still in her pyjamas, Phylida stirred her rolled oats and milk. She'd been house-sitting and dog-minding since Saturday while her father and Eve were away in Rome. A text arrived. He sent one every day always around lunchtime: *Hi Phy. Still having a lovely time. Hope all is well. Love Dad*

She placed her dish on the cast-iron table and keyed a reply: *All is well. The house fire is out! Dogs getting plenty of exercise. Weather still good* xx

But for the house fire it was true. For half the week it had been sunshine and clear skies and the dogs had been walked three times a day. Her phone chimed again. This time it was an email, an automated message telling her not to forget the birthdays of two of her Facebook friends, Jenny Fellows and Phillip McMullan. Jenny had been a Facebook friend for five years, though they hadn't seen or spoken to each other since the sixth-form at Sawbridgeworth Grammar School. While they had been classmates during their A-levels, and both had played hockey for the school, they had never socialised. They were friends only in the sense that a computer programme had identified a shared past.

Phillip McMullan was Phylida's last boyfriend. They split-up two years ago, on the day before his thirtieth. He gave her an ultimatum, saying that, '...things had to change...there's no point in carrying on...I never see you...we don't do stuff...when we're on holiday you're still at work.' He wanted to be centre stage, or at least not an extra, but when he finished talking, she simply shrugged her shoulders and told him her work was important. And that was it. They hugged and said goodbye. There were no tears and no false promises to stay in touch, and nothing was said about being

Facebook friends. His thirtieth birthday present, a pair of Paul Smith shoes, was still wrapped and collecting dust under her bed.

The birthday email reminder annoyed her for another reason. It meant another sex-free year had passed by, a year of no dates, no prospects, not even a drunken snog at the Christmas party. She deleted the emails and went upstairs to her office/bedroom. At her laptop she scanned the latest version of the *Millwall Risks/Threats Matrix*. She moved the cursor from one cell to the other, deleting a full-stop, inserting a colon, changing a hyphen to a back slash, a might to a could, a probable to a possible. She had made progress of sorts, there were now fewer empty cells, more words than white space, but still most of it remained supposition.

Her meeting with Hobson at the LPFL had been useful; it had clarified their priorities (they were purely financial) and their capacity to damage Millwall, but meeting Sir Harold Meade, MBE, the Chairman of the Footballing Association, had been a waste of time. Like Hobson, she had pushed Meade for an opinion on the Millwall situation, and in response, he bit his bottom lip and drew down his eyebrows, his face frozen in puzzlement. As she thought about re-phrasing the question to help him out, Meade's face relaxed into a broad smile. An answer had arrived.

'I met him you know, the Archbishop, a lovely man. I'm sure he's doing the right thing. Why wouldn't he?'

And when she asked Meade if the Church had set a dangerous precedent, he frowned again. But this time the smile came with a knowing nod. He simply said, 'I'm a Christian, you know.'

His answers confused her. They weren't denials or opinions, they were just wholly irrelevant. She wondered if he was acting, playing the buffoon. If he was, he was wasted at the FA. It was acting of the highest calibre. When she asked about Gülen, he said he'd not read 'Lord of the Rings', but that he'd enjoyed the movie. With each subsequent answer it became clear that it wasn't an act. They were his best and only answers. They were the answers of an honest man with early-onset dementia. She left his office as soon as

165

she'd finished her cup of tea. Afterwards, she wondered if there were others at the Association whom she should meet. But when looking on their website at the photographs of the other board members, she decided not to bother as most of them looked like Meade's younger brothers.

She moved the cursor to cell *D6: Gülen Movement*. The stories about Izir Manas moving in for Chelsea still hadn't been confirmed. There had been emphatic denials, but they came from an unnamed source in the Corporate Affairs Department of his company, Anadolu Netcom AS. She figured that until Manas personally refuted his interest the rumours would continue.

As she saved and closed the file her phone rang. 'Hi Carol.' Carol Lindeman worked for BSM, heading up the small team that monitored the media output on Millwall. She usually sent through her weekly report late on a Friday.

'Are you okay to talk?' said Carol.

'Yes, go ahead. What's happened?'

'Tom's in today's Sketch, but not on the back pages. He's inside. I've just scanned and emailed it to you. It's on their website too.'

'What's it about?'

'It's a photograph of Tom with a young Filipino woman. It looks like a smear. It claims he's been unfaithful to his wife.'

'I'll have a look. Have you contacted Tom?'

'No.'

'Okay, I'll call him.' She brought up the Sketch website and clicked *News Headlines*. On the right-hand side of the screen was the photo of Cowly and an unnamed woman, but her eye was drawn to the left side of the screen and a photograph of a cabbage. Underneath it stated that under controlled clinical trials, pickled cabbage was twice as effective as 100 mg of Viagra. The article caught her eye because downstairs, on the kitchen table, were five jars of homemade sauerkraut, all labelled and dated by Eve's curlicue hand. As far as Phylida could remember, he mother had never made it and her father had never eaten it. She wondered if this was another of Eve's cures. She imagined

166

them together, in the evening, at the dinner table, with Eve laying down the ultimate ultimatum: 'William, eat your cabbage or my knickers stay on.'

The photograph on the right of the screen showed Cowly hand-in-hand with Imee waiting for a cab outside Nahm, a Thai restaurant in Belgravia. The caption read:

CHRISTIAN FOOTBALL BOSS CHEATS ON WIFE

An inset photo showed Jocelyn Cowly, alone, walking with her head down. The two paragraph article read:

> *'Tom Cowly, the newly appointed CEO of Triboarde Ltd, the Church appointed owners of Millwall FC – and currently on sabbatical from his employers BSM – was seen leaving Nahm with an unknown Filipino woman.'*

The second paragraph repeated the headline about Cowly cheating on his wife, then adding that Jocelyn Cowly was believed to be overseas with her twin daughters. It then quoted an unnamed diner who had apparently said:

> *'...the couple looked besotted and very much in love.'*

She called him.

'Hi Phylida. I've seen it. The phone's been ringing since seven. I'm not answering it anymore. There's no point.'

'I'm in Braney. Shall I come down?'

'No,' he said, 'there's nothing you can do. I'm working on a statement for the Board. If Ken wants to pass it on to the Church Commissioners, that's up to him. I'll email it to you. Have a look and let me know what you think.'

'Okay. Speak to you later.'

The press coverage over the past month, mostly supportive, some negative, had gradually died back. She had started to believe that perhaps they had misjudged the situation, and that Hobson was right, Millwall had nothing to fear and the Church's involvement had been accepted. She read the Sketch article again and concluded it was either tabloid tittle-tattle, annoying but not wholly unexpected, or a deliberate attack. Thirty minutes later, Cowly emailed his statement:

Hi Phy,
Have a look through and tell me what you think. There's a board meeting next week so I'll include this as an agenda item. Tom

> In light of recent press coverage concerning my private life, I would like to express my sincere regret that a national newspaper has sought to embarrass my wife and family. I also regret that this newspaper, for reasons unknown to me, is also seeking to damage the reputation of the Church and Millwall Football Club. From my perspective the article is a dishonest smear, nothing more. There has been no cheating or betrayal. Jocelyn, my wife, has been a wonderful mother, but our marriage was never a happy one, and we have been leading separate lives for many years. Throughout this period we have maintained a family home for the benefit of our daughters. They are now at university and so, this year, my wife and I commenced formal divorce proceedings. The lady in the photograph is a dear friend whom I have known for several years. She, like my wife, is also an innocent victim. I would like to assure the Millwall fans and the Church Commissioners that I remain fully committed to the task of making Millwall a successful League Premiership club.'
> Tom Cowly, Triboarde Ltd/Millwall FC.

Her first thought was that his statement was over the top. The Sketch would argue that the public had a right to know that the CEO of a club owned by the Church of England was seeing and, most likely, having sex with a young Filipino woman. It had no obligation to give a full and balanced account. She printed Cowly's email and then underneath she wrote:

a) Irritating, unwanted distraction.
b) Not necessarily an attack on the Church.
c) We manage the situation.

She called him. 'How are things now?'

'I had to leave the house. There were press in the front garden, and then someone started chucking fruit at the front door. I'm in a cab on the way to The Mandarin, up near Hyde Park. I've booked in for a couple of nights.'

'Anything I can do?' she said, knowing there wasn't.

'No. I'm waiting to hear from Ken.'

'I saw your statement. It's fine, but it won't be the end of it. They'll want to wring it dry. They'll want to know about your companion, who she is, where you met, and whether she has a visa. They'll probably be chasing Jocelyn.'

'I agree. They'll also want a response from the Church.'

'Have you spoken to Jocelyn?'

'I've emailed her, but she's not replied. She's in France.'

'Shall I contact the Sketch? See what they've got to say. I'm guessing they bought the story.'

'Yes, do that,' said Cowly.

— — — — — — — — —

There were a number of other calls that Wednesday afternoon. The second was between Vince and Ailish. He called her from the EuroCar office in Tarbes, in the Midi-Pyrénées. 'How are you?' he said.

'Fine, and you?'

'Not good. Malisse came along with his body guards. They tried to grab me. I ran off. I didn't get to speak to him. He knew I wasn't Groenig.'

'Is that it then?'

'I guess so.' Then he realised for the first time that he might have put her at risk. Barros had his Tooting address. He decided not to mention it or that he was heading to Spain. 'I should be back in a couple of days. The weather's good, so I might have a look around.'

'See you then.'

169

Before she had a chance to ring off, he said, 'So how did it go with Spinks?'

'Nothing really happened. He wants to see some evidence.'

'What do you mean?'

'I'll tell you when you're back, it's complicated.'

The third call was a missed call. Phylida called Vince and left him a message: *'Mr Wynter, this is Phylida Cranson at Millwall. We met at the press conference when Kevin Furling signed. I'd like to have a chat. Perhaps we could meet up. Can you call me back?'*

Vince listened to the message after he'd spoken to Ailish. He'd not expected the call, because he didn't think there was anything to discuss.

The fourth call, an hour later, was between Spinks and Ailish. He called while pacing his garden in Primrose Hill, his head down and a bottle of beer in his free hand. She stepped from the bath and answered without checking the caller's name.

'Miss Brady?'

'Yes.'

'It's David Spinks. Can you talk?'

'Yes..err...go ahead.'

'I thought after our meeting that it might be useful to meet again, before you return to Dublin. Are you still in London?'

'I am. I'm here all week. When were you thinking?'

'Tomorrow, somewhere a bit more relaxed. Just you and me, no lawyers or agents.'

'Tomorrow would be fine.'

'I'll book a table at Amaya. Shall I pick you up?'

'No, I'll meet you there. Text me when.'

'Okay, see you tomorrow.'

The fifth call was between Barros and Kevin. As usual there was no greeting. 'Have you seen Wynter? Have you spoken to him?'

'Not since last week,' said Kevin. 'He called about the ebook. He said that you two were going to be meeting up.'

'So what's he doing in France?'

'How should I know? Ask him.'

Barros cut the connection and flicked his finger down the screen of his phone sending his contacts into a blur. Wynter was his last. He called, but Vince chose not to answer and Barros chose not to leave a message.

The sixth call came ten minutes after the fifth.

'Hi Vince,' said Kevin. 'I've just had Ángel on the phone. He was asking after you. He seemed a bit on edge.'

'He's just tried to call me. I didn't answer it. I didn't want to spoil my holiday.'

'He said you were in France.'

Vince changed the subject. 'Was it about the ebook?'

'He didn't say. Are you following him?'

'Sorry Kevin, but I have to go. Just catching a train. I'll call you when I'm back.'

The seventh call went to the front desk of Sketch Newspapers Limited.

'I'd like to speak to Craig Crozier,' said Phylida.

'Can I ask what it's about?' said the receptionist.

'I'd just like to have a chat. I have some information he might be interested in, it's about Millwall.'

'One moment, I'll see if he's in.'

Thirty seconds later Crozier came to the line. 'Can I help?'

'I hope so. You wrote the piece about Tom Cowly?'

'Cowly?'

'Yes, Tom Cowly, in today's paper. My name is Phylida Cranson. He's a colleague of mine.'

'The guy with the Filipino?'

'Yes that one.' The sarcastically, she said, 'I wondered if you'd like some information about me. I'm an atheist. I look nice, I ride, but I don't have a boyfriend. That sort of thing. You can take some photographs while I'm out riding.'

'I don't...'

'Sorry, what I mean is, shall we meet for lunch? How about the Roof Garden? Friday at one, my treat. I'll come to your offices.' She rang off, not giving him the opportunity to say no.

Then she rang Kevin.

171

'Hi Phylida. How are you?'

'Good. How's Brighton?'

'I'm buried in letters,' said Kevin.

'Why?'

'Some fans still write letters. The club sends them through once a month. I try to reply to all the ones that like me.'

'I was thinking that maybe we should meet? Are you in London at all?'

'I wasn't planning to be,' he said, 'but I can be.'

'Well perhaps another time.'

'Why don't you come to Brighton? We could spend some time on the beach if the weather's okay.'

'What about all your fan mail?'

Kevin looked at the rising mound on his lap. 'I'm nearly done. I'll text you my address.'

'I'm in Braney until Sunday. How about Monday or Tuesday?'

'Any day is fine.'

'I look forward to it,' she said.

'Me too.'

She rang off and quickly pulled off her breeches and knickers. From a shoe box at the back of her wardrobe she took out her vibrator. Wet and tingling, she eased it in. Meanwhile, in his bathroom, Kevin pumped his cock over the hand basin.

31

Tarbes France, Wednesday 22nd June

'Voila Monsieur, suivez moi.' The man behind the EuroCar counter handed Vince his keys and a folded copy of the hire contract. Then he led Vince to a computer in the corner of their back office, their staccato conversation following a pattern of alternating English and French.

'Thank you,' said Vince, as he rolled his chair up to the keyboard. 'I'll be two minutes.'

In his inbox he had two responses to the posts he'd left on YouTube the previous week. They stated that de la Rosa lived in Llivia and his parents in Saneja, both villages on the outskirts of Puigcerdá. Back at the counter, Vince said, 'Do you have a map?'

'Une carte? Oui.' The man reached down to retrieve a folded road map.

Vince opened it up, checking first for Tarbes and then Puigcerdá. 'How much?'

'C'est libre.'

On the back of the hire contract Vince listed the roads and towns that would take him over the French/Spanish border to Puigcerdá. Fifteen minutes later he joined the A64, a motorway that paralleled the railway line and the Garonne's ancient flood plain. To the south were the foothills of the Pyrenees. Vince looked ahead. He drove on through the arrondissement de Saint-Gaudens, a district of the Haute Garonne. The detail was all on the map, in the footnotes, in French and Spanish, including a brief summary of the local geology.

He stopped for food and petrol west of Saint Martory. Later, on the D117, beyond Saint-Girons, the valleys narrowed; the road and river now forced to follow the line of least resistance across the Massif de l'Arize. The footnotes said nothing about this particular leg of his journey. He trailed a caravan for sixty kilometres until he reached the E9 at Tarascon. The last leg, eighty-three kilometres, passed through Ax-Les-Thermes − the footnotes mentioned skiing and hot springs. At its highest point, the map showed the road's red line twisting and doubling back, again and again, but from inside the Mégane − the air-con maintaining a steady nineteen degrees − the hairpins and warnings of falling rocks went unnoticed. He cruised round the corners in first and second gear, his thoughts on Malisse, de la Rosa, Barros and Kevin. When on the outskirts of Puigcerdá, he followed the signs for Centro de la Ciudad and parked up outside the first pensión he spotted: Pensión Terese Victoria, in Carrer Querol.

Unfolding stiffly from the Megane, he swung his arms above his head and then down to his toes. Holding the position, he gathered his right trouser leg up to his knee and turned his foot outwards. The two-inch scab had hardened to resemble a strip of beef jerky. He straightened, shook out his trouser and went inside. The receptionist, a woman somewhere in her twenties, looked up and smiled. Vince smiled back, holding up an index finger. When she nodded, he pointed to his chest, his eyes and then the ceiling.

'Sí señor, por supuesto.'

She led him upstairs to the second floor and a room at the end of a stone-tiled corridor. No television, air conditioning or mini-bar, just a bed, a fan and a balcony view of the street. He paid for one night, retrieved his bag from the Mégane and returned to his room. Resisting the temptation to lie down, he showered and dressed in the same clothes. In reception, he asked the woman if she knew Adriano de la Rosa?'

'Sí, a footballer. He lives in Puigcerdá.'

'Where does he live?'

'No sé señor. No me gusta el fútbol.'

Hearing the word no, he assumed she couldn't help. He leafed through his phrase book and said, 'Hablar con el director del hotel? He sounded like a robot from a fifties sci-fi.

The woman stifled a laugh. 'Lo siento señor...he come in the morning.' Then she waved her hand towards the door over her right shoulder.

He frowned, wondering why the door was relevant, but also in disappointment that his first attempt to track down de la Rosa had come to nothing. He had half a backup plan. In Balham Library, he'd read about the Padrón Office, where the town council kept records of local residency – it was Spain's version of the Electoral Roll. In most towns the office was in the town hall.

'Padrón Office,' he said. She shook her head. He found town hall in his phrase book and placed the edge of his thumbnail above the word *ayuntamiento*. He held it up to her face. She nodded and reached under the desk for a map. In biro she circled the town hall.

He stepped back and studied the map, tracking the route from Carrer Querol. But he suspected the Padrón Office records wouldn't be available to non-residents. He smiled and leant over her desk. He wrote DE LA ROSA on the back of the map, and then CASA, and underneath CASA he wrote PADRÓN OFFICE. He turned the map around and slid it across to her. She read it and shook her head. Then he took two twenty euro notes from his wallet and placed them by her forearm.

She looked at the money and back at the sheet of paper. 'Un momento por favour.' She stood and left the room through the back door.

Vince heard two women's voices, one raised. Seconds later the young woman reappeared. She quickly shut the door and held the handle with both hands. She looked over at Vince, and said, 'Disculpa, mi madre, she is not happy.' When her mother's voice trailed off, she released the door handle and returned to her desk. She handed Vince his map and said, 'No señor.'

'I'm sorry,' said Vince. 'I didn't mean to cause you a problem.' He nodded toward the door.

'No problem.'

'Can you help with a taxi?' Vince paused and flicked through the phrase book. 'El taxista...habla inglés.'

'Your Spanish is good now,' she teased. She looked at a list of taxi companies sellotaped to the right corner of the desk and swayed her head from side to side, chewing the end of her biro. 'One moment señor.' She made a call and scribbled a name and number on a slip of paper. 'This taxi man speaks English.'

'Thank you,' said Vince. 'One more thing. Is there a shop near here, a supermarket?'

'¿Supermercado? Caprabo.' She reached for his map and marked the pensión's position with an X. 'You here, Caprabo here...cinco minutos.' She circled a building on the corner of Carrer del Claustre.

At Caprabo he bought washing powder and underwear, and on the way back he ate at Tap de Suro, a smoky wood-panelled tapas bar opposite his pensión. An hour later, full with cheese, chorizo, and potatoes, and heady from a bottle of red, he was back in his room. He stripped down, washed all his clothes in the bath and hung them out on the balcony hoping they would be dry by the morning. In bed, and guilty that he'd not warned Ailish about Barros, he sent her a text. *Hi A, I'm in puigcerda. Just thinking, I've upset barros and he knows where I live. I'm sorry. I should be back at the w/e V*

A minute later his phone chimed. *Thanks for waking me!*

He keyed in a reply, then changed his mind and pressed delete.

– – – – – – – –

The next morning, in reception, in damp clothes, he looked down at the slumped body of an old man. 'Aparcamiento?' said Vince. The man didn't move. Vince's hire-car, parked out front, half on and half off the pavement, had to be moved before eight. 'Aparcamiento?' he repeated.

The old man, the night porter, the grandfather, slowly raised his head, his neck muscles knotted. He leant back in his chair and wiped the dribble from the corner of his mouth.

Vince tried a third time, putting the stress on the *miento*. The impact was discernible, if not decisive.

'¿Que?' said the man, gazing at Vince's midriff. Vince opened his phrase book and pointed to the word for car park. The old man raised a wrinkled hand and turned away as if averting his eyes from a bright light. Vince gave up. He dropped his room key on the desk and walked out. After driving twice around Puigcerdá's one-way system he parked up at the train station. From a kiosk he bought a postcard, stamps, envelopes, and a pad of paper. Then crossed the main road in front of the station and sat down outside a crêperie.

'Desayuno?' he said to the waitress. She nodded and disappeared inside. While waiting for his breakfast, he wrote a postcard to his sister.

> *Dear Hayley,*
> *I hope you are well. I'm taking a break in Spain for a few days. Got paid recently. I'm working on a story. Can you do me a favour and keep this letter? It contains some documents that I don't want to carry around with me. I'll explain another time. It's nothing to worry about. Take care and I'll speak to you soon. Vince*

He put the postcard inside an envelope. The waitress returned with a café con leche, water and a plate of sweet bread rolls. He began writing about the blackmail of Kevin, his encounter with Malisse, and his planned meeting with de la Rosa. He said that if anything should happen to him, Barros was responsible. He tore the page from the notebook and put it inside another envelope, sealed it and wrote confidential and c/o Hayley Wynter on the front. Then he folded it in half and placed it inside the envelope containing the postcard.

He drained his coffee, stuffed the last sticky roll in his mouth, and set off in search of a post box. When the letter arrived it would be a surprise for his sister. They were rarely in touch. She had no idea what he'd been doing since the Spinks' libel case, and she only found out about that from a neighbour. Five minutes later and back at the pensión, the young woman, the dutiful daughter/granddaughter, was

177

back.   Vince booked another night and handed over seventy euros.

'You find your taxi man?' she said.

'No,' said Vince. 'Would you call him for me?' He took a wilted slip of paper from the back pocket of his trousers. 'I'd like him to come here.'

'Sí, I know.'

The driver, Agapito, arrived fifteen minutes later. On the way to the station, and in his mangled English, he told Vince of his three years in London, cleaning and driving, and how he had been many times to Tooting. When they pulled up alongside the Megane, Vince asked him if he was free for the day.

'How do you mean?' said Agapito.

'I need some help for a few hours, maybe longer.'

'I am working today.' Agapito began tapping out a beat on the centre of the steering wheel. Then he turned to Vince. 'This is not my taxi.'

'I'll pay you three hundred euros for helping me find someone, and for being my translator.'

'And if we cannot find them?'

'It doesn't matter. I give you one-fifty now and the rest when we're finished.'

'And who is this man?'

'I want to speak to Adriano de la Rosa. Do you know him?'

'Sí señor. He is a Freeman of Puigcerdá. We have a bridge after him.'

'That's good. Do you know where he lives?'

'He lives in Llivia, not here.'

'Can you take me to his house?'

'One moment.'   Agapito made a call, then another call and then a third. When he'd finished he said, 'Adriano is in Saneja at his parents' home. Why do you want him?'

'I'm a football agent. You understand?'

'Oh yes, the money man.'

'I have an offer for Adriano.'

'Okay, but I do not want him to know I tell you where he live.'

178

'I understand. Just show me the house.'

Agapito looked out through the windscreen and then back at Vince. He nodded and held out his right hand.

Vince took out his wallet.

'No, we shake hands first, then the money.'

Vince smiled, shook his hand and counted out the notes.

First, I must make a call and return the taxi.' After some heated words on the phone, he said, 'I am yours today.'

'I'll follow you,' said Vince. Ten minutes later they were together again, but this time Vince was at the wheel of the Megane and Agapito in the passenger seat. From the station they joined the one-way system, crossed the railway line on the northern outskirts and then turned right onto the GIV-4035. After a few kilometres Vince parked up by a field gate just on the outskirts of Saneja.

'Their house is three houses after the church,' said Agapito. 'There are big forests in front. You cannot see it from the road.'

'If I need your help I'll call,' said Vince.

Agapito nodded and they exchanged mobile numbers. When Vince reached the first grey-bricked house, he could see the church up ahead, also in grey brick, distinguishable only by a golden cross on its pitched roof. Passing the church he saw the de la Rosa residence. From Agapito's brief description, he'd imagined a high line of cypress bordering a large garden, and a driveway snaking up to a villa. The actuality was more ordinary. The cypresses were leylandii, and their villa much like a British seaside bungalow. Only the vehicles on the driveway, a Mercedes soft top and a red X5, suggested affluence. He turned off the pavement and passed the white Mercedes, not noticing the tick of its cooling engine. Then losing confidence, he stopped, looked up at the house, back to the road and then into the tinted window of the X5. He saw the squinty eyes of a bald man in wrinkled clothes. Then he looked down at his cheap sandals. He decided to abort, buy some new clothes and come back later.

'Señor?'

He turned to face the house and saw a woman at an open window. He waved his hand and forced a smile.

'¿Qué desea?' she said.

As he walked towards the front door she disappeared. Then from inside a dog barked. Something large, thought Vince, an Alsatian or Doberman. Seconds later the front door swung back revealing a slim woman dressed in tight jeans and a red blouse, attractive, but old enough to be a footballer's mother.

'¿Señora de la Rosa?'

'¿Sí?'

He knew there was little point in being anything but direct. 'My name is Vince. I am English. Can I speak to Adriano, your son?' She shook her head. He delivered his one prepared sentence. '¿Puedo hablar con Adriano?' It made no difference. 'Ángel Barros,' he said. 'It's about Ángel Barros.'

'Un momento,' and she walked away, leaving the door open. Toward the end of the hall she shouted her son's name and disappeared. Vince heard her mention Barros. Then Adriano appeared in shorts and t-shirt. He was shorter than Vince had imagined, the height of his mother. Only his muscled legs hinted that he might be a sportsman.

'Señor,' said de la Rosa, stopping short of the doorstep.

Vince smiled, but didn't offer his hand. '¿Habla inglés?'

'Sí, yes I do.'

'My name is Vince. I am a friend of Kevin Furling. Do you know Kevin?'

'I know he plays for Chelsea.'

'He is at Millwall now. His agent is Ángel Barros, the same agent as you.'

'What is it you want?'

'I want to ask you a question.'

De la Rosa looked over Vince's shoulder, towards the driveway and the road.

'Don't worry I am on my own. I'm not a journalist.'

De la Rosa nodded toward the front lawn. Vince backed up and de la Rosa followed.

'Kevin needs your help,' said Vince. 'He has a problem with Mr Barros.'

De la Rosa held up his hand, indicating that he'd heard enough. 'I can't help you. I have to go.' He turned back to the house.

'I just want to ask a question.' Then louder, Vince said, 'I know that Kevin is gay.'

De la Rosa stopped, and gesturing with open hands, he said, 'I am a footballer and that is all.'

Vince noted that it was neither a denial nor an admission. He pressed him further. 'Do you know Patrick Malisse?'

'Yes.'

'He is gay too. His agent is Barros. Do you understand what I'm saying?'

'No.'

'I'm going to stop Barros,' said Vince. 'If I succeed you will need a new agent.'

De la Rosa looked again toward the main road. 'Take your shirt off, empty your pockets.'

Vince slapped his trouser and raised his arms to show he had nothing to hide.

'Do it,' said de la Rosa.

Vince pulled off his shirt and then turned out his pockets.

De la Rosa stepped forward and whispered, 'You have nothing. You cannot help me.'

'I want to help Kevin. That's all. Just tell me if you are gay.'

De la Rosa nodded.

'Thank you,' said Vince. 'Please don't mention this to Señor Barros.' Then he picked up his shirt and walked calmly away not looking back. As he reached the road and turned towards the church, he punched the air in celebration. His trip to Spain was over. In the Megane, he said nothing to Agapito. He started the engine, spun the car around and set off for Puigcerdá.

At the railway station he counted out another one-fifty euros. Smiling, Agapito folded the notes into his shirt pocket and said, 'Buen viaje'. They shook hands, and as Agapito walked across the station car park, he called his boss to see if he could get his taxi back. Then he called his bookmaker. It was his lucky day and he intended to make the most of it.

Vince retrieved the rental agreement from the glove compartment and called the EuroCar office in Tarbes. A woman answered and in faltering English she told him that it would be okay to drop his car at Toulouse Airport.

32

Ailish lay on the bed with a towel across her eyes, breathing slowly, trying to clear her head. In two hours she was supposed to be at Amaya's in Belgravia for her evening appointment with Spinks. She was trying to decide whether to go and or make an excuse. While not going was the easy option, it didn't appeal. She wanted to meet him again, but she didn't want to continue with the half truths. She recalled again his words on the phone: '*somewhere a bit more relaxed...just you and me...no lawyers...shall I pick you up?*' They weren't the words of an adversary. They hinted at intimacy. She wanted to believe there was no subtext, that Vince was wrong, and that Spinks didn't fuck with people's heads. But would Amaya's be a business meeting, a negotiation or a dinner date? *Was it a trap? Would the police be waiting?*

There was no way of knowing, so she pushed the uncertainty aside and threw the towel to the floor. She dressed and redressed four times, finally settling on three inch heels, a navy sleeveless dress cut four inches above the knee, and on her bosom, a lucky charm, her Nana's gold pendant. She took a taxi to Balham and the tube to Knightsbridge, by which time she was running late. She hurried as best she could in her heels, cutting through the arcade near Starbucks. Then she saw him, pacing slowly outside the restaurant. He turned and looked up at the sound of her footsteps, and then, as she closed in, slightly breathless, she started to apologise.

'I'm so sorry Mr Spinks. I couldn't...' She paused, and unknowingly rubbed her Nana's pendent between forefinger and thumb. 'I was held up and...I couldn't find a cab.'

'No problem,' said Spinks, raising his hand, 'and it's David or D. It's up to you.'

She smiled. 'I have a friend called Dee...for Deidre. She's very blonde.'

'So?'

'You're not blonde. I can't see you as a Dee.'

'And what does Dee get up to? Is she an artist?'

'No, she's not. Shoes mainly, she's big in shoes.' Has it started? she wondered. Is he already adding up my lies?

'A blonde with big feet?' said Spinks.

She laughed. 'No, it's her business.' Deidre was one of her loyal eBay customers and because she was local, Ailish would sometimes drop round with new stock before she listed it.

Spinks nodded. 'Well it's good to see you again.' Then he leant towards her, his arms raised, his head angled slightly to one side. She swayed back at the last second leaving his air-kiss dangling. He quickly straightened and said, 'Sorry, I...'

'No, my fault. I just wasn't expecting it.' She blushed.

'You're right. Why would you? I get to meet a lot of people. All the hugging and kissing is kind of automatic.'

'I suppose our situation is a little unusual. We have a legal dispute of sorts, but we're meeting for dinner.'

He nodded. 'It's like a handshake isn't enough anymore. Though I like a handshake, it can still be intimate.'

She shrugged her shoulders. 'So what shall we do?'

He offered his hand, and simultaneously they moved together and gently pressed cheeks.

As they parted, he said, 'Where were we?'

'Well you're David and I'm Ailish.'

'Ailish. A great Irish name.'

'To be honest,' and putting on her thickest brogue, she whispered, 'I fuckin' hate it.'

Spinks laughed, and as she smiled at his laughter, she noticed the quarter-inch gap in his lower front teeth. She wanted to ask him about it, but their small-talk was cut short by Amaya's maitre d'. He pushed back the restaurant's front door and invited them in.

At their table, Spinks suggested champagne.

'Are we celebrating?' she said.

'Probably not, but we can pretend.'

'Bubbles and curry?' she said, frowning.

'Trust me,' and Spinks turned to the sommelier. 'Do you have a Gosset?'

She sniggered.

Spinks and the sommelier turned their heads.

'Sorry, forgive me,' she said. Then under the table she pinched her thigh for behaving like a teenager, and for forgetting who she was supposed to be.

The sommelier turned back to Spinks. 'Yes Mr Spinks, we have a Celebris Blanc.'

'Excellent.'

When the sommelier returned and filled their glasses, Spinks said, 'Here's to a lovely evening,' and then, raising his flute, he added, 'and your enduring beauty.'

She laughed. No one had ever said such a thing to her before.

'What's so funny?'

'Well, you're being so...so charming.'

'I mean it.'

'No you don't.' She was certain he was playing games, trying to knock her off-guard. They touched glasses over the table and then with hers just inches from her lips, she said, 'And here's to you David, and your enduring success.' She smiled, pleased at her counter compliment. She sipped enough to wet her lips and then placed the glass to one side. 'I'd prefer to get our business out of the way first...keep a clear head.'

'Of course, fire away.' He place his glass on the table and then leant forward as if something important was about to be said.

She gestured with an open hand at all the other diners. 'As this was your idea, I kind of presumed you were going to make some sort of offer.' She deliberately avoided the mention of money or compensation. It was way too soon for that.

'An offer for what?' he said.

She refused to answer, and keeping a straight face, she slowly pushed her glass to the very edge of the table, to the limit of her reach.

He smiled and nodded, as if conceding a move well made. He was tempted to advance the pepper pot over the small vase of peonies, and then reach over and kiss her full on the lips. Instead, he flicked his fingernail against the side of his glass. 'Okay, but if I make an offer, I'll need some evidence.'

Fuck me, she thought. *This can't be happening!* Then her phone chimed. 'Do you mind?'

'Carry on.'

She reached down and opened her bag, having forgotten about the prearranged text from her sister Bríd. She'd figured that if the meeting with Spinks went badly, she could use Bríd's text as an excuse to escape. *Hi A. Still got your panties on? Bríd.* She smiled and put the phone away. She hadn't told Bríd who she was meeting, just that she was going out for dinner and that it wasn't with Vince. 'Sorry, you were saying?'

'Evidence, I'll need evidence.'

'Of course. I can provide affidavits if you can wait a few days. I can also send you a statement.'

'A statement?'

'Yes. In the presence of a solicitor my artist described his idea for what you call Art-Vision. That was two years ago. That statement could be made public.' She glanced at his drumming fingers, pleased that she'd made him think. 'So in the absence of an offer, that's one way we can go...and if you're not happy with that, you can seek damages.'

Spinks nodded. 'I assume you're talking about Vince Wynter?'

She didn't flinch. 'That is correct.'

He laughed and shook his head. 'And how much did you pay him for his art? Not much I hope?'

'That's of no relevance.'

'It is if you're seeking compensation. Was it cash in hand?'

She ignored his jibe. 'Mr Wynter's statement will be made public if you and I cannot agree a settlement.'

'But Wynter never had a solicitor. He represented himself.'

Is that it? Is that your best shot? At any moment she'd been expecting him to demolish her story and expose her as a pedlar of second-hand shoes.

She said, 'Yes, I believe you're right, but when he received the initial letter from Brewer and Copthorne, he made a statement in the presence of a solicitor. Mr Wynter recounted everything that was said during your meeting at Heathrow, a safeguard if you like.' She raised her eyebrows encouraging him to respond, wondering if he saw the loose parallel with his own death-bed letter.

He scratched his stubble and nodded. 'Okay, so how much do you want?'

Though softly spoken his words stunned her. *This is too easy. It can't be!* She looked straight ahead, her eyes fixed and unfocused on his chin.

'Ailish...Ailish are you alright?' When he touched her hand she broke her stare.

'Sorry,' she said, 'you were saying?'

'I said, you want money, so how much?'

'For what?'

'So you'll go away, so you'll send me all your evidence and Wynter's statement.'

'You want the evidence?' she said, trying to buy some time. She hadn't given the matter of compensation much thought, because she didn't believe she would get that far. For her, success was simply conning her way into meeting Spinks.

'Yes, evidence, it's quite straightforward.'

She glanced at the diners at the next table and said, 'I can't do that.' She was about to say that she didn't trust him, and that she wanted the money first, but Spinks jumped in.

'Don't you have the evidence?'

187

'No, it's not that, it's because...' She decided to blame someone else. 'It's because I don't trust your lawyers. They'll want to win.'

'But they're not here,' he said, raising his voice. 'This is my decision.'

She realised she'd annoyed him. She picked up her serviette and unfolded it on her lap. 'David, I like your work and I like Art-Vision. I think it's good to mess with people's heads. I think it's your strength. I even like Cock 'n' Bull.'

'Man's Best Friend,' he corrected. Man's Best Friend (MBF) was Spinks' signature piece and it still rankled when people got the name wrong. The critics, press and bloggers called it Cock 'n' Bull. The work was a six-foot penis shaped out of red house bricks and mortar (Chemfix) and for the eighteen years it had been jutting out from a wall at the Hayward Gallery, it was still making people laugh and frown. And just three feet to the right of MBF was a brass plaque which read: **Touching Permitted**, and in tiny writing in the bottom corner of the plaque, it read: This too!

And over the years tens of thousands had, smoothing and darkening its surface. For Spinks, it had been no more than a joke, a final piece he had hurriedly constructed for the Artgasm exhibition. The work had gained added notoriety because during the show a rumour had spread that Spinks had used his own semen in the mortar mix. It was a rumour started by Spinks and spread by Witherspoon.

One critic described MBF as 'grotesque and narcissistic'; another called it 'a wonderful paradox of the static and the animated; while Zac Quell, of the London Evening News, said 'it was a futile construction parodying the inherited clichés of the male libido.' Later, when asked on Radio 4's Front Row what he'd meant, Quell had replied, 'My dear, it's simply car boot material.'

'Of course, Man's Best Friend,' she said, 'I'm sorry.'

'Don't worry. Perhaps I should give in and rename it. Maybe Cock 'n' Bull is better.'

'No, definitely not,' she said. 'The name and the object, they're indivisible. You can't change it now. Your only option is to...' and then she paused, conscious that she was about to tell an artist of world renown what to do.

'Go ahead,' he said. 'What's my option?'

'Nothing, it doesn't matter.'

'Please, I'm interested.'

'Well you could make another penis and call that Cock 'n' Bull. Physically, it should be exactly the same, but because it would have a different name, it would have a different meaning. It wouldn't be a copy.'

He laughed. 'I can see the headline now: Two Cocks and More Bull.'

As their laughter subsided, he said, 'So what about this evidence then?'

Her smile dropped, she sipped some champagne, and said, 'David, you know you've benefitted. Mr Wynter's career is over, and I know that's not your fault, but you gained and he lost.' She wanted to ask him why he had taken such a risk in using Vince's idea, but she knew now wasn't the time.

Spinks replied with a question. 'What is it you do? Are you a lawyer?'

'No.' She shrugged her shoulders. 'I help people, I paint.'

'You paint?' She'd surprised him again. 'And do you sell your work?'

'No, it's just something I like to do. It's more of a serious hobby.'

'But I could buy one of your paintings?'

'I suppose, but why would you want to do that?'

'I'm also an art collector. I might be interested in buying something of yours.' Then he reached inside his jacket, placed his cheque book on the table, and then signalled to a passing waiter that he wanted a pen. 'So?' He stared at her, waiting for a number.

'What do mean, so? She shook her head and then the penny dropped. While he wasn't prepared to compensate Vince directly, he was prepared to buy a painting.

'I mean, how much do you want for one of your paintings?'

'Which one?'

'Any one,' he said, 'it doesn't matter.' He was testing her. Could she put a high price on her own work? The psychology of pricing was something Spinks had learnt from Witherspoon, who had told him never to be timid on price. And he'd been right. At all Spinks' exhibitions, the most expensive pieces were always the first to sell.

'I'm not sure,' she said. 'I've never sold one.' Her first thought was maybe two hundred pounds, maybe three, but then she recalled how much Spinks was charging for his Art-Vision exhibits. She said, 'You're selling your visions for fifty thousand and they're not originals.'

He smiled at her joke.

'How about we decide on the number of zeros?' she said.

He nodded. 'Okay, three?'

She shook her head.

'Four?'

She stared back, unblinking.

'Five then?'

'Five seems reasonable. Now we just need a digit to go in front.'

'Two?'

She visualised the number, two hundred thousand. It looked very good, but she decided to press for more.

'Well?' said Spinks.

'Four,' she said.

'Three,' he countered.

She paused, not wanting to appear overly keen. 'Okay, I'll accept three,' and then she smiled and he smiled back. Their business was over. While he made out the cheque, she emptied her glass and decided to leave as soon as it was in her hand.

'There you are,' he said, sliding the cheque across the table.

Without inspecting it, she slipped it into her clutch bag. 'I'll arrange for the painting to be delivered when the cheque's cleared.'

'I'll want a disclaimer signed by Mr Wynter.'

'You don't want the statement from his solicitor?'

'The disclaimer will do,' said Spinks. 'That should stop him from coming back.'

'And where shall I send them?'

'My studio. I'll text you the address. Come round if you like.'

She looked at him quizzically, unsure what the invitation meant.

'You're an artist,' he said, 'so you might be interested in seeing my studio.'

'Maybe I'll do that. That would be nice.'

He lifted the bottle of champagne from the ice bucket. 'More?'

'Another time. I should go now, I have to speak to...to my client.'

He nodded. 'Well it was nice meeting you Ailish. Until next time.'

They stood and kissed cheek to cheek without hesitation.

'See you soon,' she said.

Outside she ran through the arcade, crossed Motcombe Street without looking, and then entered the familiar safety of Waitrose. She stopped by the tills and looked back across the street. There was no sign of him.

'Are you alright Miss?' said the security guard.

She turned. 'Pardon?'

'Is someone chasing you?'

'No, no I'm fine.' She took the cheque from her clutch bag and held it up to the light. The date and amount were correct. It all looked beautiful, but for his signature. Above his printed name, he'd drawn a heart and arrow.

33

The Roof Garden, Friday 24th June

Phylida studied the colour photograph on the back of the Roof Garden's menu. The image's title, printed across a blue sky, read: *London's Iconic Landmarks.* Looking out of the restaurant's window, and lined up on her left, she saw the scaffolded Shard, and in the foreground the old hemisphere of the Royal Albert Hall, and between the two, the London Eye. All three were clearly labelled on the photograph. She wondered, in what sense they were iconic? They were merely large regular-shaped constructions. Earlier in the week, she'd read a newspaper article about Millwall, where the journalist had described it as an iconic East London club. After that, she started seeing and hearing the word everywhere. Even her local curry-house was in on the game – describing one of its specials as iconic Tandoori Chicken.

As a precautionary measure she decided against meeting Crozier at the Sketch's Derry Street office. At 12.50 she called him to say she would see him at the restaurant. 'The reservation is in my name, Cranson. If you have any problems, give me a call.'

Stepping out of the lift on the seventh floor, Crozier said, 'Cranson' to the red-coated receptionist. While she checked the lunchtime bookings, he looked around for the toilets.

'Mr Crozier?' she said.

'Yes.'

She gestured to her left. 'If you go through, the maitre d' will show you to your table.'

He pointed to the men's room and she nodded. Inside he washed his hands and then wiped his face and teeth with a damp hand towel, finishing off by smoothing his fringe to one side. Out in the reception area, he followed the maitre d' into the restaurant, giving his damp hands a final wipe on the back of his shirt.

'Mr Crozier,' said the maitre d'. Phylida turned and smiled. She guessed at early twenties, and thought boy-band material.

'Sorry I'm late,' said Crozier. 'I had to check a story and then make a phone call.' His right index finger began zigzagging the air as he plotted the sequence of events, 'and then someone called me, and after that...'

'Never mind,' she said, rising from her chair and offering her hand. 'Take a seat.'

He sat opposite, his back to the city skyline.

'What would you like to drink?'

He glanced at the neighbouring table for ideas and then at her glass of juice, and said, 'A shandy, do you think they do shandies?'

'I'm sure they can.' She looked at the waiter who nodded and moved away. She asked Crozier about his day, and how long he'd been a journalist, where he'd studied, and what his plans were. He replied: busy, two years, Cardiff, I don't really have any. The waiter returned with a chilled glass and bottles of Broadside Bitter and Fevertree Lemonade. Crozier half-filled the glass with lemonade and then trickled in the Broadside, worried it would over-foam. They ordered mains and passed on starters.

'Any developments on the Cowly story?' she said.

He shrugged. 'No, not that I know of.'

She wondered if he'd been instructed to keep quiet, to take the free lunch and leave. 'Craig, I thought meeting up face-to-face, might be helpful. We're happy to talk to anyone about anything. You ran a story attacking Tom Cowly, but you never bothered to contact us. I mean, what was the story? That his marriage failed?'

'Kind of. He's been in the news 'cos of what's happened at Millwall. He owns a Christian club and he left his wife for a Filipino. I don't see what's wrong with that.'

All of it she thought. 'How do you know she didn't leave him?'

'I don't. I didn't have time to check. We just stuck to the facts we knew.'

'You weren't interested in the whole story?' She knew it was a stupid question.

'Someone gave us some photographs and we used them.'

Thank you Craig, she thought, that's all I need to know. 'So the Sketch didn't start this?'

'They arrived in the post and I was given a couple of hours to put something underneath.'

'There was no discussion about who'd sent them or why?'

'Not that I know of,' said Crozier. 'It was the sub-editor's decision. He said if we don't use them someone else will.'

'What about Millwall? What's the editor's view?'

'I don't know. He doesn't talk to me.'

That morning she'd reread the Sketch's coverage on the Millwall situation. One leader, written days after the acquisition, described the Church's involvement as an *act of desperation*, while a more recent leader had picked up on the rumours about the Gülen Movement's interest in Chelsea, saying it was:

> *'a worrying trend, and that the Government and the LPFL needed to act decisively to prevent the sectarianisation of the national game.'*

'Someone's worried,' she said. 'Don't you read the leader columns?'

'Never.'

Their mains arrived. They had both chosen crispy duck with mixed herbs and a smoked rapeseed mayonnaise.

'Looks nice,' said Crozier, pushing the herbs around his plate, wishing he'd ordered soup.

'Your editor thinks the Church's involvement is a worrying trend.'

'I wouldn't know.'

'Can you get me a meeting with him?'

'I can ask.'

With their business complete they had little else to talk about. They hurried the food and Crozier left. She stayed behind for ten minutes walking in the roof garden. She wanted to be sure he was well clear of the building before she came out onto Kensington High Street.

34

Victoria Embankment, Saturday 25th June

At a bench table down the side of Gordon's Wine Bar, Ailish and Bríd were one bottle down and half way through another. They usually met somewhere on alternate Saturdays, when Jim, Bríd's husband, had the kids for the day and evening, and it usually involved food and wine, sometimes a movie, sometimes a gallery. Ailish was hoping to see *No Man's Land* at the Cornerhouse, but Bríd wasn't keen. 'It's too nice to be inside and you still haven't told me about your date.'

'What date?' said Ailish.

'Don't mess with me sis. Thursday, your dinner date.'

'It wasn't a date. I met with Spinks. It was business.' Previously she'd told Bríd that she was due to meet up with Spinks' lawyers, but not when, nor the outcome. As with Vince, she didn't want to raise expectations.

'Why didn't you tell me?'

'I'm telling you now.'

Bríd leant forward, fixing on her sister's eyes. 'Did you sleep with him?'

Ailish peered back. 'No I didn't, we just talked. It was a negotiation.'

'What about?' said Bríd.

'Compensation for Vince. He gave me a cheque for three hundred thousand.'

Bríd shrieked, covering her mouth with both hands. Heads turned at the tables on either side.

Ailish slapped her sister on the arm. 'Ssh.' The deal with Spinks was supposed to be confidential. 'You can't tell anyone Bríd, you hear me? No one, not even Jim. Spinks is buying one of my paintings, but the money is for Vince.'

'Three hundred?'

'Yes, but he didn't sign it.'

'What do you mean?'

'He signed the cheque with a heart and arrow.'

'What?'

'He just drew a picture.'

'Like Dali?'

'What do you mean?'

'Salvador Dali used to draw pictures on the back of every cheque he wrote, knowing that people would never cash them. The fucker never paid for anything.'

'I don't think so,' said Ailish. 'Anyway, I banked it yesterday. I should find out on Wednesday if it bounced.'

'Three hundred for Vince? Why?'

'Yes, remember? Art-Vision? Vince's room with chairs for seven billion people.'

'Whatever, it ain't worth three hundred grand.' She leant forward and whispered. 'Have you told Vince?'

'No.'

'Then you should keep it, keep every penny.'

Ailish shook her head and looked at her watch. 'Come on, let's go. I've had enough.'

On the way to Tooting they bought more wine and spent the evening talking about money: how it didn't make you happy and then how it did make you happy, how London was a shit place if you were broke, and then about what they'd like to buy. Then the chemicals in the wine started to encourage alternative ideas. Ailish said, 'I could keep some it. I could keep a hundred thousand. He wouldn't mind. He needn't know.' Bríd was flat out on the sofa resting her eyes. 'Bríd,' she shouted. 'Did you hear me?'

'What is it?'

'I said Vince will want me to have some of the money. He likes me.'

Bríd sat up and laughed. 'He *liked* you, you mean. You're supposed to be kicking him out or have you changed your mind?'

'I'm not kicking him out,' said Ailish. 'He wants to move out.'

'Look as I see it, Spinks wants to fuck you. Why wouldn't he? You've got good legs. He doesn't give a monkey's about Vince or your painting and he wouldn't be giving a penny to some flabby-assed minger. It's about fucking. Jim's with me, because I'm a good fuck.'

'Was,' said Ailish.

Bríd picked up a pizza crust and chucked it across the room, missing and hitting the far wall.

'You don't know Vince. He'll want me to take some.'

'Whatever.' Bríd dropped down and closed her eyes.

'Spinks paid me because he's worried about his reputation. It's worth a lot. He's not paying three hundred to fuck me.'

Bríd laughed. 'Too right he's not. He'd have to be the craziest fucker on the planet. I mean fuckin' fuckin' crazy to think your arse is worth that much. But whatever he's up to, he'll be in your knickers in a week.'

'What if he is? I still reckon I deserve a commission.'

'Yes you do,' said Bríd. 'A fuck for a bounced cheque is a fair deal.'

They continued arguing about what commission Ailish deserved until they both fell asleep with the television on.

— — — — — —

During the drive to Toulouse and his flight home Vince's thoughts continued to circle around the one problem: how to expose Barros while ensuring Kevin's anonymity? He came up with nothing. Following the money wouldn't work. He was sure Barros would have a contract that legitimised the extortion. Even if he could obtain evidence of the blackmail, it would be too risky to use, the story would probably leak and Kevin's name would be out in the open. It seemed that Barros was untouchable unless Kevin came out.

From Heathrow he caught the Piccadilly and Northern lines to Tooting. On the way he sent Ailish a text: *Hi A, back in an hour.* Then another: *I'll move out this week.*

She didn't reply and when he opened the front door and saw the empty wine bottles it was obvious why. She was flat out on the recliner, while Bríd was face down on the sofa, her mouth open. Neither roused as he shut the door and switched off the television. In the kitchen he ran the cold tap and downed a glass of water without pausing. Then he took two quilts from the top shelf of the airing cupboard. As he laid them over the two women, he said, 'See you in the morning.' Ailish mumbled, pulled her legs up to her chest and rolled onto her side.

He woke just after three regretting the text he sent her. He figured he'd need at least a month or two to find another house share. He didn't want to hurry it. Then he thought about staying on. *I could offer her more rent and pay something toward the bills. She could have half the book money.* In the semi-darkness he climbed out of bed, grabbed his mobile and walked naked into the lounge. He sent her a blank text and a second later her handbag chimed. He took the bag to the bedroom, shut the door, and picked out her phone. He deleted the three texts he had sent. But as they vanished from the screen, a text from *DavidS* moved to the top of her inbox. He opened it:

Hi Ailish, The studio is on Rhuddlan Road. Call me when you're there. See you soon. Don't forget your painting. D

– – – – – – – –

When he entered the lounge mid-morning they hadn't moved. Ailish was staring at the opposite wall and Bríd at the ceiling. 'Do you want this?' he said, holding a glass of juice in Ailish's line of sight.

'Can you put it down?' she said.

'Bríd, do you want one?'

'Please, and some paracetamol. I feel like shit.'

It wasn't an unexpected response. Always, the day after the night before, Bríd was the unfortunate victim, the villains being the wine and those that hadn't prevented her from drinking to excess. Vince suspected her heavy hangovers were no worse than anyone else's. When he'd mentioned it to Ailish, she had an explanation: 'It's because she's a redhead. It's well known that they feel more pain than others. She can't help it.' When Vince had pointed out that

199

she too had red hair, she'd replied, 'It's not a law of nature, it's just a stats thing.'

From the kitchen he shouted, 'Coffee?'

'No,' came their joint reply.

'What was the celebration?'

'Nothing,' said Ailish.

'Do you want toast?'

Ailish silently mouthed to Bríd, 'Not a word. You understand?' Bríd frowned. She'd forgotten that her sister was only going to tell Vince about the money if and when the cheque cleared. 'Not a word,' whispered Ailish, firmly.

Bríd nodded.

'Toast, do you want toast?' he repeated.

'No thanks,' they shouted back.

After his coffee, Vince walked to the paper shop on the corner of Robinson Road. On the way he called Andy. 'It's Vince.'

Andy was on the sea front unlocking the Pump Room's metal shutter. 'Aye.'

'I need a favour,' said Vince. 'I might need somewhere to stay for a few days, maybe a week.'

'Okay, no problem. Bring some bedding.' There was no hesitation. Andy's offer was open and unconditional.

'I'll probably be down tomorrow.'

'Come down. I'll give you the key.'

– – – – – – – –

Bríd left after lunch and Ailish spent the afternoon catching up on her eBay sales, packing three pairs of shoes for posting to Canada, Denmark and Dublin. Mid-evening, in front of the TV and feeling sick from a cheese omelette, she asked him about his trip to Europe.

Standing behind the settee, he said, 'It was a waste of time. I didn't get a chance to speak to Malisse.'

'So what now?'

'Nothing.' He wasn't going to tell her about de la Rosa. Not yet.

She hit the mute button as the ads started.

'I'm going to move out. I'll go down to Brighton.'

'Okay.'

He knew she was hung over, but he had expected more than an okay. 'I'll go tomorrow. I can't take everything at once. I'll have to come back another time.'

'Why Brighton?'

'I have a friend there...Andy.'

'And if Barros drops round, what shall I tell him?'

'Barros?'

'Yes, Barros. Is there another one?'

'I'll speak to him,' said Vince. 'If he turns up, just tell him I've left.'

'Right, I'll tell him you're not in Brighton and you're not staying with Andy.'

'I'll call him, okay? Don't worry. I'll tell him I've moved.'

'Good. Make sure you do.'

He paused and said, 'And what about your meeting? What did Spinks have to say?'

'Not much. He talked about copyright. Stuff about not owning ideas.'

'Is that all?' He wanted to ask why she was lying. 'He didn't admit he stole it then?''

'No, he said he'd thought about Art-Vision before he met you.'

'So that's it?'

'Probably.'

That night Vince slept on the sofa.

35

The Mandarin, Sunday morning 26th June

Tom Cowly had arranged to meet Ken Ffooks on the Monday to discuss the story in The Sketch, but the paper's Sunday edition forced a change of plan. This time Ffooks was the target, and much like the story on Cowly, it did little more that imply impropriety. The photograph, taken in Regent Street, showed Ffooks talking to a woman in a short skirt and extreme heels, his face seemingly inches from her ample chest. The caption underneath read:

> *Ken Ffooks, the Archbishop's investment guru, discusses tactics with new signing and ex-prostitute Shelley Abrahams.*

The article stated that Ffooks had been the man behind the Church's acquisition of Millwall and that Abrahams had a police record for soliciting.

Cowly called him just after ten. 'What's happening?'

Ffooks' hands were shaking. 'I don't know who she is Tom. She stopped me in the street.' He was in his kitchen, in his pyjamas and slippers. He'd found out about the story two hours earlier when his wife's sister, Jane, had called. Not long after that the first photographer knocked on his front door.

'Is Eileen alright?' said Cowly.

'She's upstairs with Jane. She's taken a sedative.'

'You've seen the article?'

'Yes, Jane brought a copy round.'

Because there had been some truth behind the Cowly story – Cowly had left his wife, and he was having a relationship with a Filipino – Ffooks was worried that people would also believe that he used prostitutes. At his golf club, he imagined it would be the news of the day. There would be speculation on every fairway and green – *dirty old man, lucky bastard, randy Ffooks, poor Eileen* – the punning and nudging sustaining some members all the way to the clubhouse bar.

He could barely remember it happening. But as he looked again at the photograph in the Sketch, a few details came back. She'd stopped him just after lunch with Eileen, and because she'd spoken so softly, he bent forward so he could hear her words above the traffic noise. She asked him the time and directions to the nearest tube station, and then thanked him for his help. But when he called out to tell her she was heading off in the wrong direction, away from Regent's Park Tube Station, she didn't stop.

'Ken, is anyone outside?'

Ffooks moved into the front room so he could see the driveway. 'I can see six or seven.'

'There'll be more on their way. Is there somewhere you can go? Not a relative, perhaps a friend? If not, come here. I'm at the Mandarin.'

'I don't think Eileen's well enough to...'

'Ken, do it. If you stay, it'll be worse for her. They'll be outside for days.'

'I could do an interview on the doorstep,' said Ffooks. 'I can give them a statement.'

It was an option that Cowly had also considered and then quickly rejected. 'It won't help. Come to the Mandarin, pack some things and call a taxi.'

'Okay,' said Ffooks, with little conviction. He wasn't sure Eileen would leave their home and he wasn't going anywhere without her.

'Call me when you're near. I'll meet you outside.'

Cowly rang off. His immediate thought was that Ffooks would resign. He was what Cowly called a 'back roomer', someone who had spent his career focussing on the numbers and the analysts' reports, never in the limelight. He would have made a perfect Director of Investments, if the Church's strategy hadn't changed, but with Millwall and the Church making front and back page headlines, the role now demanded someone with different skills, a communicator, someone relaxed in front of camera, someone that could think on their feet. Cowly knew Ffooks couldn't do that and so did Ffooks. After a stuttering performance on BBC's Panorama, Ffooks had refused to do any more interviews, passing them all over to Cowly.

Two hours later, outside the Mandarin, Cowly slipped a twenty pound note to each of the red-coated doormen with instructions to keep the photographers at bay. 'At least make it awkward for them,' he said.

One doorman nodded to the other and they both disappeared into the hotel, emerging twenty seconds later each with a hand hidden inside their unbuttoned coat.

'Sir,' said the taller of the two, 'it would probably be safer if you stood somewhere else.' The doorman gestured to the stone steps leading up to the hotel's entrance. Cowly nodded and moved away. When the Ffooks' cab arrived, four other cars and a motorbike pulled up behind. Within seconds doors flew open and cameras flashed as the paparazzi rushed forward. But before they got close, the two doormen threw open their coats, and standing shoulder-to-shoulder, and each clutching a plastic spray bottle, they fired a watery mist over each and every lens. Like cold water over fighting dogs, the impact was immediate and final.

– – – – – – – –

Later that evening Cowly was in the Mandarin's piano bar waiting for Ffooks and his wife. They were already late and he was beginning to regret his decision to meet them for dinner. He wanted to be upstairs in room 514, with Imee, tickling her neck while proofreading her latest college assignment: *'What's to stop another Bernie Madoff?'* He always checked her grammar and punctuation before she handed anything in, though he never touched the content. Earlier, when she had been writing the concluding paragraph to her five thousand word essay, he'd asked her to summarise her answer to the Madoff question. She'd shrugged her shoulders and said, 'Not much.' Cowly was inclined to agree.

Cowly glanced at his watch, drumming his fingers on the arms of his chair. Opposite, in line of sight, Adrija Sen, the hotel's resident pianist, began a medley of easy listening tunes from the fifties, sixties and seventies. After thirty seconds of *Magic Moments*, Cowly said to himself, 'Perry Como.' Sen moved seamlessly into *Twenty-four hours from Tulsa*. 'Pitney,' said Cowly. *Walk on by* followed, but Cowly couldn't put a name to the singer who had made the song famous. Then, as Sen picked up the tempo for *Do you know the way to San Jose?* Cowly slapped his thigh. 'Dionne Warwick.' Then he realised, they weren't just any old random hits from the second half of the last century, they were the songs of Burt Bacharach and Hal David, and they were all familiar to Cowly because his father had had a huge collection of LPs, and on every Sunday and Wednesday evening in the Cowly household, winter or summer, the television was switched off and the radiogram on. Dissent or debate weren't tolerated and the teenage Cowly wasn't allowed to retreat to his room, his father maintaining that it was all part of his musical education. And on the rare occasions when Cowly refused to be bowed, his father would swap the Bacharach, Dylan and Guthrie for the nightmare of forties bebop.

Cowly looked at his watch again and called Imee.

'Hi Tom,' she said. 'How is your meal?'

'I'm still in the bar. They've not arrived yet. What are you doing?'

'No much.' She touched the mute button on the TV remote. 'Maybe they don't want to have dinner? Perhaps they are tired?'

'I'll call him.' Then as he rang off Ffooks entered the bar.

Cowly waved.

'Sorry I'm late,' said Ffooks, 'Eileen's not coming down. She's resting.'

'That's fine, we don't have to eat. Have you time for a quick drink?' Cowly had a couple of things he wanted to discuss.

'I'll have a scotch, a small one.' The waiter hovering behind Ffooks' chair nodded and left.

'Is the room alright?'

'Yes, it's fine and thanks for sorting it out. I think you were right to get away. When we left home there were cars blocking the road and the police had just arrived.' Ffooks grimaced as he recalled the scene. 'She's not sure what to believe. I told her it's a smear, but I can't explain it. I don't have an explanation.'

'I'll speak to her if you like?'

'Maybe tomorrow,' said Ffooks.

'We'll need to respond,' said Cowly, 'so I was thinking of bringing the board meeting forward to Wednesday. We could hold a press conference in the afternoon and make a statement on the Sketch stories.'

'And then what?' said Ffooks.

'And then we get back to work as best we can. There's not much else we can do.'

When Ffooks' whisky arrived he took a mouthful, looked into the bottom of the glass and emptied it. 'I was thinking I could contact this woman that was named in the paper, Shelley Abrahams. I could get her to make a statement that we've never met. I need something Tom, and so does Eileen.'

'Well we can try,' said Cowly, 'but you shouldn't do it. I'll call Phylida. She's already met the journalist who did the story on me. I'll call her later.'

Ffooks nodded and then looked over his shoulder towards the bar. 'Do you want one?'

'Not for me Ken. I'll see you tomorrow, about ten.'

Ffooks raised his glass to the barman.

– – – – – – – – –

The Saddle-up Livery, Braney, Sunday 26th June

In rural Hertfordshire, away from the air-conditioned hum of The Mandarin, Phylida pushed her shoulder against the lopsided gatepost.

'I'll get the Landrover,' said Alice, a devoted animal lover and the livery's sole owner. Someone earlier in the day had reversed into the yard and clipped the post, and now the slam-catch and striker-plate wouldn't line up. The gate wouldn't lock. Security was a constant worry for Alice. Over the years, horses, saddles, buckets, and even bags of manure had gone missing.

Phylida stood back, knowing the plan wouldn't work. Alice crunched the old Landrover into first gear and nudged the post back to vertical, but as soon as she backed off, the gate sank again, a little further. She'd made the situation worse.

'We'll have to brace it and reset the post,' said Phylida. She knew this because her father had had a similar problem, though then it had been time and gravity that had caused the misalignment. 'If you can wait a couple of days, I'll drop by and give you a hand.'

'Thanks,' said Alice, putting her hand on Phylida's shoulder, grateful for the offer. 'I'll park up against the gate tonight and remove the distributor cap.'

As Phylida rolled her bike out of the yard her phone rang. It was Cowly. He explained about the photo of Ffooks and asked her to contact Abrahams and find out what she could.

36

Tooting, Monday 27th June

On the sofa, Vince slept in ten and twenty minutes segments, and between each one, he adjusted his body position, turning, stretching, curling up, on one shoulder then the other, reshaping his pillow, each time trying to find a position that wouldn't wake him up. He rose at eight feeling like he'd had a good kicking. Ailish was already in the kitchen towelling her damp hair. In striped underpants and t-shirt, he broke with routine; he spoke to her before breakfast. He asked her again about her meeting with Spinks, testing her for the truth. 'So you'll be hearing from him?'

'What?' she said, her head still buried in a towel.

'Spinks, he'll be in touch?'

'I don't know. Nothing was agreed.' She was determined to stick to her plan. She didn't want to do or say anything that might disrupt Vince's voluntary departure. She didn't want the money to be a complicating factor.

'What else did you talk about?'

She stood up and dropped the towel over a stool. 'I told him you left a statement with a solicitor, a signed statement, and that you did it before the trial started.'

Vince shook his head. 'Why?'

'Because it seemed like a good idea.'

Annoyed at her continuing deceit, Vince grabbed the Friday Ad and disappeared into the toilet.

She shouted after him. 'I said the statement described Art-Vision. I told him he'd ripped you off.'

Vince didn't respond.

She walked up to the bathroom door. 'He said he would think it over. Look, if he gets in touch, I'll call you, and if you need my car, take it.'

They didn't speak after that. Vince packed a rucksack and just after eleven they hugged in the hallway without kissing, and then he left for the station.

_ _ _ _ _ _ _ _ _

Phylida's attempts to track down Shelley Abrahams proved fruitless. Crozier had taken the day off and no one else at the Sketch would talk to her. The Sun and Mirror had picked up the Ffooks story and had printed two new photographs. One showed Abrahams on a street corner, again in a short skirt and heels, but this time with another woman whose face had been obscured.   The other image showed her outside a school clutching the hand of a small child.   Each paper repeated the Sketch storyline. She called the newsdesks of the Sun and Mirror and got nowhere. She googled Shelley Abrahams and found nothing. On LinkedIn there were eight women of the same name, and on Facebook a few dozen, but none matched the profile of the woman with Ffooks.

37

Amsterdam, Monday 27th June

While Landuzière and Spilotti took precautions, using open-access wifi, public phone networks, untraceable mobiles, always assigning names to numbers and bank account numbers to names, they still found it useful to meet face-to-face, somewhere where they could talk freely and sign and exchange documents. In the summer they met at the Black Crow in Amsterdam, flying in and out on the same day, dressed in their own version of Dutch incognito – Oakley sunglasses, t-shirts, and knee-length shorts – in the hope of blending with the thousands of cannabis tourists who frequented the city's smoker-friendly cafes. For September, October and November they joined up at Le Belgica, a gay bar in Brussels, both freshly bearded. For the winter months they chose the Aqua Spa Centre in Madrid, and for the spring, a café in the Galeries Lafayette, a large shopping mall near the centre of Nice.

Spilotti pushed back the heavy door of the Black Crow, took five tentative steps into the darkness and stopped. He closed his eyes to speed up their adjustment, while holding out a cautionary arm like a blind man guarding against the unfamiliar. Then from behind, Landuzière kicked his heel.

'Attendi,' snapped Spilotti. He counted to ten in his head and then opened his eyes. 'Ça va.'

The heavy beat of Black Uhuru filled the room. Spilotti moved forward and nodded at the bulky Rasta behind the counter. He ordered two espressos and an internet terminal. He placed a twenty euro note on the counter and said keep the change. The Rasta said nothing. No smile, no thank you for the tip, just a barely perceptible nod toward the door at the rear of the room. It was service without a smile, a

210

business model that only worked because the cannabis was cheap.

As they descended the unlit stairs to the basement, Landuzière reluctantly grabbed the handrail, knowing it was layered with the filthy sweat of countless deadheads. He hated everything about the Black Crow; the music, the customers, the darkness masquerading as atmosphere, but most of all, he hated the fug of floating cannabinoids. He'd complained to Spilotti that the place made it difficult to think straight. After their meetings, which could last from ten minutes to three hours, he always had a sense of bewilderment, that their discussion hadn't really happened, and most worrying of all, that their decisions were flawed.

On that particular afternoon, and to the relief of both men, the basement was empty of smokers. They could see easily from one side of the room to the other. Spilotti began by updating Landuzière on two players whose deals had gone through to completion – two Cameroonians had been signed by English clubs, bringing in one hundred thousand dollars of Camorra commissions. Landuzière talked about his forthcoming trip to South America, a fact-finding mission to see if they could establish a parallel operation. Their last item for discussion was Millwall. Landuzière keyed in www.millwallfc.co.uk and clicked on *What's New?* Then he clicked again on: *Millwall Boss Reaffirms Commitment.* Cowly's statement filled the screen:

> *In the light of recent press articles that have sought to disparage myself and others connected to Millwall, I feel it is necessary to restate my commitment to the club and my determination to continue with the project of establishing Millwall as a regular League Premiership side. The motives for these slurs and inferred allegations remain unclear. Moreover, we expect this cowardly campaign to continue. I hope all Millwall fans will pull together and continue to support the Board of Directors and the players. I can assure you*

that I have the resolve to see through these difficult times.

Tom Cowly, CEO Millwall FC.

Spilotti said, 'We need to do more. We need to destroy this man's resolve.'

'We could take her out,' suggested Landuzière, sliding his finger from left to right across his throat.

'Okay, why not? It can't do any harm.'

Landuzière nodded.

'And Goosen?' said Spilotti.

'We will owe him five thousand for the graffiti when he does it.'

'When are you seeing him next?'

'Nothing has been arranged.'

'Cut him off. We don't need him anymore.'

38

Brighton, Monday 27th June

In Brighton, Vince sat on the low brick wall that bordered
the beach volleyball, immediately regretting that he had left
his sun hat in London. He had timed it badly; Andy's game,
with two Poles, Tomek and Patryk, and a Serb, Predrag, had
only just begun. They'd be on court for at least an hour.
Jadranka, Andy's Croatia helper, was in the Pump Room
serving. After five minutes, and bored at the stop-start
game, Vince circled the court and shouted to Andy, 'I'll be
on the beach.' Andy raised a hand and nodded.

He stretched out on the shingle using his rucksack as a
pillow, and through the noise of gulls and breaking waves,
he dreamt of camping on an old railway line with a
punctured airbed. Then, with his eyes still shut, the dream
was broken. He rolled over, his face now away from the sun.
He dreamt this time of a muddy shoe hanging by its laces
under the West Pier, and underneath the shoe was a small
sign: ART-VISION. The dream rolled forward and Ailish
appeared from nowhere. They didn't speak. They undressed
and began having sex. But the act went unconsummated
because she was forced to stop. She had sand up her fanny
and she was still cleaning herself with a toothbrush when
Vince was disturbed by the coolness of Andy's shadow.

'Here's the key,' said Andy, his body a patchwork of
sand and sweat.

Vince lifted his head, squinting.

'You alright?'

'Just tired,' said Vince. 'I was on the sofa last night.'

Andy dropped the key on Vince's stomach.

'Thanks, I'll get one cut and come back later.'

Andy looked over at the queue in front of the Pump
Room. 'I'd better go. I need oranges.'

On his feet with his rucksack onto his back, Vince crunched along the beach in the direction of the wrecked West Pier. He sent a text to Kevin: *I'm in Brighton. Can I drop round?*

Seconds later he had a response: *Sure. I'm in. K*

He left the beach, crossed the Kingsway, and cut up to Western Road. Unshaven and red-faced, his belongings on his back, he had the look of a man of no fixed abode. He turned left towards Adelaide Crescent and on the way, at *Gill's Home and Garden*, Gill cut him a spare key.

– – – – – –

'I'm staying with a friend in Seven Dials,' said Vince to Kevin. 'He owns the Pump Room.'

Kevin shook his head. The name didn't register.

'In one of the arches, by the beach volleyball.'

'The Scots guy?'

Vince nodded.

Kevin poured hot water into two mugs. 'What are you going to do?'

'I'm not sure,' said Vince. 'What I'd like to do is...' Then he hesitated, knowing that their friendship might soon be over. 'I'd like to do something about Barros.'

Kevin turned to face him, a spoon and steaming teabag in his hand. 'It's not your problem Vince, stop worrying about me.' He dropped the spoon in the sink, picked up the mugs tea and walked into the lounge.

Vince followed, undiscouraged. 'I went to see Malisse and de la Rosa.'

'I thought you might have.' They sat down either side of the coffee table. Then knowing there was more to come, Kevin said, 'Go on.'

'First of all, Malisse and de la Rosa are gay. All Barros' players are gay...or bi.'

'So?'

'So that's his business. It's his speciality.'

Kevin nodded, nothing more. Then he picked up his tea.

'They're gay,' repeated Vince, thinking that perhaps Kevin hadn't quite understood his revelation.

214

'I heard you. It doesn't surprise me. I met Malisse once after a match. It was a charity event. I was only there for a few minutes and...'

Vince jumped in. 'And you could tell he was a bender?'

Kevin laughed. 'That's right. But it wasn't quite like that. He spotted me.'

'What did he say?'

'Nothing. It was just a look.'

'And you looked him back?'

Kevin shrugged. 'Not intentionally, but I guess we all give off signals we're not aware of.'

Vince thumped the arm of his chair. 'So why didn't you tell me? I've just driven halfway across Spain and France. I needn't have bothered.'

'Sorry Vince, but it's none of your business.'

Raising his voice, Vince said, 'They could have killed me.'

'Who?'

'Malisse's bodyguards. They tried to kidnap me, but I got away.' He lifted his right trouser leg to show off his scabby calf.

'Nasty.'

Exasperated, Vince leant forward and said, 'I'm trying to help you.'

'No Vince, you're confusing me with you.' Then Kevin pointed his finger. 'You're looking for a story. You need a story, but I'm not it.'

Vince held up his hands. 'Okay, I should have told you. I'm sorry.'

'No Vince, you were wrong to go. You said I could trust you, but...' Kevin sat back in his chair shaking his head, lost for words.

'Okay, but let me finish,' said Vince.

Kevin nodded once.

'Barros looks for people like you and Malisse. It's no accident he's your agent. He didn't just happen to see you kiss someone. Somehow he found you.'

'So he's smarter than we thought.' Then Kevin smiled. 'Perhaps he's gay and he used his gaydar?'

It was an explanation that Vince hadn't considered. 'Are you serious?'

'No, but anything's possible.'

Vince paused and said, 'He knows I was in France. I was photographed.'

'So what are you going to do?'

'I don't know. I don't have a plan.' Then half-heartedly, and because he couldn't help himself, he said, 'You could speak to Malisse and de la Rosa. Maybe Barros is up to something else illegal. We could get someone to investigate him, they could look at his finances, see if he has underworld connections, see if...' Vince trailed off.

'Listen Vince, forget it. You need to worry about yourself, not me. If Barros knows that you know about Malisse and de la Rosa, he'll do something. He has to.'

'That's why I've moved. He's got my London address.'

Kevin stood up and disappeared into the kitchen. He returned with two bottles of Grolsch and handed one to Vince. 'So your theory is that Barros goes round Europe spotting queers.'

'I don't know how, but he does. My guess is he starts with the internet.'

'What, he googled: *Kevin Furling gay?*'

'Err...not just that.'

'I've done it, there's nothing.'

'But some of your life is on the net. There are hundreds of photographs of you, mostly playing football or training or with the team, and sometimes with a woman, but there are none of you with a long-term girlfriend or partner.'

'It's not that easy,' said Kevin.

'I know that. But there's other stuff. Chat rooms where they talk about footballers that have or don't have girlfriends, and who's been dumped, and who's pregnant. So firstly, it's a desk job, a process of elimination. Barros eliminates ninety maybe ninety-five percent of players. For the League Premiership he ends up with a shortlist of around thirty. Then it's about observation. He watches each player or pays someone to watch them. He might use other gay men to make an approach. It would take time, but it's not difficult, and he knows for sure he's going to find you eventually.'

Kevin nodded. 'I suppose that's possible.'

'Not possible. It's a fact. Then the final part is to become your agent. I'm assuming you had an agent before Barros?'

'Yes, Malcolm Corby. He was with me for five years, before I joined Chelsea. There was a sort of handover, mid-contract. I was transferred from Corby to Barros. I was twenty-three and I wasn't really bothered who my agent was. The terms and conditions were the same and at the start Barros took the same percentage.'

'So Barros somehow engineered that changeover,' said Vince. 'Who vouched for him?'

'What do you mean?'

'How did you know Barros was any good?'

'I didn't. I met him...or I suppose he arranged to meet me. He said he would get me into a bigger club, which he did, and as I hardly ever saw Corby anyway, I switched. I didn't see how Barros could be any worse.'

They both stared down at the table, only the sound of gulls permeating the room.

Kevin was first to speak. 'You need to be very careful.'

'Well the worst he can do is kill me.' It was a poor joke and neither laughed.

'If he has other players besides de la Rosa and Malisse, his business could be worth twenty, thirty million. He's not going to let you threaten it. He could do anything, he could make you disappear.'

'Yes, I know, but that's risky too.' Vince was thinking of the letter he had sent to his sister Hayley when in Puigcerdá. If anything happened, the letter would come out into the open, the police would be involved.

'Why risky?' said Kevin.

'There'd be a police investigation.'

'Not if he disappears you. With no body, there would be no investigation.'

'But I've...' Then Vince paused. He couldn't tell Kevin about the letter. 'I'll take precautions,' he added. Then he wondered if Barros, or someone who worked for Barros, had followed him to Brighton. They could be outside now waiting for the right moment. 'Look, if Barros calls, tell him I came here. Say I was asking you about Malisse, but that's all. There's no need to mention de la Rosa.'

'Then what?'

'I don't know. Maybe I should leave...go overseas.' Vince took a mouthful of beer. 'I'd better go.' Then he stood and walked to the balcony window and looked out over the gardens. Just picnickers and couples. He scanned the parked cars. 'How do you pay him?'

'We have a contract. I pay his company a flat forty-five percent of all my earnings.'

Vince turned back in. 'Simple as that, no offshore accounts?'

'No, it's all legal. He even handles my tax affairs.'

'You've got a blackmailer who minimises your tax liabilities?'

'Yes. Last year he said he saved me over a hundred grand.'

'Jesus.'

Ten minutes after Vince had left, Kevin's phone rang.

'Hi Phylida, how are you?

'I'm okay thanks. I was thinking I could come down tomorrow. Would that be alright?'

'Yes, do that. I'll meet you at Brighton Station.'

– – – – – – – –

Tuesday 28th June

The next morning, with a bundle of newspapers under one arm, Phylida boarded a train to London. Over breakfast in First Class, she leafed through the tabloids searching for follow-ups to the story on Ken Ffooks. Turning each page, she half expected to see her own face staring back. But what would be the storyline? *Cowly's right-hand woman has no secrets! Phylida Cranson admits to no sex for two years! Cranson dislikes step-mother!* Then she wondered if being with Kevin would change things. Would she become newsworthy, a WAG in the boardroom? Ten minutes out from Liverpool Street Station, she called Craig Crozier and said, 'What's the story this time?'

'No different. The photographs were sent to my sub-editor. He asked me to verify that Abrahams had a police record and that was it.'

'Have you been in touch with her?'

'No.'

'And did you speak to Ffooks?'

'No.'

'Do you have Abrahams' phone number or address?' She was expecting another no.

'I'll have a look,' said Crozier. 'I'll call you back. I've got to go.'

When he finally returned her call it was late afternoon, and she was on a different train down to Brighton. He had Abrahams' address but no phone number.

As her train slowed under the double-spanned roof of Brighton Station, she studied her reflection in the sliding door. She moved in closer and pouted. Then wetting a fingertip, she traced a line along the edge of her bottom lip. Out on the platform she pulled at the cuffs of her navy jacket and glanced down at her suede Nota Bene shoes. Happy that all was in order, she looked towards the ticket barrier.

Kevin saw her; a woman dressed for business, in a dark trouser suit with her hair tied back, a laptop bag over one shoulder. He waved.

She saw a large group of people, some holding balloons and others placards. It looked like a homecoming. To the left, standing apart from the crowd, she saw a man in a baseball cap and t-shirt waving his arms. She couldn't see Kevin. When through the ticket barrier and amongst the well-wishers, she was tapped on the shoulder. She turned, her puzzled frown holding until Kevin removed his hat and sunglasses.

'Sorry, I must have walked straight past you,' she said. 'I saw you wave but I thought you were someone else.'

'My fault,' he said. 'I should have said what I'd be wearing.' They shook hands and kissed cheeks. Then a cheer rang out as the homecoming hero rolled down the metal ramp from the front carriage.

Kevin looked over his shoulder and said, 'Come on, let's go.' He grasped her free hand, and without looking back, led her out to the taxi rank. 'We could go down to the beach?'

She nodded and glanced down at their clasped hands.

Following her gaze, he immediately let go. 'Sorry.'

She smiled at him. 'No need. It was nice of you.'

Their taxi dropped them opposite the Brighton Centre. Kevin pulled his hat down low and replaced his sunglasses. They set off along the upper promenade side by side, their hands occasionally touching.

'I still haven't spoken to Vince Wynter,' she said.

'I saw him yesterday. He's just moved down.'

'Perhaps I should call him while I'm here.'

'He may be closer than you think.' Kevin pointed down to the lower promenade. 'He has a friend who runs a cafe on the seafront. We can have a look.'

They turned onto the wide ramp that led down to the lower promenade. Then heading westwards, they passed a dozen or more bars and cafes, each serving much the same fare, while striving to look different. At the Pump Room, Kevin circled the short queue by the ice cream counter and peered into the arch. 'Vince,' he said, then louder, 'Vince!'

Vince had his head half inside the deep freeze, searching for a blueberry and apple smoothie bag. He straightened and turned.

'New job?' said Kevin.

'Just helping out.'

'Can we talk?'

Vince looked at the queue. 'We're a bit busy just now.'

'I can manage,' said Jadranka, snatching the smoothie bag from his hand. 'You speak to your friend.' Given the choice, she preferred to work alone rather than with Vince. He asked too many questions and didn't clean up his mess. 'Andy will be back soon,' she added, 'you take your time.' She pushed Vince through the gap between the juicer and fridge and out onto the brick pavement.

'You know Phylida?' said Kevin.

'Yes, I got your message. I was going to call back, but...'
Phylida nodded but she didn't offer her hand.

'Would you like to talk now?' said Vince.

She looked at Kevin and shrugged her shoulders. 'I guess we could. Do you mind?'

'I'll come back later,' said Kevin.

'There's no need for that, it's not a private matter.'

Vince picked up two empty coffee cups and an ashtray from one of the Pump Room's tables and dragged in a third chair. As Phylida and Kevin sat, he said, 'What would you like?'

'I'll have a smoothie,' said Phylida, 'any flavour.'

'Me too,' said Kevin.

A few minutes later Vince reappeared with two plastic glasses, one with a mauve filling, the other green. 'Take your pick,' he said. Then he sat down, crossed his arms and looked at Phylida.

'Did you see the Sketch this week?' she said.

'No, I've not seen any papers.'

'There've been a few stories. It looks like someone's out to damage us.'

Vince shook his head. He had no idea what she meant.

'One was about Tom Cowly, you probably remember him from the press conference, and the other on Ken Ffooks. Ken heads up the Church's Investment Fund.'

'So?' said Vince, glancing at Kevin.

'Have you ever worked for the Sketch?'

'Once, about ten years ago.'

'Do you still know people there?'

'No.'

'Do you know Craig Crozier?'

'No, never heard of him. I've not worked for any paper for two years.'

'But you must have some contacts, some friends?'

'Not really.'

Phylida nodded. She didn't believe him, but she let it pass. 'What about your disagreement with Mr Barros?'

'What about it?' Vince glanced at Kevin, unsure of how much he should say.

221

'Kevin has told me about the problem over the book. I suppose what it is, we don't want Millwall dragged into some dispute that you may have with Mr Barros. You brought your problem with Barros onto club property, where there were others around, journalists and photographers.'

'I'm sorry about that, it wasn't deliberate.'

'Ángel handled it badly,' said Kevin. 'Vince did a good job on the book and deserved to be paid. As I said, it wasn't his fault that the deal fell through.'

'But is there still a problem?' she said, looking at Vince.

'Not anymore. I've read the contract. Barros was right. If it's not published, the publishers don't pay anyone.'

'We might do an ebook,' said Kevin.

'And Barros is happy with that?' said Phylida.

'Yes,' said Kevin.

'Good.' She had nothing more to say. She picked up the green smoothie and sucked on the straw.

'If that's all, I'd better get back,' said Vince. He pointed with his thumb toward the queue of customers. Then he stood, shook Phylida's hand, and told Kevin he would be in touch. A minute later, from behind the Pump Room's counter, Vince watched them walk away, laughing and zigzagging their way between skateboarders. Then he turned and scanned the spectators around the volleyball court, searching in vain for a face that didn't fit.

An hour later, after a fried egg sandwich at the Meeting Place Cafe, Phylida was on Kevin's sofa, barefooted, her legs drawn up. She decided there would be no more talk of football or smear stories or Barros and books. She was smiling when Kevin came into the room with two glasses of wine.

'You look pleased,' he said

'Just daydreaming.' She had him naked on the floor.

He sat beside her with an inch or two of separation, his right arm along the back of the sofa. 'Do you have any plans?'

'Not really,' she said. 'I suppose I'll carry on at BSM and see where it takes me.'

He laughed and dropped his hand to her knee. 'No, I mean tonight, plans for tonight. Would you like to go out?'

'Sorry I...I've train to catch.'

'If you want, you could stay over. I've got a spare room.'

She smiled and then reddened. She needed to know more about him before agreeing to stay the night. 'That's nice of you, but you've probably got plans, friends to see...girlfriends?' She sipped her wine.

He smiled. 'No girlfriends. I'm free tonight, tomorrow and next week and the week after. What about you?'

She ignored his question. 'I thought you would be fighting them off?'

'No. I guess I'm not really interested in women that are interested in footballers.'

'That can't be right. There must be others out there?'

'I suppose, but I don't seem to meet them. I'm not boasting, but on the seafront I get propositioned by teenagers...fifty-year olds...all sorts, but it's only because I played for Chelsea.' He looked down and slapped his thighs. 'I was born with lucky legs.'

She looked down too, at his hands, his thighs and then his crotch. She could see movement. She could feel a wetness spreading.

'Anyway,' he said. 'I thought you would be more of a rugby woman.'

'Not really.' She looked up and then down again. 'So you've got your lucky legs, but no girlfriend.' She tilted her head to one side and pouted. 'Poor Kevin.'

He laughed, took her glass and placed it on the table. Standing, he held out his hand. 'Come on, I'll show you around.' He led her straight into his bedroom at the front of the apartment. They stopped in the doorway, at the transition from wooden floor to deep-pile carpet. The evening sun streamed in, yellowing the room. He watched her as her eyes moved from the watercolour above the mantelpiece, to the corner armchair, to the full length mirror, and then finally the bed.

'It's nice,' she said. She walked over to the front window and looked down over the gardens. He followed her, stood behind her and put his hand on her shoulder. Then she laughed. She laughed at a man sprinting down Adelaide Gardens towards the sea, trying to create a breeze that would lift his kite. The man's young son stood to one side, licking his lolly, unimpressed by his father's efforts.

Kevin removed her jacket and dropped it to the floor. She reached back with her right hand and touched him with an open palm. Then she turned and glanced down. 'I think gravity needs some help.'

'You might be right.'

She knelt, untied the drawstring around his waist and pulled his shorts clear. Then with one hand on his thigh, she licked the underside, from base to tip and then took it in her mouth.

'Phy, just a minute.'

She froze and looked up. Kevin pointed to the window. Looking sideways she saw the kite flying father, arms folded, starring up at them. She tumbled backwards and shouted, 'Shit.'

Kevin waved once to the man, drew the curtains and then helped her to her feet. 'Are you okay?' he said.

'Yes, I guess. Sorry about that.'

'It wasn't your fault.' He put his left hand to her neck and kissed her lips. 'At least he didn't have a camera.'

'Oh god!' she said.

'I didn't see one, or a phone.' Kevin peeked between the curtains. 'He's gone.' He took her hands and led her to the bed.

39

Millwall FC, Wednesday morning, 29th June

Detective Sergeant Gateley and two uniformed constables arrived at the Den as the Millwall monthly board meeting got underway. Gateley spoke to the receptionist and then to Jennifer Halfpenny, the assistant head of marketing. A detective sergeant for three years, he used up much of his spare time playing second-row for Dorking fifths, watching the Sport Channel, and eating his wife's food. But occasionally, when boozed up and in the company of strangers, i.e. anyone that didn't work for the Met or play for Dorking, he would tell them about his plan to publish a limerick anthology; an A to Z on the world of crime.

He'd been writing them, on and off, for two years, beginning with 'Aiding and Abetting', and 'Assault and Battery', and had recently started on the Ds: 'Dangerous Dogs', 'Delinquency', and 'Death by Strangulation'. He worked on them whenever his wife was out or asleep; refining and reengineering, searching for the right balance of rhyme and rhythm, and though he had over a hundred that were ready to go, no one had seen any of his work. And to protect his intellectual property, he kept them all in a locked metal box at the back of his garage, determined, above all else, not to become a victim of limerick theft.

While Gateley talked to Halfpenny, up in the boardroom Hardwick gave a brief summary on each of the club's new signings. The Financial Director, Eric Thomas, followed on with an overview of the likely contract costs, saying that the net outlay – three players were leaving to clubs in the lower leagues – would be in the region of fifteen million. The second agenda item concerned the press articles on Cowly and Ffooks. Cowly led the discussion, asserting that the articles were fabrications. He acknowledged that while they had been expecting some criticism of the Church takeover, he hadn't expected the attacks to be so personal.

He summed up. 'These past few days haven't been good, but I'm still committed. I'm not going anywhere.' Though his words were intended to reassure, for some they had the opposite affect: Eric Thomas was wondering if he'd been photographed during a visit to a strip club in Bangkok; the Director of Licensing and Merchandise recalled his affair with a shop assistant in the Megastore while his wife had been pregnant; and Hardwick relived the night that he'd been hauled down the police station for pissing in a bus shelter.

Cowly looked over to Ffooks before delivering his final word on the matter. 'There are no skeletons in Ken's cupboard or mine, and neither of us has any intention of resigning.' It was a half-truth. Just prior to the board meeting, Cowly had spoken to Ffooks, saying that he would understand if Ffooks wanted out. All Cowly asked of him, was that for now, for the next couple or three weeks, they presented a united front.

Ffooks had agreed, but said no more. He didn't tell Cowly that he regarded the Church's investment in Millwall as an annoying distraction, or that if there was more to come, more lies and innuendo, he would resign and seek a settlement. He wasn't prepared to have his name and family dragged through the gutter just because the Church was on a mission to boost its popularity.

As Ffooks began reading out the statement he'd prepared for the afternoon press conference, Jennifer Halfpenny slipped into the room. Not wanting to disrupt the meeting, she tiptoed around the head of table, her body stooped. Ffooks paused as she whispered her message to Phylida. 'The police want to speak to Ken. They're not prepared to wait.' Then she turned and tiptoed out.

Phylida looked at Ffooks and then Cowly. 'Carry on. I'll deal with it.' She left the room and went down to reception. As she reached the three officers, she smiled, and then looked to Jennifer for an introduction.

'This is Detective Sergeant Gateley,' said Jennifer.

Phylida offered her hand. 'Hello Sergeant. I'm Phylida Cranson. How can I help?'

Gateley shook his head, irritated that he was standing in front of another person he hadn't asked to see. His eyes flicked to her ringless left hand. 'I'm not sure you can Miss. I've asked to see Kenneth Ffooks. I asked at reception, then I asked this person here.' He pointed at Jennifer. 'And now you. I don't need or want to see anyone else other than Ffooks. I want you to get him down here now.'

'He's in a meeting,' said Phylida. 'He won't be long.' Then she smiled again, hoping that her reasonable explanation would suffice.

Gateley looked down at his size twelve's and swore under his breath. When he looked up, he said, 'Go and get him.'

Phylida shook her head, feigning puzzlement, while visualising her knee rising into his groin.

Not getting the response he wanted, he tried again, 'Miss, get him down here or I'll arrest the two of you for interfering with a police investigation.'

'But what it's about?' said Phylida, gesturing with open hands. 'Why can't you tell me?' Then she spotted it; just beneath his right ear, a tiny dangling tattooed spider. She raised a hand to her mouth, fighting back the urge to laugh.

'What is it Phy?' said Jennifer, thinking something had upset her.

Gateley tugged self-consciously at his collar. Curious, Jennifer peered up at his neck. He'd had enough. He leant forward, just inches from Phylida's face. She stood her ground, but at his first shouted word, she stepped back, repulsed by the smell of sweet instant coffee and stale cigarettes. 'The reason I'm not telling you,' said Gateley, 'is because it's none of your effing business.' He straightened up and glanced at his uniformed colleagues, as if daring them to speak.

Phylida looked him up and down, and imagined an overgrown schoolboy in grey shorts, his seam busting blazer tight across his shoulders, and on his splayed feet, a giant pair of Ninja Turtle daps. 'Mr Spiderman,' she said, 'my name is PHY-LI-DA CRAN-SON. If you have a crayon handy, you can write it down.'

One of the constables stifled a laugh.

Gateley sneered and said, 'We just need to speak to him.'

'Thank you Sergeant. That wasn't so difficult was it?'

Then an unsettling smile crossed his face. 'You see Miss Cranson, Ffooks' whore is dead.'

Momentarily she didn't make the connection. 'You mean Shelley Abrahams?'

Gateley's smile widened. 'Yes, Abrahams.'

Phylida stared ahead, trying to make sense of it.

Seeing her discomfort, Gateley took advantage. 'Shot in the head, she was. Blood all over the place.'

Phylida broke her gaze and looked up. 'Is Ken Ffooks a suspect?'

'He might be. That's why I need to speak to him. It's called police work.'

'Does he have to speak to you?'

'If he refuses, we'll take him in for questioning.'

She nodded. 'I'll be right back.'

Up in the boardroom she gestured to Ffooks that he was wanted downstairs and then she signalled to Cowly that they should wind things up.

Out in the corridor, Ffooks said, 'What is it?'

'Shelley Abrahams is dead. She's been murdered.'

'What?'

'The woman in the photograph, in the newspaper.'

'Yes, I understand,' but Ffooks didn't. He forgot about his body and that he was standing. His legs started to buckle.

She grabbed his upper arm and edged him to the side wall. 'Ken, are you okay?' He lifted his head and nodded. 'The police are downstairs. I think it's just procedure.'

In reception Jennifer led Gateley and the two constables to a small room with a table and four chairs. When Ffooks appeared she waved him in and closed the door. Five minutes later the door opened and Gateley left for the Mandarin to verify Ffooks' whereabouts.

Cowly looked into the room and said, 'Ken?'

Ffooks stared blankly ahead, his fingers interlocked, his thumbs jammed together. He was contemplating a different future where his name would forever be linked to the death of a prostitute.

Cowly walked in. 'Ken, come on, let's go.' With no response, he squeezed Ffooks' shoulder.

'Where to?' said Ffooks, his gaze still fixed on the far wall.

'To the Mandarin and call your lawyer.' Cowly turned to Jennifer. 'Would you get a cab to meet us out front?' She nodded and left the room. 'Phy, grab his arm.' Standing either side, they encouraged Ffooks to his feet.

When just yards from the waiting cab Ffooks threw his arms down, breaking their grip. 'I'm alright. Leave me be.'

'Where's Eileen?' said Phylida.

'It doesn't matter. She'll be with me. We're going home.'

'Will you see he gets there?' said Cowly to Jennifer.

Ffooks raised an open hand in front of Cowly's face. He was done with taking advice, and done with Millwall. He'd accepted the job in good faith and they'd ruined him.

As the cab pulled away, Phylida said to Cowly, 'What about the press conference, shall I call it off?'

'No, we go ahead.'

– – – – – – – –

Within an hour of Ffooks' departure, the news about Abrahams had spread far and wide. The first tweeters said Ffooks had been arrested, and that he was a suspect. In the second hour, thousands of re-tweets asserted their own versions of the truth. That:

> *Abrahams had been carrying Ffooks' child, that a good/dead whore is a dead/good whore; that Ffooks deserves everything that is coming his way; that the Church and the League Premiership were managed by a bunch of whore fuckers...*

As the tweet traffic built, uninvited journalists and a hundred or so rubberneckers started arriving at the ground, homing in on the epicentre of the story. Unable to gain access to the official press conference, the journalists were forced to operate via tablet and phone from the club's car park, and soon their growing presence became an opportunity for others. Just after one o'clock the first burger van parked up and soon after that a Mr Whippy, and by two the car park had reached capacity, and at 2.16, inside the stadium, Phylida quietened the room.

Hardwick was first to speak. No one had asked him to hurry, but he knew that his news was now of little interest to any of his audience. Staring down at a yellow post-it, he cleared his throat and sped through the names of the players that would be joining Millwall for the new season. As an afterthought he added, 'and we've sold Duncan Lodden and Wayne Older,' not bothering to mention the transfer fees or where they were going. He glanced at Phylida and nodded that he was done.

'Any questions?' she said. A few heads turned, but no hands went up. 'Over to you Tom.'

Cowly leaned in closer to the microphone, unfolded his statement and placed it on the table. 'Thank you for coming along today and my apologies to those that we've been unable to accommodate.' The Sport Channel were broadcasting live and he knew that those in the car park would be listening in. 'Originally we scheduled this press conference to announce our new signings, signings that we think will ensure the club becomes an established LPFL side. Unfortunately, that good news has been overshadowed by other events. Ken Ffooks and I had also planned to make a joint statement today to refute the recent news articles about our private lives. Those articles were manufactured and fed to the press solely to damage this club and the work we're doing. I think it's regrettable that some newspapers should have taken such easy bait. They have acted as the agents of those that are too cowardly to speak for themselves.' He paused and stared at the journalist in the middle of the third row: Craig Crozier.

Crozier looked down and tapped at his phone.

'We don't mind being criticised. We expect it. The acquisition of the club and the bold steps taken by the Church of England were bound to upset some people. Stepping forward and not following the crowd always does. But as you all know, a few hours ago the Metropolitan Police announced the killing of Shelley Abrahams and I would like to express my deepest sympathy to her family. A murder investigation is now underway and we will be giving the police all the assistance they need. However, to my knowledge there is nothing linking her death to anyone at this club. Ken Ffooks has spoken to the police. We were both at a London hotel when this horrific event took place.

He turned a page. 'Ken Ffooks has been the subject of a disgusting smear story and those that have assisted in that smear should never attempt to set foot in this stadium again. So I would like to ask the reporter from The Sketch to leave now.' Crozier stood and began shuffling sideways along the row of chairs. As he made his way to the door, Cowly added, 'I realise you weren't personally responsible, but your employer was.'

When Crozier closed the door, Cowly said, 'I am prepared to take questions, but if any, I repeat, if any are to do with Shelley Abrahams they will not be answered. I never knew her, I had never heard of her until Sunday, and the same can be said for Ken Ffooks.' He nodded to Phylida.

'Thank you Tom,' she said. 'We have plenty of time, so please be patient, and please state your name and representation before asking your question.' She pointed to a woman in the front row.

'Mary Harris, The Times. Mr Cowly, who is it that you think is seeking to damage Millwall and do you think Shelley Abrahams' death is related to the Church's involvement?'

Cowly shook his head, tapping the table with his fingers. 'I think the press articles were malicious, that's what I think. And I've just said I don't know who killed Shelley Abrahams and that I've never met or heard of her. I'm not

231

going to speculate.' He raised his voice. 'Do you understand that?'

Harris nodded, accepting the reprimand.

Cowly scanned the room. 'And the photographs of me and Ken Ffooks and Shelley Abrahams that were sent to newspapers,' he pointed at his audience, 'if you want to know why and how and who and when,' with every other word he stabbed the air, 'you'd better ask your tabloid colleagues. They're in this room.' He drew his finger from left to right and back again, as if searching them out. 'Ask them after we've finished.' Cowly's forehead glistened and the room fell silent while he paused. 'Clearly someone dislikes this club, and like you, I want to know why, but I don't have the answers now.' He wiped his brow with the back of his hand and nodded at Phylida that he was ready for the next question.

She pointed to Mark Groenig.

'Mark Groenig, the Sport Channel. Tom, do you think this will make the Church reconsider its decision to invest in football?'

'Mark, that's another question I can't answer. It's entirely a matter for the Church Commissioners. Personally, I hope they will stick with Millwall. I feel we've made a good start and that we'll have a positive impact on the league. I expect to be meeting with the Assets Committee later this week and I envisage a statement will be released shortly after that.'

'So you've not spoken to the Commissioners yet?' added Groenig.

'No, we haven't. Mark, this has only just happened.' He looked at his watch. 'Three hours ago.'

Phylida pointed to a man on the back row.

'Dave Williams, The South London Press. If the smears persist or escalate, what are you going to do?'

'Right now,' said Cowly, 'we're not going to do anything. We're going to carry on, business as usual. The squad will come together in a week or two for pre-season training.' Cowly looked to Hardwick who nodded. 'Then there are warm up matches which will go ahead as planned.'

He shifted in his chair. 'Let me make it clear, the club's resolve is undiminished. We aim to build a team and a business that is an asset to the English game. This club will be a beacon for the local community and a role model for other clubs to follow. We won't be walking away because someone wants us out.'

Phylida waited a few seconds unsure if he had finished. Then she pointed at Henry Barnes, from the Evening Standard.

'Are you going to take legal action against The Sketch?' said Barnes.

'No,' said Cowly, 'but their newspapers, their employees are barred from this club. That's all l can do.' He picked up a facsimile of a Sketch photograph of Shelley Abrahams with her son outside his school. Then he turned and looked directly into the Sport Channel's camera, and holding the image close to his face, he addressed her killers. 'To me, these articles are hateful. You have no excuses, no public interest defence. You are gutless filth and soon we'll find out who you are and why you murdered this woman.' He placed the facsimile back on the table and turned back to his audience. 'And if we find that the publication of her photograph with Ken Ffooks was instrumental in her death, it will be up to the owners of The Sketch to explain why they did what they did.'

Phylida pressed her hands together, the tips of her fingers resting lightly against her lips. He had surprised her. She had never seen him angry, so passionate. After four more questions she wound it up. Most of them couldn't be answered and Cowly had said 'no comment' to anyone that mentioned Shelley Abrahams' name.

40

The Star of Princes, Wednesday afternoon 29th June

Goosen swung round on his bar stool. With sore feet and knees and nothing to report to Landuzière, he was beginning to regret his decision to arrange the anti-Gülen/anti-Manas graffiti along the Fulham Road. He had spent the day visiting skate parks in northwest London, talking to wary teenagers, telling them he was looking for a street artist to decorate his garden wall. A couple of days earlier, he'd done the same in East London, around Newham and Stratford. Knowing his story lacked plausibility, it came as no surprise that his plan hadn't worked. Over the two days he met just one person – tag-name: *miF* – who was prepared to do it. But when Goosen had explained what he wanted, miF replied, 'Look mate, I don't want any interference. I do it, like I always do...when the time's right.' Goosen then decided that he was unbiddable and too risky to use.

He starred at the television on the back wall of the bar and read the stuttering dialogue running along the bottom of the screen. Then the news reporter's face was replaced by a photo of Shelley Abrahams. He cursed the barman's absence and scanned around for the remote control. Seconds later the news reporter reappeared. Goosen's eyes jumped from lips to text and back to lips.

> . . .THE METROPOLITAN POLICE HAVE YET
> TO. . . ASCERTAIN A MOTIVE FOR HER
> BRUTAL MURDER. IT HAPPENED SOMETIME
> BEFORE MIDNIGHT THE POLICE ARE
> APPEALING FOR WITNESSES. . .

He slammed the bar with a flat hand. Then the camera cut to two police cars and an unmarked white van, and then to a

234

zoned off pavement and a dark puddle-sized stain. He knew it was a hit and that no matter who the police questioned or fingerprinted, they wouldn't pin it on a pimp or any drug-fuelled mugger. They had both been used, and for reasons he couldn't guess at, she'd been sacrificed. He turned away from the screen and glanced at the three other drinkers in the pub, each at a separate table. The one to his far right he had seen before in the pub car park. He was a window cleaner with a white escort van. The second man, wearing socks and crocs, was asleep, his head resting against the yellowed wall. The third seemed to be fully absorbed in his newspaper puzzles.

Turning back, and with the barman still away, Goosen picked out a fiver from a bunch of notes and left it for the pie and chips that hadn't yet arrived. He walked out, crossed the road and waited just out of sight from the pub's entrance. He doubted any of the men inside were watching him, but he wanted to be sure. He called Landuzière, and as expected, the number didn't ring.

Goosen had staged the photograph of Ffooks talking to Abrahams soon after he'd taken the pictures of Cowly and Imee. He first saw her at Liverpool Street Station while on another assignment; her heels were so high, she couldn't bend her knees. Then he realised she was working the crowd. For fifteen minutes he watched her chatting to strangers, all businessmen, all in suits, and after each conversation she would offer her card and move on. Goosen thought he could use her. He bought a newspaper and went over and stood beside her.

Within seconds she came round to face him. 'Been waiting long?' she said. Before he could answer she told him she was meeting a friend on a train from Norwich.

Goosen nodded, encouraging her to make her pitch.

After thirty seconds on the weather and the busyness of the station, she said, 'Do you live here? Are you staying in London?' Then she raised her hand, her fingers and thumb framing a glossy business card. 'You might like this', she added.

Goosen swayed back, trying to focus on the white on red writing.

'The Healthy Living Centre', she said, recognising his difficulty. 'It's a therapy and massage clinic off Whitechapel Road. Take it. You never know. We're online and it's all legal.'

Goosen thanked her, took the card and merged back into the crowd. He continued to watch her. When she had shaken hands and said goodbye to two more potential clients, he approached her. 'We spoke a few moments ago. I was wondering if...'

'No,' she said, cutting him off. 'You need to call the...'

'No, not that,' said Goosen. He handed her her card. 'My name and number is on the back. Give me a call if you want to earn some extra cash. Don't worry it's not for sex.'

She nodded and tuned the card over. 'Maybe I will.'

He offered his hand. 'Robin Lithgow.'

'Shelley Abrahams.'

Goosen walked away and she called him that evening.

'Mr Lithgow, we met at the station. It's Shelley.'

'Yes, I remember,' said Goosen. Earlier he'd asked a former colleague at the Met for a CRB check. She had a police record for soliciting and had done time in Holloway. She was perfect.

'You said you had some work?' said Abrahams.

They met up an hour later at the cafe inside the Park Royal ASDA off Western Road. Goosen was first to arrive. He bought a pot of tea for two and a couple of iced buns and sat down at a corner table away from the counter and the till.

She arrived out of her work clothes and clean of make-up, dressed in a pink tracksuit and trainers. She sat down and said, 'I can't stay long. I have to pick my son up at nine.'

Goosen nodded. 'Ten minutes, that's all. I need some photographs, photographs of a man talking to an attractive woman.'

'You mean a hooker?'

He smiled. 'Well, someone that can look like a hooker. I want you to stop him in the street, ask him a question...the

236

time...directions, anything. Then I'll take the pictures. That's it.'

'How much?'

'Five hundred.'

'And then what?'

'That's it, job done.'

'And the photographs?' she said.

'I'm doing them for someone else. I'll hand them over. They could end up in the papers.'

'Is he famous?'

'He's a businessman, a sort of banker.'

'Is he dangerous?'

'No, he's harmless.'

'So what's he done wrong?'

'I don't know. I'm just being paid to get the photos.'

She took a bite from the bun. 'Five hundred in cash?'

'And another five hundred if it goes well. I want to do the same thing with another man.'

'And that's it?' she said.

'If anyone asks you what it was about, if it gets into the papers, tell them an Australian called Lithgow paid you.'

'You don't mind?'

'I can't stop you and you might be offered some money for your story.' As far as Goosen was concerned, everyone's life, whether they were a Prime Minister or a hooker, was governed largely by risk/reward ratios. He reckoned the prospect of more money would ensure her co-operation.

'Okay I'll do it,' she said.

Still on the pavement opposite The Star of Princes, Goosen opened the back of his phone, removed the battery, and slid out the SIM card with his thumb nail. Bending down, he dropped it all through a roadside drain. Then as he waited a few more minutes, scanning the road on either side, he wondered what would happen to her orphaned son. She had talked about his talent for drawing and mimicry, his energy, and his obsession with tractors. And while they'd waited two hours for Ffooks to appear, she never once complained. She talked of cleaning kitchens and offices, of helping out on a stall in Camden Lock, and without

237

embarrassment or shame, of her occasional evening work for a blowjob agency in Brixton. The blowjob jobs, she said, were her backstop for when money was tight.

Inside the pub the three men hadn't moved, and behind the bar the television continued to report on the Shelley Abrahams' murder. Beside a grainy image of a black BMW, the screen read.

> . . .THE METROPOLITAN POLICE HAVE JUST ISSUED A PHOTOGRAPH OF THE VEHICLE USED BY SHELLEY ABRAHAMS' ATTACKERS. THE POLICE WOULD LIKE TO HEAR FROM ANYONE WHO RECOGNISES THIS CAR.

From the CCTV footage and information provided by Abrahams' family, and with the help of a Metropolitan Police lip-reader, the initial police report on the incident stated:

At 10.37 pm the victim, Shelley Abrahams, was walking home along Kimberley Avenue after spending the afternoon at her sister's in Clapham. She was wearing jeans and white trainers and a long-sleeved top. Her head turned as she saw a black saloon car (BMW 520i) pull up in front, close to the curb. She slowed and stopped just back from the rear bumper. She transferred her bag from her left hand to her right shoulder. The window of the front passenger door opened. An unshaven, middle-aged man smiled at her. The man had thinning hair. The man said, 'Hello, we are lost. We are looking for the Northern Circular.' Immediately Ms Abrahams was attacked from behind by a second man. The second man grabbed her wrist while his other arm came over her left shoulder around her neck. The second man forced her down onto her knees. He pushed her forward, closer to the car. Then a third man, from the rear door of the car, fired one shot at her head. The second man released his grip and she fell to the pavement. The second man wiped blood and fragments of skin and bone from his face, then he picked up her bag, stepped clear of the body and climbed into the rear of the BMW. The car accelerated away.

The digital clock on the CCTV tape showed that it all happened in twenty-eight seconds. But there was more. As the tape ran on, a man in a hoodie stopped and stared down at her body. He quickly looked up and down the street. Then as he bent down to search her jean pockets, his dog raised a rear leg and squirted two jet of piss onto her bloodied head.

Back at his flat Goosen packed two bags and caught a train to Gatwick Airport.

41

Robert Caldicott had spent the last working week rewriting a report on 'The Revitalisation of UK Manufacturing'. The original draft by DoB had been quarantined. Sir Terrence had deemed it unfit for publication, a problem of increasing regularity affecting all Government departments. Some blamed the cutbacks. The budget for external consultants had been slashed and civil servants were being forced to do their own thinking and writing. At DoB the situation was particularly serious. The Department's Permanent Secretary had overdone the redundancies and then been forced to recruit outsiders from the private sector; people that knew nothing of the ways of Government.

The draft Revitalisation report had been written by a small team headed by Hugo Stormance, an Oxford graduate who in 1999 started a dotcom business called *IronMaidens*. It offered an on-demand and bespoke ironing service for time-short Londoners. He raised £25 million in venture capital and spent most of the money on a fleet of mopeds that cruised the city night and day, each one with a fold-away ironing board and iron strapped to the rear.

Stormance's report, according to Sir Terrence, contained too much opinion, too much criticism of past initiatives, and far too many objectives. He had handed it over to Caldicott with the instruction to neuter it.

'...the police say they have no reason to believe the Archbishop of Canterbury is linked to the murder of Shelley Abrahams...'

Caldicott smiled and switched off the TV. 'You couldn't make it up,' he said to himself. Then Sir Terrence called. Caldicott assumed it was about the DoB report.

240

'Are you busy?'

'Not especially,' said Caldicott.

'Drop round would you?'

He pulled on his jacket, grabbed his diary and headed down the parquet corridor to Sir Terrence's office. The door was open so he knocked once and walked in.

'Robert?' The voice came from the bathroom/annex to the rear of Sir Terrence's office.

'Yes.'

'Sorry for the late call. Was about to leave myself.'

Caldicott heard an unzipping, then a damn, and then, 'I'll be with you in a moment. I'm just trying to...'

A minute later Sir Terrence appeared, red-faced and barefooted, clutching a cycle helmet and shoes, clad from neck to ankles in a skin-tight body suit. 'Sorry about the...,' and he gestured to his outfit. 'I'm in training. Got myself talked into joining the local cycle club. Better for your knees you know.'

'So I've heard,' said Caldicott, though he hadn't.

Sir Terence placed his shoes and helmet on his desk and picked up his remote. 'What it is Robert, is this.' The wall-mounted TV screen lit up and he began scrolling through a list of pre-recorded programmes. 'I meant to mention it to you earlier.'

But Caldicott's eyes weren't on the screen. They were looking down at Sir Terrence's feet and his yellowed, crumbling toenails.

Sir Terrence looked down too and wriggled his toes. 'They say technology is the future, but I suspect for many of us, it's fungal.'

Caldicott nodded sympathetically and turned to the screen. The recording was a Sky News broadcast from the central lobby of the Palace of Westminster. Caldicott recognised the bearded face of John Woodendale MP, the Chair of the Culture, Media and Sport Select Committee.

'I'm afraid I didn't get the very beginning.' Sir Terrence pressed play.

A question, from an unseen Sky reporter, came first. *'Isn't this going to dilute the Committee's principal aim?'*

Woodendale: *'No, I don't think so. It'll simply push back the date we intend to report. We'll spend more time interviewing and taking evidence. As I've already said, in light of recent press reports, we think it would be prudent for the committee to look in some depth at the impact of religion on club ownership.'*

Sky Reporter: *'You're doing this because you believe the Gülen is involved?'*

Woodendale: *'No, not at all. When the Church acquired Millwall there were concerns amongst some of my colleagues that such a development could escalate.'*

Sky Reporter: *'You've spoken out on this matter before?'*

Woodendale: *'Not publically, no I haven't. But that's not really the point. There has been unease for some months.'*

Sky Reporter: *'So your decision is nothing to do with the Gülen Movement's Islamic affiliations?'*

Woodendale: *'No, but we feel that if Parliament is to intervene in this area, we need to do so before the situation escalates.'*

Sky Reporter: *'Are you going to investigate...'*

'That's pretty much it,' said Sir Terrence, halting the recording. 'There's an article in today's Financial Times that Chelsea is in negotiation with a Gülen Movement backer. I'd like you to look into that, see if the rumours have any substance, see if Gülen are active in the UK and what they've done in the US. I was going to ask DoB to do it, but it's a domestic matter and you already know the background. See what you can find out for next week. Is that clear?'

'Okay,' replied Caldicott, 'but I've...'

'You've other things on?' said Sir Terrence.

'A few, yes.'

'Push them back and if there are any problems let me know.'

Caldicott nodded, and as he turned to leave, Sir Terrence said, 'And Robert, good work on the DoB report. I've handed it back and told them not to touch it.'

That evening, from his apartment, Caldicott sent a text to Mathew Groves: *Hi Matt. Sir Terrence wants us to work on gulen asap. Come round first thing. If you've stuff on push it back. See you at 8.30. Robert*

42

The Gherkin, Wednesday 29th June

Frank Hobson's bad week started to go wrong on the Friday
before with the delivery of a couriered envelope to his office.
When Jeanie, his PA, had placed it on his desk, she stepped
back dutifully, waiting for his instruction to file it away.
Hobson flipped the envelope and read the sender's address:
'13 Calamity Canyon, Aturperil. Looks like we've upset
someone again.'

Jeanie nodded. Like Hobson, she assumed it was hate
mail, most likely a photo-shopped image of Hobson in some
perverse act of sexual congress. He was often pictured
coupled with dogs and pigs, though the most popular theme
had him with his trousers down, knee-deep in money,
buggering a football fan. Such mail tended to arrive in
waves, peaking whenever he appeared on television trying to
defend a new broadcasting rights deal.

He tore off the security strip and pulled out a colour
photograph. He frowned and turned it over.

'What is it?' said Jeanie.

He pushed it across his desk.

She raised her eyebrows, surprised at the absence of
farmyard animals. 'Who are they?'

'It's me,' said Hobson, searching the envelope for an
accompanying message.

She moved in closer. 'Oh, so it is. I'm not used to seeing
you with your trousers on.'

Hobson studied the photograph. 'It was taken outside
here.'

Jeanie leant forward again. 'She's rather hot, isn't she?'

'I think she asked where the nearest tube was. A few
weeks back.'

'But why?'

'Beats me.' Hobson shook the envelope, double checking for a note.

'Shall I put it with the others?'

'Not just yet.'

'And you've not seen her since?' She's not been hanging around outside?'

'No, but I haven't been looking.' Hobson stood and walked to the curved outer wall of his office. He peered down at the traffic and pedestrians moving along and across St Mary's Axe, trying to recall the exact spot where she'd stopped him. He turned back in. 'I'll deal with it.'

He put the photograph in the bottom drawer of his desk and forgot all about it until early Sunday morning. He was having breakfast with his wife in the garden. She'd made the coffee while he made the brown bread toast. The Sunday papers, tabloids and broadsheets, were by his feet, neatly stacked and unread. Then a phone chimed from inside the house, the mobile he used only for family and friends.

'Probably Josh,' he said, as he passed through the French windows into the kitchen. It was a text from an unrecognised number: *morning frank seen the sunday sketch?* He moved back out to the patio still peering at the message.

'What's he want?' said his wife.

'It's not Josh, it's something else. I think it's work.' Then his other phone rang, his Blackberry, the one he used for business. He went back inside. It was the same message, the same unrecognised number.

When he reappeared holding a phone in each hand, she said, 'What's up?'

'I'm not sure. There's something in the papers.' He spread them out with his slippered foot and reached down for the Sunday Sketch. He leafed rapidly from front to back, expecting to see a scandalous headline above a footballer's face. On reaching the back page, he started again, but this time more slowly. On page 12 he paused. He moved his breakfast plate to one side and placed the open paper on the table. The photograph was oddly familiar. He read the caption underneath. While the names meant nothing, he noticed the woman's shoes, her red platforms, and her check

245

patterned skirt well above the knee. It was the woman who had asked him for directions outside St Mary's Axe.

His wife leant forward to study the picture. 'Is that it?'

'Maybe.' He summarised the first paragraph. 'It says he's a fund manager for the Church of England and she's a prostitute. It's something to do with Millwall.'

'So why's that your problem?'

'I don't know.' He looked at the Blackberry and said, 'Perhaps someone will tell me.'   But his inability to come up with a plausible explanation ruined the rest of his Sunday.

When news of Abrahams' death reached him on Wednesday his worries doubled. He guessed at extortion. Hobson had a few enemies or rather people that didn't rate him, and periodically there were sniping press reports on the LPFL's need for fresh faces and ideas. He dismissed them all.   As far as Hobson and his fellow shareholders were concerned, money, and promises of more money, is what made the LPFL function, and certainly not fresh faces. But this was different; any story linking him to a dead prostitute couldn't be ignored. He called Jeanie in and showed her the article in the Sunday Sketch.

'Does it look familiar?' he said.

'Oh no,' she shouted.

'Don't worry, it's not me.   It's someone called Ken Ffooks. He's involved at Millwall, but it's the same woman. Her name is Shelley Abrahams.'

'She was the one outside?'

'Yes she was, only now she's dead.'

'Oh my God!'

Then he lied. 'Jeanie, I've spoken to someone at the Met. They said to sit tight.   They said I should speak to you as you're the only other person that knows about the photograph from last Friday.'

'I see.'

And he lied again. 'And I've called Diane Bellot. She said the same, to sit tight.' Bellot ran a public relations consultancy that specialised in resurrecting the reputations of the famously rich, and as a consequence, was now also famously rich.

'Jeanie, we'll need to keep this quiet, not a word to anyone. The police are investigating this.' He tapped his finger on the photograph of Ffooks and Abrahams.

'Of course Frank, not a word.'

That evening in his study, via his landline, Hobson received the call he'd been expecting.

'Mr Hobson?' The caller was Henri Landuzière.

'Speaking.'

'I have a photograph in my hand.'

Hobson couldn't place the caller's accent.

'You were talking to the dead prostitute,' said Landuzière. 'You were wanting to fuck her.'

Hobson imagined an unshaven Russian, overweight with nicotine stained fingers and teeth. 'You're setting me up.'

'You were talking to a dead prostitute. You probably fucked her. You can deny it, but she cannot. Maybe you killed her.'

'You set up the story on Ffooks?'

'Not at all. Like you, he used his money to fuck prostitutes. He fucked many young women.'

Hobson leant forward, his hand on his forehead, realising any attempt at reasoning was pointless. 'What do you want?'

'We have a problem and now it is your problem. The Church of England and the Gülen. You have heard of the Gülen?'

'Yes.'

'Religion in football is very bad. It will cause you trouble. You must get rid of it.'

'I don't understand. Get rid of what?''

'You make the Church sell Millwall. You keep religion away from football.'

'I can't do that. I don't have...'

'You must find a way. Don't forget, someone is already dead and we are not short of bullets.'

43

Brighton seafront, Wednesday 29th June

Vince leant back against the two-toned iron balustrade that separated the pebble beach from the promenade. He was in Hove, the quiet end, well away from milling day-trippers. In his line of sight a dozen or more novice bladers practiced their spins and turns, while to his left, a static group of six talked and laughed; this group apart, sporting bandanas, lycra, and top of the range boots, were the fully-fledged, the blade-masters; the practitioners now so expert they no longer practiced.

Rollerblading was another of the many sports that Vince had never tried, his self-excuse being his dodgy ankles. The nearer truth was his fear of public humiliation; that strangers, passing day-trippers, young children, even the infirm on their motorised scooters, would laugh at his clumsiness.

He turned and faced the other way, towards the sea.

Kevin called. 'I've had Ángel on the phone.'

'Did he ask where I was?'

'He did. I said I thought you were in London.'

'I might go back. I can't stay at Andy's much longer.'

'If you're really stuck you could stay at mine for a few days.'

'What if Barros turns up? He could be watching me.'

'Maybe, but that doesn't change things. He can't stop me offering you a place to stay. Anyway, I think you should meet him or speak to him. You need to find out what he's thinking. I can ask him down to Brighton. You need to tell him you're not going to do anything about his gay players. That's what I want you to do...and if you do all that, we could do some work on my next book.'

'What do you mean?' said Vince.

'I mean, if Millwall go straight down, I'll retire. I'm not playing in the Championship. I'll come out, so I'll need a book.'

Vince turned and began striding eastwards down the centre of the promenade, his accommodation problems temporarily forgotten.

'I'll pay you twenty for the first draft,' said Kevin.

'Shall I come round today? We can kick around a few ideas.'

'Next week sometime.'

When their call ended a text arrived from Ailish: *Hi Vince. Can you come to the flat tomorrow morning? It's urgent.*

44

Whitehall, Thursday morning 30th June

Mathew Groves placed two lattés on Caldicott's desk.

'We've got a week,' said Caldicott as he continued tapping at his keyboard. 'Did you see Woodendale on Sky News?'

'No. What's he done?'

'He's getting worried. His committee is going to widen its review. They're going to look at religion and sport, and while they're doing that, Sir Terrence wants us to look at the Gülen Movement. He wants us to see what they've done in the West. I want you to do a review on what's on the net and then make some calls. Start with the US and Canada. Is that alright?'

'Yes,' said Groves, then adding with a hint of sarcasm, 'Anything else?'

Caldicott looked up and smiled. 'Sorry Matt. I know it's short notice. While you're doing that, I'll chase up the FT report about Chelsea and then visit Hobson at the LPFL. He should know something about the Chelsea situation. We'll get together first thing each morning to review progress.'

'Sure.' Groves picked up his coffee and made for the door. 'I'll start now.'

– – – – – – – –

On the train into London Vince sent Ailish a text saying that he was on his way. He'd never known her to be urgent about anything. It puzzled him. She could be impatient, she could talk fast and think on her feet, but she didn't do urgent. He assumed it was about the books and clothes he had left behind, and that she probably wanted everything gone, no reminders.

He put the key in the front door, pushed it open and then paused. Though he had only been away a few days, he no longer felt that he had the right to enter unannounced. He pressed the buzzer for her flat and started up the stairs.

She met him on the landing. 'Have you lost your keys?'

'No, but...' He took them from his trouser pocket and dropped them into her open hand. They went inside.

'How are things?' she said.

'Alright, I suppose.'

'Settled in at Andy's?'

'Not really.'

'Why?'

'I need somewhere where there aren't any cats. I might move in with Kevin...just for a week or two. He wants me to work on another book.'

'Another one?'

'Well, it's more of a revision. He wants to add some new stuff. It's no big deal.'

'As long as you get paid.'

'It's Kevin's idea, so nothing to do with Barros.'

'Ah Señor Barros. Have you spoken to him yet?'

Vince decided it would be best to lie. 'I called, but he didn't answer. I left him a message.'

'Like what?'

'That I'd moved out. He didn't call back so I'm assuming he's happy.'

'Why would he be happy?'

Vince shrugged and changed the subject. 'I guess you want me to shift my stuff?'

'Yes, I might be moving soon, so it's best you do.'

Vince nodded, unconvinced, and made for the bedroom.

'I've left a couple of bags out,' she said. On the bed there were two holdalls, the bags she used for carrying her shoes. 'You can drop them off another time.' She paused briefly and added, 'I've some good news.'

Vince unzipped one of the bags. Then recalling the text from *DavidS*, he said, 'Have you sold a painting?'

'Kind of. Spinks has been in touch.'

'Oh yes.'

251

'He's agreed to pay you some money for your idea, for the Art-Vision thing.'

Vince moved to the bedroom doorway. 'Why's that?'

'Officially, he's buying a picture from me.'

Vince shook his head.

'What I mean is, he's not compensating you, he's not admitting anything. He's giving me some money, lots of money for one of my paintings and he wants you to sign this.' She handed him the disclaimer:

FAO: Mr David Spinks,

C/o Brewer and Copthorne,

Bouverie Street,

London.

I, Vince Wynter, of 15 Suffolk Road, Tooting, hereby declare that I claim no intellectual property rights or ownership of the term 'Art-Vision' or of any of the ideas that have become associated or linked with the 'Art-Vision' concept. I recognise and fully acknowledge that 'Art-Vision' is an idea that was conceived and first demonstrated by Mr David Spinks.

Vince Wynter:

Witnessed in the presence of:

Ailish Brady

Vince read it once, and then again and then looked up. 'How much?'

'Three hundred thousand.'

'Bullshit.'

'He's already paid me. It's in my account.' She handed him an ATM print out. 'That's my balance.'

Vince stared at it and shook his head. 'There'll be a twist. Why would he give you that much?'

'Probably because he can. To him it's pocket-money. I told him I would tell the press that he stole your idea. He believed the story about your witnessed statement. That got him worried.'

'It was that easy?'

'No, it wasn't easy.' She went into the bathroom, slammed the door, and shouted, 'If you don't want the fucking money, don't take it.'

Vince looked again at the ATM slip. He checked the date of deposit. He turned it over. He wet his thumb and rubbed the navy-blue logo of the NatWest Bank. He walked over and tapped gently on the bathroom door. 'I just find it hard to believe he would do this. He's not like that.'

'Know him well do you?' she said, her jeans and knickers around her ankles. 'Anyway, he did get something. He got your silence.'

'I know, but...'

'It's your decision Vince. If you don't want the money, fuck off and take your junk with you.'

Vince returned to the bedroom and began stuffing the holdalls with books.

When she came out she had calmed a little. 'You can have it now. I've written you a cheque.'

'I didn't do anything. You should keep it.'

She moved to the bedroom doorway. 'Don't be a twat. I met Spinks. I just made up a story and he swallowed it. You knew what I was doing.'

253

'Exactly, you did it. You saw the opportunity, so you should keep it.'

'You're homeless Vince. The money is compensation, it's not a gift.'

He zipped up one of the holdalls and straightened. 'We'll split it then. I'm not taking it all.'

She moved to the edge of the bed and removed a folded cheque from her back pocket. 'Here.'

He looked at the amount and then tore it in two. 'Write another.'

'Are you sure?'

In the kitchen over coffee she described her second meeting with Spinks, and then wrote out another cheque for two hundred thousand.

'Sign the disclaimer. No disclaimer, no money.' She slid it across the table. 'I said I'd deliver it today with the painting.'

'To his studio?' said Vince, as he signed his name.

She frowned. 'Did I mention that?'

Realising his error Vince stood up. 'I think so.' He went back into the bedroom.

She stared blankly at the disclaimer, thinking over each line of their conversation. Then she shouted, 'How did you know I'm going to his studio?'

He shouted back, 'I didn't. I just assumed his studio was his office.' She didn't reply.

By the bedroom window he looked at the cheque. He turned it over and over, as if it were some unworldly object. He folded it in half and put it in his shirt pocket. Then ten seconds later he touched the pocket with his hand to make sure that it was still there. He looked around the room. While he had used the bed for two years for sleep and sex, the room was a mix of the familiar and unfamiliar. As always on the bedside table was her moisturiser, her alarm clock and a book – the same book she had been reading before he moved out – but he'd never noticed the flecked pattern in the brown carpet or the damp patch on the ceiling above the window. The wardrobe he knew; its size and colour, the shoe boxes on top, but not the intricate wood

grain of each door or the missing door handle. Hanging
from the curtain rail were clothes he didn't recognise, two
summer coats, a green jacket, and a pair of Abercrombie and
Fitch jeans. He wondered if they were eBay stock or new
purchases bought to impress Spinks. He lent forward and
sniffed the duvet, detecting only the faintest trace of washing
powder. Then he jolted at the sound of ripping parcel tape.

'You going to be long?' she shouted. 'I have to go soon.'
She was in the kitchen taping bubble wrap around a newly
framed painting.

'Nearly done,' he replied, 'but I'll need to come back. It
won't all fit.'

She tore off another strip of tape. 'Take the keys just in
case I'm not in next time.' Then she came into the bedroom
and dropped them on the bed. She grabbed some clothes
from the wardrobe and then went to change in the bathroom.

He watched her shut the door and heard the bolt slide
across. As an ex-lodger/lover, he had lost all viewing rights.
He finished packing and carried the holdalls into the lounge.
'Okay, I'm off now,' he shouted.

'Hang on. I won't be minute.'

She came out wearing a cotton coat belted around the
waist, tight white jeans and a pair of short boots. 'Are you
going to be alright with those?' she said, nodding at the full
bags.

'You look...' Stunning he thought, but he couldn't say it.
He'd never said it before, so what was the point of saying it
now. 'You look nice.'

'It's my Spinks outfit,' she said.

'Oh yes,' but he had no idea what she meant.

'What I mean is, it helps me. If I'm going to lie, because
that's what I've done, it helps to dress like someone else.'

'It suits you.' Then with a hint of sarcasm, he added,
'Maybe it's the new you?'

She smiled, picked up the wrapped painting and opened
the door. Not looking back, she said, 'Don't forget to lock
up.'

45

Sunningdale, Thursday 30th June

Frank Hobson called in just after nine and told Jeanie he would be working from home for the rest of the day. He had slept fitfully, and sometime after four in the morning his wife banished him to the spare bedroom. Lying awake he came up with a plan that he thought might satisfy Landuzière. He called Arnold Lesley, the Chairman at Liverpool. He told Lesley about his concerns about Manas and the Gülen Movement and that, in retrospect, the Church's acquisition of Millwall was perhaps not a good precedent. 'We might have to take action,' said Hobson. Lesley agreed and suggested they raise the matter at the forthcoming AGM. Next he called Karl Greene, the retail magnate and owner of Spurs. Much the same conversation led to the same outcome. Greene was also happy to have the matter on the agenda. Hobson left it at that. He even relaxed a little. Next week he could tell his unknown caller, Landuzière, that the matter would be discussed by the LPFL board. He hoped it might be enough.

– – – – – – – –

Tower Hamlets, Thursday afternoon

Ailish caught a cab to Rhuddlan Road and then watched from the pavement as the driver did a u-turn and headed back towards the city. Only then did she call Spinks. 'It's me.'

'Where are you?'

'Outside some blue metal gates and a pine furniture place.'

'We're opposite. We're Redfern Rendering, Traders in Offal. I'll buzz the gate and meet you where it says reception.'

'Okay, I see it.'

She arrived at the white steel door as Spinks pushed it open, the dry hinges screeching.

'Hello,' she said.

He smiled and lent forward and kissed her left cheek. She felt his lips touch the corner of her mouth. It was no air kiss.

'Nice to see you,' he said. 'Shall I take that?' and he nodded at the wrapped painting in her hand.

'No, it's fine.'

'If you go in and up the stairs I'll lock the door.'

She had been to studios before; she had even shared one for a year when she first came to London, but never to one with such an uninviting entrance. Through the rusting metal stair she could see oil drums, a tangle of ropes and wiring, and a rotting tarpaulin. She could smell creosote. On the corner landing stood an old desktop computer and a swivel chair with ripped upholstery. She squeezed past, turned and looked down. Spinks was looking up, smiling. He had watched her all the way.

'Carry on in,' he said, 'along the landing and through the red door.'

As she moved into the centre of the studio, she heard the metal door slam and then a clang as Spinks slid the security bolt. Tight against the outer walls were a dozen or more irregular objects all covered in dustsheets. The room was silent and empty of people. She had imagined something much different, a noisy workshop with huddles of technicians and trainee artists, with Spinks, when present, moving from one creative pod to another, directing his staff and refining their work. Only the scratched and paint splattered floorboards suggested a studio.

When he appeared, she said, 'Big on security?'

'We have to be. We had a few break-ins, though since we became Redferns we've been okay.'

She turned away and scanned the room again. 'What's to steal?'

257

'Not much at the moment.'

'It's not what I expected. Where are all your helpers?'

'I don't need any at the moment. Other than Art-Vision I've not been doing much, and I did that from home.'

'So why are we here today?' she said, then quickly adding, 'Not that I'm disappointed. In a way I'm glad.'

'Why's that?'

'We've no distractions and...' She raised her wrapped painting. 'I didn't really want a pack of young guns pouring over this.'

He smiled. 'I wouldn't have let that happen. Anyway, I'm sure it's excellent.'

'Dangerous words Mr Spinks. This could be the worst thing you've ever seen.'

'It won't be.'

She handed it over, then spun round on the heel of her boot and walked to the far wall. She lifted the edge of a dust sheet. 'A band saw?'

'Yes, it's all machinery. I've only one piece here and it's up there.' He nodded to the upper level. 'I just need a couple more days on it. It's too big to work on at home.'

'I see.' As she walked back to him, she retrieved the disclaimer from her shoulder bag. 'This is for you too.'

He took the envelope and slid it into his inside jacket pocket. 'Thanks.' Then he held up her painting in both hands, trying to see the image through the bubble wrap. 'Is it a water colour?'

She nodded. 'Sorry.'

'Nothing wrong with water colours. Do you mind if I have a look now?'

'If you must.'

He walked over to a covered bench and removed a Stanley knife from a side drawer. He sliced at the tape and bubble-wrap and leant the painting against the wall. While he studied it, she studied his face, afraid. The picture was in black ink and water colours, float-mounted in an ash frame under glass.

'Expensive wasn't it?' she said, clasping a hand over her mouth, as if she'd just witnessed a terrible accident.

258

He moved two paces to the left to avoid the reflective glare. The central image depicted a garden strimmer leaning against a water butt with the strimmer's electric cable trailing off to the left, unplugged. The background wash suggested an open landscape, uninhabited and desolate, scrubland or desert, while an unseen and low-lying sun cast shadows from left to right. There was no human presence but for the objects of human endeavour: a strimmer without a garden and a water butt with no plants to nourish.

Then he turned and smiled. He walked up to her and gently pulled her hand away from her face. 'I've decided, I like it.'

She shook her head. 'There's no need to be polite. I don't mind if you don't.'

He took her hand and led her back to the bench and her painting, and standing side by side, he said, 'Is this your style...this balloonist's view? The sense of neglect and isolation.'

'I suppose. I've done about ten like this.'

'I've seen similar, but not so sparse. I'm worried by it.'

'Oh dear,' she said.

'No worried is good,' and he gently squeezed her hand. 'I wish my own work worried me more.'

'I'm just an amateur,' she said. Only then did she realise he was still holding her hand, that Vince's tough negotiator was holding David Spinks' hand. She slipped it free and brushed her hair back. 'I dabble,' she said, trying to regain her confidence, 'and I have my other work.'

He moved a step closer to the painting. 'We're all amateurs. I just happened to break through.'

She shook her head. 'Break through what?'

'The art market. I'm an insider and you're an outsider. It's principally a competition for attention, because the market can only sustain a few.' He turned to her. 'We're not so different from people that sell cars or shoes. The market makers don't want hundreds of top-end suppliers. If you have fewer insiders, supply is more predictable and prices stay high. Otherwise it would be chaos. Buyers would get confused and worse of all, prices would fall.'

But she wasn't listening. She was thinking, why shoes? *Does he know I'm an ebayer?*

Spinks continued. 'So the trick is to break through. Get into that top echelon and make sure you stay there.'

She shook her head. 'Just a trick. It can't be that easy?'

'Trick's probably the wrong word. It was hard work, but hard work towards a specific objective. The art still has to be right for the moment, for the time, and then we priced it high. High price infers high quality. People with money like to buy expensive things, much like the people that wear Balenciaga.' He smiled and nodded at her sharp-toed boots.

She looked down to her feet. *He knows. He knows all about me.*

Spinks continued. 'So someone like Gorky, who lived and died on the breadline, all he probably needed was a hard working agent.'

'Perhaps Gorky didn't care for money?' she said.

'Maybe, but he was born into poverty. I doubt he wanted to stay there.'

She nodded. She was no believer in the romance of the penniless artist. 'So what was your trick?'

'I studied the competition and found a partner with contacts. Then I made things that, at least for a year or two, appeared to be interesting. When I started out it didn't seem that difficult.'

She stepped forward and peered at her painting. 'So I'd need an agent?'

'Yes, eventually.'

She faced him and said, 'But I'm not going to break through with these?'

'No, you're not. But that doesn't have to be your objective. I like your painting and I'm sure others do too. That can be enough. I used to destroy lots of work that was probably okay, but just a fraction too derivative. You have to self-edit. For a few years we used to submit everything to the crusher test.'

'The what?' she said.

'We had a conveyor belt out the back of the studio which fed into a crusher. Every piece we made was put on the

260

conveyor, and everything was crushed unless someone wanted to save it. If they saved it, they had to say why. From one end to the other took thirty seconds.'

'So who decided what to save?'

'Whoever was around...me, my mother, Chris, the postman.'

'The postman?'

'Why not? Everyone has an opinion. Those were the rules.'

'How many people needed to be there?'

'The minimum was Chris and me, but there were usually more. When busy, we had about twenty outside in the yard.'

She smiled, and wondered if he was teasing her or testing her. 'I didn't see it in the yard.'

'No, it's gone now. We stopped using it about six or seven years back. We sold it to a Russian. He bought it for five million.'

'Why?'

Spinks shrugged. He couldn't defend the absurdity of the price. 'We were never sure. He didn't speak English and he paid in cash.'

'So no regrets about what was crushed?'

'Maybe one or two. Some works were saved but they went straight into storage. They've never been shown. They're works with no hinterland, so they'll stay there until I think the time is right.'

'Until you're dead?' she said.

'Maybe.'

'So no more crushing?'

'Now I use an animator. If it's going to be expensive to make, I get him to mock it up in 3-D. Then if I'm not a hundred percent certain, we don't do it.'

'How come I've never heard or read about this?'

'Because no one's ever asked.'

'Really?'

'I've never talked about it and the people who work here are under contract to...'

'Keep their mouths shut.'

'Kind of,' he said. 'There has to be some control.'

261

She nodded. 'Sorry, that was rude of me.'

She looked back at her painting again, its simplicity now starker than ever. 'We're miles apart David.'

'Don't be so hard on yourself. I've just been more systematic. I started out with a different objective and I had help. It also depends on how serious you are. You have your other work. It's difficult when there are other priorities.' He picked up her painting and inspected the back. 'You've not signed it?'

'No. I never do.'

'Well sign it for me. I'm taking it home. I have a place for it.'

'The garage?'

'My bedroom, by the window.'

She scoffed. 'You'll be posting it to that Russian with the crusher.'

He laughed. 'No, I'm serious. A painting, or whatever it is, is a reminder of the person I met. For me they're better than a photograph. I'll remember the day you came here, the weather and what you said and what you looked like. So it will be a reminder of you.'

'And a reminder of Vince?'

He nodded.

She crossed the studio and peeked under another dustsheet. 'Furniture,' she said.

'Yes. The chairs are over there.' He pointed toward another dust-sheeted shape in the far corner. 'They're for my sister. They just need staining then they're finished.'

'Any more talents?'

'I've no talent with wood, just persistence. One of the guys that works here helps me out. I'm still learning.'

'So where's this other work you mentioned?'

'MBF2?'

The name didn't register. 'I don't know. Is it big?'

'It is.' He set off and she followed him up the short staircase to the upper studio.

From ten yards away she said, 'Of course, MBF2. I wasn't thinking.' Against the left wall, cradled in a rectangular scaffold, was Spinks' follow up to Man's Best

Friend. It had the dimensions of the brick and mortar original, but from a distance it appeared grey. 'You were ahead of me,' she said.

'What do you mean?'

'At Amaya's, I said you should do another one and call it Cock 'n' Bull.'

'Yes, but this isn't quite what you were suggesting.'

From outside the scaffold, she said, 'Can I have a look?'

'Help yourself.'

She stepped inside. Close up it was white. She tapped it gently with her knuckle and ran her hand along the cool shaft. 'Steel?' she said.

'Yes, then powder-coated.'

Along its entire length and head were words, the lettering no more than five millimetres high. She leant forward and started reading. All the words were referenced quotations, each one comprising a statement, the author's name, the date, and the publication's title. Some were from web pages and others from events where the author had spoken. Each statement was a comment, interpretation or exposition of Man's Best Friend. They were set within a grid of dashed lines that ran lengthways and around the shaft's circumference. She read half a dozen. They were all critical.

She straightened and said, 'Any particular order?'

'Chronologically, from base to tip.'

'And the dashed lines?'

'No reason. Just to keep things neat. They're not inlayed. They'll come off with some solvent.'

'And when are you going to show it?'

'Early August at the Hayward, next to MBF.'

'Looks like a lot of work.'

'On and off nearly twenty years. The fabrication was done right after MBF. Then as the comments came in, I started the engraving. I've probably spent three or four days a month on it. I'm just tidying it now.'

'All your own work?'

He knew what she meant. 'Yes, all mine this one. It's been good... therapeutic, like making the furniture.'

At the very tip she read another scathing comment. 'It's not your revenge?'

'No, but I'm sure that's what people will say. It's the obvious thing to say, but it's not. For me it's an exposition of criticism. If you read them all, you'll see there are themes. One person picks up on another and that theme might run for a year or two. Then there'll be nothing for a while until it's exhibited again, perhaps somewhere overseas, and that generates a whole new batch of interpretations. Some of it's completely contradictory.'

'And you've been collecting these comments for twenty years?'

'No. That's the bit I didn't do. Someone does it for me. They translate them, if they need translating, and pass them to me.'

'And what are *they* going to call it?' she said.

'The press?'

She nodded.

'I guess More Cock 'n' Bull.'

'I suppose they will.'

'They'll hate it,' he said, 'but I couldn't have done it without them.' Then he nodded toward her hands. 'How are you finding the orifice?'

She had two fingers of her right hand inside, while her left cupped the rim of the helmet. She quickly pulled them away, hiding them behind her back like a naughty child. 'Sorry.'

'No, it's good to see someone engage with it.'

She stepped out of the scaffold and they both turned and walked down the steps to the main studio floor.

'I suppose I'd better be off,' she said, 'Thanks for showing me around. It's been really interesting.'

'My pleasure.'

As she made for the door, he said, 'What about this evening?'

She turned, frowning. 'What about it?'

'I mean would you like to have dinner? I still owe you a meal.'

She smiled. 'I'd like that.'

264

'Eight o'clock. Shall I pick you up?'

'No, I'll meet you.'

'Come to my house then and we'll go from there. Eaton Place. I'll text you the address.'

Out in the yard he keyed in the security code for the gate. 'See you later,' he said. Then he watched her walk away until she turned left onto Brick Lane.

46

Merton College Oxford, Thursday 30th June

Outside Oxford Station Cowly glanced at his watch. He had nothing prepared for his meeting with the Assets Committee, no risk-weighted scenarios or strategy options. For once, he had no past experience to draw on. None of his colleagues at BSM had any advice other than an orderly exit, and there was nothing in his management consultancy textbooks on how a chief executive was supposed to respond when faced with acts of indiscriminate violence.

He calculated that he there was just enough time to walk to Merton College. He hoped that the fresh air might provide some last minute inspiration. As he walked his thoughts turned to his future. *What to do after Millwall? Where to live? How to live? Marry Imee?* He had no appetite for returning to BSM.

Arriving at the Breakfast Room a few minutes late, he raised a hand in apology and sat in the only empty chair. At the head of the table, in Ffooks' place (Ffooks had resigned and refused to work his notice) was Sir William Denham, The First Church Estates Commissioner. Though Cowly had never met Denham in the flesh, they had spoken on the phone and he knew Denham was a keen advocate of the Church's new investment strategy. The only person around the table that Cowly had had no contact with was seated directly opposite; he was the Chair of the Church Commissioners, Dr Philip Prendergast, aka the Archbishop of Canterbury. In a grey suit and purple shirt, he smiled warmly at Cowly.

Welcome Tom,' said Sir William. 'We've just finished the introductions. I think you've meet everyone before except the Archbishop.'

Cowly smiled back at Prendergast, unsure of the protocol. Then the Archbishop rose from his seat and reached out. 'Please to meet you Tom. I've heard a lot about you.

'Not all bad I hope?' said Cowly.

'Quite the contrary,' said the Archbishop as he sat back in his chair. 'The Commissioners I've spoken to are more than happy with the way you've handled a very difficult situation.' The Archbishop looked towards Sir William who nodded in agreement.

Before Cowly could reply there was a knock on the door. It eased open and a trolley appeared steered by a white-haired woman in a blue dress and apron. 'Teas and coffee,' she said.

'Bring it round here,' said Sir William. 'We'll sort it out.'

As she rattled around the table and passed the Archbishop, he touched her arm. 'That's fine. I'll do the honours.'

'Are you sure?' she said, not knowing who he was.

The Archbishop manoeuvred the trolley closer to the table while the tea lady backed away. He glanced around the table. 'I can assure you it's not an act of humility. It just gives me another chance to remember your names.' A few laughed and everyone smiled. 'So William, what's your preference, tea or coffee?'

When the sugar, milk and biscuits had gone full circle, Sir William began. 'Thank you for all coming along today at such short notice. In particular, I would like to thank the Archbishop for taking time out of his busy schedule. I suppose in some respects I would prefer it that you weren't here, as your presence is itself an indication of the seriousness of the situation.'

'Before we start,' said the Archbishop. 'I suggest we stick to first names. I'm Philip and you're William.'

'Agreed,' said Sir William. 'As you know there is no agenda for today's meeting because we only have one issue to discuss.' He turned to face Cowly. 'Tom, I'd like you to start off and give us your thoughts on what's happened and

267

what might happen. We've all seen the press coverage, but we'd like your insider's view.'

Cowly recounted the events since the publication of the first photographs in the Sketch up to the time he was notified of Ken Ffooks' resignation. Then he said, 'Those are the known facts. We had expected some opposition and we did some risk analysis. Our thinking was that the Church would attract most of the flak, but what we didn't expect was the sort of personal attacks we've seen, certainly not the violence. Something is going on here that we don't fully understand. The smear stories and possibly the death of Shelley Abrahams seem to be about making things so uncomfortable that we'll be forced to back out. The only conclusion I've come to, on the basis on what I know, is that it's not ideological.' He looked at Sir William and then across the table at the Archbishop. 'It's not much, but that's my view.'

'Thanks Tom,' said Sir William.

'You don't think it could be a fringe group?' suggested the Archbishop. 'Perhaps some extreme atheistic or Catholic organisation?'

'I don't, but then I'm not an expert in that area. Maybe that was a possibility, but not now, not if Shelley Abrahams is part of this. I can't see how killing her helps anyone with an ideological objective.' Cowly paused and then added, 'Does that make sense?'

'I think it does,' said the Archbishop. 'Caveats accepted, they are clearly people who see no sanctity in human life. They have cast aside a young woman, a young mother, simply because it served their objective.' Addressing Cowly, he added, 'You don't think it was a random killing, and therefore unconnected to events at Millwall?'

After Tuesday's press conference, Cowly had asked Phylida to check on London gun crimes against women. 'It could be,' he said. 'We know her bag was taken, but she had nothing to steal, and most shootings involving women are domestic incidents. Apparently, it's been ten years since a woman was shot for her handbag.'

The Archbishop frowned, his face unable to hide his sadness. 'She was executed.'

'I guess she was,' said Cowly.

'So what can we expect next?' said Sir William. 'More of the same?'

Cowly nodded. 'We should expect the worst. Whoever they are, they want a result.'

'They want the Church of England out of football?' said the Archbishop.

'My feeling is that it's any religion,' said Cowly. 'If it isn't ideological, then I doubt it is specifically against the Church of England.'

Sir William shook his head.

'What I mean is, if the Catholic Church had bought Millwall all this would have still happened.'

'Okay,' said the Archbishop, 'So you're saying that it's probably anti-religious, anti-faith.'

'Yes, but I've no idea why,' said Cowly.

'My communications office monitors all the negative mail we receive,' said the Archbishop. 'It's not increased significantly since the Millwall acquisition. Most of what we get, we classify as extreme Protestantism, and most of the rest is from angry Catholics and Muslims. It's all doctrinal, nothing to do with Millwall or the new investment strategy.' He paused and said, 'In some respects, I sense that leading the Church of England is not so dissimilar from being a football manager, there's never a time to relax and there are always plenty of critics on the sidelines.'

Cowly nodded. 'I think you're right,'

'So we're saying,' said Sir William, 'the motivation is anti-religious, but it's not coming from other faiths. Atheists then?'

'I doubt it,' said Cowly. 'If it was some extreme atheistic organisation I think we would have heard from them. To me it's someone or some organisation with vested interests who wants religion out of football. For some reason they see the Church's presence as a threat.'

'Criminal interests,' suggested the Archbishop.

'They have to be,' said Cowly.

For a few moments no one spoke, each person searching for a credible explanation.

Sir William broke the silence. 'So how do we respond?' Then sensing that the Archbishop's presence might be stifling a more open debate, he glanced round the table to indicate that the question was directed at everyone, 'I think we should consider anything, no matter how extraordinary.'

Derek Connelly was the first to offer an opinion. 'Either way, it looks bad to me. If we want to save lives, then we back out and disinvest. These people, whoever they are, will win and the Church will look weak. I don't favour that route, but we can't expect people to put their lives at risk because of an investment strategy. We can't put profits before lives.'

The Archbishop responded. 'We have an age-old moral dilemma. How to deal with the bully? To fight or flee?' He smiled and added, 'I'll spare you the scripture.'

'But it's worse than that,' said Sir William, 'because we don't know who the bully is.'

Cowly came in. 'I think everyone here would agree it would be regrettable to walk away from what the Church is trying to do just because we were threatened. If we feel the risks are too high, then we need to take precautions. I'm not sure what, but I'm sure we could do something.'

'I think you're right,' said Sir William. 'It would be a catastrophe if the Church retreated. It would be seen as a victory for...'

'For evil,' said the Archbishop.

'So if we get some advice on security,' said Cowly, 'and take precautions, I'm for carrying on. I'm prepared to go down that route.'

'That's all very well Tom,' said Connelly, 'but you might not be the target.' Connelly looked around the table for some sign of support. 'I'm really struggling here. We made an investment decision, a relatively small one at that, and now we're discussing security so that more people aren't killed. This is crazy.'

Cowly responded. 'I hear what you're saying, Derek. I don't want to be a dead CEO or a dead anything. What I

270

suggest is that we make this more about me and not the Church. The decision to stay with Millwall needs to be seen as my decision. We present it as though I'm the only one they need to target.' It sounded heroic, but Cowly figured at most, he only had a few years left.

Connelly shook his head 'What about your family and your friends? These people will target anyone that's vaguely connected to the club. That's why Shelley Abrahams is dead.'

Cowly nodded. 'Possibly, we still don't know that for sure. All I'm saying is that we could take precautions and I'm prepared to do that.'

Sir William said, 'Let's go back a step. Firstly, we don't know that Shelley Abrahams' murder was connected to the club, and secondly, what do these people have to gain by more killing? I accept that more violence is a possibility, but to me it's not likely unless they reveal why they're doing what they're doing.'

'I'm afraid,' said the Archbishop, 'our dilemma won't be resolved through deductive analysis. We're dealing with human nature and issues of power, and most likely, money.' He paused and smiled at the unintended irony of his statement. 'I don't favour backing off, but I also don't want any more lives destroyed. If it will help, I'll make a statement on the matter condemning the smears and the cowardice of Shelley's killers, and take full responsibility.'

'Thanks Philip,' said Sir William, 'but I'd rather you weren't drawn into this.'

'Except that I already have been,' replied the Archbishop. 'Ultimately, I am responsible for this.'

'You're not,' said Sir William, emphatically. 'We all supported the changes. Look, let's have a break for five minutes, get some fresh air.' He stood up and stepped over to the French windows. As he pushed them out a cool draft swept inwards. Balancing on the door frame Sir William filled his lungs and exhaled, blowing out his cheeks.

The Archbishop came to his side. 'You alright old boy?'

Sir William turned and smiled, and looked back into the room to see if anyone was in earshot. 'Could be better, but nothing a good night's sleep won't put right.'

The Archbishop eased Sir William out onto the lawn. Then he turned and beckoned to Cowly that he should join them. They walked along the gravel path that cut down the left side of the college lawns, all three with their heads angled down; Cowly in the middle dwarfed by the two six-footers on either side. No one spoke until they reached the old summer house.

'Philip,' said Sir William, 'I don't think we have a choice. I don't think we can or should back down. We need to stay resolute. I'm prepared to back Tom, that's if you've not changed your mind.' Sir William looked at Cowly.

The Archbishop put his hand on Cowly's shoulder. 'Are you happy with that Tom?'

Cowly nodded.

'I know the Deputy Commissioner at the Met,' said Sir William. 'He can advise us. We can share the responsibility and take precautions. With the Met's help perhaps we can lure these people out into the open.'

Cowly and the Archbishop nodded in agreement and then all three turned and walked back to the Breakfast Room. The round table discussion resumed for a further twenty minutes, covering much of the same ground. At twelve-thirty, the Committee members dispersed by car and taxi, and the Archbishop headed back to London and Lambeth Palace. Cowly and Sir William stayed behind to draft a press statement.

The Office

of :

The First Church Estates Commissioner.

Chairman of the Commissioners' Assets Committee

Church Confirms Commitment to Millwall FC

In response to the tragic death of Ms Shelley Abrahams and recent newspaper articles concerning Mr Tom Cowly (CEO Millwall FC) and Mr Kenneth Ffooks (the former Assets Committee Director of Investments), Sir William Denham, The First Church Estates Commissioner has issued the following press statement:

As Chairman of the Assets Committee, I remain fully committed to the Church of England's new investment strategy. I will continue to support UK enterprise and British businesses. Moreover, the Church will not be selling or diluting its interest in Millwall Football Club. Tom Cowly has my complete support and together we intend to see this project through and establish Millwall as a successful and financially stable LPFL club.

Sir William Denham

Church of England Media Centre, Church House.
Great Elm Street, London W1P 3LZ

'What now?' said Cowly.

'I suppose we do some sort of security assessment. I'll call the Deputy Commissioner. I'll state our concerns, see what he says.'

'There was something else that I should probably have mentioned earlier.'

'Go on,' said Sir William.

'Before all this happened I'd been planning to take a holiday, just a couple of weeks. All the player signings have gone through and the new season starts in a month.' Cowly grimaced, not happy with the timing.

'Don't worry Tom. I think you should. You deserve it. I'll stay in touch with Phylida, and we can talk on the phone if anything urgent comes up.'

'You know it won't look good...heading off in the midst of a crisis.'

'We'll deal with it. You get away and we'll meet up when you get back.'

They shared a taxi back to the train station. Later that afternoon the Church of England's Media Centre released the statement and an hour later it was posted on the Church Times website.

47

Monday 4th July

A week on, Phylida dropped the paper to the floor. As Cowly had predicted his departure hadn't gone go unnoticed. The front page of the Sketch announced:

MILLWALL BOSS FLEES AWAY

Cowly and Imee had been photographed on Sunday evening in a departure lounge at Heathrow. The paper slammed him for cutting and running while the club was in crisis. It also alleged that:

> ...*Cowly and his Filipino girlfriend had booked one-way tickets to Manila and were unlikely to return.*

She emailed Cowly to let him know and then left for Brighton.

– – – – – – –

Vince, meanwhile, headed for Tooting on the train. It he was thinking it might be for the last time. He had banked his cheque and on the Saturday moved into a furnished flat on Wilbury Road, only a few minutes walk from Adelaide Crescent. The night before he'd sent Ailish a text saying that he would pick up the rest of his belongings first thing in the morning. He planned to be back in Brighton for the afternoon as he'd promised Andy that he would help out at the Pump Room. She'd not responded to his text, so as the train pulled into Clapham Junction he sent it again.

Ailish had spent her Sunday afternoon at Spinks' house and later they went to a party in South Clapham. She met some of his friends, some artists, and some of the people that had invested in his work. But before they got drunk, and while they were sharing an armchair in the lounge – she was on his lap, her right elbow resting on his shoulder – she told him what she suspected he already knew.

'David,' she said.

'Yes Ailish.' He widened his eyes as if startled.

She flicked his ear lobe. 'Now listen. I've something to tell you, and it's not easy for me.'

'Like what?'

'You need to know who I am, what I am.'

'I know who you are. You're a part-time artist. You're a good negotiator.'

'No there's more.'

'I know there's more.' He craned his head forward and kissed her cheek. Then in his best Southern Ireland accent he said, 'You're short and red, very fuckable, and one day I'd like to...'

'Shut up!' She clamped her left hand over his mouth. 'Now listen.'

He grunted okay through her fingers.

'Promise?

He nodded and she removed her hand.

'It's about me and Vince. I helped him because he's a friend. He's not my client.'

'Okay, that's fine.'

'And I sell shoes. Did you know that?'

He nodded.

'It's just that...'

This time he stopped her. He held his right index finger against her lips and said, 'I'm not with you because of what you do or who your friends are. I'm here because...'

She'd heard enough. She grasped his chin and kissed him hard on the mouth.

– – – – – – –

Spinks sat up and stuck out his tongue, regretting the cigarettes he'd smoked the night before. Ailish was out of sight buried under the duvet. He went into the kitchen with a

276

full morning-glory and returned with two glasses of water. He placed them on the bedside table.

Sensing movement, she stirred. 'Where are you going?'

'Nowhere. I've already been.'

'Good, I need a cuddle.' She threw back the duvet, inviting him in.

Spinks rolled onto his side, kissed her neck and shoulder and placed a flat hand between her thighs.

'Did we drink too much?' she said, returning his kiss with a kiss.

'I suppose we did.'

'And we had sex?'

'Sort of,' he said.

'What do you mean?'

'You murdered my nipples and then fell asleep.'

She laughed. 'I don't think so. Something else must have happened.' She reached down and grabbed him.

'Yes, you showed me some paintings and...'

'You bought them all.'

He laughed and said, 'I wasn't that drunk.'

'Don't be so mean.' Then feeling him harden, she turned and dipped under the duvet. 'Have you got a torch and a pen? I'm feeling inspired.'

'Why have you got something to say?'

'Oh I have, but there's so little space.' Then she threw back the duvet and facing the end of the bed she raised her bottom. 'Put it in.'

Spinks edged round on his knees and slipped his cock in halfway.

'I thought it was,' she whispered to herself. He was fractionally wider than Vince.

'What was that?'

'Nothing, carry on.'

He pushed in hard and she groaned. Then the door bell rang.

'Shit,' they said together.

'I'll get it,' said Spinks, still inside her.

'No don't. It's probably just a neighbour.'

Then the bell rang again, and when they heard a key in the door, Spinks pulled away.

'David,' she said, 'don't...' But he was already gone, naked into the lounge. She heard the door shut and then silence. 'Who is it?' she shouted.

'It's Vince,' said Vince.

'Oh fuck.' She jumped from the bed and pulled on her bathrobe. In the bedroom doorway, angry and embarrassed, she said, 'Why didn't you tell me?'

'I did,' said Vince. 'I sent you a text.'

Spinks went back to the bedroom.

'I've come for the rest of my stuff.' Vince raised the empty holdalls in his hand.

She glanced round and saw Spinks pulling on his underpants. She turned back to face Vince. 'Can you give me ten minutes?'

'I'll come back another day.'

'Don't be stupid. Ten minutes.'

He dropped the empty bags and left.

She moved into the bedroom and picked up her phone. 'Sorry about that. He kept some of his stuff here. I left him a key just in case I was out.'

Spinks sat on the bed buttoning his shirt. 'Another time?' he said.

She brushed her fingers across the back of his neck. 'I hope so...soon.'

Spinks nodded. 'Did he live here?'

'Yes, for a while. He was homeless. He moved out a few weeks ago. It was your fault we met...and his fault I met you.'

He smiled at her explanation. 'Come over this evening or meet me at the studio. I'm going to spend the afternoon there.'

'That would be nice. I'll call you later.' She bent forward and they kissed. Then straightening up, she said, 'Have some juice before you go, you need liquid.' She left and came back with a pint glass of orange juice and ice.

He emptied the glass and took an ice cube into his mouth. 'I'll eat on the way.'

278

On tiptoes and with a steadying hand on his shoulder, she kissed his wet lips.

– – – – – – –

Vince sat on the wall opposite her flat staring at the pavement. He was more annoyed than angry; annoyed at his inability to control events, and at his apparent dependence on the behaviour of others. A few minutes passed. When Spinks came through the front door, Vince lifted his head, and when Spinks passed through the front gate and waved, simply in acknowledgement that these things happen and that no offence was meant, Vince waved back. And when Spinks was finally out of sight, he kicked a flattened coke bottle into the road and went back inside.

Ailish was dressed and in the kitchen, cleaning the cafetière. At the sound of the door, she shouted, 'I'm sorry about that. It wasn't deliberate.' With no reply, she shouted, 'Vince?'

He moved into the kitchen doorway and lent against the frame. 'It doesn't matter. I hope you'll be happy together.'

'Don't be stupid.' Then glancing over her shoulder, she added, 'We only had sex.'

'Like us then?'

She ignored his gibe. 'He invited me to a party. We got drunk and we came here. That's all.'

'An expensive fuck.'

She laughed. 'I guess it was.' She turned to look at him. 'Like I said before, if you don't want his money, just hand it back.'

Vince picked up the two holdalls and went to the bedroom to pack.

She called out, 'There was no plan Vince.'

'Slag,' he said to himself.

She didn't hear him. 'There are more bags in the wardrobe if you need them.'

He knew what she meant. She meant: take all your stuff and don't come back. Then the confirmation came.

'You can keep them. I don't need them anymore.'

Two minutes later he dropped the keys on the bed and left without saying goodbye. By the time he reached Colliers Wood High Street his forearms and shoulders were burning. He dropped his bags by the bus shelter and in the minutes before the arrival of the 219 to Clapham Junction, he decided it was time for a change. Today would be the day when he broke from the past. As the bus came to a halt he jumped on empty-handed, and when seated at the back of the bus, he started deleting all his phone contacts, all the people that he used to know that never called.

On the train to Brighton he moved down the centre aisle to the rear carriage, to the rearmost seats, and as far away as possible from the other passengers. When the train sped though Haywards Heath a text arrived:

Hi Vince. Barros is in the UK next week. If I invite him down to Brighton next Thursday will you be around? Kevin.

Vince replied: *Thanks for offering. I'll deal with it. It'll save time. V*

Beyond caring, He called Barros who answered immediately.

'How are you Vince?'

Thrown by the friendly but disingenuous greeting, he forgot his reason for calling.

'What do you want Vince?'

'Err...we need to sort something out.'

'I am busy. What is it?'

Though the nearest person in the carriage was eight rows away, Vince raised his free hand to cover his mouth. 'It's about you and your gay players.'

Barros laughed. 'There is nothing to sort out Vince. Business is good.'

Then remembering the letter he'd posted to his sister from Puigcerdá, he said, 'But it won't last. I know about you and so do others. You're finished.'

'Vince, I think you are mixing me with yourself. You are finished. You have nothing. Your Irish girlfriend is fucking a rich man. You have no home.'

'I have a letter. If anything happens to me, the police will find out. Do you understand?'

'I understand your words Vince, but not what you are saying.'

'I'm saying,' said Vince, 'if you want my silence you have to pay for the letter.'

'You are blackmailing me with a letter?'

Then Vince heard Barros talking in Spanish sparking a chorus of laughter in the background.

'Sorry Vince,' said Barros, 'that was rude of me. You were saying about a letter?'

'If you want my silence, you give me two hundred thousand.'

'That is a lot of money for a man who makes up stories, for a man who is a convicted liar. Vince, be clear about this, I know how to keep you quiet. It won't cost that much.'

Vince cut the call, dropped his phone onto the seat and covered his face with his hands. As he replayed their conversation, Barros called back. Vince turned the volume down and put the phone on loud speaker. He didn't want Barros' voice up against his face.

'Next stop Burgess Hill,' said Barros.

Vince looked out of the window. The train was in a cutting just north of Burgess Hill Station.

'I have thought about your offer Vince. It was a good offer, but only for you. So I am going to make a counter offer. Listen very carefully. You never contact me or Kevin or any of my players again. You keep your mouth shut and I leave your little Irish lady alone. You need to...'

'Fuck off,' said Vince and then he cut the call. He assumed that either Barros was tracking his movements via the phone network or someone was tailing him. He stood and walked slowly along the aisle glancing at the other passengers. He passed a young couple, Goths, sharing an iPod, and then three rows on, a middle-aged woman holding a book close to her face. Opposite her was a man, seemingly asleep, with his head against the carriage window. Further along, just beyond the second set of doors, were two men, lookalikes, possibly brothers. They were both fingering their phones. Vince continued to the end of the carriage, turned and walked back to his seat. He assumed the 'brothers' were Barros' men. And when he climbed into a taxi outside Brighton Station, they were there again, leaning against the station wall, heads down, fingering their phones.

Vince spent the afternoon at the Pump Room, and occasionally, while he blitzed a smoothie or loaded the juicer, he would scan the crowd around the beach volleyball looking out for the brothers.

Andy closed up at seven and Vince took a taxi to the corner of Wilbury Road and sat outside the *Greenhouse Effect* with a pint. Ten minutes passed and a police car crossed over from Second Avenue, its siren set to deafening. A fire engine followed close behind. After his second pint he left the pub and turned up Wilbury Road. He saw the fire engine parked halfway along, two police cars either side. A gathering of eight was standing out on the wet pavement looking up at No. 23. Vince had the top floor flat and without breaking stride, he started up the steps.

'You can't go in,' said a woman's voice.

'I live here,' said Vince without bothering to turn.

'So do we,' she shouted, and then more quietly to the woman beside her, 'I've not seen him before.'

Vince stopped in the doorway. 'What's the problem?'

This time a man replied, 'A fire in the top floor flat. Someone broke in.'

'When?' said Vince.

'About an hour ago,' said the man. 'I put it out and called the police.'

Vince climbed the carpeted stair to the second floor. On the landing he smelt damp and smoke. A single strip of yellow tape stretched across the entrance to his flat. He peered in. 'Hello?'

A uniformed policewoman appeared from inside. 'Sir, you were asked to stay outside. Now please leave the building.'

'I live here.' He pointed to the floor. 'In this one, flat 4.'

She turned and shouted, 'Sarg.'

A woman replied, 'What is it?'

'The owner's arrived.'

Moments later a woman ducked under the tape and peeled off her latex gloves. 'What's your name sir?'

'What's yours?' said Vince. He guessed from her accent that she was Eastern European. Then noticing her donkey jacket and short hair, he assumed she was part of the 'woman/lesbian/foreign quota'. Back when Vince had lived in Brighton, Sussex Police had been renowned for its community engagement, in particular its efforts to recruit a force that mirrored the population it served. They had been the first force in the UK to publish mandatory quotas based on gender, sexuality, disability, ethnicity, nationality, age, and educational attainment. At the time, the education quota had caused uproar. To fully reflect the local population it meant Sussex Police had to recruit a number of officers with no GCSEs or NVQs, and even a few that couldn't read or write. But mindful that some applicants might try to fake their illiteracy, the force's HR department was compelled to interview, under oath, the family and teachers of all their supposedly illiterate applicants. It took them nearly five years to hit all their quotas, but when they did, the Chief Constable proudly announced that 0.8% of Brighton's police officers were functionally illiterate.

The officer smiled at Vince and repeated her question, but this time adding, 'I won't ask again.'

'Vince Wynter.'

'Good, well I'm Detective Sergeant Bezek. Can I see some I.D?'

Vince took his wallet from his back pocket and handed over his driving licence.

She flipped it from one side to the other and handed it back. 'This is not your current address.'

'I moved in yesterday. What's happened?'

'Someone broke the door open.' Bezek nodded toward the busted lock and the wood splinters on the floor. 'They started a fire in the bath and your neighbour from number two put it out. I'm afraid it's wet inside. Brighton's bravest got a bit carried away.'

'Who?'

'The fire brigade. They like to leave their mark.'

'Can I see inside?'

'I have a few questions first. How long have you lived here?'

'A day. I rent it.'

'Who from?'

'Brighton Lets.'

'Can I see your keys?'

Vince removed his keys from his pocket.

She said, 'You didn't lock the mortice.'

Vince shook his head. 'What d'you mean?'

'The brass key...it's for the mortice lock. If you'd locked that they might not have got in.'

'I left in a hurry,' said Vince. 'I wasn't expecting arsonists.'

'Did you have anything valuable here?'

'Clothes mainly.'

'So why would someone want to burn your clothes?'

'I've no idea. Perhaps they were after the previous tenant?'

'What does that mean?

Vince shrugged his shoulders. 'Maybe someone had a score to settle.'

'But not with you?'

'No, like I said, it was probably to do with the previous tenant. They must have pissed someone off.'

'Mr Wynter, I like to stick with the facts.' She knew Vince was lying and he knew she knew too. 'You have enemies?'

'No, I'm a writer.'

'What sort of writer?'

'A ghost-writer. I write for people that...'

'Yes Mr Wynter, I know what it is. So what are you writing now?'

'Nothing.'

'And where were you before you came here?'

'Living with my girlfriend in London.'

'So why are you here?'

'Because we split up.'

'And her name?'

'Ailish Brady.'

'I'll need her address and phone number.' Vince read out the details and she pencilled them in her notebook. 'Have you ever been in trouble with the police?' But before he could answer she said, 'Think about it Mr Wynter, because I'll be checking.'

Vince shook his head.

'Okay, we'll go inside now, but don't touch anything.'

In the bathroom they stared down at a soggy heap of charred clothes.

She said, 'Tomorrow I want you to come to the station to be fingerprinted.'

'Can't we do it now?' said Vince.

While walking to Hove Police Station Vince left a message with Brighton Lets saying the front door needed replacing. He didn't mention the fire. He figured the whole flat would need decorating and that they would probably want him to move out.

Half an hour later he was on a bench seat outside The Cricketer; this time with a pint and some rolling tobacco. A non-smoker for ten years, after four lungfuls, he'd had enough; he flicked his rollie into the road and tossed the tobacco onto the nearest empty table. To take the taste away he swashed a mouthful of beer. Then he called Ailish and left her a voicemail. 'Hi. Sorry about leaving in a hurry. Someone's just broken into my flat and set it on fire. I've just left the police station. I think it was Barros. He's watching me. I gave the police your phone number and address. They wanted to know where I've been staying in London. I said we'd just split up. If they call you, please don't mention Barros.'

Next he called Kevin.

Not wanting to wake Phylida, Kevin rolled out of bed and took the call in the bathroom. Vince told him about the fire, but not about his conversation with Barros.

'Where are you now?' said Kevin.

'In a pub up by the cricket ground.'

'And where are you staying tonight?'

'I'll stay at the flat. It smells, but it's okay. Do you still want to meet up about the book?'

'Let's leave it for a while until you've settled things with Barros. There's no hurry.'

As Kevin rang off and slid back into bed, Phylida switched on the light above the headboard. 'What's he up to?'

'God knows.'

'God and you you mean.' She stared at him waiting for an explanation. With no response she moved closer. 'Kevin, can you hear me? What's his problem?'

'He calls me because I'm the only person he knows that knows Barros. It's nothing to do with Millwall.'

'Yes, so you said.' She rolled onto her back disappointed that he wouldn't confide.

'Phy, I will tell you, but not just now.'

'Okay, if that's what you want.'

He kissed her cheek.

She smiled. 'There was something I was going to ask you...a favour.'

'What?'

'Would you mind if I stayed here for a while?'

He hesitated and said, 'Okay...I suppose.'

'Sorry, I shouldn't have asked. It doesn't matter.' She rolled away and disappeared into the bathroom.

He called out. 'Of course you can. I wasn't expecting it that's all. Is there something wrong?'

From the bathroom, she said, 'It's to do with the Abrahams' murder. We've been told to take precautions.' She reappeared with a glass of water, and standing at the foot of the bed with her legs apart, she said, 'I suppose what I'm saying is, will you have me?'

'I'd love to have you,' said Kevin, smiling. 'You can stay as long as you like.'

'If it doesn't work out I can go to Braney.'

'Phy, I like having you around.' He held open the duvet and patted the bed.

– – – – – – – –

286

Vince drained his fifth pint. *Fuck them all. Barros, Ailish, Spinks...seagulls, cats, dogs, fags, smoothies and volleyball, staircases and books and footballers and letting agents.* He wondered if the internet cafe opposite the Greenhouse Effect was still open. He could splatter his story everywhere. *Kevin will get over it. It'll be good for him. Spinks can sue Ailish for breach of contract. Barros can fuck off back to Spain. People will thank me. I'll write a book. I'll go to South America. Ecuador. They can't touch me there.*

He closed his eyes and took a deep breath. *From tomorrow...from tomorrow things will be different.* He smiled and promised to smile more often. Then opening his eyes he glanced at the discarded packet of tobacco still on the table where he'd thrown it. *One last cigarette before tomorrow.* As he rose to his feet and stepped forward, a woman brushed past. It happened so fast all he noticed were her flip-flops and her tangled yellow hair. She snatched the tobacco from his outstretched fingers and said, 'Beat you old boy.' Then she grinned, pirouetted and jogged back to her friends waving the tobacco above her head.

Vince walked towards her and without stopping or turning, he said, 'I hope you fucking choke.' He didn't look back. All he heard was laughter.

Outside his flat the pavement had dried. Inside, he staggered heavy-legged up the stairs. He thought of Alex. They hadn't been in touch since March. *Perhaps he's found someone else, someone cheaper? I'll call him in the morning. Tell him about Spinks and the book and the trip to Spain. He can update Kirsty.* He peeled off three strips of tape that held the door shut, rolled them into a sticky ball and tossed it over his shoulder. Then he froze. He could hear voices and laughter from inside. *Squatters? They must have come in when the police left.* He listened for a few moments and then knocked. 'Hello?' But no one came, no one answered. He pushed back the door. *Why are they in the dark?*

'Hello?' he repeated. Between the shrieks of laughter he could tell they weren't British. Then with a steadying hand against the wall he moved from the front room to the kitchen and then to the rear bedroom. He had his answer when he looked down from the open window. In the garden were ten men around a trestle table loaded with bottles. Their barbeque over, they were now in the drinking phase, their daytime voices carrying in the cooling air. Vince lowered the sash, dragged his mattress into the lounge and shut the door.

He fell asleep in his clothes and then woke when he couldn't breathe. He had a leather-gloved hand tight around his neck and another over his mouth. A knee on his chest pinned him down. Vince gripped his attacker's forearm trying to force it away.

'Kick his head.' Unseen, the toe-end of a boot thumped into the side of Vince's head, centring on his right ear. Vince stopped struggling. 'Now shut up!' The man removed his gloved hand, leant forward and sniffed. 'The fucker's drunk.'

'So?' said the standing man

'He's drunk, so he won't remember. Tape him.'

The standing man tore off a yard of gaffer tape, dropped to his knees and wound it twice around Vince's head, covering his nose and mouth.

'You trying to kill him?'

'You what?'

'He can't breathe.'

The standing man dropped his tape and took out a small knife. With his knees either side of Vince's head, he nicked the tape around Vince's nostrils.

'Good, now give me the knife.' He took the blade and swiped it hard and fast across Vince's forehead. 'Let's go.'

'I thought we were supposed to warn him?'

'What do you think that is?' He pointed at the blood oozing from the four-inch cut. They took Vince's phone and wallet and left.

Vince clawed the tape from his mouth and spewed beery vomit into his lap. Fearing he might bleed to death, he hurried downstairs. Through the front door, he tripped at the base of the stone steps and hit the pavement face-first. And there he sat, his face a mask of blood, until a police patrol car picked him up and took him to A&E. None of the medical staff that patched him up – eighteen stitches across his forehead and five in his lip – asked how it had happened. They simply assumed he was a drunk drunk, and that his injuries were most likely self-inflicted.

He left the hospital late morning and walked to the Pump Room.   Andy gave him a hundred pounds and the key to his flat.   Vince walked to his bank, then Brighton Lets and finally to Kevin's.

Phylida answered through the intercom: 'Hello?'

Surprised at hearing a woman's voice, Vince wondered if he'd pressed the wrong buzzer. 'Kevin Furling?'

'Yes, but he's out right now.'

'When will he be back?' Vince assumed he was speaking to Kevin's cleaner.

'Who's this?'

'Vince Wynter, a friend of Kevin's.'

'Okay, come on up.'

When he reached the first floor landing, she said, 'My god, what happened?'   She barely recognised him through the patchwork of dressings and bruising.

'I was mugged last night.   They took my wallet and phone and...' Then he pointed at his face. 'My head hit the pavement.'

'You'd best come in,' she said.

'I can come back another time.'

'Don't be silly. He won't be long.'

'I just want his phone number.'

'Okay, I'll get it.'   She beckoned him in and shut the door. 'Go ahead, you know the way.'

She offered tea and disappeared into the kitchen. A minute later she came back into the lounge with two mugs of tea. 'So what are you working on now, another book?'

'Nothing really.'   He wondered if Kevin had told her he was bi or about his plans for a sequel.

'And how's Mr Barros these days?   You two still at loggerheads?'

'I don't really know.   I've not seen him since that day at the club.'

'So no problems?' she said.

'Not really. I hear you've had a few.'

'How's that?

'Didn't someone get killed?' Vince had only seen the headlines. 'Sounds like a right mess.'

'Yes, things could be better.' She picked up her phone and wrote down Kevin's number on the back of a takeaway menu.

'Do you have Barros'?'

She added Barros' number and then handed him the menu.

'Thanks, and thanks for the...' He nodded at the steaming mugs of tea.

'No problem. I'll let Kevin know about what happened.'

48

Whitehall, Tuesday 5ᵗʰ July

Caldicott had spent the morning pulling together a presentation for his afternoon meeting with Sir Terrence. He sat with his laptop on his knees wirelessly connected to the projector on his right.

'Go ahead,' said Sir Terrence.

He clicked on his first slide. 'This is a definition from Wikipedia. It's as good as any I found. The Gülen movement is a...'

'It's okay Robert, we can read, can't we Mathew?' Sir Terrence nudged Groves with his elbow.

> *The Gülen Movement is a transnational civic society movement inspired by the teachings of Turkish Islamic theologian* <u>Fethullah Gülen</u>. *His teachings about hizmet (altruistic service to the "common good") have attracted a large number of supporters in* <u>Turkey</u>, <u>Central Asia</u> *and increasingly in other parts of the world. The movement is mainly active in education and interfaith (and intercultural) dialogue; however, it also has aid initiatives and investments in media, finance, and health...'*

Caldicott added, 'There doesn't appear to be an official Gülen Movement website, not an English version anyway. It's a bit of an amorphous entity. It clearly exists, but it's hard to pin down. Fethullah Gülen has his own personal site but that's about his teachings.' He clicked on his second slide. 'And in 2007 the Gülen Institute was formed in Houston.'

The Gülen Institute

...The Institute aims to promote academic research as well as grass roots activity towards bringing about positive social change, namely the establishment of stable peace, social justice, and social harmony by focusing on the themes of education, volunteerism and civic initiatives.

'That's marvellous,' said Sir Terrence, 'but no mention of Islam?'

'Officially no,' said Caldicott. 'Fethullah Gülen is an Islamic scholar and his themes are about cultural understanding and tolerance. He's been living in a small town in Pennsylvania for years. He was forced out of Turkey and in 2013 received a prize for peace building.'

'So what's their motivation?' said Sir Terrence.

'Diğergamlık,' said Groves, taking the opportunity to make a contribution, 'Though I'm not sure on the pronunciation. Diğergamlık is based on altruism.' Groves looked down at his notes. 'Then there's personal responsibility or mesuliyet duygusu, and the passion for giving... verme tutkusu.'

'Very good,' said Sir Terrence.

'YouTube,' said Groves. 'It's all there.'

'So they're a peace movement,' said Sir Terrence. 'What's the harm in that?'

'Yes, but peace originating from the east,' said Caldicott. 'Not the west. There are bound to be suspicions given where we are.'

'They have some serious backers,' said Groves. 'There are claims on the net that Bill Gates funded a Gülen-backed foundation, though I haven't been able to verify that. Most of the Movement's corporate backers are Turkish.'

'And what have they done in the UK?' said Sir Terrence.

'Before we discuss that,' said Caldicott, 'I'd just like to show you what some outsiders think.' He clicked on his third slide. 'According to 'Liberate our People', an organisation based in Alaska, the Gülen Movement wants to establish a caliphate.'

Liberate our People state that:

...Gülen seeks the re-establishment of the Ottoman

Empire and through its network of madrassahs, it seeks

the indoctrination of Turkish culture and religion and

the establishment of an international caliphate.

'A caliphate?' said Sir Terrence.

'It's a sort of unified Muslim government,' said Groves. He turned over a page of his notes. 'It's an aristocratic theocratic constitutional republic.'

'Not much to do with democracy then?' said Sir Terrence.

'Not much,' said Groves, 'but then it's probably not true.'

Caldicott read through more critical opinion, all of which stated that the Movement sought cultural and political homogenisation. Then adding, 'There seem to be a lot of people who fear it.'

'And how big is it?' said Sir Terrence.

'It's a volunteer organisation,' said Caldicott. 'Maybe five or six million, in over a hundred countries. The numbers are probably guesses. Much of its funding comes from the business sector and it's not short of money.'

'And who's interested in which football club?' asked Sir Terrence.

'All we have are press articles,' said Caldicott. 'No public statements. If we ignore the web chatter, the first mention came via Reuters.' Caldicott brought forward the next slide which summarised the article:

...Turkish telecoms billionaire, Izir Manas, a known Gülen supporter, is looking to buy an English League Premiership side. His likely target is Chelsea, whose current owner, Edik Martinov, is seeking an exit following the Russian Government's attempts to repatriate his oil and gas assets. Martinov's office has refused to comment...

...Mete Kocak, a Turkish journalist, was recently gaoled following the publication of an online article which criticised Manas after his company was awarded a billion-lira contract by the Turkish military...

'The implication here is that if you criticise a Gülen Movement supporter, you can end up in prison. Manas has since issued a statement via his company's press office saying he's not interested in Chelsea, but it's difficult to tell what the real situation is.'

'We can get the Foreign Office to look into it,' said Sir Terrence.

Caldicott continued. 'There have been a number of reports of Turkish journalists being gaoled, hence the claims that the Gülen Movement has infiltrated the judiciary and the police.'

'A bit of a mixed bag then?' said Sir Terrence.

'If you set aside those that believe the Gülen Movement is some sort of covert Islamic plot, most of the criticism is that being a Gülen supporter buys you power and influence.'

Groves came in. 'It's possible that it was well intentioned, but overtime it's been subverted. Their founding principal is altruism, but now it's accused of fostering a network that embodies favouritism and self-interest.'

'Something of a paradox,' said Sir Terrence. 'But from what you know, do you think it's a genuine peace movement or something else?'

'I'm afraid we haven't got a clear picture,' said Caldicott. 'There are respected academics outside Turkey that hold completely contradictory opinions on what its real aims are. Some say it corrupts while others say it's the basis for a harmonious civil society. My own view is that it may not matter.'

'Go on,' said Sir Terrence.

'It won't matter what the Select Committee do or find or what the Foreign Office tells us, it's about perception, and the perception, based on web traffic, is that people are vehemently against any Gülen supporter taking over at Chelsea. Even if we gave it a clean bill of health, we can't change that, it's too late.'

Sir Terrence nodded.

Caldicott continued, 'Since the first story appeared linking Manas to the League Premiership the internet and blog traffic has exploded.'

Groves nodded and said, 'Over the last couple of days I've tried to quantify and categorise the web activity from before and after the Manas story. I've looked at the sites close to Chelsea, the fanzines, the blog sites and forums.' Groves paused, unsure if Sir Terrence was following.

'Carry on Mathew, I'm with you.'

'These sites are full of comment and it's all negative. It's anti-Turkey, anti-Gülen and anti-Islam. Though Manas' office has denied his interest in Chelsea, there are now other rumours about other Turkish companies. Last week Türkiye Enerji were linked to Chelsea and the week before that a shipping company. Both companies are Gülen backers and both have been implicated in contract scandals and the funding of madrassahs.'

Sir Terrence raised his hand as if about to speak, but Groves continued.

'And there's a Facebook campaign to block Islamic involvement in English football.'

'So we do have a problem,' said Sir Terrence, and then looking at Caldicott, he added, 'Have you spoken to the League Premiership?'

'I'm seeing them tomorrow.'

'Good. Anything else I need to know now?' Caldicott shook his head. 'Okay, well keep looking at it. I'll get the Foreign Office to do some work and I'll brief the PM. Let's meet again on Thursday.'

– – – – – – – – –

By Wednesday morning the situation had changed. Home Office data supplied by several Internet Service Providers confirmed Caldicott's initial findings. There had been a dramatic rise in internet activity opposing any Gülen connection with English or Scottish clubs. The Facebook campaign had over a half a million supporters. The PM told Sir Terrence that the situation had to be brought under control and that the sport's governing bodies must act decisively.

At midday, two hours before Caldicott was due to meet Frank Hobson, Sir Terrence called.

'Robert, are you alone?'

'Yes.'

'What time's your meeting with the football people?'

'This afternoon at two. What's happened?'

'The PM's worried,' said Sir Terrence, deepening his voice. 'He wants the League people to put a stop to it. He doesn't want Gülen or any other faith organisations involved in British sport. He wants us to be the messenger.'

'I see,' replied Caldicott. 'I was planning to leave at one-thirty. Do you want me to arrange a taxi?'

'I'm afraid you'll have to manage on your own. It's quite straightforward. A warning shot. Spare them the detail, but make it absolutely clear they understand the Government's position and where it's prepared to go.'

'Is there anything in writing?'

'No, but we're talking regulation. The PM wants religion out of football. If they don't respond favourably, the Government will regulate. Do you follow me?'

'I think so,' said Caldicott. 'Is the PM thinking of regulating ownership or something more wide-ranging?'

'If I knew Robert, I'd tell you.'

'Okay,' said Caldicott, realising he'd asked one question too many.

'These League people must take whatever action they deem necessary, but if they don't, we might have a new regulator...*Ofsport*.'

'Can I mention that?'

'See how they respond. Use it if you have to.'

'Understood. I'll speak to you when I get back.'

'Tomorrow Robert, we'll do it tomorrow.'

— — — — — — —

Five minutes before Caldicott arrived at the Gherkin, Frank Hobson read his diary entry for the 16th June: *Meeting with Robert Caldicott, Cabinet Office. Talked generalities about closer engagement between Government and LPFL. Actions – None*

They shook hands and Caldicott introduced Groves. 'Mathew has been working with me on the sport side, so I thought it would be useful experience for him.' More importantly, Caldicott wanted Groves along as a witness and record-keeper.

'Keen sports fan or are you a player Mathew?' said Hobson, offering his hand.

'Architecture and design are more my thing,' replied Groves, 'but I am interested in the politics of sport.'

'The politics?' said Hobson, encouraging Groves to elaborate.

'Politics is probably the wrong word. I'm interested in the way businesses work and evolve and as I see it, football is primarily a business.'

Hobson reckoned Groves was in his early twenties, so barely a teenager when he'd taken over as the League's CEO. 'That's very interesting Mathew.'

Groves smiled, knowing that Hobson was mocking him.

'Please take a seat.' Hobson gestured to the two swivel chairs and then walked around his desk and sat opposite. 'How can I help this time?'

Caldicott went straight to the point. 'The Prime Minister and the Secretary of State for Sport have some concerns about your organisation.'

Hobson leant forward with his hands clasped. 'In what way?'

As Caldicott spoke, Groves started taking notes. 'The PM is concerned about club ownership, about owners having religious affiliations. It's not a direction that the Government supports.'

'Are you saying the Prime Minister objects to the Church investing in football?'

'It's not about one religion or another.' Caldicott thought that perhaps it would be best to steer responsibility away from the PM. 'It's a direction that the Cabinet feels could be destabilising.'

'He's worried about the Gülen Movement?'

Groves made a note that Hobson had been first to mention Gülen.

'As I said, the Cabinet is worried, but not specifically about Gülen. They're worried about a trend. There could be civil unrest and that can't be ignored, it's unaffordable.'

'In what way?' said Hobson.

'Politically, socially, economically, and the Government wants the LPFL to stop it.'

'I see,' said Hobson, nodding. 'And is this urgent?'

'It is.'

'And what's the penalty?'

'The penalty is regulation.' Caldicott glanced at Groves, wondering if he'd sensed it too. It was all far too easy. Hobson was offering no fight.

'And what exactly is it you want us to stop?'

'The LPFL will be regulated unless you stop organisations with religious affiliations taking ownership of League Premiership clubs.'

Hobson took a pen from his jacket pocket and scribbled a couple of words. Then he said, 'But what about...'

Caldicott knew what was coming and cut in. 'We'll be putting the same case to the Footballing Association. It applies to all professional sides.'

Hobson made another note on his pad, and said, 'We can't do that, we don't have the authority.'

'I'm sure you can find a way.'

'We can't stop people going to church.'

'Sorry?' said Caldicott.

'If an owner wants to go to church we...'

Caldicott cut in again. 'I think you know that's not what I'm asking. As I understand it, you do checks on prospective owners?' Hobson nodded. 'Well you'll need to widen those checks. I don't see the problem. Either you do it or the Government will arrange for it to be done on your behalf, and they won't be doing it for free.'

'That sounds a little threatening,' said Hobson.

'Not at all. I'm sure you're aware that a select committee is looking at this issue now and it's highly likely they'll come to the same conclusion. I can't see Parliament not backing their recommendations. I'm just here to let you know the way things are heading. There is no room for manoeuvre.'

'I'll have to get the clubs together.'

Caldicott nodded. 'And when you do, the Government expects decisive action, nothing less.'

'And if someone leaks to the press?'

'Leaks what?' said Caldicott.

'That you're putting pressure on us to kick out the Church of England.'

'I never said such a thing.' Caldicott looked to Groves, who nodded. 'The Cabinet, the Prime Minster and the Secretary of State have nothing to hide. There will probably be a Government statement on the matter next week, so you've got a few days to prepare your response.'

'We have an AGM in two weeks. Can you wait till then?'

'All I'm prepared to say is that you need to act quickly.'

Hobson nodded.

'I think we're done,' said Caldicott. All three stood and shook hands over Hobson's desk. 'Perhaps we should speak later in the week?'

'I'll be in touch,' said Hobson.

As soon as his visitors had left Hobson called Jeanie in. 'We need to contact all the board members. We need to bring the AGM forward.'

Jeanie frowned.

'Don't ask,' he said. 'I'll draft an email and I'd like you to phone round and see who's in the UK and what days they're available next week. Let's try for Wednesday or Thursday. Tell them it's urgent and put them through to me if they're not happy.' After an hour Jeanie had only been able to contact four board members. When she called Tom Cowly, she was diverted to Phylida.

'I can make it,' said Phylida, 'but Tom's overseas and won't be back until the end of next week. If you can let me know what's it's about, he might fly back or I can stand in for him.'

'You'll have to speak to Frank,' said Jeanie.

After the usual pleasantries, Phylida said, 'I understand you want to bring the AGM forward. Unfortunately Tom's not around, but I'd be happy to step in.'

'To be honest,' said Hobson, 'I'm in a bit of an awkward situation. We have an urgent issue that I need to present to all the shareholders, but the way things are going we'll probably be sticking with the original date. Tom's not the only one that's not available.'

'Okay, well I'll see you on the twenty-first.'

'I look forward to it.'

Hobson put the phone down and called Jeanie in. 'Thanks for trying, but it's not going to work.'

'Is there anything else that needs doing?'

'No. Email everyone and let them know we're sticking with the original date.

49

Amaya, Knightsbridge, Sunday 10th July

Ailish dressed the same; the same skirt, blouse and shoes. She told Spinks that she wanted to recreate their first dinner date, the same time, restaurant, and table. He was happy to go along with it and didn't ask why. If he had, she would have told him, I want to go back to before we knew each other, to before the cheque. They met outside Amaya's and as before she was late.

'You look familiar,' he said. Then he grasped her hands and kissed her on the lips.

She smiled. 'That's not how I remember it.'

'Have I done wrong?'

'Yes and no. I'll forgive you.'

The maître d' led them to their table, topped their glasses with champagne and headed back to the front door.

'We're going back to June the twenty-third,' she said. 'So I know nothing of MBF2...and our lips have never met.'

He pouted like a toddler on the naughty step. 'I don't want to go there.'

She mirrored his face. 'Try your best Mr Spinks.' She edged her chair in closer to the table and leant forward. 'I would like to go back to the day when you decided to use Vince's idea. When was that?'

Without hesitation, he said, 'It was the day after Vince lost in court.'

'Why then?'

'No particular reason. I'd been thinking about it before that. I thought about it on the flight to New York.'

'New York?'

'I flew to New York after I met Vince.'

'I thought you and Vince were drunk?'

302

'A little, but alcohol doesn't stop me thinking. It can stop me remembering, so I always carry this.' From his inside pocket he took out a small notebook no larger than the palm of his hand. 'It's just for stray thoughts.'

'So on that flight you noted down Vince's idea?'

'Yes and no. It wasn't Vince's idea.' He flicked quickly through the pages. 'Here we are.' Then he passed it across the table.

Underneath the date, she read out, *'Mid-Atlantic, heading to New York. Look again at the boundaries between the visual and prose. Concepts in words.'* She looked up. 'So that shows you made a note suggesting something similar to Art-Vision directly after you met Vince.'

'Yes, but I have earlier notebooks. I can show you them. Also I used the word 'again'. The idea wasn't new to me.'

She hadn't expected him to contest the very origin of Art-Vision.

'Vince mentioned it to me at Heathrow, but that really doesn't mean anything.'

'I think it does,' she said, reaching forward for her glass. 'Without meeting Vince you wouldn't have made another entry in your notebook. You wouldn't have looked at it *again*. You wouldn't have created the one about the Nobel Prize winning scientist.

He smiled. 'I agree. All I'm saying is that someone else probably thought of it before Vince, even the one about the scientist, just as someone would have thought of MBF before I did.'

She frowned. 'I think they call this obfuscation.'

'No, I'm serious. Lots of people have the same ideas and they get passed around and never used. Have you heard of Calista Graham?'

'Should I?' she said.

'She paints like you.'

'Okay, so I'm not original. I never said I was.'

'No, and I never said you copied her.'

'And you never met the person who first dreamt of building a brick cock?'

'No I didn't, but does that matter? They didn't realise it or see its potential. Maybe they didn't have the opportunity.'

'But you did?' she said.

'Yes, and Vince didn't see the potential of Art-Vision. He came across the idea but he didn't use it, and he didn't own it. Whatever he said to me, or whatever ideas he thinks he passed to me, it was all unconditional, without obligation. But it wasn't all one way. At Heathrow I passed him some ideas too. It was a drunken exchange. There was no contract.'

'So you're saying no one can have an original idea?'

'No, but they're much rarer than you might think. I passed him an idea for a story, but I'm not claiming it was mine.'

'Like what?' she said, unsure if he was being serious. She now felt she was back to the twenty-third, and once again unsure if Spinks was playing mind games.

'I told him about a book I'd always wanted to write. It was about an explorer who walked across Africa in the late 1930s. He walked from west to east, from the Atlantic to the Indian Ocean, and every few hundred yards he stopped, took out a stone pendulum from a silk-lined box and timed the pendulum's swing. He wasn't alone. He had a hundred Africans with him carrying supplies, chains and theodolites. He took thousands of readings. So while blood was flowing in Spain and Hitler was building his army, this man was swinging a pendulum across Africa. That's what I told Vince. He could have used it.'

'Is that it?' she said, expecting more.

'Pretty much.'

'It's not the same. That's not a story.'

'It could be.'

'What of, The Adventures of Pendulum Man?'

He laughed.

'Mr Spinks, I'm starting to think you're completely obsessed with things that dangle.'

He laughed again. 'Whether I am or not, I didn't own that story. I didn't write it and Vince didn't own Art-Vision.

Like everything, it had predecessors. I thought Art-Vision had merit, Vince thought it was a joke.'

'So why the two-year delay?'

'I needed to test it. I finished it about fifteen months ago. I had all the visions on the walls in my house and I left them there to see if they had staying power.'

'You weren't worried that Vince would object once you went public?'

'Not really. When you've lost two libel cases people stop listening.'

'What?'

'Vince has history. He libelled someone about ten years ago. His paper apologised and they settled out of court.'

'I didn't know that.' She paused and then waved her hand as if it was of no consequence. 'Nevertheless, it was still risky of you. He had nothing to lose.'

'And nothing to gain. He had no case.'

'But what about his statement to his solicitor?'

'I thought we've covered that. Witnessed or not, it's still his word against mine. He didn't exhibit Art-Vision. He was never going to.' Spinks leant forward. 'And I didn't believe your story about Dublin.'

'Not for a minute?'

'If you'd done that, you'd have shown us your evidence straightaway. It's happened before so we are naturally suspicious.'

'The same thing?'

'Not exactly. The solicitor's letter was a new twist.'

'So why did you pay me, if you knew it was all bullshit?'

'Because I like you. I liked what you were trying to do.'

'Do you *like* all the people that try to screw you?'

'No, you're the first.'

'So it was just because you *liked* me?' She looked away. 'What an idiot. It's embarrassing.'

'You wanted the truth. And it's not embarrassing. You were the reason I gave Vince the money. We all make mistakes and he paid a heavy price.' Spinks rose from his seat and grabbed her wrists but she twisted free.

'You were laughing at me.'

305

He sat down. 'I wasn't laughing. I'm glad you did it. I was happy to buy your painting. I'm still happy. It was a worthy cause.'

'Because you liked me?'

'Does there have to be another reason? You're forgetting, you were the one trying to screw me. Your plan succeeded. Don't be upset because I paid up for the wrong reason.'

She nodded. 'You're right. I suppose I should apologise. I haven't done that.'

'It's not necessary.'

'It is. I'm sorry for what I did.'

'Forget it. You were helping a friend.'

'There's something else though. I have a hundred thousand in my bank account. Vince took two hundred. He refused to take it all. You can have the hundred back.'

'I don't want it and I won't take it back. Give it away if you want.'

'Are you sure?'

He nodded. 'So are we finished now?' he said. 'Are we back to the present?'

'Not quite.' She opened her clutch bag and glanced at the post-it note stuck to her phone.

1. *Art-Vision?*

2. *D Spinks – real deal or faker?*

3. *Vince to court?*

She looked up. 'It's not important...perhaps another time.'

'Come on, let's do it.'

She sipped some champagne. 'There's no need. I'm sure it's been said before. It's probably all written down on MBF2.'

'If that's the case,' he said, 'I'll have an answer.'

She smiled. 'It was about your work, your art. Mr Spinks, are you an artist or a player?'

'Both...neither. Right now I'm a part-timer.'

'But was it ever a passion?'

'Does it have to be? I was determined. Is determination a sign of passion? I suppose like you, like everyone in this restaurant, I filled a niche.'

She shook her head.

'I made art because I thought I could make money and because I thought it might be fun. I was twenty-one.' He shrugged his shoulders, as if to suggest that youth alone was explanation enough. 'I was sure I could make stuff as good as anyone else. The ideas seemed to come fairly easily, and art, irrespective of what it does or means, is a business. I knew that much.'

'That's such a shame,' she said.

'No it isn't. No one's been hurt or misled. If you like, I'm redistributing wealth. I employ people and give others something to write about. I try to keep the debate alive and give people experiences.'

'So what of the artists, the really good British painters, the ones without a business head, who never get recognised? What about them?'

'What do you mean?' he said.

'I mean you come and knock-up MBF and make a fortune and they're still living off crusts.'

'Like you?'

She laughed, 'No, not like me. I said *good* artists.'

'Are you suggesting that stop knocking up stuff and let others take my place? It sounds like you want to regulate art. You want a panel that decides what's worthy and what isn't.'

'No, not that.'

'I've never had a penny from the Arts Council. I never went to Art College. I've not deprived anyone of their

307

opportunity. Why should I stop making things that people want to buy?'

'Like the crusher?'

'No, not like the crusher.' He smiled. 'But people like to buy and own things. The reason doesn't matter and I can't change that.'

She believed him. 'I'm sorry.'

'No need to be.'

They leant forward and kissed over the table.

'Are you ready to order?' said the waiter as they dropped back in their chairs.

'Five minutes,' said Spinks. The waiter nodded and moved away.

'I didn't mean to be critical,' she said. 'I like your work.'

'Are we finished then?'

'One more question. Did you have to take Vince to court? He did apologise.'

'He did, but he didn't say it was untrue.' Spinks looked away at nothing and then back to her. 'I knew of Vince before we met at Heathrow. When he told me what he did and his name I recognised it.'

'You knew him?'

'No. I remembered his name. He'd written a review of a programme I was in. He wasn't complimentary.'

'So it was revenge?'

'No. Lots of people criticise me. That's normal. But part of my function is to protect myself, to defend what I've done. I don't rollover if people accuse me of doing things I haven't done. Vince asserted something that wasn't true. The so-called death-bed letter with Christopher was an idea I'd been thinking about, but we hadn't written it. I hadn't mentioned it to Christopher.'

'Now you're getting me confused,' she said. 'Are you saying Vince didn't know you told him a lie?'

'No he didn't, but Vince is a journalist, so he should know to check his facts. He should have asked me before he wrote what he did. If I hadn't sued for libel, his assertion would have been believed.'

'He was wrong?'

'Yes, when he wrote about it on the internet, he was wrong. Spinks held up his hands, fingers splayed. 'I can't see any other way it could have gone. Honestly, I have nothing personal against Vince.'

'So we'll eventually see this letter when you and Witherspoon are dead?'

He raised his eyebrows and winked.

She decided there was little point in pressing further. 'Okay, I'm finished.'

'Good. So are you still staying at mine tonight?'

'Definitely.'

50

The Gherkin, Wednesday 20th July

On the morning of the LPFL's annual general meeting, Frank Hobson handed Jeanie two plastic boxes, each no bigger than a packet of cigarettes. She turned them over looking for clues to their function. 'What are they?'

'They're phone jammers. I don't want any leaks or interruptions...not while the meeting is going on. Put one in the boardroom, somewhere where it can't be seen and leave one in reception. Turn them on ten minutes before we start.'

She raised her eyebrows. 'If that's what you want.'

'Please...I'll explain later.'

At two o'clock there were thirty-six in the boardroom with tableside seating for twenty-four. Phylida sat behind Cowly and on either side of him were the CEOs from Southampton and Newcastle. Hobson began with an apology about the loss of phone reception, blaming it on a localised mast failure. While he talked, Jeanie passed around the agenda.

'As you can see,' said Hobson, 'I've added another item: *Regulatory changes with respect to club ownership.*'

Speculative conversations immediately broke out. Phylida leant forward, her chin close to Cowly's right shoulder. She whispered, 'Do you think it's to do with us?'

'Could be,' said Cowly.

Hobson continued. 'If I can have your attention.' He waited a few seconds for the chatter to stop. 'My apologies for not forewarning you about this additional item. I'm afraid recent events have led me to be a little more cautious than usual.' His eyes flicked towards Cowly. 'I didn't want any discussion about this matter until each of you had heard the background directly from me. Two weeks ago some civil servants came to see me. They delivered a message directly from Number 10 and the Cabinet.' Hobson then recounted his meeting with Caldicott and Groves, occasionally referring to his notes. He made no mention of Millwall or the Church of England.

'In a nutshell, we've been given a warning. If we don't take measures to keep religion out of club football, the Government will do it for us. That's basically it.'

John Shrimpton, the CEO from Everton, spoke first. 'You mentioned regulation. Does the Government want us to regulate or just to put a stop to it? They're different.'

Hobson suspected many around the table were thinking much the same. 'Thanks John. I think that's the crux. I'm assuming most of us are against any regulation.'

'Just a moment,' said Cowly. He looked at Shrimpton and then Hobson. 'You're getting way ahead of yourselves. Are you saying the Government wants the Church of England out?'

'They weren't that specific,' said Hobson. 'They want to stop a trend and they don't want the Gülen involved in English football.' Hobson looked toward the Chelsea CEO. 'But Gülen isn't the issue. The Government doesn't want *any* religions involved.'

'Okay,' said Cowly, 'So does that mean they want us out?'

'They didn't say,' replied Hobson. He looked down at his notes, as if double-checking.

'Well I think we need to know,' said Cowly, emphatically.

'Personally,' said Hobson, 'I've no objection to the Church staying on as the owners of Millwall, but that may cause us problems and it may not satisfy the Prime Minister.'

Cowly tried again. 'Therefore, we need to know for sure exactly what they want.'

The Arsenal CEO, Leonard Ledeby, spoke. 'I know what I want and it's not regulation of any sort. It's already scaring off investors.'

'That's as maybe,' said Cowly, 'but Millwall isn't the problem.'

'Yes and no,' said Ledeby. 'I've no problem with Millwall's ownership, but it sets a precedent. We'll be in all sorts of trouble if we discriminate in favour of the Church of England. I don't think we can make an exception for you.'

Hobson smiled inside. He couldn't have made the point any better.

Ledeby continued. 'If we have Government regulation, they'll have to crawl all over us. It would be a nightmare.' He looked toward Hobson for support.

Cowly hit the table with a clenched fist 'That's the point! No one knows where the money's from and that's the way you want it to stay.'

'That's not fair,' said Hobson, 'We're as open and democratic as any other business.'

Cowly groaned at the absurdity of Hobson's statement. 'You're forgetting my background Frank. I know all about the ways of UK Plc. What you really fear is financial transparency, not regulation.'

'Tom,' said Hobson, 'that's a completely different matter which we're not here to discuss. The issue is religion. The Government wants religion out of football, and as Leonard said, I don't see how we can make an exception for Millwall. We'd end up in court.'

Cowly shook his head. 'So what are you going to do?'

'I'd like to see how you all feel. I suggest we have a simple show of hands.' He paused and looked around at the nodding heads. 'Who's happy with some form of Government regulation?' No one moved. 'What about some form of internal regulation that would bar religious bodies from owning LPFL clubs?' Thirteen hands went up.

'So how does that help?' said Cowly.

'It shows that there is a clear majority against any form of external regulation,' said Hobson.

'There are other options Frank,' said Ledeby. 'If the Church refuses to sell Millwall, we can exclude them because they would be a threat to the League's commercial viability.'

'How's that?' said Cowly.

'We don't have to prove it,' said Ledeby. 'If the majority of us think you are, then you are. I think it's undeniable that greater regulation would be a commercial threat.'

'So what if a company that was known to support the Gülen Movement took over Arsenal?' said Cowly.

'I wouldn't let it happen. It won't happen.'

Cowly scoffed. 'It could happen and you wouldn't even know about it.'

Hobson tapped the table. 'Gentlemen, let's get back to the central point. The Government has made it absolutely clear that they want religion out or they'll intervene.'

'Okay, so stop the Gülen, but let us stay.'

'We'd be tied in knots,' said Hobson. 'As Leonard said, it would be discriminatory.'

Cowly laughed at the irony.

Hobson paused and looked slowly around the table, eye to eye with each CEO, and without exception they nodded their assent. Then he looked at Cowly. 'Tom, we've established that this board is against regulation. What we have to do now is show the Government that we've taken action and the only way we can do that is by excluding Millwall.'

'So you're kicking us out?' said Cowly.

'I think the Church should sell Millwall. I think that would be the best outcome for all of us.' He didn't wait for Cowly to come back. 'Can we have a show of hands if you think the Church should offload Millwall?' Their hands rose quickly, no one hesitated. Cowly was furious.

'Good,' said Hobson. 'We'll take a short break.' He looked at his watch. 'Ten minutes. Everyone back here at eleven. The toilets are down the corridor, and please no phone calls, no texts, nothing about this to anyone until the meeting is concluded.'

Cowly stood up and set off to confront Hobson, but Phylida reached out and gripped his wrist, bringing him to a halt. 'Tom, let's go outside. Let's get some air.'

He looked over his shoulder and down at her hand still tight around his wrist.

'Come on,' she said.

Outside the meeting room they took the lift and didn't speak until they were in the Gherkin's foyer.

'What do you think?' said Cowly, looking down at the floor, pacing one way then the other.

'I think Hobson's been sitting on it for two weeks,' she said, 'ever since he called me about bringing the AGM forward.'

Cowly stopped and looked up. 'He's a fucking idiot.'

It was the first time she'd ever heard him swear. 'Whatever he is, we only have his word on this. It could be a conspiracy.'

'Like what?' said Cowly.

'We've seen nothing in writing. Perhaps Hobson wants us out and is blaming it on the Government.'

'I suppose that's possible, but the outcome's the same. I think all the Gülen talk about Chelsea has spooked everyone, and blocking something like Gülen might also be a popular move for the Government.'

She nodded. 'So what can we do?'

Cowly didn't hesitate. 'The Assets Committee will have to disinvest. I can't see any other way and the sooner the better. We need to act before the season starts, before we lose any matches.'

'That gives us a couple of weeks.'

'Not long, but it's not impossible. 'I'll call Sir William now and let him know what's happened.'

When the AGM finally ended there had been no vote to exclude Millwall and no vote to regulate club ownership. The minutes of the meeting simply stated that: *Tom Cowly informed the LPFL board that Millwall FC was up for sale and that a new owner was being sought.*

In the taxi from the Gherkin, Cowly made another call to Sir William. He told him it was done, but for the detail.

'I'm meeting the Archbishop tomorrow,' said Sir William. 'We've scheduled a Committee meeting for the afternoon at the usual venue. Can you make it?'

'Yes.' Cowly looked at Phylida and she nodded. 'We'll be there.'

'It'll be presented as an exit by the Church, rather than an expulsion. So we need to think about how we handle that.'

'I agree,' said Cowly. 'See you tomorrow.'

Back at the Gherkin, after everyone had left, Hobson called Landuzière. 'It's done. The Church is selling Millwall, there won't be a repeat.'

'Good,' said Landuzière.

'Are we finished?'

'Yes.' Landuzière left the phone box and called Spilotti on his mobile.

51

Oxford, Thursday 21ˢᵗ July

At the conclusion of the Assets Committee meeting, Sir William Denham's office issued a press release:

The Office

of:

The First Church Estates Commissioner.
Chairman of the Commissioners' Assets Committee

<u>*Sir William Denham confirms Church to sell Millwall*</u>

The Commissioners of the Church of England have today instructed the board of Millwall Football Club to seek new ownership. The club is profitable and the Commissioners believe it has tremendous potential should it secure its place in the LPFL. The sale process will be coordinated by Mr Tom Cowly, the club's CEO, and all enquiries should be directed to his office at Millwall FC. The Assets Committee, under the stewardship of Sir William Denham, believe that at this current time professional sport is not an appropriate investment sector for the Church of England.

Church of England Media Centre, Church House,
Great Alder Street, London, W1T 9ZZ

316

On their drive back to London, Cowly asked Phylida to contact Newsnight.

'You don't have to,' she said.

'I know, but now's not the time to hide.'

She called the programme's producer. 'Phoebe, it's Phylida Cranson from Millwall. Are you okay to talk?'

'Yes, go ahead.'

'Would you like Tom Cowly on your show again?'

'Why, what's happened?'

'The Church is selling Millwall. They've decided to get out. We thought you might like to know why.'

'When did this happen?'

'A couple of hours ago.'

'When's he available?'

She turned to Cowly. 'When?'

'Tonight,' said Cowly.

'We're only doing the one interview,' said Phylida. 'So tonight, if you want an exclusive.'

'Yes, we'll do it. I'll call you back'

Phylida turned to him. 'Do you want me to come along?'

'No, you can watch from home.'

She didn't argue. She'd already made arrangements to be with Kevin in Brighton.

– – – – – – – – –

The first-half of the programme were on the developing crisis in South Africa. Sixteen were dead and forty-three in hospital. Newsnight's Peter Marshall, reporting live from Johannesburg, said the demonstrators' only demand was for adequate housing. Cowly watched from the sidelines, uneasy with the juxtaposition of Marshall's report with the minor upheavals of an English football club. At five minutes to eleven Lakin turned to the autocue:

BARELY TWO MOONS AGO THE
CHURCH OF ENGLAND ANNOUNCED ITS
INTENTION TO CLEAN UP ENGLISH

FOOTBALL.   MILLWALL   FOOTBALL
CLUB   WOULD   BRING   SOME
RESPECTABILITY AND HONOUR BACK
TO THE NATION'S FAVOURITE GAME.
THE   PLAYERS   AND   MANAGEMENT
WOULD PRACTICE CHRISTIAN ETHICS
ON AND OFF THE FIELD OF PLAY. BUT
THAT WAS THEN. NOW THERE'S BEEN A
VOLTE-FACE. WE'RE NOW TOLD IT WAS
ALL   A   SILLY   MISTAKE   AND
PROFESSIONAL   FOOTBALL   IS   NO
LONGER A PLACE FOR MEN OF THE
CLOTH.   I'M JOINED BY TOM COWLY,
MILLWALL'S OUTGOING CEO.

As the camera closed in on Cowly, Phylida continued her steady rise and fall.

Kevin said, 'Phy, I can't watch it like this, they're hideous.' He was lying on his back with his head hanging over the end of the bed. 'Can't we stop for a bit?'

'No, just shut your eyes and listen.' She hadn't told him why the Church was selling Millwall.

Lakin swung his chair round to face Cowly. 'So what went wrong?'

'Paul, nothing went wrong. There has been no folly, no disaster. The club is ready for the new season. It's simply the case that the Church Commissioners have decided to recover their investment. The club is up for sale.'

'Yes, but why the exit?' said Lakin.

Cowly's ignored the why. His aim was to use every opportunity to portray the club as an attractive investment opportunity. 'We believe the club is in a stronger position now to establish its presence in the League Premiership and we hope to make a small profit on the sale.'

Lakin laughed. 'Yes, that's all well and good, but the viewers to this programme want to know why, otherwise they will be switching off and I'm not prepared to let that happen.' Lakin raised his eyebrows.

'We've invested in the club and cleared its structural debts...'

Lakin cut in. 'Were you pushed out?'

Cowly shook his head.

'Did the LPFL threaten to kick you out?'

Cowly realised he had a second to answer. Any longer, any slight hesitation, and it would come across as a lie.

Phylida lifted off.

'What you doing?' said Kevin.

'Nothing,' she said. 'Just stay where you are. Think of Millwall.' She couldn't bear to watch Cowly's humiliation. She turned round and slipped it back in. All she really wanted was to think about was the cock she was riding, but she expected Cowly to call when the programme ended.

'Are you working?' said Kevin.

'What d'you mean?'

'Are you putting this down as overtime?'

She pinched the inside if his thigh. 'Definitely. We at BSM...' She paused between each downward grind. '...have chargeable...fees for everything...including fucking...the client. Technically...I'm contracted...to work...for Millwall. So I'm paid...to watch Tom...and sit on...your cock. It's basic...multi-tasking. Then she turned her head to the mirror so that she could see the reflected image of the TV.

Cowly continued, '...the personal attacks and the death of Shelley Abrahams have been a factor. The Commissioners feel that these sorts of factors could be disruptive and damage the club and the Church.' Cowly knew immediately his explanation lacked credibility.

'Factors?' said Lakin, laughing. 'That's a new one. A woman's death is now a mere factor.' He turned to the camera and shook his head as if to say: are you hearing this? Then the smile disappeared. 'As far as I understand it, Shelley Abrahams' death had nothing to do with Ken Ffooks or is there something you're not telling us?

Cowly nodded. 'It looks like someone wanted to link her death to the club.'

'Is that what the police have said?'

'No.'

319

'So because of some possible link and a few tabloid headlines, you're running away.'

'We don't have to sell, but we feel it's in the best interest of the club that we seek a new owner.'

'And if you don't?'

'The smears will continue. I think there are some who will continue to attack us until the Church is out of professional football.'

'Like who?' said Lakin, leaning forward.

'I don't know.'

'You're running from ghosts? A few smears from who knows where and you chuck the towel in.'

Cowly had no answer. He looked down at his hands. He wondered what Imee and his colleagues at BSM were thinking.

Lakin shrugged his shoulders, and said, 'Who kicked you out?'

Cowly raised his head. 'No one is kicking us out. We could stay, but...if the club's ownership is continually being questioned we feel the football will eventually suffer. So the Commissioners and the board have decided to sell to ensure the club's future success.'

'Most odd,' said Lakin. 'It looks like a surrender.'

'Derek, it doesn't matter to me what you think it is, the club is in a good position and the Church is disinvesting with some regrets. We feel that the partnership had a lot going for it.'

'This is a heavy blow for the Archbishop.' Lakin was given the signal to end the interview.

'I don't think so,' said Cowly. 'I can't speak for him, but I understand that the Church will continue with its policy of investing in Britain, in British skills and innovation. As far as I know the Archbishop remains right behind that policy and I think he should be commended for it. Sometimes decisions don't work out as one might have planned and this just happens to be one of those occasions.'

'Tom Cowly, thank you very much.'

Phylida lifted off and leant forward on her elbows. 'Okay, let's do it.'

Kevin sat up. 'So what happens to you? You go back to BSM?'

'Right now I don't care,' she said, keen to get thoughts of Millwall out of her head.

Kevin reached for the Pjur on the bedside table and then coated two fingers. 'Ready?'

'I guess so.'

He circled her rim and then inserted the tip of his index finger. Her buttocks tightened. He slid his finger in halfway. 'How's that?'

'Interesting.'

He leant forward and kissed her shoulder. Then moving back again he turned his hand over, palm upwards and inserted the other finger. 'Push back a bit if you want.' He stroked her neck and slid his fingers all the way in. She rocked back and forth back against his hand. 'Okay, shall we try it?'

'Go for it,' she said.

He smeared lubricant on his cock, and then inching forward on his knees, he gently pushed into her.

'Is there any more?' she said.

'I'm halfway.'

She eased back until it was in all the way in. After half a dozen gentle thrusts, she said, 'It's okay, but...'

'But what?' he said, worried she wasn't liking it.

'I can't see the telly.'

He laughed, picked up the remote and hit the mute button, cutting off the weatherman mid-sentence. Then he held her hips, fully penetrated.

'What's wrong?' she said, looking into the mirror.

'I think that's enough for now.'

'I'm happy to carry on.'

He withdrew and kissed her neck.

She turned and sat back against the headboard. 'Your turn tomorrow and I promise to be gentle.'

'We don't have to,' he said.

She glanced at his cock. 'It was your idea, you're not backing out now.'

321

Later they lay side by side in the dark and talked about Millwall; about who might buy the club and whether or not the Church would lose money. They were questions neither could answer. Then he asked her if there were other reasons behind the sale.

'Not really,' she said, 'but if there were, I'm not allowed to tell anyone, not even my boyfriend.'

'Okay, well you can tell me then.'

She pretended to laugh.

He kissed her shoulder and said, 'I like you.'

'And I like that you like.'

'Will you stay here afterwards, after this is all over?'

'Live with you?'

'Yes, live with me.'

'And why would I do that?' she teased.

'Because I want you to.'

– – – – – – – – –

The day after his trip to A&E, Vince had transferred his belongings back to Andy's, and to make his stay more bearable he bought a folding bed, a new sleeping bag and a laptop. He even began to bond with Andy's flat-bound cat now that they no longer shared the sofa. For the first three days of his recovery, he sat to one side of the balcony window with his laptop on his knees, peering down onto Vernon Terrace. He made notes on a spreadsheet of everyone that crossed the road, parked their car, or loitered on the pavement, describing their clothing, approximate height, weight and age, and the date, time and duration of their visibility. But on the fourth day, having accumulated over five hundred observations, he gave up. Not one person had even glanced up at Andy's flat.

From then on most mornings he would venture down to the Pump Room with Andy, stay for a coffee and then head back to the flat, stopping on the way at the supermarket for food and a newspaper. He remained inside most of the time because wandering around Brighton with a bloated bottom lip and a bandaged forehead attracted too many questions from strangers. Most were just casually nosey, wanting to know how it happened. Some though (an addict with pin-cushioned forearms, a smoker with pleurisy, and the owner of a three-legged dog) saw Vince's misfortune as an opportunity to talk about themselves, quickly seguewaying the conversation in their own direction and boring Vince with their tales of injury and disease.

In the middle of the night on the seventeenth day of his recovery, he peered into the bathroom mirror. The swelling and bruising had almost gone. He traced the pink scar line that divided his forehead, picking at the last remnant of scab. Then he made a decision. 'An eye for an eye,' he said. He sat on the toilet and keyed a text to Kevin. *Sorry for not being in touch but lost my phone. Phylida probably said. Hope you're enjoying it* ☺ *Hope we can work on the new book soon. Perhaps meet up? Think things are smoothing out with Barros. I'm meeting him but I lost his London address. Can you send it? Vince.*

Kevin didn't stir. Phylida rolled to the side of the bed, picked up the glowing phone from the bedside table and read the message. She put it down and then picked up the tube of Pjur. She sniffed it and squeezed it, and wondered why it was nearly empty. Then she rolled back to the centre of the bed. She wanted to wake him and ask about the new book and why he hadn't mentioned it, and why he'd used so much lubricant. When he woke around eight she mentioned the text, but not that she'd read it.

Then, mid-morning, as she was leaving for London, they kissed on the doorstep. And as she climbed into her taxi she looked back at him and said, 'We'll need some more lube.'

'Okay, I'll get some.'

Back inside he replied to Vince's text: *54 Cumberland Grove, Barnes. Not far from the duck pond. But I don't think he's around until next week. We're meeting up on the Saturday after the Chelsea match. Speak soon. K*

323

52

Friday 22nd July

After the BBC's limo had dropped him home, he sat in the lounge, lights off, replaying the interview in his head. He realised his evasiveness had been more akin to a politician than a CEO, and deservedly, Lakin had made him look a fool. It was the nearest he'd ever come to public humiliation. He wished he was back in Manila with Imee.

At The Den the next morning, the phone calls began and he soon forgot about the embarrassment of the night before. He spent three hours talking to the intermediaries of prospective buyers, and though some were clearly tyre-kickers with no serious intentions, two seemed credible and were happy with his valuation. The first of these, Jesper Olsen, a London-based Dane, claimed to be acting on behalf of a Qatari. Olsen said his client would pay in cash. For Cowly this was ideal; he didn't want to rush through a sale that would leave the club mired in new debt. The second offer came via Evan Limes, whose client was British and apparently a long-time supporter of the club.

Cowly met Olsen at the stadium that afternoon. A towering blonde in a pinstripe blue suit, he told Cowly in perfect English about the deals he had brokered in *La Liga* and *Serie A*. Olsen said he'd also steered through the sale of Liverpool to Curry Lomax, the billionaire and co-founder of Furry-Friends Inc, the USA's leading pet insurance business. On the following Monday, Cowly and Olsen exchanged non-disclosure agreements. It was then that Olsen revealed his client's name: Hārūn al-Rashīd.

'What's his business?' said Cowly,

'Mainly construction.'

'Is he a football fan?'

324

'I'm not sure. He instructed me to find a club in the League Premiership, so I suppose he's not a Millwall fan, not yet anyway.'

Cowly didn't enquire further on Al-Rashīd's motivation. For the rest of the week he worked flat out with the club's legal advisors, drawing up the Contract of Sale whilst feeding documentation to Olsen's office. But not wanting the sale to collapse because of Al-Rashīd's unsuitability (the LPFL had a 'fit and proper' test for all prospective club owners which barred anyone convicted for drugs offences, rape and killing, from owning an LPFC club) he asked Phylida to check Al-Rashīd's background, and whether or not he had any affiliations with the Gülen Movement.

She discovered he was a property developer worth over $700 million, with business connections to the ruling *Al Thani* family. He had a brother-in-law who was on the organising committee for the 2022 World Cup, and one of his businesses, Agwed Falcon, had won the contract for an eighty-thousand seater stadium in the new city of Lusail. On Al Jazeera's website, she found an archived interview he'd given from the site of the proposed stadium. Looking and sounding like a Qatari version of Brian Blessed, Al-Rashīd blared at the camera: '*Agwed will transform this coastline into Arabia's most modern city...*' Then, pushing his female interviewer to one side, he waved his arm at the sun-bleached flatland that stretched to the horizon. '*...the Cup of 22 will bring many glorious opportunities for the Qatari people. There will be roads and hotels and shopping and a frozen mountain for the outdoor skiing. Everything will be here for the football fan, and one day the people will call me Soccerman!*' Then he laughed and thumped his chest with both fists.

On the 27th July, Olsen and Cowly met Al-Rashīd at The Ritz. Al-Rashīd talked of his love for England, recalling his three years at Durham University, and then of the unrest across the Arab states, and what they should do to stamp it out, and why it would never happen in Qatar. Olsen eventually brought the conversation round to Millwall; on a four percent commission, he was as keen as Cowly to secure a deal.

'Tom,' said Olsen, 'it might be useful to run through the proposed revenue funding from the Sport Channel. I have mentioned it to Hārūn, but it would be good to hear it directly from you.'

'I don't think that is necessary,' said Al-Rashīd. 'The future is for the future. I think the price you want for Millwall is a fair price. I think we can agree that.' Al-Rashīd looked to Olsen who nodded. Then he turned to Cowly. 'Jesper mentioned that you are keen to complete a sale.'

'Yes we are. Financially there is no hurry. It's more a matter of strategy. The Church would like to exit this particular market as soon as possible and reinvest.'

'Yes, I understand. I think it is a wise decision for the English Church...and wise also to make a decision before the new season begins.'

Cowly nodded. 'You've no objection to making a down-payment to secure your offer? We do have other people who are interested.' Cowly had told Limes, that he wasn't out of the picture.

'I understand,' said Al-Rashīd. 'And the down-payment?'

'Fifteen-percent,' said Cowly.

'Six million sterling,' said Olsen.

Al-Rashīd nodded. 'Okay Tom. I am happy with that.' They all stood and shook hands, and Al-Rashīd touched his heart with the palm of his hand. The deal was done but for the paperwork.

53

Chiswick, Thursday evening, 29th July

Phylida rang the bell and turned the key.

'In here,' said Kevin from the kitchen.

She dropped her bag in the hallway and slipped off her shoes. 'Sorry I'm late.' She found him at the breakfast table, his dinner plate clean. 'I couldn't call,' she said. 'I was in a taxi with the new owner and then on the tube.' She bent down and kissed his lips. 'Umm...risotto.'

He pulled her down onto the bench seat. 'You must be hungry. I can warm some up.'

'Not really, perhaps later.'

'What kept you?' he said.

'Hārūn asked Tom if he would stay on as CEO, just for a few months until he appointed a replacement. Tom said no, so Hārūn said...' She paused and tickled the underside of his nose.

'Who?' said Kevin, throwing his head back.

'Guess.'

'I've no idea. It could be anyone. Olsen?'

'No, someone a bit closer, someone you know quite well.'

He shook his head again.

'Me! I'm your new boss.'

'You're kidding?'

'No, and don't sound so surprised.'

She tried to stand, but he pulled her back. 'Sorry, that's great, really great. I just didn't think he would appoint...a woman.'

'I know. It surprised me, but then it's only for a few months. Tom thought it was a good idea.'

'And what's Tom going to do?'

'He's flying to Manila next week to see his girlfriend, but I wouldn't be surprised if he stays. He told me he's been told to rest. Apparently he has heart trouble.'

Kevin nodded.

'How did it go down with the players?' Cowly had taken Al-Rashīd and Olsen to meet the first team after morning training.

'Nobody said anything,' said Kevin. 'Tom said a few words and Al-Rashīd wished us good luck against Chelsea. That was pretty much it. Hardwick said it would...' and then he stopped.

'Go on, what did he say?'

'Nothing, just changing room talk.'

'Is he not happy?'

'No, he's all for it.'

Phylida wasn't convinced. 'Are you sure?'

'He thinks it'll be good for Millwall.' What Kevin couldn't tell her was that after Cowly and Al-Rashīd had left, Hardwick had ranted against the Church, saying that football was no place for fucking do-gooders and that his players should forget all the bollocks about Christian ethics. He'd called Al-Rashīd a raghead, and said the bastard will need to spend some of his oil money if they were to have a chance of staying up. When Hardwick finished, no one said a word, the players realising that the man who would lead them out at Highbury and Stamford Bridge was a Jekyll and Hyde, and someone that couldn't be trusted.

'Why good?' said Phylida.

'He thinks Al-Rashīd will spend money. He thinks he's an oil man.'

'He is rich, but he's not in the big league.'

'Is he going to spend anything?'

'I don't know. It's not been mentioned, but don't tell Hardwick or anyone else. And don't tell anyone I'm your girlfriend. Keep it quiet until I've moved on.'

He smiled and winked at her. 'Of course boss.'

54

The Den, Saturday 6th August

On the first Saturday of the new season Kevin arrived at the ground three hours before kick-off. Hardwick had called him two days earlier to see if he would do an interview for Mark Groenig. Groenig wanted to know how Kevin felt about his move to Millwall and what it would be like facing his old club. Hardwick said, 'Give him the usual crap.' The manager's mood had soured on the news that Al-Rashīd wasn't going to sanction more spending in the summer transfer window. On the club's website, in his match-day blog, he tried to reassure the Millwall fans that on the footballing side preparations couldn't have gone any better:

...the players focus has been 100% on the game against Chelsea. Training has gone well and there are no fitness worries. We are all pros and backroom changes and issues of ownership won't affect us. I'm look forward to working with Mr Al-Rashīd and I am confident we can build an established LPFL side. The players we signed over the summer have greatly strengthened the team and I'm sure Kevin Furling in particular will look to impress the club that let him go. Kevin's a big game player, a model professional with a great temperament. That's one of the reasons we brought him to Millwall. He's bound to get some barracking from the Chelsea fans, but that's football. He'll deal with it...

Kevin met Groenig and his cameraman in reception. The interview was to take place in one of the hospitality boxes in the Dockers Stand. As they climbed the stairs to the upper tier, Groenig asked Kevin if he was nervous.

Kevin said nothing. his thoughts were elsewhere.

Groenig tried again. 'I guess you'll want to do well against your old club?'

This time Kevin turned and smiled, but still offered no reply.

'I see Hardwick's backed you in his column.'

'Has he? I've not seen it.'

When they reached the door to the hospitality box, Groenig said he needed ten minutes to set up and then he would be ready to go.

'Okay, I'll come back,' said Kevin. 'I've some calls to make.' He watched Groenig and his cameraman disappear inside and then turned and moved down the corridor in search of another empty room. The third door he tried was unlocked. He knocked, walked in, and called Phylida. He went straight through to her voicemail and he didn't leave a message. Then he tried Vince, but Vince didn't answer because he was driving a hire car around Barnes. Finally, he called his mother.

'Hi Kevin. How are you? I was going to call you after the game. Is everything alright?'

'Yes, pretty much. I just thought I'd say hello, see how you're doing.'

'I'm okay, busy. I could do with a break from work.'

'Are you in later?' he said. 'I may need to speak to you.'

'What about?'

'Nothing much. I'll call you. Take care now.'

He checked his emails and then returned to the hospitality box. Groenig attached a lapel mike to Kevin's collar and positioned him with the pitch as the back drop. Groenig sat six feet back with the cameraman over his right shoulder. 'How's that?'

'Fine,' said the cameraman.

Looking at Kevin, Groenig said, 'We'll just start, see how it goes, and we can stop anytime. If you'd like to repeat an answer that's fine too. We're looking for about three or four minutes to broadcast.' His first recorded question was a banal opener and an equally banal answer was expected. 'Are you looking forward to playing for your new club?'

Kevin nodded and said, 'I was really looking forward to playing more regularly. The people that signed me here seemed to be doing a good job, but things have changed.'

'What do you mean?' said Groenig, immediately sensing that he was about to get a headline.

'The new owners...the Qatari owners, I'm not sure I want to play for them.'

'Because?' said Groenig, leaning forward as if worried that he wouldn't hear Kevin's answer.

Kevin pulled a folded sheet of paper from his top pocket and started to read. 'Because Millwall's new owners are Qatari. As I understand it, the Qatari State will deport gay and lesbian workers. Homosexuality is illegal. People are imprisoned because of their sexuality. I've read that some have been lashed. I know Mr Al-Rashīd is not the Qatari State, but his businesses do work for the Qatari State. He has connections with the Qatari rulers.'

Groenig tried to jump in. 'So you're...'

Without looking up Kevin held up a hand and continued reading. 'In recent months the Church of England has made much of its disinvestment from countries without democratic representation or basic human rights...including gay rights, yet they seem to have no ethics when it comes to selling their assets. They seem to have found nothing wrong in selling to a Qatari who will make millions from the World Cup in 2022 by employing thousands of foreign nationals on poverty wages.' Kevin nodded at Groenig that he was ready for the next question.

'So you're keen to support gay rights?' said Groenig.

'I'm not keen, but I will speak up from now on. I've not spoken about this before because I thought my career was more important. That's a fact, and I can't change that now. All I'm saying is that as a bi-sexual man I do not support Mr Al-Rashīd's purchase of Millwall Football Club.'

Groenig nodded and smiled, encouraging Kevin to continue.

'I realise this could be the end of my career. I think it's regrettable that the Church has sold the club. I am not a religious person, but I think under Tom Cowly's stewardship

Millwall would have had a positive impact on the game. I think most people, most fans, would like to see some changes in football. Finally, I would like to say to the Millwall fans, that while I am against the recent takeover, as a professional footballer I will do my utmost on the field to make Millwall a successful side.' He folded his sheet of paper and then smiled, as if in apology for going off-script.

Groenig hesitated. He looked down at the floor, searching for a follow up question, but he was too distracted by the knowledge that he'd just hit the journalistic jackpot.

'Mark,' said the cameraman, sharply. 'What's up?'

'Sorry,' said Groenig. 'I was just wondering what to ask next.' Then he said, 'Are you sure about this Kevin? You don't have to do it.'

Kevin nodded. 'I'm sure, but can we leave it at that. I've said enough.'

'Okay, let's wrap up.' As Groenig stood, he said, 'You know Kevin, this will go out today, before the game.'

'Yes, that's what I want.'

'Well good luck...and I hope you score.' For the briefest of moments Groenig was tempted to reach out and hug him, a hug of gratitude for this once in a lifetime gift. Instead he turned away and began planning his live transmission from the club's car park. The interview, he thought, could go as it was, without an edit.

Kevin made his way down to the staff canteen; kick-off was still two hours away. On the way a girl from admin passed by and wished him well. He didn't see her. And when he walked into the canteen and toward the buffet, he didn't see his five teammates playing cards. He picked up a plate and spooned baked beans onto two pieces of unbuttered brown bread – his usual pre-match meal. He turned slowly and scanned the room and then sat at an empty table facing one of the seven TV screens that hung from the canteen's walls. Then he looked down at his meal. Though he'd not eaten breakfast, the sight and sweet smell of the beans made him feel nauseous. He wondered why he had eaten them all these years. He pushed the plate to one side, leant back in his chair and looked up at the TV. As always, the volume was down.

Then Phylida called. 'Hi Kevin. I was in the bath.'

'Where are you?'

'I'm just about to leave. Are you alright? You sound a bit down.'

'I'm okay, but I've done something. It'll be on the news soon. Switch on the Sport Channel.'

'What do you mean? Are you injured?'

'No, I'm fine, but I want to apologise for not being honest with you.'

'What is it?'

'It'll be on the news. Look, I'd better go. I can't talk here. I'll see you after the game.' Then he cut the call. He read the headlines running along the bottom of the screen:

COLIN JEAVONS, THE MANCHESTER UNITED MIDFIELDER HAS PULLED A HAMSTRING AND WILL BE OUT FOR THREE WEEKS; SVEN GORAN ERIKSON IS TODAY'S SPECIAL GUEST ON THE SPORT CHANNEL'S MATCH-DAY PANEL; FA CALLS FOR FIFA TO REDUCE THE SIZE OF THE PENALTY AREA; MILLWALL'S . . .

His heart jumped:

NEW OWNERS DENY CASH INJECTION....

He rubbed his face, trying to clear his head. Then he walked over to the buffet and brought back a mug of tea.

In the stadium car park Mark Groenig sent a text to Bryan Hardwick. The Furling interview would be aired in minutes and Groenig wanted to exploit his opportunity and be the first to get an official response from the club: *Bryan, Mark Groenig here. Why is Kevin Furling refusing to play?'* Groenig waited a minute and then called Hardwick's number.

'What is it Mark?' Hardwick was standing outside the door to his office.

'I've just interviewed Kevin Furling, and...'

Hardwick cut him off. 'Yes, I know that, so what?'

'He's bi-sexual and he's just dissed the new owners. He said they imprison people in Qatar if they're gay.'

'What the fuck you on about?'

'Is that the club's response?'

'Hang on. I've not seen it and until I have, I've no comment. Is that clear?'

'Switch the news on Bryan.'

Hardwick cut the call as he saw Al-Rashīd and Olsen walking towards him. They shook hands and Hardwick steered them into his office.

'We won't keep you long,' said Olsen. 'Mr Al-Rashīd wanted to wish you well. He's hoping you might at least get a draw.' Olsen looked to his client, but Al-Rashīd wasn't listening. He was staring above Hardwick's head at the wall mounted TV.

In the canteen, Kevin sipped his tea and looked up at his image on the screen. On the right-hand side was the headline: FURLING ACCUSES AL-RASHĪD OVER GAY RIGHTS, while along the bottom appeared the stuttering transcript of his interview. He quietly mouthed the words he couldn't hear. Then a scouse voice from over his shoulder said, 'Look at you, you tart.'

Kevin didn't look round, he didn't need to. The voice belonged to Steven Jones, the team's left-back, and the only scouser in the squad. 'Yes,' said Kevin, still staring at the screen. 'I've only just done it.'

Jones paid no attention to the headline or the words underneath. 'Are you coming over, or are you gonna sit here on yer own like a saddo?'

'I think I'll stay here.' Kevin turned to face him. 'Don't tell the boss, but I'm feeling a bit iffy.' He pointed to the untouched beans on toast. 'No appetite.'

'Okay then Big Man,' said Jones. 'I'll see you later.' Jones was two inches taller than Kevin; the *Big Man* epithet was simply in recognition of Kevin's years in the top flight.

He watched Jones return to his card game and then turned back to the TV. The image had changed. Mark Groenig was holding a microphone and talking to camera. Kevin took out his phone and sent a text to Hardwick: *I'll be outside your office if you want to talk.*

– – – – – – – – –

In Barnes, sporting a three-week beard, a baseball cap and sunglasses, Vince had his back tight against the trunk of a sycamore. At the sound of a slammed car door, he edged round, craning his neck. He saw Barros heading up the driveway of 54 Cumberland Grove towing a trolley bag. Vince had been in the Barnes area for twenty-four hours, occasionally driving or walking past Barros' house looking out for signs of occupancy. He'd spent Friday evening in the local pubs and then a sleepless night in his hire car.

When Barros entered the house Vince ran across the road and along the pavement to his car. He keyed in 141 to withhold his number and then called Barros.

He raised the pitch of his voice, 'Mr Barros?'

'Yes.'

'I'm calling from DHL. We have a package for you, but we need a signature. We have tried several times. Are you at home today?'

'Who is it from?'

'One moment.' Vince counted to ten in his head and said, 'The sender is the Professional Footballing Association, Oxford Road, Manchester. A driver will be in your area in the next hour. Would that be convenient?

'Yes,' said Barros.

'Thank you. Have a good day.' Vince cut the call and noted the time.

– – – – – – – –

Hardwick, Al-Rashid and Olsen stopped their argument when they saw Kevin in the doorway. Hardwick ushered Al-Rashid and Olsen out and said, 'Give me five minutes. I'll sort it.' Then he grabbed Kevin's forearm, pulled him inside and slammed the door.

'Sit down,' said Hardwick, glancing at his watch.

Kevin remained standing.

'What the fuck have you said?'

'You've not seen it?'

'Yes.' He nodded to the TV screen on the wall. 'Have you lost your fuckin' mind?'

'I don't think so,' said Kevin. Then he took the slip of paper from his pocket and glanced at his statement. 'No, I meant every word.'

Hardwick sneered. 'Why now?'

'Isn't that obvious? Groenig asked me what I thought about the new owners, so I told him.'

Hardwick kicked the chair beside his desk sending it toppling across the room. 'Look Kevin, your queer. That's tough for you, but it's not our fault. And get this, we don't care, we don't need to know.'

'I'm bi-sexual,' said Kevin.

'You don't know what you've done,' said Hardwick, pointing to his door. 'That raghead out there, he pays our wages, your wages, my fucking wages. You've fucked him off.'

'So?'

'I want you to apologise. Think up an excuse, a good reason, you've got to tell him something.'

Kevin shook his head. 'I meant it, every word.'

There was a knock at the door. Hardwick stepped across and inched it open. It was Olsen. 'What is it?' said Hardwick.

'We need to speak.'

'Where's Mr Rashīd?' said Hardwick, peering down the corridor.

'He's just gone. He heard you. He wants Furling out and he wants to see you now.'

Hardwick looked at his watch. It was two-fifteen. 'I can't,' he said, 'I have to be with the players. Tell Mr Rashīd I'll see him after the game.'

At two-thirty, in the Millwall changing room, no one spoke, but everyone knew.

Hardwick said, 'Iain's going to do the team talk.' Iain Harvey was the assistant manager. 'I have to go. I'll see

336

you at half-time. You're all going to defend. I want a nil-nil. Is that clear?' A few murmured. 'Is that clear?' he shouted.

In miserable unison they replied, 'Yes boss.'

Hardwick pointed at Kevin. 'You're on the bench. Eliot, you're playing.' Then he left the room slamming the door.

– – – – – – –

Hayward Gallery, Saturday afternoon 6th August

Spinks' installation team had been busy all week. On the Monday, in his studio, a metre square steel plate had been welded to the base of MBF2. The half-tonne unit was then secured in a wheeled gantry and delivered to the Hayward Gallery. Tuesday morning was spent drilling and grinding a shallow recess into the concrete wall three metres to the right of its brick forerunner. In the afternoon, they rolled the gantry up to the recess, bolted in the base plate and cover it in mortar. On Wednesday the plasterers arrived, and on Friday they painted the entire wall with a white that matched the white of MBF2, giving the impression of a seamless penetration.

Saturday morning, the gallery's Director, Richard Crevinson, suggested they erect a curtain to keep the invited guests in suspense until the moment of unveiling. Spinks said not to bother. He said he didn't want to encourage comparisons with the terminally ill. He told Levinson to rope it and cover it with a sheet.

At 2.45 Crevinson unlocked the door to the White Room and the ruly crowd of critics, photographers and friends filed in. Spinks, standing to one side, dutifully smiled and shook hands. Without instruction, they gathered five and six deep in a semi-circle around the exhibit. Ailish, anxious for Spinks, stood apart, leaning against the back wall. He had told her that morning, over breakfast, that most of the people attending would probably be disappointed, and that the critics would claim that he had run out of ideas. Then he told her he didn't really care as long as there was some reaction.

Crevinson, on the other side of the rope, asked those that were working, the photographers and critics, to stand to the right, with everyone else to the left. And while they shuffled left and right, he shouted, 'David, where are you? I need you here now.' Crevinson rose on tiptoes and peered over the moving heads.

Spinks walked over to Ailish at the back of the room and grabbed her hand. When he tried to lead her away, she shook herself free.

'What are you doing?' she said, 'It's not about me.'

'I need your help...please?' He grabbed her hand again and like a father towing a reluctant child, he led her round to join Crevinson. As he passed MBF, he slapped its shiny head with his free hand.

Crevinson said, 'Once again welcome. It's wonderful to see so many familiar faces.' He looked down at the rope and pointed. 'We'll take this away once the photographers have finished.' Then he turned to look at the sheathed exhibit. 'Some of you,' and he paused and smiled, 'have probably guessed what it is.' A few cameras flashed. Then Crevinson said to Spinks, 'David, why don't you show the good people what you've been doing?'

'Sure,' said Spinks. He lifted Ailish's hand to his face and kissed it. Cameras clicked and flashed. He looked at her. 'Will you do it for me?'

She shook her head, not understanding.

'Just unveil it, that's all.'

She wanted to argue, but couldn't. 'Just you wait,' she mouthed. A few behind the rope laughed. She walked over and not waiting for permission or a cue, she grasped the sheet and with the single flourish revealed Spinks' metal penis.

'Oh, it's white,' was the first comment from someone at the front.

Crevinson lead the reluctant applause which quickly died away. 'David, would you like to say a few words?'

'One moment Richard,' said Spinks. He walked over to Ailish and whispered in her ear. 'One more favour. We need to give them a photo to remember.'

338

'What do you mean?' she said.

'Will you sit on it for me?'

'No way.'

'Just for a few seconds.' They turned their backs to their audience. 'Please?' he said. 'It could make all the difference.'

'You're in such big trouble,' she said.

'I know.' He kissed her on the lips, and said, 'Have you ever ridden a horse?' She nodded. Then she moved to the side of MBF2 and placed her left hand on to the back of the shaft. 'Careful you don't go over, there's no saddle.'

'I'm not fucking blind,' she whispered.

Spinks bent down and she offered up her right calf. 'One, two, and up,' he said.

She dropped down lightly to another volley of clicks and flashes. Then she realised he'd planned it all along. Before they'd set off to the gallery, he asked her if she'd wear her jeans and cowboy boots. He refused to say why, other than it was a look he liked. She sat there for twenty seconds until he lifted her off. Then Spinks nodded to Crevinson to remove the rope and at the back of the room corks popped.

– – – – – – – – –

Vince parked up on a side road to Cumberland Grove. Still wearing sunglasses and cap, he jogged along the pavement and up the driveway to Barros' house. Holding an envelope up to his face he rang the bell. As the door opened he forced his way in.

'What are you doing?' said Barros.

Vince extended his arm pushing Barros back. He removed his cap and glasses, and said, 'I thought I'd pay a return visit.'

'Get out,' shouted Barros.

Vince slammed the front door and gestured to Barros to turn around. They entered a white-walled and cream-carpeted room at the back of the house. Above the marble mantelpiece was a flat screen TV of equal width. Barros stopped in the middle of the room and then looked down at Vince's shoes. Vince looked down too.

'Take them off,' said Barros.

'What?' said Vince, shaking his head.

Barros picked up the remote, hit the mute button, and then dropped it on the coffee table. 'I said take your shoes off.'

Vince looked at Barros' bare feet and laughed. Then fixing his gaze on Barros, he wiped the sole of each shoe across the carpet as if scrapping off mud.

'What do you want?' said Barros.

'I haven't decided. Maybe to give you one of these.' Vince touched the scar on his forehead. 'A slicing for a slicing.'

'I have friends coming soon,' said Barros. Then he looked at his watch. 'They will arrive soon.'

Vince laughed again. 'Friends. I don't think so.' Then Kevin's face appeared on the screen behind Barros. Vince pointed. 'He might be coming round, but no one else.'

Barros turned. The Sport Channel were repeating Kevin's interview. On the right of the screen they summarised the main points.

- *FIRST PROFESSIONAL PLAYER TO ADMIT BEING BI-SEXUAL*

- *CRITICISES MILLWALL'S NEW QATARI OWNER*

- *BLASTS CHURCH OF ENGLAND FOR SELLING TO QATARI*

'Fuck,' said Vince.

Barros reached down for the remote and pressed the volume button. Kevin's flat voice filled the room.

> *'...a fact, and I can't change that now. All I'm saying is that as a bi-sexual man I do not support Mr Al-Rashīd's purchase...'*

Knowing that one sentence had destroyed his business, Barros slung the remote across the room. 'Coño!' he said, Then he lunged forward at Vince's throat. Vince side-stepped easily and Barros stumbled past. Barros turned and tried again. Once more Vince swayed back at the last moment, but this time Barros' right knee met with Vince's left leg. Barros' top-heavy body, briefly airborne, landed head first against the hearth.

> '...most fans, would like to see some changes in football...'

Vince bent down. He drew back the hair covering the side of Barros' face to reveal an unblinking eye and the right-angle of the marble hearth embedded in his forehead. Vince straightened up facing the television. Kevin's head was angled forward, his eyes down, as if in witness to the body on the floor. Vince looked around the room, at the carpet where he'd wiped his feet and at the broken remote by the window. He ran from the house.

– – – – – – – –

The Den

As the Millwall players went through their final warm up, the stadium announcer read out the two teams. He paused between each name allowing the fans time to show their appreciation and loathing. When he came to the subs and Kevin's name, the ground erupted. Kevin held up his hand in acknowledgement, but kept his head down and continued firing shots at the Millwall keeper.

By half-time Millwall were 2-0 down with two forced substitutions, a mid-fielder and their centre-forward. Fifteen minutes from the end the deficit increased to three and Millwall's left-wing pulled a hamstring. Hardwick sent Kevin on and in the eighty-ninth minute he scored; a left-foot shot from the edge of the box flew to the top corner of the net. And there the game ended: 3-1 to Chelsea. But as both teams walked off the pitch, shaking hands, some smiling, some despondent, in the corner of the West Stand a woman with a Millwall tattoo started singing to the tune of an old Madness song.

> *We're not going to Qatar*
> *We don't care who you are*
> *Kevin takes it up the arse*
> *He's alright he's a star*
>
> *We're not going to Qatar*
> *We don't.....*

Her boyfriend, who had a matching tat on his right forearm, joined in. By the fifth repetition another hundred or more were singing along. By the fifteenth, the Millwall fans had stopped leaving and the imperfect rhyme was carried around the ground and through the window of the Director's Box. Phylida looked at Al-Rashīd. She smiled and shrugged her shoulders and said, 'It's just their way of saying welcome.'